The Good Family Fitzgerald

ALSO BY JOSEPH DI PRISCO

Novels
Confessions of Brother Eli
Sun City
All for Now
The Alzhammer
(Or: Keep Your Friends Close and…I Forget the Other Thing)
Sibella & Sibella

Memoirs
Subway to California
The Pope of Brooklyn

Poetry
Wit's End
Poems in Which
Sightlines from the Cheap Seats

Nonfiction
Field Guide to the American Teenager (Michael Riera, coauthor)
Right from Wrong (Michael Riera, coauthor)

EDITED BY JOSEPH DI PRISCO

Simpsonistas: Tales from the Simpson Literary Project (Vol. 1)
Simpsonistas: Tales from the Simpson Literary Project (Vol. 2)

The Good Family Fitzgerald

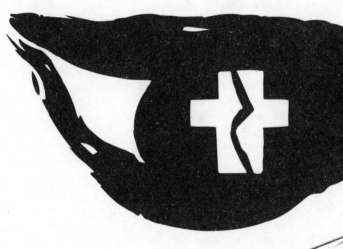

A NOVEL

JOSEPH DI PRISCO

Rare Bird Books
Los Angeles, Calif.

THIS IS A GENUINE RARE BIRD BOOK

Rare Bird Books
453 South Spring Street, Suite 302
Los Angeles, CA 90013
rarebirdbooks.com

FIRST HARDCOVER EDITION

Set in Dante
Printed in the United States

10 9 8 7 6 5 4 3 2 1

Library of Congress Cataloging-in-Publication Data

Names: Di Prisco, Joseph, 1950– author.
Title: The Good Family Fitzgerald: A Novel / Joseph di Prisco.
Description: Los Angeles, CA: Rare Bird Books, [2020] | "A Genuine Rare
Bird Book"—Title page verso.
Identifiers: LCCN 2019051729 | ISBN 9781644280782 (hardback)
Classification: LCC PS3554.I67 G66 2020 | DDC 813/.54—dc23

LC record available at https://lccn.loc.gov/2019051729

Sent 2020

For Paul
& the Better
Family Wilmer.

For Edith Maude Fitzgerald's great-granddaughter

The water is wide, I cannot get o'er
And neither have I wings to fly,
Build me a boat that can carry two
And both shall row, my love and I.

Could the truth be so simple? So terrible?

Tim O'Brien, *In the Lake of the Woods*

PART ONE

Chapter One
Anthony & Francesca

FRANCESCA NEVER FORGOT THE day Anthony, who was no fisherman, failed to bring home the fish. She did the math. Say the heart beats eighty times a minute, forty-eight hundred times an hour, one hundred fifteen thousand times a day. That meant in the three years since, the muscle that was her heart had contracted one hundred twenty-six million, one hundred fifty thousand times. The calculation was simple, if nothing else was.

That was an incredible number—*one hundred twenty-six million, one hundred fifty thousand.* To her, though, it felt more like *one* heartbeat ago. She couldn't wrap her mind around that number, either.

—

FRANCESCA RESIFTED MEMORIES OF what had seemed to be an ordinary day, the day her husband didn't return with the fish as he promised. Sparkling summer had mercifully descended after a pitiless winter. The fat heirloom tomatoes were ripening bright red in their raised beds: the prospect of a bountiful harvest. Honeybees zoomed and hummingbirds darted, peony to sage to goldenrod and beyond. She answered mail, returned calls, paid bills, did chores, ran errands, scheduled meetings, worked out, watered plants, watered plants again, ate lunch. How genially purposeful was her routine. That was before everything changed for Anthony and for her and for everybody she cared about. Memory is a funny thing, even if it isn't a thing and there is nothing funny about it.

So that was a lifetime or a minute ago, a Thursday, typically the most vexed day of the week. Not weighted with deferred obligation like a Monday or Tuesday, and not freighted with implied expectation like a Friday or Saturday. Not hollow like a transitional Wednesday or wistful and lonesome as a Sunday, either. Sundays could be particularly hard. That's when rain ought to fall, sunrise to midnight, or when owls should hoot and hoot and hoot some more. But back to Thursday: that's when you swivel, backward and forward, when you are open to surprise, prepared for anything. But that is Thursday's reliably broken promise. Nobody's prepared when *anything* takes place.

She had been the recipient of well-meaning, hopeless advice—advice she should *stay in the moment*. That's the last place she wanted to be. All around her, people seemed to be manically meditating, too, when they weren't rushing off to spin classes and resistance training, or eating more plants and antioxidants and less animal protein. They were undivided, aggressively striving to *stay in the moment*. She half-wished she could heed their counsel and stay in the freaking moment, if only she could fathom where and what and why the *moment* was. Their intentions were well-meaning, probably, and they made a sort of sense because consider the unappealing alternatives. Living in the foreclosed past meant trudging through the mucky sludge of regret and nostalgia, while living in the clouds of the inconceivable future meant taking up residence in the land of make-believe. And yet, and yet, and yet: loss and remembrance and the continually imploding present were the fundaments of her existence.

—

ON THAT THURSDAY WHEN Anthony did not return with the fish, dawn broke with uneasy intimations, sly premonitions. Francesca was already late for something urgent—but what that was, she could not name. She walked into the garden beyond her bedroom door in hopes that the scents of rosemary, basil, and freesia might elevate her spirits. Hopes were quickly dashed; the garden didn't help. Honestly, it never did. The night before, empty Wednesday night, she and Anthony had had an extraordinary spat—extraordinary in that they rarely tangled. They took no pleasure in marital swordplay, so it didn't take long before they both lost interest. Not that either was ADD. If anything, the two of them suffered from a surplus, not a deficit, of attention.

Thus it was, that awkward Thursday morning, she found herself stopping him dead in his tracks on his way out the door: "Not so fast, buster. Not done with you yet."

If she were not who she was and he were not who he was and they were not who they were, she might have been shouting, and the wedding china might have been rattling inside cabinets. The sentiments might have been accompanied by glassware flung, doors slammed, ultimatums delivered, and miserable zig-zaggy lines of mascara running down her cheeks. But not a chance when it came to her—and him—and them.

Her husband was bustling about, getting organized to go to work. The instant he heard *Not so fast*, deferential Buster—Anthony, that is—histrionically screeched to a halt: "Road Runner, *meep meep*, meets rock wall."

"*Meep meep*, Road Runner? Just curious, *meep meep*, Anthony darling."

"Go for it, Frankie."

"You're a smart guy."

"Full disclosure: there was cabinet-level consideration as to whether or not I ought to repeat second grade. Everybody knows second grade is a scholastic juggernaut."

She shook her head side to side, a miserable metronome. "You sleep soundly, like you're an innocent man. How come when you wake up you're a knucklehead?"

Because about last night: a little snark and snip, a passing complaint, a minor grievance, an eye roll, a self-defensive pushback, one glass of wine too many, all right maybe two, and they drifted into their respective corners to lick their superficial wounds. But hours later, they got through it and slept in each other's arms. Well, one of them slept. But no, marital triage was not on the docket, and as per usual there wasn't a lot to clean up today.

"Knucklehead? You said *knucklehead*?"

"What, you've never been told before?"

"Objection, badgering, as well as hearsay, but let us stipulate semi-lovable. At the same time, kind of immaterial, too," he added, "as well as leading, your Honor. Calls for a conclusion. Exhibit A: Counsel is testifying and is way too foxy, especially with respect to the earliness of the hour."

At this point an outside observer would be hard-pressed to appreciate that Anthony was well-versed in raising logical and coherent and strategic objections in legal proceedings, unlike the frivolous, nonsensical ones he raised with Francesca. That's because, for his day job, he was a litigator specializing in criminal law. Lawyers are often justifiably saddled with a bad rep, but if you had a genuine problem, and the money, Anthony Fitzgerald was the up-and-coming barrister you wanted to have your back. You didn't necessarily have to be Irish or be personally acquainted with any of the Fitzgeralds, and you didn't always need to have all the cash for the retainer up front, but it didn't hurt.

"Where you think you're going?" she asked, not that she had suspicions. "Want to track me?"

"Ankle monitor, never thought of that. You can borrow one from all your clients under house arrest."

Then his forehead wrinkled and his shoulders slumped and his eyebrows arched and his lower lip did that signature goofball overhang. That was his go-to Parisian street mime move, which was practically indistinguishable from his trademark dejected clown.

She gave up and smiled and threw up her hands, like somebody on the church steps showering the bride and groom with confetti. What had they been fighting about? She could barely recall. Once more her vision was drawn to the shadowy mini Zeus thunderbolt scar on his forehead, directly beneath the scalp line. It was a marker of Anthony's storied past, and it set off right on schedule a high-voltage erotic charge. Such yearning made her woozy, as if she zip-lined from a great, great height.

She braced herself, leaning a hip against the kitchen counter, arms folded. She was wearing gray sweats, her black mane of hair was tied back, and her reading glasses were perched on top of her head. To him this made her resemble a college girl who had crammed all night for a final exam. In fact, her efforts at sleep had been sheet-twisting, pillow-punching restless and wracked. Meanwhile, alongside her, he seemed to enjoy the serene slumber of the guilt-free. She had briefly entertained slapping him awake so they could resume talking, but in the end didn't follow through.

That morning the big blue sky beckoned, and, dressed in a bespoke black suit and gold Marinella tie with contrasting orange la-di-da silk pocket square, he was going to work, as he usually did at this hour. Where else did she imagine he might be going? He stole a glance at the wall clock over her shoulder. He was on schedule.

"You look snappy," she said, and he did. A while ago, she had supervised his wardrobe makeover. He hadn't a clue how badly he required such intervention, which is one thing all men who desperately need a makeover have in common. He resisted at first, but soon his once-upon-a-time standard-issue corduroy sport coats and wrinkled chinos, which made him look like an assistant professor possessed of pronounced Marxist leanings, were relegated to Saint Vincent de Paul, supplanted by a rack of Italian designer suits fashioned of sumptuous fabric whose folds embraced him in an elegant caress. When he risked a glance in the mirror, he wondered what mystifying road he had taken to become a guy wearing a suit like that. It was easy to map the path: he trusted Frankie's lead, and she never misguided him. Though, true, he would stipulate for the record, early on she did buy him a pink shirt, which constituted a low point, but how could she have known then that his father would disown him if his son swanned around in such a fey garment?

Francesca was inclined to be conciliatory. Her *snappy* was punctuated by a wry smile, as if she had made a poker hand, drawing to an inside straight—but honestly, no, she did not have one of those poker faces, at least when it came to him. Fighting was so, so dumb. She could shift direction quicker than one of those shimmering hummingbirds suspended outside her kitchen window. Pure Francesca Scalino.

As for her last name, before she affirmed her Catholic wedding vows she contemplated taking Anthony's, becoming Francesca *Fitzgerald,* which ethnic mash-up would have qualified for major points on the mellifluousness scale. Maybe she had inhaled the dispersed current of pop feminism or maybe she preferred her maiden name, not that there was anything wrong in her mind with becoming a Fitzgerald. Or maybe professional considerations held sway, insofar as she had earned during the boom her successful entrepreneur's reputation as a *Scalino*. Her father did not enjoy a vote on the matter, though he expressed no displeasure when his precious daughter elected not to assume a new—and quintessentially Irish—last name. Keeping hers did not betoken ambivalence. She was not hedging her bets. She was not the type to hedge a bet, or question her heart. Anthony was her soul mate and would be her husband, and she his devoted wife. Wasn't that obvious?

As for him, the issue of a last name was more inconsequential than his defunct corduroy coats. He didn't care how her name appeared on the marriage certificate or mailbox as long as the two of them were bonded in perpetuity.

Anthony's parents may have been initially critical of what they construed to be the girl's radical decision to retain her name, but then again, they cultivated generalized skepticism with regard to the younger generation. There was no getting around that she *was* indeed Italian, and this would be what they would term with pruned face and wrinkled mouth a mixed marriage. So yes, definitely very old school. Yet their son proclaimed he was in love. That could be true, but what was he *thinking*? And with *what* was he thinking? An *Italian* girl? Well, that's what his mother wanted to know: handsome boy like him, oldest of her four children, smart as a whip, setting such a poor example for the siblings, and—Holy Jesus, child of Mary!— whatever happened to that cute curly-haired colleen he was cavorting around with not so long ago, a girl who was gentle as a lamb and whose name she did not recall? Anthony didn't always remember her name, either, and that former girlfriend's sweetness, which was authentic and abundant, cloyed over time. His baby sister was actually christened Colleen, but he was through cavorting around with any and all other colleens, if that was the way to put it, because he had found the one and only. He didn't mount an argument or defend himself in the Fitzgerald Court of Family Law because—because what was the question again? Why couldn't they be happy for him? For him, that wasn't a rhetorical question.

His father, whose temperament nobody would dare characterize as lamblike, had not been half so wary as his mother. In fact, he cultivated a measure of grudging respect for those he spoke of as the *Eye Talians*. In his specialized arena of business, dealings with them were hard to avoid. They proved competent businessmen, erratic and blustery, certainly, but finally bottom-line pragmatic, and prosperous, too, in all these respects much like him. Not only that. He had in his garage an Italian trophy car, a gleaming, gorgeous, classic, low-slung Maserati. His wife refused on principle to ride in it, though what that principle was must have seemed so transparent that it had never been adduced. Driving the car was reserved for what was termed "special occasions," but since few occasions were deemed sufficiently special, she hadn't many opportunities to spurn getting in, not that that mattered. For her, the point remained.

"Oh, you want me to buy an *Irish* car?" he once asked. "Henry Ford's da might have been Irish, but our kind don't have the corner on automobiles, and if we did, their pistons would be cantankerous as a tubercular deacon from Cork—and they'd all be slathered with seasick green paint."

That may be, but Anthony's mother ardently celebrated the bounty of Irish blood flowing in her unashamed veins. In contrast, his father's feelings were muted if not mixed on that score. Decades after that soul-crushing November 1963 day of national reckoning, President Kennedy's framed, fading photo still assumed a place of honor on their mantle, positioned alongside family portraits, all of them faithfully dusted. John *Fitzgerald* Kennedy, after all, you see. Then again, there was a time when it would have been borderline implausible to saunter into any Irish home or pub bereft of iconic images of the rascally handsome Jack and gravely good-looking brother Bobby and, as she often implored the heavens, may they rest in peace and let perpetual light shine upon them, amen.

—

ONE AFTERNOON THE ENGAGED couple came over to the baronial Family Fitzgerald home. Francesca and Anthony and his parents enjoyed a pleasurable lunch in the patio gazebo with the panoramic view of woods and water, and afterward Paddy offered Francesca what he and his son should have offered before: a tour of the grounds. In due course the three of them ended up in the garage. He wanted to show off that classic car of his—and to signal, almost undoubtedly unconsciously, his open-mindedness on the budding Italian controversy.

"Oh, my God," she said, gasping, "a 1959 Maserati? Oh, my God. I would love to drive a car like this once in my life. Anthony, sweetheart, what's it like handling this beauty?" She extended her arms as if she were begging to be handed a newborn to swaddle.

Following Francesca's lead, Sweetheart himself lifted up his own hands, in his case pleading for understanding from whatever deity existed above. He didn't know the first thing about handling this or any other beauty, and less about cars, especially his dad's prized vehicle. He was never permitted behind the wheel of the bone-white two-seater the family reverentially referred to as the Maz. As a young boy he may have been assigned numerous domestic chores to hone his sense of family obligation, but he wasn't ever allowed to wash, much less drive, the car.

"There can't be many of these left in the world," she said to his father. "Where did you find this gem, a 3500 GT?"

"Knew a guy who knew a guy. Took one look, had to have it. It's almost as old as me, so we both needed work on the body and under the hood. I hear Maserati made a grand total of eighteen of them."

"Everybody raves about Ferrari, and they're obviously marvelous engineering works of art, but for my money Maserati makes the most beautiful cars. And this one, it's so sleek and sexy, the automotive equivalent of, I don't know, a soaring raptor."

"You know your cars," said Paddy, beaming.

She didn't really know her cars, and was normally unawed by anything on wheels—though she was invested in all matters Italian. She had evinced more exuberant interest in the Maz than Paddy's son ever had. The father didn't have the heart to tell his prospective daughter-in-law that his 3500 GT was not a 1959 but a 1957, an easy enough mistake to make, and it was christened an Italian name. He knew the name meant "white lady" but he would never risk pronouncing it and embarrassing himself with his wretched accent. The man had his faults, which were spectacular and which his son could enumerate at length if compelled by a subpoena, but pedantry was not numbered among them.

"A Maserati *Dama Bianca*, unbelievable, what a showstopper," she said.

"When I take it out? It loves to fly. I got up to a hundred twenty a couple times, on the open road, and it roared, so happy. My accountant regards this car as an investment, a terrible one, but I would never sell it, never, at any price."

"It must feel like a racehorse—a Secretariat, Affirmed, Citation, Seattle Slew—winning wire to wire."

"And now I find you also know your ponies."

"My dad. He spun some tales."

"He owned horses, trained them?"

"More like a speculative interest."

Paddy let this information seep in. How did he not put this together? Of course, this Scalino was the daughter of *that* Scalino, Mimmo Scalino, who used to be the biggest and most reliable bookmaker around, back when. He hadn't heard much about him lately, assuming that unless he'd gone over to the other side, he'd turned over a new leaf. He now had newfound respect for his own son's taste and judgment. It was not insignificant, either, that she had major means of her own, which were not derived from her own family business, and was therefore not likely to be tracking breadcrumbs on the trail to Fitzgerald riches. Overall, this girl might simply be too good to be true.

Paddy's wife would come around to the proposed marriage, he would see to that, because Francesca's response to the car, not to mention her own family lineage, sealed the deal. He was enchanted. This dark-eyed, olive-skinned girl was a keeper. A woman who knew her way around classic automobiles and the race track wouldn't get vertigo approaching the lightning-fast learning curve required by familiarity with the Fitzgeralds. He had the passing thought that the Maz would make for a sweet wedding present, but reconsidered. Perhaps a tenth wedding anniversary gift.

"Next time, we'll take the venerable dame for a spin, Frankie."

"Fabulous, Mr. Fitzgerald."

"Please, deary, please. *Paddy*." His teeth sparkled. "Pass along respects to your dad from me, would you? Someday, he and I can catch up. We all have much to celebrate."

Anthony came this close to rubbing his eyes. He'd witnessed the man unleash his charm offensive on business partners, lawyers, school administrators, clergy, reporters, occasionally even law enforcement—on almost anybody, that is, not named Fitzgerald. Anthony had to admit, the day had gone better than expected.

In any case, Paddy Fitzgerald adopted the long view. As far as he was concerned, his son's brood would be perfect and those Irish babies to be would be a shade Italian, true, but *their* last names at the baptismal font and in Catholic school would be *Fitzgerald*. So this was a small price to pay for what one day a grandfather presumed would be many, many grandchildren in need of being spoiled. Consider the immense bounty promised by their commingled genes: these babies would bring out the beautiful best of both families.

—

"ROBIN'S-EGG COLORED SHIRT, HIGHLIGHTING your baby blues," she declared that morning three years ago, taking stock of him as he was heading out the door. "Got a hot date, buster?"

Snappy. Hot date. Buster. Anthony had fallen forever for a woman who lifted her dialogue from broads straight out of central casting in the old black-and-white movies she fell asleep watching. That was where gents favored floppy fedoras and padded shoulders and packed their gats in violin cases, and babes popped bubblegum or chain-smoked a bluish haze and had gams all the way up to here.

As it happened, Anthony did have a date. A very hot *court* date alongside his client, the owner of Limerick Jewelry & Loan, under indictment for laundering cash to further an intricate criminal enterprise whose intricacies were insufficiently intricate to misdirect the district attorney. Maybe all pawnshops traffic exclusively in used guitars and universally refrain from maintaining two sets of books. Maybe leprechauns also frolic in the woods. Silver-tongued, golden-throated, platinum-haired Slip McGrady was entering a plea of not guilty today, but not because anybody capable of making change for the uptown bus presumed for a second he was innocent of anything. Nonetheless, everybody was entitled to a vigorous defense.

Enter Anthony. He was the kind of lawyer you needed in your corner if, let's say, you owned a pawnshop fronting for the genuine money-generating. Counsel therefore advised his client that the chances of a killingly charming lender by the name of Slip getting a walk were remote, comparable to those of a train conductor named Casey with a gambling jones next day reclaiming his hocked vest pocket watch after cleaning up in an overnight craps game. Anthony reminded McGrady what everybody in town knew, that the man was so jovial, so hail-fellow-well-met that even desperate losers at the pawnshop window cage hardly begrudged him. And yet, unless boyo wished to croon *Oh, Danny Boy, the pipes, the pipes are calling* and serenade his fellow inmates for the next five to ten, he would be wise, so counsel advised, to shut the fuck up today in court.

Branded upon her memory was something else he said that morning. Anthony promised Francesca, the love of his life, that he was not going to die today. These were the words he uttered:

"I'll pick up some fish."

He was referring to dinner tonight, when last night's conflict would be a dim reminiscence.

At that early hour she was unable to stomach the prospect of dining on fish, but that was Anthony the litigator's MO: move ahead undaunted, burn no bridges, coalesce around mutual interests—like dinner. Before she got to know him, she would have assumed all high-paid lawyers were hardwired to be disputatious, if not belligerent. It was indeed the case that by reputation he was a bulldog in court, though never with her, never. His blond hair curling down over his shirt collar cried out for a trim at Scanlon's barber shop, but this was not the opportune moment to offer such a suggestion.

"All right, you young buck," she said. *Young buck*: there she went again, quaint as ever. Upon reflection, she didn't have anything left to say to him after all. Getting in the last word was an overrated pleasure, an empty victory that might have been prized when she was in her early twenties, whenever that was.

Besides, that was as good a way as any to put distance on their scuffle, by looking forward—dinner, domesticity, ordinary life. Not that some outside observers might have predicted as much, given their ethnic roots, families for whom—so go the Irish and Italian stereotypes at least—confrontation amounted to a jig, a boisterous magic show, an irresistible if dangerous *festa*.

Irish and the Italians. The Irish may have invented talking, but the Italians invented never shutting up. The Italians may have originated fashion and style and design (the French may take a number), while the Irish originated not giving a knee-wobbler what anybody thought about how they looked. They were both cops and mobsters, sometimes simultaneously. They were equally connoisseurs of contemptuousness: Italians looked down upon somebody not born in their hometown, and the Irish, anybody who wasn't born Irish and (as far as the Fitzgeralds were concerned) sipped anything other than Jameson. And yet they both fancied themselves experts in matters of the heart, too, natural-born poets and artists and die-hard loyalists to the bitter end when it came to their friends. Most were what you might call Catholic, but Catholics couldn't confidently articulate what Catholic meant anymore. All their emotions were operatic in scale and their glasses were not empty indefinitely. They deplored their countries but with patriotic conviction. They were generous with their money, and even more generous with yours. They trusted you around their spouses and with other precious possessions, but kept a close watch, because all men are dogs and you never know. They were both dedicated to the idea of the family, for which they would die if they didn't demolish it first. They both served up tragedy all day long, breakfast, lunch, and dinner—and comedy for dessert—but speaking of cuisine, that's when equivalence evaporates, as only the Italians can be said to have one. And they both lived and died for and with soccer, which they called football or *calcio*, and wholeheartedly believed in the vagaries of luck, as when the two converged in the latest penalty kick of misfortune. Stereotypes like these may come in handy, insofar as each contains a germ of truth. Thus only a fool subscribes. Italians and the Irish. They were exactly the same, only completely different.

Francesca recognized that some married couples maintained they benefited from learning how to fight fair, because, to their way of thinking, clashing was inevitable once the honeymoon glow dimmed. If you believe the rom-com movies and TV shows, fighting amounted to an aggressive, ritualized form of foreplay, or anthropological display. Ultimately, married people fought not so much to defend themselves or to draw blood, that is, but in order to be intimate. That could make a kind of sense, she supposed, though that made it sound tactical, and the notion of erotic strategizing, a frat boy's wet dream, depressed her. She'd concede this much: post-battle sex could sweep the decks clear, exchanging one sort of emotional intensity for a more satisfying kind—at least when each member of the couple suspends self-interest and stops to care for the other more than achieving the goal of scoring points. Then interests overlap as bodies and souls merge in mutual consent. Arguments melt into meaninglessness in the heat of passion. But sex was not the result, and not the byproduct, of a negotiation (at least not the kind of sex anybody really craved). It was more like reciprocal submission, which sounded both logically impossible and absolutely real. As a rule, as far as she was concerned, being a devotee of marital combat meant not being good at being married. On the street, in the boardroom, in the financial markets, in court, every fight must have a winner and therefore must have a loser. But for her in a marriage, fighting risks leaving two losers on the sweaty mat, or at least two un-winners. Of course, she was guessing, a rank amateur. When it comes to intimacy and marriage, everybody was an amateur, hazarding wild hunches. All her friends—this was a stat drawn from an idiosyncratic small sampling—well, many of her *female* friends had maneuvered their mates into going on a couples counseling peacekeeping mission, a type of mediation. In practice, somebody was often wishing to commission a psychic makeover on her partner. Or somebody was lodging a kind of criminal complaint, in which case couples counseling functioned as a branch of law enforcement. Couples counseling never crossed Anthony and Francesca's minds, not once. They knew they were lucky, but they didn't know how lucky. Until one day they were not.

—

"I'LL PICK UP SOME fish." Anthony was unequivocal and, to reference his lawyer lingo, dispositive.

She posed no alternatives as he rushed out the door. He had a big job as a criminal defense attorney that he loved. On the way home, he would take a number at bustling Mulvaney's Fish Market, stand on line, and consider what the sea was offering Frankie and him for supper tonight.

The morning of the fateful promise, he had that crucial McGrady date at the courthouse, and he did appear preoccupied, a little frazzled, and he abhorred being late, so he absent-mindedly neglected articulating *goodbye*, but there is no question he loved Francesca from the first and loved her without reserve and there is no doubt he did assure her he would select and bring home some fish and did therefore imply—not that she had a sliver of a doubt—that he would return for dinner, to her, his wife. With his haul from the sea.

He packed his backpack with the files he needed and slipped it through his arms and over his suit coat. This image always made her smile. So *Anthony*: high schooler's backpack on top of his Zegna suit on the way to his max-billable-hour, corner-office job—a comprehensively mixed metaphor. She had wrested from him the corduroy coat, and she was confident she'd have success one day jettisoning the backpack.

They were making a solid life together. Someday they'd have a child, or two, who knows, maybe they'd go crazy and have three. They had been together for five years, the *tick tock* of the clock resounding like a blacksmith's hammer on anvil.

As it happened, she never again revisited the backpack, they never did have children, and he wouldn't come back home.

Fish. The last word he said to her that morning was *fish*.

That was it. What kind of irresponsible thing was that to say? This from a man who had honored every one of his promises—big or small, better or worse, richer or poorer, sickness or health.

—

FRANCESCA WAS SPEAKING ONCE again to Anthony, but he wasn't responding because he was no longer available. He had not been there for three years. Yet she addressed him in her mind despite his reluctance to respond. He was not being rude. Their whole life long, he was never unkind to her. There was a rational explanation for his reticence. The reason is that one afternoon three years earlier, a few hours after the grandiloquent Slip McGrady swallowed his tongue, copped a plea and, thanks to his attorney, got a better deal than he deserved or anybody expected, Anthony Fitzgerald keeled over without warning at his office desk, brain aneurysm, age thirty-nine, and that was that, end of story. Road Runner met rock wall.

It could happen to anybody, somebody familiar with the actuarial tables might verify.

But no, it couldn't, Francesca believed every single unbelievable day.

For someone no longer there, he inhabited the emptiness inside Francesca. He was not there coming through the door, arms open wide. Not there fixing the lampshade, the leaky faucet, the running toilet, the tilting fence, the cable connection, the computer backup. He was handy with repairs, but at some point everyone realizes some problems can never be rectified. He was not there making coffee on the kitchen counter or pouring from a beautiful bottle of decanted Tuscan wine on a candlelit vintage country farmhouse table. Not there with his nose in the travel guide on the cobbled lanes of Dublin or Rome. Not there driving around town at five miles above the speed limit—not two, not ten, five. Not there napping Saturday afternoons in the garden with a book splayed open upon his chest. "Reading with my eyes closed," as he put it. Not there wading into the bath-temperature Maui surf. Not there polishing his shoes before bed. Shoes are, he contended, the first thing a perceptive client notices, and scuffed-up footwear signals a disordered mind—and unreliable professional counsel. Mostly, he was not there in bed. Not there in bed. Not there in bed, sleeping alongside Francesca, who was herself swept up in the dream he would never die.

He was nowhere, he was everywhere. He shuttled daily, or hourly, between those two poles, and she was haunted by memories often more urgent than her own existence.

So yes, it does seem a lifetime since the Thursday that Anthony Fitzgerald failed to come home with the fish—or with himself. Or as it felt to Frankie—a heartbeat ago. And she would never make peace with Thursday. *What a cruel day on which to die*, she thought. *Just like all the others.*

As we all learn sooner or later, there is a kind of story that never comes to an end as long as we live. And some stories, like that of Francesca and her Anthony, along with the whole good Family Fitzgerald, are always beginning again and again, and then again.

Chapter Two
Paddy

PADDY FITZGERALD WAS IN a spot of trouble. But let's get something straight. He wasn't bellyaching, wasn't feeling boohoo sorry for himself, and wasn't seeking any pantywaist's sympathy. Not Paddy Fitzgerald, not then, not ever.

All right then.

About that *trouble* of his: right there, that's one freighted term the Irish, according to legend rarely if ever tongue-tied, don't casually invoke. If you ever hear them utter the word *troo-bull*, you would be wise to backtrack swiftly for the closest exit. But there are troubles and there are *troubles*. He had the worse kind, which ought not to be confused with the capital-T Troubles that once embroiled his ancestral hated homeland— beloved, far-off Ireland. But his *homeland*? He wouldn't overplay his ethnic identity, such as it was. He would also not suffer to be compared to, say, his wretched immigrant of a father, man of unsainted memory: encrusted black fingernails, wobbly whiskey bottle on the rickety dinner table, child- and wife-beating belt buckle at the ready, venom dripping from his lips for the fecking Protestants and the fecking Brits, both sharing a seamy bed in the selfsame scummy bog. The son of a bitch was not in error in that estimation, but if he issued another truthful utterance in his not-foreshortened-enough life, his son missed it. Rest in peace. As if that were possible for a Fitzgerald.

"You hear the one about the Irishman who left the bar?" Paddy's old man trotted out this one a hundred times. Two bilious beats later: "Yeah, it could happen."

No wonder Paddy had zero tolerance for the loathsome shamrocky caricature and the Saint Patrick's Day posturing, and the chances of his crooning "When Irish Eyes Are Smiling" while pub-crawling were a long, long way to Tipperary. He supposed there was no escaping being typecast as an Irish American, whatever that augured, not with a name like Padraic Fitzgerald, though few knew how to pronounce the Irish. Paw-rick? Pah-drake? Pahd-ray-ack? So Paddy would do. But if Paddy swore any allegiance to anything it was to God Bless America—and he didn't, not quite.

He had never been a tonsured monk and taken a vow of cloistered silence, but no thanks, he didn't care to talk about any of his troubles.

—

YET SAY HE DID, where to start? Family? Business? The new girl? Some kind of trifecta. And come on now, at his advanced age, what was he doing with a new girl? If you ever once laid your lucky eyes on her, the answer might seem thunderously obvious. For another thing, the deal he had been counting on swinging, selling a prime piece of property at a healthy profit, looked to be heading south. He didn't *need* the money, not in the way most people need money, because he had more than he would ever use, but he needed to swing the *deal*. One scuttled transaction amounted to little on his balance sheet in the grand scheme of things, though it was also *something* because in the grand scheme of things there may be no such grand scheme of things, and certainly not for a man with his sort of pride—or for anybody else. Compounding matters, his mirror had broken the incredible news, that he had metamorphosed overnight into an old man. How did that happen? And now there was this new skirt, who made him feel older when she didn't make him feel younger, and did double duty during the course of the same hour, while wearing or not said skirt. He had to ask himself how come, in the midst of all his troubles, when he had pressing, immediate business to tend to, he was also thinking about her?

He may have been outfitted in a midnight-blue dinner jacket, but this was no Michelin-star restaurant, and even if it were, nobody would mistake him for some suck-up maître d' sticking out his hand, trolling for an Alexander Hamilton, an Andrew Jackson, a Ben Franklin. No, his fists were clenched and his arms drooped like an exhausted boxer in his corner waiting for the bell to ring, and he looked out across the city skyline through the penthouse window as if he were prepared to mix it up with an upstart opponent in the opposite corner ready to charge across the mat, exhaling raw onion, fists flying.

Lights glittered down below, and from high above the street he imagined enemies lurking in the shadows. The world had changed over the decades before his very eyes. As God was his witness, a world changed not for the better, and he had his doubts about his supposed witness. People had become harder to manage, downright truculent. Not that he was intimidated by anybody. An old-fashioned donnybrook makes the blood flow, and a soul-satisfying smack drains the sinuses, and after all that blood flows, you get your second wind, you stand taller, you see clearer, scales walloped from your eyes.

In the city vista, through undulating, sparkly sheets of rain squalls, he also glimpsed opportunity. The opportunity he sensed everywhere on the other side of the triple-pane safety glass was unrealized, untapped, unexploited opportunity, which was the worst kind.

Deals not cemented.

Men who needed to be brought to their senses, knocked off their high horses.

Obstacles that cried out to be obliterated.

People who ought to be shown in no uncertain terms the advantages of being reasonable with him.

Everybody should be more like me, he often remarked to himself. If they were, he had no question the world would be a much finer place. He'd make more money, sure, but so would everybody else. People would dress presentably, too. The ridiculous rags grown men and women threw on when they went out, it was embarrassing, it was disrespectful, they had to be kidding, at the baseball game, at the store, at the airport, looking like they had rolled out of bed for an early trade school class or their fry cook job at the greasy spoon. Snap to it, slackers, make the fucking effort: that was his summary judgment. And don't get him started on the unsanitary flip-flop contagion.

Once while he was being chauffeured along on a beautiful day, his head snapped back witnessing a stomach-turning spectacle. From his back seat window he saw a shoeless man on a park bench clipping his toenails. The park was called Fitzgerald Green, because Paddy's civic consciousness, and his money, caused it to exist: a safe place for children to play, for the elderly and infirm to stroll in the sun, for birds to take wing, for dogs to romp—in other words, no such place where a man could with impunity give himself a goddamn pedicure. Paddy told his driver to stop. He instructed his people to speak directly to the man, in order to have him immediately amend his ways. So they did. The self-groomer didn't appreciate the attention they paid him, but he appreciated even less the actions they undertook to ensure he would not be able to resume his revolting regimen in Fitzgerald Green ever again.

Troubles, troubles. Who doesn't have them? The one and only consolation strictly reserved for the departed: no more troubles, no more problems. Problems signaled you were still breathing, still yearning for air, still seeking a sliver of fading sunlight. Same time, when drastic measures were indicated in order to solve a problem, Paddy Fitzgerald had no qualms becoming somebody's worst solution.

—

He wasn't alone in the penthouse with his reflection in the window. "Baby, if I was a young man…" he started, but then hopped off that rattling, cow-catching train of associations.

The young woman on the other side of the great room was long-legged, lithe, and bright-eyed, and she was wearing without a single perceivable regret a shimmery kimono. She gave every mortal indication she had major plans in store for it. She took a stab at uttering some semblance of a thought: "Yeah, if you was a young man, we might've went to high school together. Go, Mighty Honkers. Never did pass algebra either time, but you could've saved me, let me see your answers on the exam." She called herself

Caitlindee and was channeling her inner scamp, all that champagne she solo consumed having gone to her breathtakingly pretty head.

He was amused. He was often amused around her, which was not the primary reason she was around. "Honkers? Get outta here. *Honkers.*"

"*Mighty* Honkers, my school mascot. Like, you know, ducks?"

"Which then you gotta mean geese, gorgeous. Ducks'd be the Mighty Quackers."

She giggled, conceding in effect that he may have made a solid point and that she may have had a little too much to drink.

Paddy's midnight-blue shoulders relaxed and his chilly, single-note, silvery laugh wanted to qualify as one. He enjoyed having the girl around, she partied like a pro, which in fact she was, and she took his mind off some of those famous troubles of his for a few minutes, and what a great few minutes they were. Long flowing red hair, creamy flesh, rosebud mouth, traffic light green eyes—she was certified to take any man's mind off his problems, if only temporarily. Then again, *temporarily* was often all a man desired. And sure, in theory, *sure* it might have been nice to know her twenty, thirty years ago, but *high school?* He didn't know about that. In his day, goals did not include caps and gowns in processional, and her name was never posted on the Honor Roll in the hallway, either.

And yet, if time bent back in a hypothetical universe or, say, in a strip mall somewhere across town, who knows, they might have locked up, a couple of mighty, mismatched Honkers. Stranger things have happened.

Before he showed up tonight unannounced at the apartment, Caitlindee had powered through most of the champagne bottle that was sweating on the high-modern, trapezoidal glass coffee table. It was a Friday evening, after all, and champagne was the ideal prelude to date night. But to judge by how she was dressed—and how she was not—she wasn't going to be viewed in public soon.

Paddy kept staring out the apartment-wide floor-to-ceiling wall of glass, and he watched the brake lights and headlamps down below filtered by the driving rain. He did have affection for the girl, who—so far so good—appeared mostly uncomplicated in the way that he wished everybody to be and hardly anybody was, including his own adult children, who traveled paths antithetical to his, and including also their mother, his late wife, whom he remembered with fondness—until he recalled she was perennially one step ahead of him. He missed her, he did, but he also had to admit that he found it simpler to conduct his business free of her encumbering awareness.

He mourned his oldest son, as well, every single day, and there was no upside whatsoever to Anthony's loss.

"Feeling low, Sweets?"

Saying that, she referenced Paddy's street name, but he didn't mind, which wasn't the case when law enforcement or reporters rashly presumed otherwise. It was important, what you called yourself. For instance, she had been christened at birth Caitlin Cahill, and to her nothing was amiss with Caitlin, except how for some reason these days there was a gaggle of Caitlins milling about, not as many as the Jennifers and the Samanthas and the Heathers and the Madisons, but a virtual Calling All Caitlins Flash Mob Convention nonetheless. So when she ventured upon her specialized career path, she wanted a handle that was unique, memorable, Southern belle-ish, for coquettish brand appeal. She briefly contemplated naming herself Destiny. The name itself was fun to say, and she couldn't wait to speak of herself in the third person and propose to a potential client, "Would you like a date with Destiny?" Accurate enough, but a little bit too darling to live. So in a burst of inspiration, she tacked *dee* onto Caitlin, hence the Caitlindee, and it stuck, like gum on the sole of her thigh-high black leather boots. To entertain herself she creatively varied spellings. On her driver's license she was Catelindey, and on her checkbook it was Caitlindy and she entertained Cait Lindy, too. Katelynd didn't cut it, however, a position she couldn't defend, not that she was asked. Spelling, like algebra and bird calls, was not her strong suit.

"What's eating you, Daddy Bear?"

He was feeling wistful and talked to his own face in the glass, his back to her. "Like I said, if I was a young man, I'd own this whole damn town."

Her lantern-green eyes opened wide, and she didn't know what to say, because along with every Caitlin and Jennifer and Samantha and Heather and Sarah and Madison around, she assumed Sweets Fitzgerald already owned the whole damn town, and then some.

—

MUCH AS HE LIKED the penthouse, and even more the girl he'd installed there, so far he had elected never to spend the whole night there with her. He made it a point to return home before sunrise, because that's where he lived, and lived alone, and where he had not once taken her.

She never asked for an invitation and the topic never came up for discussion. Other smoldering topics, including the obvious ones, assumed primacy when it came to her. She deduced that his home was simply off-limits. She never assumed he was telling the complete truth, not that this disturbed her terribly. Maybe he had a wife, or something or someone else to conceal—how could she know? Men had their secrets. You should count on that. Oftentimes it was their most endearing trait, their predictable unpredictability. In that regard she thought she was not so different from him. Whatever it was, whoever it was, she could adjust. When it came to men, she was clever as a chameleon: she changed to fit circumstance.

As far as he was concerned, it was as if he would be betraying not someone but something precious he couldn't identify. It had nothing to do with the memory of his late wife, either. Her memory was sacrosanct. Some fool might be tempted to call him a sentimental Mick—but unless you preferred the view of the sky from the horizontal plane, it wasn't advisable.

The Family Fitzgerald house stood out on top of the lofty peak of Haymarket Hill, and Paddy loved to hunt the view from high up, instinctive as a hawk in soaring flight. This was the choicest neighborhood, and his secluded property constituted in and of itself an enclave, accessible by turning off the street, passing through tall iron gates, and going up the steep winding private road a quarter mile to the circular drive at the top. Records were not crystal clear, but the house seemed to have been originally constructed at least a hundred years ago. Shortly after he was married, before Anthony and the rest of the children were born, Paddy bought it from an aged onetime bootlegger who was down on his luck, who himself had bought it from an older wildcatter who was also further down on his luck, and with each passing year Paddy appreciated more and more what a sharp deal he had struck. From his front room, he could see out the bay windows to the headlands in the distance, and the forest of evergreens swaying beyond. At that altitude the wind seemed always to be blowing. He could spy the tiny ships down below inching slowly into port, and he could study the cottony cloud formations rushing by in the blue distance.

Two six-day-a-week housekeepers and one Monday-through-Friday cook surreptitiously tapped the bottles of Irish whiskey throughout their shifts, but since the Chilean ladies were pleasant and respectful (they referred to him as *Don* Paddy, nothing he could do to discourage them), he turned a blind eye and a deaf ear. After all, the house had not burned down a single time under their watch, and the windows sparkled, and the floors gleamed, and the larder was invariably brimming. The cook hadn't yet mastered Irish stew, but since he recoiled from the old country dish, he was indifferent. "Almost there, Hilda, almost got it, *signora*," he would politely say, not quite savoring a forkful. "*Grazie*, Don Paddy." His three full-time gardeners were born-again Christians and teetotalers occupied the year round. The domestic bustle didn't diminish his sense of isolation, and if anything deepened it.

As for the groundskeepers, they manicured shrubbery and greenery and tended to two acres of olive, fig, and apple trees as well as the beautiful multicolored flower beds. Roses never took because temperature on the Hill plummeted at nightfall, including in the summer. The pious gardeners carefully tried to talk him out of planting them, but for a man without evident weaknesses, Paddy had a weakness for roses. Not having a green thumb, he assumed one day the roses would be intimidated, obey his command, take root, and bloom already. As a result, every other year or so new bushes would be planted, and every other year they would fail. You could call him mule-headed, but again, there was no percentage taking a risk like that.

In theory, he had neighbors beyond his property lines, but he wouldn't recognize any of them if their paths should converge, which they likely never would. He literally looked down on them, but not metaphorically, not disrespectfully. Neighbors were by definition inconsequential. That sounds harsh, but they weren't Fitzgeralds, his flesh and blood.

As for the Fitzgeralds, they lived in a world of their own on Haymarket Hill, though now there was only *one* Fitzgerald remaining who walked the echoing hardwood hallways not covered by dozens of Persian carpets dispersed throughout. The ten-thousand-square-foot Georgian could have modeled for a pretty postcard, complete with turrets and towers and stained glass windows, limestone floors, and redbrick chimneys, and tapestries big as schooner sails stolen long ago (not by him) from Irish monasteries. Mansard roof and half-round dormer windows and fireplaces big enough to roast a stag. Gothic was the darkness gathering everywhere inside, spooling in the mahogany bar, his favorite room, where he would meet with his crew when necessary. There was also a black-bottom swimming pool, which he occasionally forgot he owned, but though the gardeners kept it in pristine condition, it was rarely warm enough to swim, and nobody could remember the last time anyone was foolhardy enough to dip a toe in.

He may have lived by himself, but memory played its predictable, mundane tricks. His wife had possessed the designer touch, and she had executed all the decorating decisions, the impact of which lingered, and which sometimes made him feel glad. Once the house used to resound with the elevated voices of his four children, with the clatter of scampering dogs' paws, with the music of Irish ballads playing on the turntable. His wife used to organize parties in the gardens, and the children and their school friends would squeal and the batshit Irish setters would bark, and for big occasions the diddly-aye bagpipes she inexplicably loved would bleat nostalgically across Haymarket Hill. When night fell, a more credulous man might have believed ghosts gamboled about. When Paddy heard thumps in the walls and creaks on the stairs, he recalled that his own father had no doubt about the existence of banshees, witches, and ghosts. So when he heard strange noises in the dark, he checked for the loaded handgun underneath his mattress. Paddy may not have believed in spirits, but if that were his old man, returned to pay a visit to square up accounts with his son, he had a high-caliber greeting at the ready.

As a thought exercise he considered selling, but that would have been nothing but a prudent business move. And where was he to go and why? Besides, the Fitzgeralds were sensible only as a last last last resort, when something else more compelling didn't qualify. Truth was inarguable: he could not relinquish the family home, though the Family Fitzgerald wasn't what it once used to be. He would clear millions by selling, of course, and some spec developer would subdivide the prime Haymarket Hill property into numerous lots and reap obscene returns. But that was money he didn't need—even if money was money, and for his own family of immigrants who fled the famines, there never could be enough of it, and whatever you had was at risk. Nonetheless, odds were he would never sell. He'd leave the whole homestead to his three surviving children, equal shares to each. Let the remnants of the clan duke it out.

He did love his olive trees, how hardy they swayed and self-possessed they loomed. The Italians had a saying that resonated: plant vineyards for your children, olive trees for your grandchildren. He didn't have a single grandchild, a fact that routinely rendered him downcast. His gardeners took delight in the harvest and the boutique pressings, and the spare cash they generated for themselves by pedaling it on the side, but Paddy never acquired a taste for the olive oil—too Italian. It was the rustling trees that meant the most.

He did harbor one fantasy, one he would share with no one as long as he was alive, a fantasy of being buried on Haymarket Hill, in a clearing beyond the olive trees. That prospect almost cheered him—at least to the extent that any thought pertaining to mortality could cheer anybody. He went to the lengths of adding a codicil to his estate plan, specifying where he wanted to be laid to rest, assuming rest was ultimately conceivable for somebody like him. He added another set of terms for good measure including: *Bagpipes at my funeral, I'll haunt you forever.* To which his children, reading that one day, would likely nod and say in one voice, *Even in the afterlife you're consistent.*

In his advancing years, Paddy remained busy, busy, and as a result he spent much less time at the house than when he was a new husband and father. When he indulged himself in a vanquished mood, he'd sit for hours ruminating in his Moroccan red easy chair under the forty-foot high beams and listen to scratchy vinyl records cut by classic tenors from the Emerald Isle, sipping tumbler after tumbler of Jameson's top-of-the-line, Midleton Very Rare, each bottle of which cost more than his own miserable da earned for a month of backbreaking labor at the ironworks. When his whiskey glass clinked on the table, the echo seemed to bounce all over Haymarket. Over time he had come to regard his solitariness the way the lighthouse keeper on some remote cape views his isolation— as his single confidant.

—

CAITLINDEE AND HER PENTHOUSE existed on another, altogether rarefied plane. So did that short black silk kimono of hers, one with a red dragon coiling up her spine and reaching over her shoulder to paw her breast, a garment that in the moment was hanging tenuous and shimmering as a burnished autumn leaf. That's one very fortunate dragon, Paddy considered.

She untied the belt, as if it were a ribbon wrapped around a surprise present, and she shimmied out of her auspicious kimono, letting it fall in cascading folds to the white carpet, and stepped in her heels beyond the dragon, impatiently waiting for Paddy to come over to her. She quivered like the plucked string of a guitar.

She hadn't expected him tonight. Not that he ever cleared his calendar with her—why would he? He did mention he was going to some splashy benefit—and not with her in tow. She liked to believe she didn't take such decisions personally. After all, men didn't first make her acquaintance at the symphony or a poetry reading or the environmental fundraiser. And true, men had an unblemished record of disappointing her. That's what men were used to doing around somebody like who they thought she was, which she wasn't anymore and never would be again if she could help it, and for the first time in her life she believed she could. Because thanks to Paddy, she now believed she was exempt from disappointment when it came to men.

As for him, he did not disapprove whenever she cast off that kimono. He *did* wonder why she was wearing it since he wasn't expected.

"Champagne?" she said, to get his attention. Pilates, yoga, kickboxing— she was committed to working out every day, toning her body, her inflation-proof asset. She picked up the bottle on the coffee table and struggled to read the name on the label of what Paddy had left in her refrigerator along with five more bottles of the same. She mangled the pronunciation of *Veuve Clicquot*, but she gave it her best shot.

If it were imperative that a mistress also be talented linguistically, Paddy would have insisted. *Mistress,* he said to himself. *Who says the word "mistress" anymore?* He didn't care, and in any case he only did what he wanted— and whom he wanted. And he wanted her available when he wanted: the benefits of his advancing years and his status and his wealth—and the terms of their arrangement.

"Enjoying the bubbly?" he said to the window.

She certainly did, and she had a follow-up suggestion: "Should I lift up your mood?"

Her purring tone of voice aroused his attention. "Just having you here, just you living here and being here whenever I come over, that cheers me up."

Paddy Fitzgerald turned away from the window and walked across the vast expanse of the living room. "You're kinda gorgeous, aren't you," he said, and it was true. He presumed you needed to state the obvious to a woman, even one as young and dazzling as Caitlindee, on the off chance either of them forgot. And nobody like her doesn't like to be reminded anyway. So far he hadn't called upon the services of a blue pharmaceutical when it came to her. That day would arrive, he figured, soon enough.

"All for you, Sweets."

He fanned a set of hundreds on the glass coffee table like the winning hand in a casino. "Enough pocket money, get you through the week?"

She nodded. The man took care of her, as promised.

"No drugs, baby, right?"

"Clean as a whistle, since you."

"I mean, drugs, you know, pretty girl like you, be an unfortunate development."

That was his only stipulation, that she stay clean—and also that she entertain no other men here or anywhere else on the planet. And keep the kimono handy and disposable.

"This apartment, should I get you a different one?"

The stunning penthouse was a dream come true for her, how could she not like it? She sidled up to him, who towered over her. She put her arms around his waist. She once asked him if he wanted her to get implants, because she worried her demure breasts were a little too understated, and she would gladly go under the knife for him or do anything at all he wanted, but that was unnecessary. A girl with breasts that filled his mouth didn't require the services of a surgeon. To him, she was perfect and those were deadly excellent toys in her sachet.

"Might see you later. Watch your TV shows, don't wait up."

She pretended to sulk. She didn't sign on any dotted line, and taking contract classes in law school did not loom in her future, but she grasped the nuance-free message.

"Daddy Bear always gotta work," she pouted. She placed her head against his pristine ruffled white shirt but he didn't mind. She no longer wore lipstick because Paddy did mind that. To him, that made women look cheap, like dolls. Besides, her full lips didn't require cosmetic enhancement to brighten the room.

"Work's how come you can drink Veuve Clicquot anytime you want in your penthouse."

She looked baffled, but he was sympathetic.

"That's the name of the champagne you been downing. In my sad French, named for a widow."

When she laughed she sounded like a child on a roller coaster, unleashing a series of delighted and frightened musical notes. What a weird name for champagne. Was she the luckiest girl who ever lived, or what? Drinking what she considered fabulous champagne, living in a fantastic apartment on top of the world, her bank account flush, diamonds on her fingers, the most powerful man in town in her bed—now and then, when he said he could.

Her cell phone rang on the coffee table. Paddy glared at the thing as if it were a personal antagonist, which it was except for when he called her. He had instructed her to turn off her phone when he was around. He would remind her more pointedly when he got the chance. His eyes darted toward hers and he saw something he wished he hadn't seen. Fear. And not for the first time. He would figure all this out. It was relatively early in their relationship—if *relationship* was the word for their arrangement. He'd known her five or six months. He could make a few guesses as to what might account for her uneasiness about a call coming in. Maybe she was tying up the loose ends of her previous life, where he found her and from which she had been scooped up by him. But he was a realist. He had a little patience. But as his business associates, and especially his rivals, would testify, that was a commodity in limited supply.

"Like my cufflinks, the bow tie?"

She rallied, as he went in that direction, away from the telephone complication. "You look good enough to eat, Sweets. Fancy Dancy in your pretty tuxedo." She stepped out of her shoes.

He explained tonight was all about business, couldn't be avoided. For a minute he had contemplated taking her to the big Catholic benefit, but in the end determined no, he had work to do before, during, and after. More to the point, he wasn't ready to go public, and a good chance he never would be. Besides, he was having nothing but difficulty with regard to the big real estate deal he had been offering the diocese, and tonight he would take advantage of the opportunity to move the right people in the proper direction: his. He didn't have unbridled high hopes on that score, and that recognition bleakened his mood tonight. The Catholics were playing hardball. How did they ever imagine they had leverage over him? They would learn sooner or later nobody enjoyed leverage when it came to Paddy Fitzgerald. To be clear, they might indeed possess leverage, but they wouldn't *enjoy* it, certainly not without paying a price. He had no alternative but to school the Catholics.

"You and them Catholics," she said. "Like, you religious?" She had never asked.

"Like I said, all business, doll baby."

"But your son, he's a priest, for *real*? Can I meet him?"

He shrugged. That rendezvous would never take place if he could help it.

"Is he going to be there tonight?"

"Usually is, events like that."

"Some of them priests, they're up to funny stuff."

"You know any? Talking about priests?" That was an offhanded question that was anything but, and part of him wished he hadn't asked.

"Didn't grow up no Catholic, never been much to church, except a wedding one time, funeral couple times."

He waited three beats. Then he shot her a look to make it clear she knew precisely what he was asking, and what he didn't want to know.

"No," she said, "don't think I ever."

"Tell you what, week or so, we jet to New York, spend a few nights at a nice hotel, Upper East Side off the Park, catch a show, some restaurants, have fun, buy you new clothes. You seem to be running out of things to wear."

That made her smile. "I dress up for you." Or not, she didn't bother to elaborate.

"Find you another kimono. You look fabulous in yours, or out of it. Where'd you get it?" His own probings tonight surprised him. He could tell from the blankness in her eyes and the immobility of her lips she was thinking hard. He appreciated she was not a gifted liar, which was one sterling character trait they did not happen to share. And if you couldn't find a girl who had a weakness for telling the truth, at least get one you could tell when she was lying. Paddy didn't play poker anymore, a younger man's game, but he could read in faces what cards people were holding when they weren't holding any.

She concluded this was a moment, perhaps a test. "Some swank consignment place, downtown, can't remember, long ago. Wait, wait, no, no, my crazy aunt got it for me in Japan."

He directed his manicured right hand between her legs, and leaned in to cup his mouth around her taffy-sweet ear to inquire in a throaty whisper if she liked that. She reflexively elevated to the tips of her toes. He considered himself a gentleman, most of the time. And he might have congratulated himself on that score, because a guy like him, he didn't have to be a gentleman unless he wanted.

"What's her name, crazy aunt, Japan?"

"What? *What?*" It took her a second, the question rattled her but not as much as his hand, and it required concerted effort to speak. "Sarah," she said, which sounded like she was exhaling, which she also was, "Sarah, Aunty Sarah..."

"You like *this?*"

His cologne intoxicated her, lemon trees and spices, but the expensive kind, not off the drugstore shelf. Older men splashed on cologne, she learned from past experience, and it worked like catnip. She gasped when her phone rang once again and she whispered yes, she did like what he was doing, but then he pulled back his hand, tantalizing her.

"Sure whoever's calling will leave a message." The implication was obvious as to how pleased he would be over that development.

"I don't care." He couldn't tell for sure that she didn't. That was okay, for now. If the girl became a problem she wouldn't remain a problem for long. He knew how to conclude arrangements that turned sour. And yet that made him ask himself if he did have feelings for her, after all. He'd file that under bizarre complications, which he also knew how to deal with.

With two hands she guided his back to where it had been and shut her eyes as her mouth rounded into an O.

"You want to go out tonight—with a girlfriend? If you have one of those, I mean. Do you? Have a girlfriend?" Every so often it would occur how little he knew about her, and how minimally that mattered.

Words were halting, and she leaned weak-kneed into his chest. "No, Pad. Stay here, be here. You come back. Af. Ter." She wasn't complaining and she wasn't explaining. She had learned from the jump that was not the thing to do.

"I would like to trust you to be here, when you say you will be."

He'd keep her out of the limelight. For a man like him, that's what having a low-maintenance beautiful mistress was useful for—as long as she remained low-maintenance. He pulled back his hand once more and she opened her eyes, communicating with some intensity that she preferred where it was before.

Her voice dropped two octaves. "Have to leave so soon, Sweets?"

She had a point. Liars, including beautiful incompetent liars, are capable of a good point. He took out his phone and advised his driver he'd be downstairs eventually, but not to hold his breath. His driver expressed concern as to timing.

"Jonesy, I have a watch, and a nice one, too. If we're a little bit late, so be it. Why don't you read your book of poetry?"

His driver, Jonesy O'Dell, was more than his driver, and a man whose reading predilections were opaque to his boss. Nothing wrong with being a chauffeur, according to Jonesy's radical democratic inclinations, but his job profile was multifaceted and his assignments were limited only by the range of Paddy's problems and needs and wishes. Only thing Paddy wished for is that Jonesy didn't attempt to micromanage him.

Paddy sighed, indicating he might wish to continue the phone conversation—but not now. "Jonesy, later. My biscuits are ready to come out of the oven."

Paddy slipped off his midnight-blue jacket, folded it precisely, and draped it on the arm of the white leather couch.

"Biscuits in the oven?" she said. "Really?"

"You know Jonesy."

She couldn't say that she did. "It's coming down pretty good outside. Got your raincoat in the car?"

It was indeed bucketing down, but the tilt of his head indicated the weather failed to elicit his slightest interest.

"What'd you have in mind before you go, besides those famous biscuits of yours," she said. "Cards?"

"Yeah? Keep thinking, little Honker."

"That's *Mighty* Honker to you."

Chapter Three

Terry

THERE SHE WAS, BEING dogged down the street by a greasy tweaker in two-dollar drugstore flip-flops. The whole thing was hilarious and sad, and Terry wasn't really scared, more like curious as to how long before he'd trip and face-plant. This was the dragon-breath guy who hooked up with her buzzed, blasted mom in the dope fiend insane asylum that never passed for home sweet home, and he was moving in slo-mo, like somebody doing dumbass water aerobics in the shallow end of the pool at the Y. A dreamlike moonless night pursuit like this qualified as a new experience for the going-on-eighteen-year-old girl, but it didn't portend a bright future on her Instagram account. It also didn't loom as the future subject of her college application personal essay. That was where, she assumed, she was supposed to address grave, weighty topics like global warming and world hunger and prison reform, about which issues she had emphatic, inchoate feelings. She dreaded the college app, though not with the same immediacy she dreaded her mom's jacked-up moronic squeeze. Here it was the beginning of her senior year, and she should get her life in order. She should also graduate from high school. Something told her that was not going to be in the cards for her, either.

"Get back here, you little bitch whore!" *Clip clop.* His flip-flops *clippitty clopped* on the pavement like tiny rhythmic lashes on a bondage grubber's latexed ass.

Fuck a duck, she pondered, he uses words the way an unhousebroken dog uses a shoe. She'd read that a smart dog, such as a Border collie, has a vocabulary of about two hundred words, but she doubted a single one of them was *bitch* or *whore*. What the man had yelled constituted a high percentage of his working vocabulary. Then again, his working vocabulary was as unemployable as he was, given his persistent crystal stupor, and any self-respecting Border collie would score higher on the SAT than he would. And the way she was lately regarding her college prospects, higher than she would, too.

When it came to drugs for Terry, like addys or rids or X, the usual, all of which were everywhere for the taking, that wasn't happening. She was no altar boy slash girl but she couldn't explain. Don't bother bringing up weed: weed, man, come on, weed was boring as a baseball game or religion class. She'd sooner cut herself to get high, which she did experiment with a few times, but for her it wasn't the rush girls like Joneen swore it was, just stupid, just sad, not judging. Waterboard her, she might concede being a naturally adrenalized freakazoid girl who, angling for inclusion among her nonexistent peers, accepted dares, especially those decreed by idiots at school, who are expert at one thing, which is promulgating dares, but even so, she never missed a chance to jump off bridges real and figurative with the sluggiest of them.

"Butter buns, over here." That was Joneen talking to Terry, the other day, stretched out on the bed in her room painted ceiling to baseboard glossy black and red, in a geometric design matching the club she loved to sneak into, and which kept throwing her out. Joneen must have had parents, Terry presumed, but they always seemed to be out of town—they certainly were never home when she showed. "Take a look, this is cool."

Terry clambered over and gazed into the girl's laptop. She laughed, and wished she hadn't. "Get out."

"I know, right? Porn's for girls, too."

"Not this girl." She froze, couldn't pull her eyes away from the video. "Shoot me, that's totally gross. Girl looks, like, what? Fourteen?"

"I'll send the link, this site's my fave."

Terry climbed off the bed, semi-amazed and fearful she had been transformed by Joneen into another kind of person, at the same time wanting to find a way to erase what had been flash-imprinted on her brain.

Joneen kept speaking to the monitor. "You got a lot to learn, princess, grow up."

"I think they call people like you a bad influence."

"So's your moms and you're welcome." She scooped up her phone.

As far as Terry was concerned, being a bad influence was not a completely objectionable thing, because a friend's a friend, though she found herself at the stage of her life when she had few friends and the friends she did have she wasn't always sure she liked, which is where Joneen came in. Terry's phone pinged.

"You got a text," said Joneen. "Check it."

Terry didn't want to, but she obeyed. She stared in disbelief at her phone. "What's wrong with you?" She was referring to Joneen's naked-above-the-waist pic.

"Now you, me."

"Sorry, fresh out of white-trash selfies."

Joneen didn't consider herself trashy, that sext of hers was anything but, it was classy and cute and punk fashion, and she was trying to guide the little girl along because she needed help only Joneen could provide. "No wonder you have trouble with boys. You gotta sex boost your profile, guys go goo goo from selfies, being the dumb shits they are."

——

UNDER CURRENT CIRCUMSTANCES, NAMELY, hustling down the street late at night, her adrenaline was flowing. Not that everybody understood adrenaline, which didn't crank up the reptile brain chain, it calmed you down. She was no track star, but she was confident the slob in pathetic pursuit enjoyed no shot of gaining on her, and stood a better chance of causing himself a heart attack and crashing onto his saggy hog jowls, the jiggly sight of which nauseated her. But hold on, somebody explain this. Meth was supposed to burn off pounds, which is why it became all that back in the day, so how come the dude looked like a pure porker? Her mom, the total opposite. She looked like a POW in old-time grainy footage on the History Channel, fingers hooked through barbed wire, cellophane skin, cheeks like sparrow heads, cigarette burns for eye sockets.

All things considered, tonight was not an experience she would post on Facebook either, which she was done with now that grandparents were crowding out everyone else with darling baby pics.

"Motherfuck, you little skank!" *Clip clop.*

She stopped, turned. "Didn't know you cared, Dad!" And took off again. She shouldn't have called him Dad. Bad move, taunting him, technical foul, two shots and the ball. At the same time, she was impressed her troll had the wind in his lungs to uncork so many words in a row. That along with his loping down the street constituted the greatest display of purposeful physical and mental activity he had ever exhibited.

Two minutes earlier she had tiptoed down the back stairs and sneaked out the kitchen door, where the cracked window was held in place by silver duct tape, closing the door with the faintest click, and headed down toward the dark street. The instant she reached the sidewalk she could breathe again. Being a feral creature, the guy must have sensed her absence and came out flying.

She did what she had to do. Nobody else would see it that way but that was their problem. She knew she was going to survive and she felt liberated, as if from some as-seen-on-streaming jailbreak, to which this run was not unrelated. She had a question for herself: *What took you so fucking long, Terry?* And another dawned in quick succession. *Why didn't you put on a fucking bra?*

This brought up for her a troubling association. Joneen told her she ought to get a breast reduction. ("'Less you're gonna be a pole dancer someday, but hey. What's it like holstering those bad girls?") Joneen fantasized about becoming a model so she was lucky not to be afflicted with big boobs, or so she claimed. Terry advised her more than once: "Least you never gotta tell some jerk, *Hey, my eyes, they're up here.*" Something she said every other day to one dickish guy or another. Joneen kind of had a point, or maybe, Terry thought, she was jealous.

Wait: *envious* or *jealous*, which was it? Mr. Fitzgerald once explained the difference as if it mattered, or mattered to him, but it went over her head like a lot of teacher talk. *Jealous* sounded right, but in itself *that* made her think it could be wrong.

This was the night she had taken out paper and made two underlined columns at the top: <u>Reasons 2 Stay</u>. <u>Reasons 2 Jump</u>. An hour later both columns were blank, so that made her decision-making process easy. She didn't require a decision-making process, she needed some air.

Her mom should have bought stock in duct tape. Not that she had a lot of what she called scratch to invest in anything besides her precious ice, not even groceries and the electric bill, not as long as she was scheming for a fix. She used the tape on the array of broken items in her possession. At some point everything inside the house seemed busted, cracked, or frayed, including her mother herself, and Terry imagined that if she could have figured out how to stick on some duct tape and put herself back together, she would have done so.

"Perfeckly good teapot," her mom would slur. "Lil' duck tape, there you glow."

And the crocodilian creepy boyfriend would chime in, "It's a lifesaver, the old tape of the duct. Only thing it don't work on is, and people don't know this shit, is…fucking ducts!"

That the guy had a glimmering as to where to locate the closest duct was gravely doubtful. Workers who knew from ducts might take actual jobs, and he wasn't going to impress any prospective employer during his interview if Mr. Men's Fitness wore either of his two unwashed, tattered flannel shirts. Not that he ever left the house in search of a job.

"You think you're better'n me, hot pants? You with your fancy school, and books you got your nose stuck in. You're wah wah crying to the molester priests what a lousy homelife you got, like you deserve better?"

"Hey, Brad Pitt, my eyes are up here."

She was on scholarship at Holy Family High, hanging on by her fingernails, but she didn't feel she was better, and here was proof. She hated his guts. A better person would use the guy's gun to blow his brains out. He had one of those.

"Holy Family, hi," he went, "your holy family is very high."

"Good news. It's open mic at the comedy club tonight."

"Face of time," her mom said wincing, as if somebody trained a flashlight on her dilated pupils. "Time has a face, you know, Terry, time has a face, a face, you know what I am talking about, about, sweetie? Rivers don't decide where they gotta go, they just flow, baby girl. Make yourself mac and cheese, there's boxes in the kitchen. Zeroes and ones, zeroes and ones, everything's zeroes and ones, everybody knows that."

Terry's backpack was bulky with stuff that made running awkward, but she didn't need to set a land speed record to keep the man at bay. She had also stolen something of his that weighed her down and that she shouldn't have taken—that handgun. But then, better with her than anywhere near her mom. She had gun rights, too, the right to get the thing out of the house.

"Your moms says get back, you tramp!"

Nobody was strolling along the street or walking dogs or collecting for victims of the latest tsunami or selling solar panels or hyping Jehovah, but here and there lights were turned on inside houses she scurried past. Houses where, unlike hers, lawns were mowed and paint wasn't peeling off like sunburned skin and presumably people weren't getting smashed and yelling at each other and scrambling around with rolls of duct tape in the wake of yet another mishap, disaster, or assault.

It was after midnight. She didn't need a clock, she could tell by the twisting knots in her belly. No idea where a girl like her ought to go, as long as it was out of that madhouse. She had had enough. Enough of the screaming, enough of the frozen pizza she stuck in the microwave, enough of the clanking vodka bottles tossed into the garbage can, enough with watching that man play with his jittery gun and pretend he knew how to clean it, television blaring all hours while he and her mother snored like freight trains on the couch after days of slamming lines on the wicker coffee table somebody put out on the sidewalk with a sign that advertised FREE. One time the tweaker asked Terry if she wanted a taste.

"Over my dead body," she said. "What I mean, I mean over *your* dead body."

"Not a little girl anymore, sweet thing." He stuck the straw up his raw-red nose. "More for me." His septum accepted the deviated challenge.

She was halfway down the block when the man cried out her name yet again, and there the slug was, in slower, agonized motion. From this distance: blurry, bad, sad, funny-failed anime. He wasn't going to catch her, not lugging that jiggling gut and not in those plastic sandals—and again, how did he retain the overhanging gut, given the meth? And where'd the slowpoke get his name? Which was Dash. The penitentiary? *Dash* not as in a tricky piece of punctuation she did not know how to use in her deathless high school composition prose, but *dash* as in half of *mad dash*? Is that what her English teacher would term *ironic*? Irony was a tough concept to handle. Every time she thought to use the word, she figured she was wrong. Sort of like *literally*. Nothing was ever literally the case when she wanted to say it was, or so her teacher told her literally a million times, but see? Right there, that *literally* might have clanged, pretty wrong. She'd check in with Mr. Fitzgerald on the thorny irony issue the first instant she caught herself caring. (Hey, would *that* be ironic?)

But she needed to keep moving, increasing the distance between Dash and herself. *Wait, that's a freaking metaphor too, or maybe an image,* both of them being terms invoked by her favorite teacher. Mr. Fitz owned an apparently infinite supply of environmentalist-slogan green T-shirts and he must have majored in English teacher terminology. He never stopped tugging on her: to wake up in class, to read the books he assigned, to rewrite the half-assed papers she submitted past the due date, urging her to "fulfill her potential." If she had any of that famous potential to fulfill, she'd probably find out when it was too late. For a guy who broadcast to the world his commitment to save the whales and the elephants and the owls and the wolves and the water and the bees and the butterflies, she believed he was also taking a shot at saving her, too. Possibly, he regarded her as another endangered species, which was not a bad connection, considering her homelife. So far, though, he wasn't wearing a SAVE THE TERRY T-shirt. Freaking metaphors everywhere, you couldn't shake them. He was pulling on her, mostly, to come to his office and talk if anything was on her mind, anything. She had assumed for the longest time he was gay, and therefore, to her mind, unthreatening. But she had begun to reconsider. Not that it mattered, because Mr. Fitz was okay. It wasn't his fault they made him her teacher. He was not the ordinary kind, either. And maybe he was queer and maybe she had misread the tiny, deniable, flirtatious vibe he threw off—and wait, didn't he once disclose in passing that he was married? He did, but gay would otherwise explain a lot. Was he bi? Was he unhappily married? Did he have kids? He never mentioned. And what made him so interested in somebody like her in the first place? Why did he ask her so many annoying questions? Why was he interested in what somebody as fucked-up as she thought? He puzzled her, but all the students respected the guy, including the hard kids, and nobody ever accused him of making any twisted moves. Nonetheless, she was beginning to think she couldn't trust her read on any member of the male subspecies. She would sooner have popped and guzzled a can of fifty-weight motor oil than have one-on-one face time with any teacher till, that is, she had Mr. Fitz, only now she took every opportunity to go to his office, and—all right, she would admit to herself—open the top of her shirt a little bit, one button, or two. Maybe she *was* a trashy girl, a claim Dash tonight bull-horned for everybody's benefit on the block.

Speaking of motor oil and her mom's boyfriend, his shitbox of a car was on blocks in the driveway, otherwise he might have hopped behind the wheel to run her down. Car on cinder blocks: possibly yet another image if it wasn't a metaphor. Recycling vodka and all the ongoing screamfests. Her whole life was amok with metaphors, images. She liked saying that word *amok*, she looked it up online, it was a Malaysian word, like *shiok*, a word that meant *wow*. Another useful Malaysian word was *orangutan*, "man of the jungle." Nothing in Terry's house worked since that man of the jungle took up with her mom. But wait, that's an insult—to orangutans. *Shiok*, she herself was running right now the fuck *amok*.

A few blocks later she slowed to a fast walk, as she had definitively separated herself—turning a corner, she couldn't see him any longer. With a little luck the man had crashed and cracked open his Neanderthal skull.

She would disappear. Or Mr. Fitz would help her. In his office today, after she had conceived her plan, such as it was, she was explicit. What did she have to lose that she hadn't lost already?

—

"Mind if I call you *Matt*, Matt?"

Matty Fitzgerald did mind, but pretended he shouldn't, though he was tough for Terry to read—and she had no idea that he'd never liked being called *Matt* by anybody, and nobody did, till she did just now. He would not correct her, and she was feeling invincible, like she could get away with anything, since she was using that off-the-top-rope tone in her voice that made people step back away from her, which is why she adopted that tone in the first place. She knew what she was doing. But she didn't know what she was hoping to accomplish.

"Are we gonna talk about college?" he said.

"Not today, or ever."

He was staring.

"What?" she said.

"What did you do to…to your hair?"

She'd chopped it up the night before, asymmetrical as shit, UFO landing strip here, wrestler slash grunge band buzz cut there, orange splash bangs sort of drooping, going for *don't even think about fucking with this girl*. She'd spent the whole day avoiding the Dean of Girls, who would bust her inappropriate ass if she got the chance. To judge by her teacher's stunned stare, the look was working like a charm.

"Glad you like, Matt. Hey, news flash, I'm running away tonight. Yeah, I don't know where I'm going, but I don't want you to tell anybody—and anyway, what difference would it make? Promise?"

He asked what the hell was going on. She gave him details, not everything, that was for sure, because she didn't want him to medevac her ass.

"All right, this is serious."

"Gee, you think?" And then winked. Winking was a purely dumb thing to do, she decided, but what's done was done. And how fucking true that was, about everything.

"Let's slow down. Think this through. Maybe I can get you some help, Terry. There's this shelter in town, Caring Street it's called, for kids." That's where Claire, his wife, was the office manager, a job that Matty's brother made happen. "I know some people there who…"

"I can take care of myself." But if that were true, she had to ask herself what she was doing in his office then, all talkety talkety talkety. Was she pleading for sympathy? To what end? Was she telling him the plan in order that she would be forced to follow through, in the process of retaining what was left of her diminished self-respect?

More than anything, she wanted him to think she wished to be hugged by him, and she sort of did wish for that, but she wasn't sure what sort of hug it ought to be. A teacher's, a dad's, a boyfriend's? He qualified as one of those at least. If he hugged her right then and there she'd figure out what she wanted from him, and he could figure out what he was offering her. Terry could escalate like a drama queen, but she was telling something like the truth. She had a real problem, and therefore so did her teacher.

"I'm worried about you. You're putting me in a difficult spot, telling me all this. I think I should report it to somebody," he said. He didn't think that, he knew that.

If he did something stupid like that, she would deny it, she told him.

He asked her if she was thinking about hurting herself. From the teacher development seminar on the subject of dealing with teens in crisis, he had learned the script.

She rolled her eyes. "The fuck-all, Matt, seriously? But that's not what's going on. If anybody's going to get hurt, it's going to be my mom's boyfriend, by me." She went too far, he didn't need to hear her say that. "He'll kill himself without help from me."

"If you don't want to go to the shelter, you should come home with me, till things calm down." That was a tremendous, almost certainly reckless leap, but any good teacher knows you need to take big risks to help a kid in serious trouble like Terry, a topic never adequately covered in any teacher training. Did it cross his mind to check with his wife? Not for a second. He was confident that she knew the lay of the land because she worked around kids, troubled kids, all day long. She would understand, he assumed.

All Terry could wonder was what he intended that offer to mean.

"My wife and I have a spare room, you could stay tonight, catch your breath, see what things look like in the morning."

So that's what he meant. As if she would ever catch her breath, as if things would ever calm down at home, he was dreaming. She shook her head and stood. Oh, well, this much was established: the man did have a wife.

"Where you going?"

"Anywhere, what do you care?"

"Get your phone out," he said and told her to text him her cell number. She complied, why not, you never know, could be interesting someday. "Okay, I got your number, you got mine, call me, if you change your mind."

"Remember what you promised, this is between you and me. Why don't you kiss me goodbye?" Now she was totally fucking with him. She shouldn't do that, that was disrespectful, but that was what Terry did.

"That's not going to help."

Was she fucking with him or with herself? "Not going to help you or not going to help me, which? *Which*, Matt?"

—

It wasn't her finest moment, and Mr. Fitzgerald hadn't come through as she wished, not that she could say what that should be. Chalk up another disappointment when it came to boys, or men, or whatever Fitz was, and more proof none of them could be trusted to come through when called upon. She was recalling every detail as she walked in the dead of night.

Her canvas bag was slung over one shoulder, like she was a hobo in an old-time movie, only thing missing was a stogie between her teeth and a nearby boxcar to jump on bound for California, where she dreamed of going one day. She had put everything in the bag she could grab in the minutes between the computer crashing to the floor and her mom being slapped around and deciding it was time to take off. There was no helping her mom. She had tried. When those two went off the rails, she'd called the cops a couple or three times in the past few months and they showed up at the door. Despite her mom's busted lips and blackened eyes, she never pressed charges and, if anybody gave credence to her fabrications, she must have been wearing roller skates when she fell descending the stairs.

Terry reached downtown and took a seat on a park bench. The big overarching sign with the park's name plastered on it cracked her up. She would tell Mr. Fitz about it if they ever talked again. The park was not much of a destination, litter and fast-food wrappers and dog crap everywhere, and she had formed no plan for the future, or for the night, for that matter. She also wasn't drafting any valedictorian speech for graduation, urging everybody to follow their fabulous dreams. She assumed she would stay awake all night and take her chances by morning light. Something would become magically clear. And she was thinking about Mr. Fitz, and what he told her last week. It wasn't right what they were doing to him.

"Are you really getting fired?" she'd asked.

"Not exactly, but basically. I can't sign the employment contract." He explained why.

"That's totally fucked. We have to do something."

He didn't approve of kids' using the F-word around him, on the grounds it was both offensive and rhetorically lazy, which was worse, but it was pick-your-battles time at Holy Family High School. "I couldn't sign the Catholic loyalty oath with a clear conscience, and unless I do, the bishop says I am gone. It's really not complicated."

All she could think was, who was she going to talk to at school now? But that point was moot, because she wasn't sticking around. Why were they getting rid of the best teacher? It wasn't fair. She was finished with home and finished with school, now that Mr. Fitz was destined to be gone—*Matt*. Something needed to be done by somebody. But the whole thing was irrelevant now. Fuck me, she said to herself, and fuck everybody else trying to stop me.

—

SHE HAD LEFT IMPORTANT stuff at home, stuff she was going to need. She analyzed the backpack contents. Roll of silver duct tape. Sweet. She couldn't resist throwing that in, you never knew when something was going to break that needed to be fixed, temporarily forever. She found her iPad, *good*, cell phone, *very good*. A few pairs of underwear, T-shirts, and a bra, too, *excellent*. Toothpaste, but damn, no toothbrush, she had been moving cat burglar fast in the bathroom. She was wearing her go-to red hoodie, so she was set in that department, and it wasn't that chilly. Also a dozen condoms, which cracked her up as much as the duct tape. Birth control was the last personal item she was going to need.

Condoms had been passed out in her mandatory sex ed class and she snagged on the sly a bunch extra for kicks. She marveled that her

Catholic school offered sex education in the first place, which was restricted exclusively to the girls, and which predictable Joneen relabeled Blowjob Busters Boot Camp. Why only girls were deemed to be in need of such instruction was a question that occurred to precisely nobody.

Inexperienced and more innocent than she wanted to be, Terry couldn't believe how much water condoms contained. That made them suitable for water balloons you could drop from the gym rooftop onto the jocks' shaved skulls below. You could also slip a bashful unsuspecting cucumber into a condom—not sure how practical that application could be, though that is what the preposterously named, new-to-the-school sex ed teacher, Tamarina Immaculata, or Call Me Tammy as she begged to be known, demonstrated for their edification, as if the students' imagination couldn't generate an image independent of Tammy the Immaculate's visual cues. Water balloon and cucumber wetsuit may not have been commercially indicated applications, but they amused Terry and her friend—technically, her last living friend and ultimately her *former* friend, Joneen of course, who outed her for having a crush on Dionte, who when Joneen sold her out to him mocked her, laughing in her face. But she got it. That's what a girl deserves for reading the guy's poetry when he super-nice pleaded, so-called poems that pretty much sucked, but a guy gets credit for trying to write one, even a cheesy one. Call Me Tammy was a big booster of condoms, which she said used to be called prophylactics, or raincoats, when she attended high school.

Joneen piped up: "Hey, Tammy, this is cool and all. But I heard the pope said you're going to hell if you strap up condoms. You sure it's okay you passed out condoms, lamby-kin or latex? Not that I'm complaining, 'cause I can always use one."

"The Church is coming around, you'll see, and someday some new pope will catch a clue. Condoms have been proven essential in stopping the spread of HIV and STDs, and anyway, Catholics are evolving on the whole question, so let's all keep it real." *Keeping it real* was a high, oft-invoked priority for Call Me Tammy, who kept it real wearing tennis shoes and jeans in class and insisting upon no fragrances and policing rogue lipstick.

Terry never had occasion to put a condom on somebody, something that would be embarrassing to admit to Joneen. But she couldn't care less how Catholics regarded condoms. The thought of Call Me Tammy's contemplating personally resorting to condom use and keeping it real when she was a teenager (around the Civil War) was to Terry fingernails-on-chalkboard cringey.

After the teacher caught her breath, she was also railing against the scourge, as she phrased it, of sexting. She proceeded to go on a red-faced rant with the girls about the dangers of the increasingly, mystifyingly popular and, according to her, demeaning-to-girls practice around school and everywhere else. She was so screaming ALL CAPS emotional, she was not easy to follow, but Terry could not fail to register the gist, and she WANTED TO COVER HER EARS. A girl might believe it was cool and a turn-on to share an intimate pic with a person she cared about and who cared about her, but the next thing she knew it might turn up in everybody else's school if not around the whole wide world. And if somebody drools over a pic like that of somebody under eighteen and distributes it to their fellow hairy-fingered bros, that act constituted child abuse or kiddie porn, which was a felony punishable by prison, and afterward somebody would be compelled to register as a sex offender for the rest of his worthless life. It would certainly get somebody in big trouble at school, if nothing else.

"Let's not forget dick pics," said Joneen. "I know I can't."

"Same same, and see me right after class," said Call Me Tammy, prompting herself. "Word to the wise," she said, and repeated vehemently for emphasis: "WORD TO THE WISE."

Joneen leaned over and whispered to Tammy: "Told you, girlfriend, what are you waiting for?"

After two sessions, the guillotine dropped. Sex education was decapitated. The girls were banished to the gym where they were supposed to play volleyball for the remainder of the term, under the supervision of the PE teacher, Mrs. Garfoyle, who herself used to teach sex ed pre-Tamarina Immaculata, who had been retained to revitalize the program and to make it "relevant to today's youth," in this case meaning, again, only to girls. In the past, Mrs. Garfoyle had made extensive use of anatomically correct dolls and colorized hazy video to highlight God's miracle of human birth, and to terrify and put on notice the sexually curious. It was hardly a surprise when Joneen was dismissed one day and sent to the dean's office when she had an unstoppable laughing fit. As for the gym reassignment, maybe somebody figured the girls couldn't get into trouble with a volleyball, but nobody bothered to explain the curricular adjustment. Until one day the principal showed up, had all the girls sit in the bleachers, and put on his serious-as-the-highway-patrol-officer face demanding you cough up license and registration. Then he explained how it was morally wrong, and against Catholic dogma, for students to be given condoms by anybody, much less a faculty member of a Catholic school, which development had only recently come as news to him, apparently. He testified that he was sure the girls had properly disposed of them, in the garbage, where they belonged. He added that he had sent a letter of apology to each of the families and also to the bishop. He didn't mention if he wrote the pope, however, and he didn't announce that the upstart teacher had been terminated, but she was never seen again on campus in her jeans and tennies while keeping it real and going all caps. Now she was presumably destined to keep it unreal and all small letters. This abrupt turn of events prompted Terry to reevaluate. One: Maybe Call Me Tammy was not so bad after all. And two: This school was getting way more fucked up by the day. As for volleyball, to her, that was a truly dumb game, and a weird and hysterical alternative to sex ed. You protect the net and jump and run around and if the opportunity arises you spike the ball off some poor girl's shocked face and make her cry or throw a punch. As for Joneen, she enjoyed the daily half hour of frantic athletic activity, though she said volleyball was better on the beach under a blazing sun, where you could show off your figure, acquire a tan, and meet hot boys.

—

IN ADDITION TO THE prophylactics hoard, *ha!*, there was another item of import in Terry's personal inventory. At the bottom of her backpack the gun had settled like a brick. Nothing *ha* about that. She gripped the handle and flinched, it was so heavy and cold. That was probably crazy, taking Dash's gun.

Sirens started blaring, fire trucks bombing down the main street that was otherwise deserted at this hour, followed by police cars. Maybe some poor lady had a heart attack. The thought that it might be her mom's disgusting boyfriend coding on the street cheered her up, and she hoped the firefighters would stop for burgers, grab a few beers, give the heart attack a chance to work its magic without their performing heroic triage.

She called Mr. Fitz, let it ring twice, then clicked off. Ten seconds later, he called. Which was the plan. If she had one.

"Really?" he said, as if slapped awake.

"Hello to you, too."

"Where?"

"Fitzgerald Green, sign says, you know, between Diablo and First." She enjoyed enunciating the park's name and could visualize her teacher shaking his head on the other end of the call. Everybody knew that Mr. Fitzgerald's old man was Daddy Big Bucks Fitzgerald and financially responsible for, among other high-visibility civic contributions, the urban park upgrade in a braggy burst of his philanthropy. Walk around town, it was hard to avoid the Fitzgeralds' moneyed shadow.

"On a park bench, can't miss me. I'll be hanging from the street lamp if you take too long. Bring Doritos, I'm famished."

"Stay put. *Doritos?*" he questioned, voice trailing off into the dusty chip void. "Those things'll kill you."

Five minutes later, *Fuck*, she was thinking. That's because a hundred yards off two beefy guys were sizing up their quarry, that is, *her*, scuzzily shuffling their grizzly bear way down the street in her direction. She couldn't make out their faces, but she didn't want to. Beanies with ear flaps, Army camo coats, hands in pockets, resembling nothing like the local hospitality committee. Then she remembered, she was equipped, she could defend herself if it came to that. "Bring it," she said to herself. If extreme measures were called for, she was happy she had the weapon. Also unhappy, on account of how she was clueless as to how to operate it. On second thought she could brandish the weapon and watch them scuttle back into hibernation. So no, she had no stockpile of useful second thoughts. She wasn't looking forward to making their acquaintance, which appeared imminent and impossible to evade. She contemplated fleeing, running back—but back where?

Then arrived good news that was bad news. A police car slowed as it drove past and the red-and-blue rooftop lights switched on, making her flinch. Terry turned to visually locate the two street guys, but they had disintegrated into thin air, escaping the police, she figured. She had to move fast. As the cop did a U-turn and lost sight of her for a second, she rustled up the gun and chucked it under the thick nearby underbrush, hoping it wasn't loaded and wouldn't go off, and it didn't. She pulled the hood over her head, magically pretending like a little kid she could hide or he wouldn't see her. Then the black-and-white pulled up alongside her on the park bench and the officer stepped out, stiffly walking toward her like he had all the answers to all the questions in the world and she didn't, which was, solidly good chance, the case. Through the open car window she could hear cop radio blather, staticky swoops and inscrutable code numbers.

"What you doing out here this hour, young lady?" the cop said as he approached, not too pleased about asking.

"Walking home."

"You're not walking anywhere, Little Red Riding Hood."

"Funny guy, anybody tell you?"

"'Less my eyes deceive me, you're sitting right here, on a bench."

She didn't praise his masterful powers of observation. "I'm heading to Hollywood, become a star." That attitude got her through the night at what used to be home, but it wasn't cutting it here with a cop. "Okay, I *was* walking home, thanks, officer." She didn't think he would buy that, either, but she wasn't feeling original. Mr. Fitzgerald would never come through. She rose to her feet, wishing she had put on that bra.

"Driver's license."

"Never got one of those," she lied. "Didn't think I needed one to walk in the park."

"Needles, drugs in your bag?"

"Why, you need some?"

"You seem to be under the assumption, Red, that I got a sense of humor."

"I would never do that in a million years."

He grabbed her backpack.

"Hey, you can't do that."

He turned his back and poked around inside, and all she could think was he was groping her C-cup bra—pervert.

"Lot of condoms, young lady," he said as he handed it back, having failed to land on, she supposed, the structural support garment she should have put on before, or he'd fondled it and chose not to mention—*total perv!*

"In comparison to what?"

"Pedaling your tail on the street?"

She laughed. Maybe Dash had called 911 to report her going missing.

"You're in the right neighborhood, but you don't look the type, I guess."

"Bitch slap or compliment?"

"I can take you down to the station and we'll find out who you are and call your family."

"My dad's in New York, where I wish I was, name's Lindsay Lohan." She guessed the cop had no clue, but she was wrong.

"Get in the car, clown, I'll take you home. The park's not safe, young girl at this hour. You got bad actors and night owls cruising here."

"Tell me about it." She pointed toward the two street guys who had resurfaced a block away to monitor proceedings.

The cop turned and waved at them, who waved back. "Nah, not them, they're a coupla good Samaritans, out here every night doing outreach, hooking up the homeless with shelters, which obviously you're not."

She saw no way around it. She did study him hard, to assess whether or not he was one of those sicko cops who trolled people, who trolled girls, she meant, because they could. Her bullshit detector whirred around inside like a juicer at the smoothie shop and spit out the sludgy judgment that the cop was probably not an immediate threat, despite the porno 'stache and aviator glasses, two generations out of style. With men, you never could be sure, so you never took chances.

She wished it was a couple of years ago. That's when she wouldn't have taken off like this in the middle of the night, her mom wasn't a washout zombie, Dash wasn't standing in front of the mirror picking scabs on his face, and her grandmother was still making cookies and slipping her twenties—and was still alive. She wished she could have told the cop to take her to her grandma's house, which sounds like a sugary fairy-tale setup, doesn't it? She missed her, she who was sort of the best possible version of her mom, so no wonder those two didn't get along. Her mom's sister, Charlene, had offered to take Terry in when her mom crashed out. Aunt Charlene was okay, if a little bit full of her crunchy self, so Terry didn't embrace that option and take her up on the invitation. The whole situation may have changed, now that Dash was the king of the dunghill, and she couldn't help her mom, who had pretty much zeroed out. As for staying at her aunt's, on the plus side she was divorced, and never had any kids, and she had an empty guest bedroom in her nice little storybook house, all of which was also on the minus side, because her aunt likely wanted somebody around to have long heart-to-hearts about LIFE, and SAVE her sister or her sister's only child. Terry had had enough heart-to-hearts with Joneen to last a lifetime, and look where that got her: on the street, bag over her shoulder, Dash's stolen gun in the bushes, standing in a park talking to a goddamn cop who was auditioning for Camp Tough Love counselor. But Charlene—she liked being called Aunt Charlie—also had a couple of tabby cats, so that was all she might have needed in the conversation department. Depending upon how things proceeded tonight, and so far it wasn't looking like Christmas was coming early, Terry may ultimately have no choice.

Why hadn't she accepted Mr. Fitz's crazy-town offer to stay at his house—and with his supposed wife? That ludicrous prospect was sounding better by the minute. But look, the guy hadn't showed. Another disappointment circled by on tonight's disappointment carousel.

"Not the front, Lindsay Lohan. Back seat, like the perp wannabe you are."

She stood by the car door and the perp told him her real name, making an implicit plea for sympathy before he took her helplessly to her house. Once he dropped her off, she would head around back and take off running again, with any luck stepping over Dash as he was bleeding out on the sagging porch.

"You go to Holy Family?" Logical question: that was the insignia on the front of her hoodie.

"When I have nothing better to do." It wouldn't take effort to convince him she would not be listed someday in the alumni hall of fame.

"My daughter's in tenth, boy's in ninth. You get good grades or are you one of them troublemakers?"

"Depends. Which is also what you're wearing."

"Sarcasm's going around these days. You're just like my girl."

"Why do fathers say shit like that? I'm not like your girl and she's not like me, poor thing."

"Okay, where we going?"

"My hunch would be hell."

That's when a chuggedy beater with a wobbly muffler on life support pulled up, brakes squealing, stopping down the street some distance behind the patrol car. Mr. Fitzgerald lumbered out of the car, like his heart wasn't in it, car door creaking and groaning like in a haunted house teen slasher movie. All that was missing was the screeched *eek eek eek*.

"Stay right where you are," said the cop standing outside his car and pointing in the direction of her English teacher. "Don't take another step."

"Officer Ryan," he said and tentatively approached, but he didn't lift his hands in the air.

"Mr. Fitz? What you doing out here?"

Terry piped up: "Mr. Fitz? You're buds with Ranger Ryan?"

"How're the kids?" said Matty, disregarding her.

"Oh, you know, *kids*, but good, pretty good."

"See you met my student Terry."

"*Your* student? Lucky you. The priests giving you hazardous duty pay? Because Miss Congeniality's been the highlight of Ranger Ryan's shift. I'm driving her home. She shouldn't be out here."

"Can you and I talk?"

And the two men walked a short distance away and Terry couldn't make out what they were saying, whether they were doing guy-bonding or girl-bashing, which can happen at the same time if high school taught her anything, and it did. She watched the cop shake his head and her teacher shrug, both of them chuckle. She noted Matty lifting his hands to the night sky, as if he were imploring nobody, *What can you do?* And the cop nonverbally communicated he wished he had never pulled up to the park that night, which was true for everybody in the vicinity.

"Thanks," the teacher seemed to say and the two men shook hands, Terry thought, like bros. She felt sorry for the both of them bros. The sight of guys bonding inevitably induced her to feel that way: exempted from understanding normal things.

"Guess that means," Terry called out, studying that primate display of male attachment, "no scared-straight ride-along with a cop tonight. Bummer."

The cop was going to say something, reconsidered, got back in his cruiser, turned off the flashing lights, and drove away, like that, like nothing ever happened, which, you know, it never did.

Matty awkwardly settled behind the wheel alongside Terry in the passenger seat, who was thinking this car needed to be washed or put out of its misery and scrap-heaped. She hadn't yet noticed somebody in the back seat. Then she did. It took no great skill on Terry's part to sense she had slipped into the aftermath of a conflict between Matt and the woman in back. The chill in the air was felt on her neck. Terry immediately had two reactions: get the hell out of the car, or sit tight and see how this plays out, because it was interesting watching two adults snarl at each other.

"Claire, Terry. Terry, Claire, my wife, Mrs. Fitzgerald."

Terry reached over to shake hands, thinking that was what somebody who wasn't a crazy girl was supposed to do, but the woman didn't have any eyes or any she could see, because she had a baseball cap pulled down on her forehead. She was wearing a big puffy jacket like she was a Teamster longshoreman off her night at the docks, but Mr. Fitzgerald, she was forced to conclude, did have a wife who did have a name, and a dumb one, too, which was *Claire*. The woman handed over across the car seat a small paper bag. Terry found inside a red apple and an unsealed bag of Doritos.

"You're going to lose your job," Claire announced for the benefit of her supposed husband. "You know that, right?"

So that's what they were fighting about, Terry realized: *her*. This wasn't a new experience for her. It used to happen every day between her mom and dad, and then later with her mom and nincompoop Dash.

"I already lost my job, day I took it."

"If you're not arrested someday, delinquency of a minor, child endangerment."

First take, to Terry: this situation didn't seem to constitute an obvious improvement of the cop on the street.

Oh, shit, she thought. "Wait, forgot something." Terry scrambled out, taking her backpack, and headed into the underbrush, finding what she was looking for and stashing it away, her back to the car, so that nobody could see.

Returning to the car in a flash, she said, "Almost forgot my library book, thanks."

"A library book," said Dean-of-Students wannabe Claire. "You always hide books in the underbrush?"

Fuck you. She wasn't worth engaging. "And thanks for helping me out, Mr. Fitzgerald." Terry chomped into the wickedest apple since all that trouble began in the Garden of Eden, even if it wasn't an apple according to her Bible study class, supposedly. Doritos, like revenge, she reserved for later. Then for effect she threw in, barely this side of a non sequitur, "Matt," thinking *what the fuck*.

"Matt? She calls her teacher *Matt*, Matty? And tell me why again," his wife wanted to know, "why isn't this girl with Child Protection Services— or Caring Street? We could take care of her there."

This girl's no child is why, Terry said to herself, concluding that the woman was hopeless, a do-gooder hall-monitor pain in the ass. "Thanks for rescuing me, *Mr. Fitzgerald*."

"Oh, yeah," said Claire, "we're like the Special Freaking Forces."

One, nobody's talking to you, and two, I got a gun, Claire, Terry said to herself. *Don't make me and Matt use it.*

"And instead of always trying to save other people, Matty, why don't you look out for your own ass for a change?"

They started to drive off toward Matty and Claire Fitzgerald's apartment, and—as if on cue—the beater of a car backfired, to Terry's way of thinking, stupendously. She had to fight off a smile. Did a backfire count as a symbol in literature? If so, symbols were goddamn lame. She would check in with her teacher to see what he thought, when she got him to herself. Then again, maybe symbols only occurred in stories big on whatever irony was and taught in high school, and she was pretty much done with high school, and therefore, with any luck, with irony, too. She had to admit: so far the night was turning out better than she had any reason to expect.

Chapter Four

Francesca

IT WAS TIME. SHE spun the tumblers, Anthony's day/month/last two numbers of his year of birth being the combination. She should get a new floor safe, high tech, biometric, electronic, digital. That sounded prudent to her. She just might prudently buy one to secure her precious possessions, right after she got a new prudent life, high tech, biometric, electronic, digital.

She pulled off her wedding ring. It was oh so simple, like doing brain surgery on herself.

She gently set the ring inside a royal blue velvet-lined box she'd kept since her child princess days, and then filed it alongside passport, pink slip, deeds, jewelry, cash, trust docs, and all the other supposedly precious possessions. But look right there, a cache of photos. She had almost forgotten she had put the album there, but she could never forget the pictures inside. For a second, the album made her glad. A second after, anything but. That's when a tear threatened—but the waterworks were bone-dry.

She slipped on her finger, the opposite hand, a new marquise diamond. This ring was elegant and stylish enough for store-bought jewelry, not a sign, not a symbol, of eternal commitment. What had she been thinking? A new ring? Why? This was the instant she discovered she had been wrong about something else: she was not cried out. She dropped like a tree snapped by a storm. The Persian-carpeted floor felt like the correct place to rest her head awhile, a minute, a month, whatever required. Maybe she was going to miss her social engagement tonight. Maybe Francesca didn't care.

New floor safe? Maybe she should get a huge steel vault and lock herself inside.

—

PEOPLE CONTINUED TO THINK of her as a Fitzgerald, as she herself did—with or without wedding ring or last name. Strangely, when she studied the new ring, she visualized her wedding ring—and Anthony. She wasn't moving on. Not today. She was also not staying put. It was impossible to explain where she was and where she was going, if anywhere. And nobody was there to ask anyway. Some days, moving on and staying put were flip sides of an untradeable coin.

After whatever was deemed the proper period of mourning, people supposedly moved on with their lives: a platitude espoused by otherwise apparently sane human beings. The terminology landed with a thud. Times like these, words themselves were overrated, but then again, everything else was too, and she had nothing else to use.

Was time like a river? She had heard people voice that view. For her, it was more like a flood, more like a blasting fire hose. She ought to have learned a lot after the passage of three years. One thing she wished she never learned is that time didn't proceed placidly, steadily, linearly by. Her traveling through time was marked by the equivalent of skid marks and roadblocks and felled walls and sink holes and downed, sparking power lines. This was a world as viewed in footage shot after a natural disaster, after what insurance carriers called an act of God on the order of tornado, earthquake, hurricane. Death was nothing but a relentless B-roll.

When first stretched upon the grieving rack, she had made her share of mistakes. In bleaker moods, she could catalogue them. She went on manic spending sprees: clothes, gadgets, shoes, wine, cookware, cars, electronics. She remodeled the kitchen—pointlessly, and then, more pointlessly, again. There were drinking and eating binges. Followed next morning by frenzied three-hour workouts. And sedatives and painkillers, some medically prescribed, some not. And more sedatives and painkillers. A few too many pills. And how could she forget a couple of one-night stands? More than a couple. Not that she cruised watering holes, and not that she was judgmental of anybody who migrated to one. It proved surprisingly conceivable to sleep with strangers, though in order for her to follow through, she perfected a little magic trick. All she had to do was slide mentally out of her body, move off to the side, and observe herself from some imaginary distant vantage point—a hill, a tower, a treetop. She thought casual hookups might constitute a path to momentary relief, at least a distraction, being immune as she was to the threat of relationship, of mutual expectation, or of the enduring dread of sharing morning coffee with somebody whose name she was unsure she caught. These liaisons, an incongruously upscale term for physical slip-slap and swapping of corporal secretions and disposal of decorum and undergarments, weren't anything she could use. One day kids would categorically reject slut-shaming—an overdue cultural advance Francesca would approve of. But as for her own hookups, such as they were, there was one night that was different. That was a night she spent with somebody she cared about, and in some true if skewed sense loved. And that amounted to the lowest moment of all.

She consulted with a psychiatrist. People in bereavement do that, she understood, that was one tried and true script to follow. She knew she shouldn't have felt ashamed to reach out to a mental health professional, but she didn't tell anybody, including her own family. She would admit to herself that Zoloft or the other benzos seemed to help a little, when their effects kicked in after a few weeks. At the indicated dosage, they blunted the razor edge of her panic attacks and anxiety. Francesca also saw a psychotherapist, with whom she felt a personal connection and upon whom she relied for counsel, insight, and wisdom. In other words, she was doing what she thought she should in order to regain footing on the shifting, illusory ground. But the more she thought about it, screw empathy and all the slope-shouldered, airheaded, bran-muffining empaths. Nobody got her pain, least of all herself. But everybody got her pain, too. Everybody except herself.

The store-bought ring was a half-hearted attempt at a useful gesture toward personal metamorphosis. Too bad she had no confidence she was capable of transformation, but she had to begin somewhere, sometime. Filing away for safekeeping the wedding ring could be the start, but she doubted it. She may have simply run out of ideas. Then one day Tommy came along. He indeed qualified as a new idea, if, that is, any man qualified as any sort of idea.

Three years, she thought. *Enough, Frankie, enough.*

But it was not going to be enough, as she would find out.

She rose up from the floor, and headed off to dress for the party. What a bizarre thing to be doing, going to a party. Well, that was the best she could do tonight. There were nights when *bizarre* was all she had left at her disposal.

—

TONIGHT FRANCESCA SCALINO WAS attending the black-tie Catholic diocese gala as a guest of honor. Her presence did not qualify as newsworthy, as she was a guaranteed A-lister for any major fundraiser in the city. A wealthy, altruistic woman such as her would naturally be on a roster of must-haves. At the same time, social occasions were not uncomplicated to navigate, considering her predisposition to anxiety, a condition exacerbated after Anthony, though nobody seemed to notice, or if they did notice, bothered to remark upon much less pry into. Maybe she should buy a Geiger Counter and measure her radioactivity. She had extensive practice faking composure, assisted by meds, different ones experimented with, on the coldblooded anxious search for the perfect pharmaceutical protocol. That was then. Now she had a shoebox full of old pill bottles, one after the other rejected, but intolerable to discard. She had wearied of the pills' side effects: the dry mouth, the psychic glass-like wall interposed between herself and the world. On this score, tonight posed a challenge. She determined she had been foolhardy renouncing pills. She could benefit from pharmacological modification of her brain chemistry in order to withstand the onrushing tides of good cheer overwhelming her at the gala.

Tonight's gaudy event would tomorrow make headlines, but regrettably for the bishop and the Catholic diocese, headlines for sensational, unfortunate reasons. The night was also remarkable for another, altogether mundane, reason. Francesca had attended countless formal parties with Anthony. During the excruciating years afterward, she would, rarely, go by herself, as often as not to get out of the house and submit herself to a diversion, any diversion. Tonight marked the occasion of Tommy Thomas and her first date for such a tony affair. This was a man she was beginning to sense she might have feelings for.

The limousines lined up around the block. Searchlights scanned the overcast sky, causing soft raindrops to sparkle as they drifted and parachuted down. On the ground, one Oscar de la Renta and YSL and Vera Wang gown-wearer after another high-heeled along the rolled-out red carpet. Rain unexpectedly contributed to the festive mood. Umbrellas were bursting open like a popped-up field of wild mushrooms moving in psychedelic slow motion, and partygoers were mindlessly laughing, sharing in their slight communal ordeal. Despite the weather, people were gathering in opulent style, ostentatiously, to raise money for the disadvantaged and the impoverished. The facile irony was noted by a few, and dismissed by others as being beside the point if not in dubious taste. After all, no money, no mission: the universal common sense mantra chanted by fundraising acolytes.

At the gala the bishop was seeking commitments in the so-called silent stages of a capital campaign; first, to build a desperately needed new high school and, second, to fund Caring Street House, the diocese's non-evangelizing ask-no-questions outreach program for street kids, an organization that had endured management and personnel problems—until, that is, the freshly installed new bishop, the new sheriff, rode in on his high horse and cleaned up the town. Caring Street was his immediate challenge. The bishop arrived almost a year ago, but tellingly, people still considered him the "new" bishop.

—

DR. HECTOR ALESSANDRO HAD been on the job as Caring Street executive director for some time, installed since practically its inception, retained by the bishop's predecessor, a man critics deemed notorious for weak judgment and for fomenting institutional laxity. Alessandro was inarguably brilliant, a charismatic, big-boned, pony-tailed, darkly handsome, work-shirted fellow who could light up a room—any assemblage at all, from runaways to clergy to fat cat donors. He could also hit the streets with uncontested authority. He himself was a product of the inner city, grew up in the hood, only member of his family to graduate high school, while his CV highlighted his doctorate in sociology and his years of counseling in public high schools and operating various children's welfare nonprofits. His religious bona fides were respectable, as well: as a young man he had been a novice in a Catholic monastery—and called *Brother* Hector. But a religious vocation was not to be for him.

Only now a few problems pertaining to him had freshly surfaced. For one thing, his CV was partly fictitious. *Dr.* Alessandro was, as it happened, not. True, he had finished the graduate coursework, and with distinction, but he hadn't actually completed his PhD. He was an ABD, All But Dissertation. This information came to light when the new bishop conducted comprehensive personnel reviews of the entire diocesan staff he inherited. In itself his misrepresentation was sufficient cause for termination, but there was one other serious matter on the table. The forensic accountants indicated that Caring Street was bleeding cash as a result of one unauthorized expenditure after another—often drawn from petty cash, and more than a few times from the checkbook. A thousand here, a few hundred there, not serious moneys in absolute terms, but cumulatively amounting to a major breach of trust that could not be whitewashed away. Everything traced back to Alessandro. The dummied vita was one thing, fraud, another order of complication.

The bishop's hands were tied. He called in Alessandro and did not provide him an opportunity to defend himself. Facts were facts. The bishop told him he was letting him go, but that he would receive a severance package on the condition he departed quietly and swiftly—and if he signed and abided by the binding nondisclosure agreement. And if he proved cooperative, the police would not be notified of the defalcation. It was Hector's choice, but the diocese had leverage and the bishop was not timid about employing it. This kind of move made self-serving sense for the bishop, too, because there was no upside to calling attention to the fiscal mismanagement of precious church funds. Alessandro pleaded and pleaded with the bishop, to no avail.

The bishop was embarrassed for the man begging for consideration, and he wished he would stop.

"Look," the bishop told him, "you've done good work, I can't deny that, and when we are asked for a reference, we will accentuate your achievements. But we can't tolerate your abuse of fiduciary responsibility, or the misrepresentation of your academic credentials. You have to go, Hector. I wish it didn't have to be this way."

"Excellence, please reconsider. I'll never do it again. I needed the money…" He couldn't explain. The money wasn't for him, he implied, but the bishop had him dead to rights.

"I'm also not bringing up something else you should have disclosed before you were hired: your arrest record."

Alessandro couldn't restrain himself. "Oh, you're *not* bringing up what you are bringing up? Fair enough, when I was younger, kind of rootless after the novitiate, I slipped up."

"Assault and battery when you were in your twenties and you put two pistol-whipped guys into the hospital. That's not slipping up, that's crashing and careening out of control." The bishop had been made furious all over again when he reflected on his predecessor's slipshod management practices; that man should have flagged Alessandro's record, which included three months in county. "You might have mentioned your checkered past when you applied."

"Yeah, right, good idea, checkered past, like I would have been considered for the job. Those guys assaulted my friend, use your imagination, and I tuned them up, which they deserved, but that was a long time ago, and since then, what? Not a speeding ticket. And yeah, sure, okay? I was once a gangbanger, it's true, and so what? I'm not proud of it, but my life experience gave me the street cred somebody in this position needed. And I've done a damn good job at Caring Street, everybody knows that. You'll never find anybody half as good as me. You yourself know that, Excellence."

That did indeed put a different spin on Alessandro's situation, and the bishop momentarily considered stepping back, moving more deliberately.

"I was a young man, it was a long time ago, people change. I'll finish the stupid dissertation if it's important to anybody. Can't I get a second chance?

That's what we're offering kids every day of the week here at Caring Street, a second chance, that's everything we're about."

But the new bishop had made up his mind. "We require transparency, and you haven't been transparent." It was an impossible convergence of disqualifications: the CV, the arrest record, the financial recklessness. "Please don't make this harder on yourself than it has to be. This meeting's over."

"You want transparent? Let me leave you with some information as to what I did with the money." He admitted taking cash and drafting the checks, but he surreptitiously spread the money around to certain kids, the ones who needed it badly, often to take care of siblings stuck at home, or to pay off the family utility bills or buy groceries. He knew it was a risk, and ill-advised, but he had to be honest. It was something he would do again if presented the chance. Was it too late to be honest?

Evidently so, as the bishop had now depleted his minimal stores of tolerance. "You'll get your severance once you sign off on the agreement, Hector. Thank you for all the good things you accomplished. I do respect you and wish you well in the future."

"Thanks for the solid when the diner calls about my dishwasher job app."

After Hector stormed out of the office, Father Philip Fitzgerald and the bishop debriefed. That didn't go well, either.

"Never realized he had such anger," the bishop said. "Though under the circumstances…"

"He's a good man, Excellence," said Father Philip, who might have been counted as his most trusted advisor in the Chancery if, that is, the bishop invested trust in any advisor, and it was not clear that he did. What was destined to come up for further scrutiny was that Philip's sister-in-law was the office manager at Caring Street, hired by Hector on Philip's recommendation as nothing more than a help to his little brother and his wife, both of whom were perennially struggling to get by. Fortunately, Matty's wife's fingerprints were not found on the shady money transactions of the organization. Philip himself had to wonder, however, how that could be possible, since her job was to be on top of such details, and nobody ever questioned her competence and diligence. Over and above all that, Philip also didn't want to think about what a headache it would be replacing a beloved ED, assuming that Alessandro would keep the agreement to go quietly. On that score, the bishop had already made his next move.

"Father Philip, you'll be the interim director, until we conduct a thorough search for a permanent replacement. You should begin as soon as possible, let's say Monday morning. Unless you think it will be a challenge for you to work with family, in which case we can also let Claire go and start from scratch. In fact, maybe we should let her go right now, make a clean break. We all know Matty is not happy these days with the new teacher's contract and his wife doubtless shares his disloyal views."

"Let's give her a chance, let me see what I can do with her." He wasn't optimistic, but that was enough change for now.

"As long as we all realize she's on a short leash. Hector and Matty might have turned her against us."

"No need to clean house top to bottom yet, Hector's departure will provide complication enough. Give me a chance to work with my brother's wife. But Excellence, I have an overriding concern. People make mistakes," said Philip in a dramatic tone of voice. "I know I have. So I'm going to ask this question for the record. Are we sure we're doing the right thing with Hector? Is it the right thing, ultimately, for Caring Street?"

This is what crossed the mind of the bishop: We *are not doing the right thing, or the wrong thing for that matter, I am.* But that would have sounded argumentative, and if he could achieve this result, he would like to retain the influential priest as an ally. For the truth was, the new bishop was feeling pressures mount. The diocese was beset with issues and couldn't withstand another controversy, and Alessandro was collateral damage, a defensible casualty. Had the political atmosphere not been so supercharged, they could afford the chance to rehabilitate the man's reputation. But that was not in the cards. The bishop had pedophile priests to expel and virtuous ones to keep in the fold if not inspire; he had teachers and other diocesan staff inciting revolt against him on account of his newly imposed employment contract requirements; and he had money he badly needed to raise—not only to help settle standing lawsuits but also to rebuild facilities in serious disrepair. Every bit as significant, he had his own reputation to cement in the minds of his flock right now.

"I take your point, Father. He's damaged, Hector is, I see that now. There's a sadness in his eyes that isn't telling the whole story, not yet, and I wonder what that story might be. Someday when you're sitting where I'm sitting you'll find there's nothing but hard options, choosing between competing versions of rotten. You'll learn this the day you take my seat and become a bishop yourself."

You didn't need to be a bishop to know that some choices are competing versions of rotten. You didn't even need to be a priest. Live long enough, truth becomes harder and heavier to bear. But if Father Philip was certain of one thing as it pertained to his ever sitting on the bishop's throne, it was this: his investiture would constitute the first miracle along his heavenly path to canonization—and nobody in his right mind would ever confuse Philip with a saint. Not to be confrontational, he could say the same thing about the bishop as well. But why bother? No point belaboring the obvious. Besides, he was now about to have his hands full running Caring Street, not to mention dealing with his brother's difficult wife. Bishop Philip Fitzgerald would have to wait his turn, till *never* happened.

—

THE BISHOP UNDERSTOOD, AS did everybody at the gala, that all this work in the diocese, all this need, called for major capital outlay. Numbers with lots of zeroes.

At one end of the social spectrum, teenagers deserved a safe new college preparatory school to replace the crumbling heap that Holy Family High had become. HFH, which was Francesca's alma mater, had deteriorated into a place where students dodged the occasional ceiling tile crashing down upon classes discussing *Romeo and Juliet* and studying the Emancipation Proclamation and learning how to solve for x, in buildings where pipes sporadically burst in lavatories and where the gym floor was warped from storms that blew in through broken windows and where mice used the cafeteria kitchen for a speedway. Mold, fire hazards, vermin infestations: the cash-strapped diocese had deferred maintenance for far too long and the entire physical plant had slipped over the years into severe disrepair. Now it was virtually a lost cause, and Francesca herself felt distressed about the fallen state of the school she retained some deep loyalty to. She was glad the new bishop seemed determined to correct the problem.

High school, everybody knows, is crucial to the development of children. It holds the key to success and stability—a game-changer especially for graduates who would be the first in their families to attend college. It's also the gateway to the Ivies as well as to the Catholic Brahmin Ivy-equivalents like Georgetown and Notre Dame, not to mention the strong state university and the admired hometown college, Saint Monica's, where Francesca was destined to be named the chair of the board. The bishop had found the perfect location to build. And significant pledges were being cultivated. But real estate negotiations were not going smoothly. Though the owner was Catholic—Catholic at least in name and by baptism—he was a man reputed to have unsavory, possibly underworld associations. Catholic fundraisers knew how to finesse such ambiguities, to work around such potential public relations debacles. More to the point, the man who possessed title to the land was holding out for a much bigger payday than the diocese was prepared for.

"Let's go to contract," the bishop tried to reason with the man. "Your property would be perfect for our kids."

The owner wasn't budging: "I know, it would be, wouldn't it? But land, they don't make too much of that stuff these days, Excellence."

"You know," said the bishop, "there is another property on the market that would make do. It's nowhere near as good as yours, but it would serve our purposes, if we had to go in that direction."

"Free country, Excellence. You gotta do what you gotta do." Clearly, this man regarded negotiation as sport, one he had long practice and success in. "And you know what they say. You get what you pay for."

"And what you don't pay for, either." The bishop himself dimly realized that statement made little logical sense, but sometimes in a negotiation you cannot be silent, you have to respond with *something*.

The two had been going round and round like that, unproductively, for some time, with no end in sight. The bishop and the seller each banked on the other to blink first.

At the other end of the social spectrum, where Caring Street House was found, many kids—not exclusively kids from Catholic families—were lost or thrown away, left to their own insufficient devices on the streets. The diocese had spent so much money tapping reserves to pay legal bills not covered by insurance related to the pedophile crisis that, as a result, services to these children stood imperiled. Street kids needed meals, hot showers, and safe beds for the night. That meant the diocese needed more money. And it was next to impossible to raise money in the service of paying off legal settlements, justified as those payouts were. But a new school or a shelter? Those were fundraising winners. Or so went the strategic planning.

The bishop had charismatically preached on behalf of both causes whenever he was given a forum—and he would do so tonight, too. He wasn't interested in laying the foundation for some personal legacy. His concern for all the children and all their families was absolute and authentic. He worked relentlessly for these causes even as he was cleaning house with regard to the sex scandals of the past, and even as he was running the Byzantine day-to-day affairs of the diocese: twenty-two parishes, seven elementary schools, and one crumbling high school, all the attendant intricacies of a midsize corporation that uneasily doubled as a spiritual big tent: a cash-strapped big tent with outsize aspirations.

—

FRANCESCA KNEW FIRSTHAND ABOUT managing complex organizations. A Chicago MBA, she had held top-level positions in the early days of dot-com startups everybody now regarded as indispensable for internet commerce and communication and social networking. As a result of her vision and sixteen-hour workdays and stock options and, to be candid, freaky good luck, she had amassed a considerable personal fortune. She lived in an *Architectural Digest* house; drove around town on ultra-flashy, fast wheels that made teenage boys weep; personally managed her vast portfolio of equities and other investments; and enjoyed choice bottles of wine temperature-controlled in Anthony's cellar. Wealth never went to her head. People might disparagingly slot her into the nouveau riche, but she never shook her self-image as the middle-class Italian American girl from hometown Holy Family High and local Saint Monica's College before she struck it fantastically rich—but she wasn't to blame for making the right bets in business. This was a subject that consumed hours of conversation with her psychotherapist. She may be overcompensating, she could not discount that probability, but she was generous with her money. She felt an overriding responsibility to be magnanimous, philanthropic—to give back, as the saying goes among the high-minded wealthy. Her father did not share what he regarded as her outlandish predilection. *Madonna*, he would call upon the name of the Blessed Virgin Mary, how the hell could Francesca defend giving so much of her own money away like that—to total strangers? All right, tax deductions were useful but again...*people outside the family?*

She had observed from a distance the new bishop. He had a huge and dirty job, she presumed. She may have had expert familiarity with the competitive corporate world, yet it was hard to conceive how anybody, no matter how skillful, conducted without turmoil the politically contentious business in the back-biting patriarchal bureaucracy that was the diocese. If she had to surmise, under every rock the bishop had to be finding snakes slithering—when he wasn't spawning new reptilian adversaries. A *good* leader has loyal followers. A *great* leader also has dangerous opponents. And leaders unaware of the existence of their opposition do not qualify as leaders at all—because they are blind to reality. If you couldn't manage both friends and foes, you couldn't manage either. The jury was out on the bishop.

On gala night, Francesca was unaware that her name appeared prominently on a very short list of people the bishop planned to have over for dinner soon, to become acquainted—and to be asked to step up financially in support of his initiatives. And yet she could hardly have been astonished. She had chaired capital campaigns; she knew everything about fundraising. If she had given the matter any thought, she would have been surprised he hadn't already made overtures to her.

The bishop had been hearing her name again and again from multiple quarters, and he had concluded she might be somebody whose expertise he should exploit. Without consulting in depth with his staff, and without doing the due diligence, he went with his gut. That's how he unfortunately characterized his management style: *going with my gut*. That was a pet phrase of his, along with *flying by the seat of my pants*. He had already decided, going with his gut and flying by the seat of his pants, to discuss with Francesca Scalino a radical idea: that she might take the lead in the real estate negotiations for the new HFH along with chairing this capital campaign. The proposition was one they could talk through in private and at leisure, over a bottle of fifty-year-old cognac he'd received as a welcome gift to the diocese and been reserving for the proper occasion, a gift he'd forgotten had come from her.

This was the substance of his thinking. A layperson, and in this case a woman, specifically a wealthy and business-savvy woman, would be in a more advantageous position to achieve success with donors—and particularly with that hard-driving property owner. Maybe the bishop and the landowner could cease butting heads like bighorn rams. At a minimum, she could take down the temperature a few degrees. This could be, under the right circumstances, a brilliant scheme.

The night of the gala, she herself had no inkling as to his plan with regard to her. And he himself had no notion as to how complex, if not impossible, such a negotiation might be for her to conduct. New bishops were entitled to make a few mistakes—and according to critical observers he had made more than his fair share. If he had done the due diligence, an exercise he deemed trivial, he would have appreciated why his was a vexed idea. Not that this would have stymied him for a moment. Vexed ideas were his favorite kind.

—

From the moment Francesca slit open the embossed gala invitation, she was sold: *All right, I'm in.* She envisioned the dress she would wear: the long robin's-egg blue chiffon, slit along the leg, off the shoulder. She had not worn that gown since Anthony, but it fit—better than she might have expected. Besides, it was time if it was ever going to be. All she needed was to pick up a tux for Tommy. Smart as she was, she might have anticipated some hurdles to surmount. Early, experimental stages of a relationship, where the two of them found themselves, may be invigorating and intense, may be a frantically fun cha cha cha of thrilling endorphins, but it can also siphon off IQ points, at least in the short term for a forty-something woman and a fifty-ish man, both of them out of practice if not awkward when it came to romance.

Nonetheless, Francesca and Tommy had indeed grown closer and closer over the past few months, since they first collaborated on the successful investigation of certain suspicious criminal circumstances that shocked the entire town: the unforeseen death of her board colleague at Saint Monica's, which prompted a search that, largely thanks to Francesca and her father, led to the uncovering and ultimate solving of a series of other unexpectedly connected crimes. Soon after that, Tommy retired, and before long he and Frankie were seeing each other. As for surprises, during this year Francesca and Tommy were both taken aback by possibly starting to fall in something like love—with, of all people in the world, each other.

On the surface, they seemed an unlikely pair. Since when, however, does anything on the surface presage the feasibility of the impracticality called love, or something *like* love? She had known plenty of men from her professional life, men with social cachet, men with more money than they could ever spend, a number of them admittedly estimable human beings. Yet it was this retired detective who took off the top of her head and jellied her knees. Money didn't do that, not for her anyway, and as for gym-toned boy-men, meticulously unshaved, tooling around in their Bentley Silver Spurs and wearing their Kiton suits and flashing Patek Phillippes on their wrists—well, she was not instinctively inclined to be impressed.

They had been tentatively discussing living together, and they were inching closer and closer. They had already practiced a sort of domesticity by raising a dog together, a rescue pit bull mix they named Dickens, and that was a success. Dickens split time between their two homes, and when convenient they alternated nights being together. Francesca had once been apprehensive around dogs, but Dickens had an amiable disposition so at odds with the commonplace misperception of the breed, and the pooch loved both of them, and they both loved him. She craved the hours and the nights they shared with Dickens—and with each other. The experience with the dog underscored for Francesca that all she and Tommy needed was a little more time together.

On the domestic front, they also liked to cook in tandem, which activity can amount to a minefield around a kitchen countertop, but he made tomato sauce that Francesca's father enjoyed, and enjoyed much more than he should have. Tommy wasn't Italian and he could make *sugo* for real? Theoretically, if her father closed his eyes and ate his pasta, this new man in his daughter's life was the definition of a keeper—theoretically.

Francesca's dad had been slowly, reluctantly, coming around with regard to Tommy—painstakingly slowly, reluctantly. The man's impressive sauce, which her dad called *gravy,* might have won the day. At first, Big Mimmo wasn't comfortable with the prospect of his daughter possibly hitching up with a detective.

"Ex-detective," Francesca told him a dozen times, as if that would make a difference, and it often seemed it wouldn't. "Ex," she reemphasized.

"Once a cop, Francesca," he would portentously begin, and leave unexpressed the implicit follow-up. At the same time, he couldn't miss that the man treated his only daughter like gold, and that—along with the gravy—went a long way with him. A detective...

"Ex-detective, on a pension, Papá."

A detective would be properly protective, at least he was schooled in techniques of protection. Perhaps Tommy was a little bit too old for Francesca, and the man certainly wasn't—and couldn't speak—Italian, though Francesca and Tommy had started taking language classes together, which warmed the heart of her dad. And before too long in Big Mimmo's mind those two did seem to click, a little. His only daughter deserved a good mate after all she had been through. He called her every morning, to check in, and lately he detected escalating hopefulness in her voice.

She herself believed her late husband would have approved of Tommy. He was the frill-free, bullshitless sort of man Anthony gravitated toward. He had contempt for dirty cops, slippery criminals with badges, and Tommy was nothing like that. She conducted imaginary conversations with Anthony, but he wasn't the problem. She had little doubt he would have given her the green light to move on with her life—but there again was that dumb expression, *to move on with her life.* Francesca's seeking the imaginary endorsement of Tommy sounds maudlin but it wasn't. She deeply desired his sanction. On the other hand, when would she begin not thinking of Anthony as her *husband*? Perhaps that was a sane objective, but was it conceivable? Then she would take a step back and ponder—and discuss everything with her cherished therapist, Ruth.

She had seen Ruth for about a year after Anthony died, then dropped her: she had nothing left to say, or nothing she cared to say. Only recently had she returned, and it felt right, and now there was a lot that needed to be said. She was younger than Francesca but from the first she struck her as wise beyond her years. She could use a dose or two of wisdom. Look at the facts: What was she doing with a seriously unmarried, widowed ex-homicide cop of blue collar origins, she a widowed woman whose stock options made her rich during the dot-com boom and whose father was a retired bookmaker—even if nobody was convinced he was retired? Francesca didn't lack for subject matter to fill the fifty-minute hour.

What were the odds a man like Tommy and a woman like Francesca could make it? Her dad could plausibly calculate them, and she could intuit he had already done so: something of a long shot. Of course, long shots do occasionally come in. But bookmakers make a living off those gamblers who fail to make a living off taking chances on a twenty to one.

Tonight also marked the occasion of the first conflict between Tommy and Francesca, which she didn't know they were having till it was essentially over. Similar observations could be made about lots of crucial moments in one's life—including possibly the totality of one's existence. A fight in which people are not fighting about the thing they are really fighting about is always the worst, and simultaneously the most revealing, fight. Which sounds blindingly obvious to anybody who is not in love, and which couples' counselors guide clients to understand.

Well, everybody had questions to answer, matters to work through, tensions to resolve. And a couple had a gala to attend.

—

UNDER THE VAST VAULTED dome of the flamboyantly ornate baroque rotunda—complete with mermaids and knights-errant and unicorns depicted on gaudy murals—Francesca and Tommy were slated to sit at a table of honor, up front where the podium loomed large on the stage and where the heavy-hitter dignitaries, like the bishop, were scheduled to hold forth—and make passionate pitches for game-changing donations.

To a disinterested observer, Tommy may have indeed looked quite handsome, turned out in the new tuxedo Francesca had gotten for him. He wasn't used to gifts on that order. But she was simply being pragmatic.

"Tommy," she had explained to him weeks before, very reasonably, "we're going to be going to these types of events, and we don't want to rent a tux some teenager sweated up at his prom." For Italians, it was no triviality how one appeared in public. Both men and women might spend an hour putting themselves together to go out for bread or to fill up their Vespas. Italians refer to cutting an attractive figure as *fare la bella figura*, a notion that has quasi-religious force—close to the force of Catholicism itself. There were worse principles to live by, Francesca supposed.

"Never went to the prom. Couldn't get a date. I miss something?"

She could have answered two or three different ways—*No, Yes,* and *Can we talk about something else?* —but elected silence. She was learning, she was open to learning more. Once she might have successfully changed out Anthony's closet and disposed of his corduroys and chinos, but when she saw Tommy in a corduroy jacket of his own, that prospect seemed foreclosed.

The intention behind formal wear for him was above suspicion, but she ought to have been better prepared for Tommy's reaction. After all, he *was* old-school, which was, frankly, part of his appeal. Naturally, he might be troubled over some woman buying clothes for him. Or to put it the way he conceptualized the problem: that some woman bought *him*. Because look, that was the man's job, to pay.

"It's not *some woman*, it's me, Tommy." And what she didn't need to say, because it was obvious, was that it was not a financial strain buying him a tux. *Dinner jacket!* The purchase did not rise to the level of a rounding error in her checkbook. But buying him a dinner jacket dredged up an issue that burgeoned for them: disparity in finances. Her dad might have been hung up on Tommy's being a cop, reasonably or not, and given her dad's past, that was at least a semi-legitimate concern. Francesca did not share her father's reticence on that score. No, if she saw any red or yellow flags, Tommy might have trouble acclimating to her moneyed status—why, even her dad had difficulty when he first realized Francesca had made a killing. When she explained how her start-up ground-floor stock options operated and how she cashed out, all he had to say was: *"Mama mia, they thought I was a crook?"*

Sex and money: that's what people say only matters when either is in short supply. Nobody ever said having too much of either could be a problem.

—

THAT NIGHT THEY RUBBED shoulders with the well-heeled designer-dressed folks. Such mingling came with gala territory, and Francesca was accustomed to it. Tommy, another story. She was glad she had in her possession some pills to tide her over tonight.

True, her anxiety intermittently flared, and the selective serotonin reuptake inhibitors and benzodiazepines had been variously prescribed over the years. She had experimented with many pharmaceuticals, like the current champion of the anxiety-ravaged set, Klonopin. She wondered, strictly as a marketing and branding proposition, how did they come up with such names? To her, they seemed more suitable to environmentally sensitive, technologically advanced automobiles.

Let's Go Places, Ativan.
Buspar, The Car That Cares.
Zoom Zoom in Your Zoloft.
Shift Expectations: All-New Celexa.
Paxil, Pursuit of Perfection.
Valium—Or Nothing.
Imagine Yourself in a Brand-New Klonopin!

So far she was not ragingly anxious. She showed up in her gorgeous gown, didn't she? She got the man his own tux. Okay, set that last one to the side. She put on blush and lip gloss, her shoes were nowhere in the zip code of sensible. Lights, camera, whatever.

But then she initiated a preemptive, precautionary action, which she took in the ladies' room. All she needed was a little *pop pop* of pharmacological leverage in the stairway-to-the-stars form of an old-school Valium 10. Hey, she herself was attracted to old school. So maybe she was more than a little bit panicky, and maybe exclusively with regard to Tommy, though drugs wouldn't help with that long-term. That's what vodka was for. Set that to the side, too. She noted the absurdity referenced on the warning label of the instant anti-anxiety elixir she had selected: *Side effects may include anxiety.* She should enhance, accelerate the process, take a couple of Vitamin Vs.

Then she returned to Tommy's tuxedoed arms. "You're the cat's meow, Detective Thomas, all decked out in your dinner jacket duds." Instantly she wished she hadn't put it that silly way. Unlike Anthony, Tommy wasn't entertained. She made a resolution: *Curtail the quaint vocabulary, he doesn't find it adorable, he thinks you sound like an idiot.*

—

SHE KNEW THAT TOMMY was a size forty-six regular, a solid number. The Fitzgeralds had indoctrinated in her their shorthand for male assessment. They categorized men by suit coat size. Thirty-eight being suspect, on account of the boyish, small shoulders, which implied a deficit of power and loyalty, and forty was but a tiny immaterial step up. Forty-two was borderline respectable, and forty-four and forty-six very sound. Forty-eight and fifty meant expansive shoulders, which translated into stature and command. Larger than that, a fifty-two or fifty-four, could lead to complications, through weakness or excessive self-regard or uncontrolled appetite.

"What do you do, grab them by the lapel and steal a peek of the label?" Francesca said to Anthony one time, finding the whole concept ridiculous.

"Don't have to, it's obvious."

"Anthony, that's absurd, men are not their suit size."

"You sure about that, Frankie? Haven't you ever looked at a guy and said, 'That is one empty suit'?"

"Sure, but come on, you're telling me you have access to a man's soul when you know the cut of their jib?"

"What, now you're watching pirate movies? Look, I'm not saying suit size is fate, but it's not irrelevant, either. I hire jury consultants and pay them way too much, but I don't hesitate to overrule them when I see a thirty-eight or a forty, or for that matter a fifty-two or fifty-four in the jury box for *voir dire*, because those guys are, good chance, unreliable, especially the slope-shouldered thirty-eight, who is totally insecure, been pushed around all his life, which makes them therefore unpredictable, and a risky wild card."

"What about my dad? He's not fit to serve on your jury?"

"He's a fifty-six, and that's a very, very good number, a noble suit size. But Big Mimmo sitting on a jury? Can you visualize that? He's the *capo di bias*, like every Italian, no offense, but you know I'm right and he'd never make it through one question before being thanked for his service and handed his hat, have a nice day."

"*Like every Italian*? Oh, you mean Italians are more chauvinistic, opinionated, and pig-headed than the Irish? No offense taken, you Mick."

They both had to laugh.

—

FRANCESCA HAD CAUGHT HERSELF thinking about Anthony's suits hanging in the closet: size forty-six. Forty-six, like Tommy.

"Cat's meow, huh?" said her bemused date. "Been wondering. About my duds, what's the diff, dinner jacket, tux?" He wasn't intending to inject a note of hostility into the proceedings, at least consciously.

"Same same. Shawl grosgrain lapel, one button, stripe down the leg. You look like somebody poured you into your tux for the spiffy party." *Cat's meow*, now *spiffy*, it was going to require concerted effort to reprogram herself.

"Whole slew of Fancy Dan people here tonight, guys in their shawl grainy collars, which I don't know what that means. The phrase *fish out of water* occurs to me."

"*Party like it's 1999* occurs to me."

Saying that, she had inadvertently alluded to a most unfortunate calendar year. Of course, she would not have phrased it that way if she had put together that that was the year Tommy's wife went into the hospital for a routine procedure and didn't come out.

"You can always cheer yourself up and make a citizen's arrest before the night is through." It never hurt to try lightening the mood, but she was misgauging his by a mile.

"I think I'll run myself in first, impersonating a big shot."

How about changing the subject? "I'm glad you're opening up your private-eye office," she said and she meant it. She could see him in that role, and if she knew anything about male psychology—an open question, certainly—men had a tough time with retirement. They needed work. And so did she, of course, but in the same kind of way? To her, retirement was the equivalent of self-immolation. That's why she was heavily involved in nonprofit causes, like Saint Monica's College, that consumed her time and imagination and gave purpose and shape to her day. She would sort this out sooner or later—with the assistance of her Rock of Gibraltar therapist. Based on tonight's conversation, resolution needed to be achieved sooner rather than later. Meanwhile, the image in her mind of a private detective might have been terminally dated, tainted by old black-and-white movies of gumshoes and cherry-red-lipsticked broads and wise-cracking tough guys with brogans propped up on their desk in some dilapidated office building while sipping Old Grand Dad from a chipped, stained coffee cup. Nowadays, private investigations were likely all about cybersecurity and surveillance and forensic accounting, but that was merely speculation. If so, Tommy might struggle to gain his footing, but if people needed some old-fashioned private detective work, he would thrive.

Privately, she also had been slowly, mostly unconsciously, fashioning for herself a little fantasy. She and Tommy could work together—she was hopeful. She knew it sounded crazy, but didn't she crack the case at Saint Monica's? She and Tommy, she would correct the record, she and Tommy, while still a cop, along with her dad as a *team* cracked the case. They could be a good team again.

"We'll see," Tommy said, with an edge. "There'll always be people who need a good private dick."

She rolled her eyes. "Really, Tommy, really? You in middle school?" She was no prude, anything but, as he knew full well, but come on.

"I'm being hard-boiled, like the eggs chopped for caviar they are spooning out around here, to feed all your fat cat people."

There it was, out of nowhere, the old gauntlet being thrown down. It had been a long time since she spied the shabby thing at her feet. The gauntlet is never a pretty sight to see thrown down anywhere, anytime. She was no knight in shining armor, and no princess, either, and it had been a while since any medieval object had made its ratty appearance in her life. Men did that throwing down thing with their gauntlets, she supposed, wherever they kept them. And she was woman—and man—enough to pick it up.

"Tommy? *You* are my people, Tommy."

The way he shook his head amounted to asking: Was she sure about that?

"Are we about to have an argument?" she said. "Because let's not." Going back to her marriage to Anthony, this was a sensitive subject.

"No, we're not going to argue, honey. Having a complicated night is all."

Each was having a complicated night, just not the same one.

"Because you don't want to argue or because there's nothing to argue about?"

His face reddened and he tugged on the top button of his ruffled formal shirt. The damn shirt collar was too tight, and the bow tie pressed on his windpipe. On the way out of his house, she had engineered for him the thing around his neck because he was all thumbs, but if she were a cop on the beat, he would have called that police brutality.

—

A TERRIBLE FEELING CREPT up on her, for the first time. Was this a mistake? She didn't only mean getting the tux, taking him to the gala, she meant everything. Was it too soon, coming with him to an event like this? Alternatively, maybe she was a fool. When would the Valium kick in?

"Do you want us to leave?" she said. The prospect unexpectedly held some appeal. Her anxiety escalated. The next pill she took would be her third today. That's two or possibly three too many.

"Do *you* want to go?"

"What I want is champagne."

"I'll get you some, baby. Me, I'm going to try to track down a beer in this joint."

Her heart sank. She hoped they served beer but wasn't counting on it at a gala like this. As soon as he turned to hunt down the drinks, she found in her velvet clutch another blue Valium 10 and covertly popped it.

After a few minutes he returned, champagne flutes in both hands. Francesca was beaming and breezily chatting—with a priest possessed of movie-star looks. Tommy didn't need to have been a crack investigator. The man's black suit and black shirt with Roman collar was the giveaway.

"Father Philip, this is Tommy Thomas…" She scrambled. How to identify him? "My special friend."

Philip reached out to shake hands but it was awkward, what with the champagne flutes, and Tommy made little attempt to smooth over the clumsiness.

"Tommy, Father Philip and I went to Saint Monica's together long ago, when he took college classes while in seminary. Back in the dark ages—like before email." She had been thrown off her game, the proof being how she had incompletely, and disingenuously, identified the priest who had played a charged role in her life dramas. She'd hold off sharing that information with Tommy.

"You're so right, Frankie," said Father Philip, amiably, suavely. "That was around the time they invented blackboard chalk."

This was Tommy's cue to say something charming. He whiffed it.

Francesca filled in the silence: "Long time, Philip."

"Let's get together soon, catch up. Hey, my dad finally showed, better late than never," said Father Philip, pointing in the direction of Paddy Fitzgerald across the way. He could tell by the way his father smiled and leaned forward that he was respectfully flirting with a lady of a certain age. "Better pay my respects, you know how touchy the man can be. But wait, before I forget. Excellence is planning to give you a call, he has an idea he wants to discuss. He wouldn't tell me what it was—but you get three guesses."

"Sounds mysterious." Though it wasn't, and she didn't need three guesses, as she assumed the bishop was going to do the money-ask in person, which was pro forma when it came to large-capacity fundraising candidates.

Francesca and the eminent and dashing Father Philip hugged as old friends might before he silkily wandered off.

"Let's do lunch, Frankie!" he cried over his shoulder as he was swallowed up by the swarm of partygoers, pawing, seeking attention.

She said yes, good idea, and hoped he was sincere, because she was. Part of her was astounded he had approached her at the gala in the first place. But then it also immediately felt natural, and right. Too much had happened between them and it had been far too long since they had talked, really talked.

Tommy couldn't help but notice that, as soon as the priest departed, so did her radiant smile.

"Special friend? *Special friend?*" It sounded to him like a designation that granted you preferential treatment on public transportation, like with a service dog. Then again, they had never agreed upon how to identify themselves in a social context. It was all too new.

She was guilty as charged. "Sorry, you're right, I clanked it. I sounded stupid stupid stupid. Don't make me feel worse than I do. But I didn't think you wanted me to say you were my favorite homicide detective, or that you're the man I am sleeping with." She had some Valium left if required, but she didn't want to fall asleep on her feet.

Side effects may include saying brainless things.

"You didn't need to make a confession that you were sleeping with me—or since he's a priest, maybe you did."

"Should have said, this is Tommy and he's with me and you figure out what you need to."

"He calls you Frankie."

"Old friends."

"They let crazy handsome drop-dead gorgeous guys like that be priests? Don't women think that's a waste?"

"Don't know what you're talking about, a *waste*, and besides, to me you're every bit as good-looking."

He didn't need to hook her up to a lie detector or to hang up a *Private Eye* shingle in thin air to determine she was not telling the whole truth and nothing but the truth.

"You do remember I used to interrogate people for a living, right?"

"Why would you want to interrogate me, Tommy?" She mentally located the pills in her tiny clutch purse, but she couldn't break the glass on the emergency pill box while Tommy was studying her.

Side effects may include taking more drugs.

"You go out with him in college—back in them dark ages?" He was not the jealous type, normally. Then again, that priest cut quite a dashing figure.

"You catch the Roman collar, Detective?"

"Ex-detective." Tommy filed away for later analysis the fact that she didn't answer the question. "Let's change the subject. How much you planning to donate? Just curious."

Francesca pretended not to be stunned, which she was. Usually, he was subtler, and not the let's-get-everything-out-on-the-table sort of man, because first, the truth only seeps out over time, and second, there's no table big enough to put everything out on. But the gala was the essence of his being out of his natural habitat, so she could sympathize—perhaps. She doubted he was being innocently curious, since nobody with current brain function is innocently curious when it comes to the subject of money. So she flinched, a reflexive response he detected, but not answering him could be construed as drawing a boundary, so she saw no alternative to being direct—since he was. She was who she was, and so was he. Time to get real, whatever that trite turn of phrase purported to mean, and everybody knows what it means. She told him how much she was contemplating. Her charitable donation exceeded his entire pension by five times or possibly ten—or so she would have guessed, not that she probed into his civil servant personal finances or the status of his IRAs. She could always use the tax deduction, but she didn't want to get into that level of detail, not to mention that tonight's causes were those she could passionately get behind. She was planning to split her gift fifty-fifty between the new high school and Caring Street. What she wasn't going to mention was that, as large as her donation may have been, this was likely not the full extent of her ultimate contribution. She would wait and see before committing what she would term serious money.

Tommy shook his head, which she feared as disapproving, so she asked him—with a tone she could not resist adopting, hard as she tried—if there was something wrong with her donation. What she was asking, of course, was if he thought there was something wrong with her.

"Not exactly, I suppose, though I gotta be wondering about the bishop, who wants a sit-down with you. He is up to some nasty crap. Forcing teachers and other diocesan employees to sign a loyalty oath, a morality clause in their employment contracts—didn't you see that in the news? Teachers have to commit to upholding Catholic doctrine in their private lives, not only at school, otherwise they can lose their jobs—because he says they're really ministers, whatever the hell that means. I hear they're about to push out some good teachers who have the gonads not to sign. Sounds dumb to me, the bishop's power play. And pretty bad if, I don't know, like, say you're gay or use birth control or march for marriage equality, which Catholics are stuck in the Middle Ages about. But you know all this."

Francesca was distraught she wasn't up to date on the latest, and the news confused and troubled her. She needed to get back into the loop or she'd one day become an old lady with a dozen cats.

"What a crushingly bonehead idea, a morality oath, loyalty oath, sweet Jesus," she said. "And here I assumed the bishop was a lot smarter, especially since he's looking to build a new school, and he could use all the good will he could get. He is a bull in the china shop, like they say." She decided to bring up this issue when the two of them met. And now she made more sense of all the protestors clamoring outside the gala as they entered. She was embarrassed to be so out of touch. She should have approached one of the protestors, one she recognized, Anthony's younger brother, and now she regretted that.

"You Catholics can be hard to figure, no disrespect intended."

"You sure about that?"

"Yeah, Catholics are tough nuts to crack."

"I meant the disrespect not intended. I'm going to talk to Philip, find out what's going on here. *Father* Philip."

There *was* information she was holding back. Isn't there always, the detective would have presumed. Tommy had knocked her off-balance.

"Yes," said Tommy, "there's *Father* Philip. Here's to the lucky church with drop-dead gorgeous priests," and he raised his glass, offering a temporary cease-fire. They clinked glasses. Given the emotional intensity, a little harder than they intended.

She tried to align herself with Tommy and toasted: "Confusion to our enemies."

"They're everywhere, aren't they?"

They sipped the second-tier bubbly, which was bitter on the palate, and they both hoped somebody would rush in to fill the gap in their conversation, or at least bless him with a beer, but nobody cooperated. Bystanders and waiters must have sensed theirs was a no-fly zone.

Tommy wondered out loud why people said they liked champagne. The appeal eluded him. "Wish they had beer," he said.

"Me, too."

"*Frankie*," said Tommy, emphatically, as if he had arrived at a fresh conclusion, "you are a very good person."

His words dropped like a spider descending onto a spun white linen tablecloth. A chill slid icily along her shivering spine. To her, this declaration sounded appalling, like half a terminal diagnosis and half a press release. She felt a passionate need to defend herself against the charge. And now would be the perfect occasion to do that, which she might if she were in fact a very good person. But she did not believe she was in fact a very good person. She could prove the point if she had to, and she hoped the day would never come when she would.

"Philip? *Father* Philip? He officiated at my wedding."

"Must have been a great day." Tommy, not normally given to self-pity or cynicism, wasn't having such a great day himself.

"It was, it was," she said, deciding to ignore the sarcasm if that's what he intended. "And full disclosure: Philip's also Anthony's brother." That was nowhere in the neighborhood of full disclosure, but it was a placeholder, and there was a lot more she might have said, but again, not now.

Tommy was thrown, but he was practiced enough not to show it. "New ring?"

What difference did it make anymore? She was silly to think this would possibly work out.

When she didn't respond, he followed up with this: "When did you take off your wedding ring?"

"Today." She noticed he was still wearing *his* wedding band.

Gong. Guests were being summoned to take their seats so dinner could be served and the program could begin. *Gong.*

She handed off the dreaded champagne flute to a passing waiter, put her arm through Tommy's as if this were her last desperate hope to hang on to him, by keeping him close, and they headed down the long flight of stairs toward their special table, and she remembered, but did not tell him, not now, not after his cheap shot, if that's what it was, which it wasn't, that it was also a pretty good day when she and Tommy met.

"Wait," she said. She scurried back up the stairs in her challenging heels, rummaged in her tiny ruby-studded purse for the pills, found them, took a deep breath, and tossed her stash into the trash, feeling instantly, strangely, exuberantly liberated. She would do this on her own, whatever *this* was, and she headed back in his direction, whatever *his direction* seemed to portend.

"Ready," she said, and hoped she was, because sometimes hope is all you can hope for. Her final old-school benzodiazepine was, as expected, working black magic upon her. She hoped she didn't nod off and nosedive into her lobster bisque. As an unconscious precaution, she locked her arm into his and held on tight. He construed this gesture as affection on her part, which it also was.

"One more thing, Tommy," she said as they walked, feeling the need to draw a line. "Just so you know, if you ever call me a good person again, I will probably kill you."

"Understood," he said, because he did. And he realized that he'd deserve such a fate. When she said what she said he remembered what it was about her that drew him to her in the first place and he looked at her anew. "You look beautiful," he said. "I'm glad I came tonight."

"You could have fooled me."

"No, truth, Frankie, honest truth."

In fact, he wasn't absolutely sure he was glad to be there, but he would also have not been glad not to be there, so it was going to take him a while to get there, yet he knew that was what he should say. And she understood him perfectly, what he said and also what he didn't say. They had a short walk ahead of them to their honorary table, and a long way to go between them, if they were ever going to arrive. Part of her was wishing she could find a soft couch, curl up into a ball, and slip off into a sweeter dream.

Chapter Five
Stanislaus Mackey

HOURS AFTER THE GALA, Stanislaus Mackey was waking up in the back seat of his limousine on the opposite, and wrong, side of town. Soon he would be talking to himself. He was not a talented listener, and he was an especially incompetent listener when he talked to himself. Lately he was talking to himself and not listening more and more.

A man who lives in a bubble like him is unaware of many things he might otherwise talk to himself about and not listen to. It would take a while for his staff to list everything about which old Mackey was oblivious. Like those new personal computers and technologies people were talking about. Those smartphones. Molly and steroids. Solar power. As one of his admin assistants once sputtered in disbelief to a coworker, "Get this. He asked me who's this Jennifer Lawrence person. Who doesn't know JenLaw? I respectfully suggested he should Google her. He looked shocked, clutching his pearls, like Googling her was some kind of sex act. Man totally lives in a vacuum cleaner."

Take this instant, for example. The man was unaware that a few feet away somebody was determined Mackey pay a price for how he mistreated innocent people.

—

At least the rain stopped. That turned into a serious storm tonight.

He had never grown comfortable being in the public eye. The jaundiced public eye. He had been a public relations question mark from the first moment he arrived in town, and he had ceased reading what they said about him in newspaper op-eds. He would never have clicked on the websites or blogs blistering him, either, because he didn't have command of a keyboard or know anything about websites or what a blog was. Nonetheless, his animal instinct told him what adversaries were likely to say, so his meager attention skills came in handy. Not that he would have preferred being cast away on some desert island. Fifty thousand souls were in his pastoral care and submitted to his authority, depending upon how loosely you defined *souls* and *care* and *submitted* and *authority*. That's because Stanislaus Mackey was the new bishop of the Roman Catholic diocese and when people spoke to him, he was addressed *Excellence*. Being addressed Excellence predictably puts a certain twisty spin on one's self-regard. In his case, it spun him toward gloom, reminding him all over again of shortcomings and failures and his anything but excellence.

He may have been *Bishop* Mackey, but no member of the flock considered him beloved and nobody for a second ever regarded him as a man of the people, unlike, say, Pope John Paul II, who was a bona fide international rock star. But then Pope Benedict one day would swoop in, God's Rottweiler, muddying up everything with his big paws. All in all, it was not an ideal time to be Catholic and quite possibly the worst epoch in which to be a bishop.

"Brendan," he called out to his driver on the other side of the limousine's partition, "what are we doing, stopping here? Engine trouble, flat tire?"

A minute ago a groggy Mackey opened his eyes, alone in the back. He had enjoyed better wake-ups in his sixty years on earth. Doing as much, he found himself in that curious corner of his personal cosmos, the intersection of Dumpster Dive and Night Crawl, on the outskirts of the sketchy neighborhood of Buzz Kill. He'd been in this place before if not technically, and aspirin was called for even if he didn't have access to any and, besides, nothing could help now. He always woke up alone but until now never in a car in what seemed to be the middle of the night.

Before long, he was talking to himself again and not listening, robotically taking stock. The principal item on his personal inventory might as well have been flashing in neon on the window of a bar and grill: *Drunk*. His parched mouth tasted like the beach and his teeth grinded with grit, but on the upside he was not quite as intoxicated as when he tumbled semiconsciously into his waiting limousine after the big event. He occupied himself with an unspoken question, but if it had been spoken it would have been along these lines:

How the hell did I get here?

He must have dozed off for a few minutes, and it wasn't the first time he had asked himself how the hell he got there and not answered the question. Something else was eating away at him. Excellence was suffering a vague, haunting recollection of his miserable, inept performance at the big diocesan fundraiser—and this despite all the donations that somehow rolled in that night. He recalled making the singularly tone-deaf remark to almost every supplicant, kiss-up, and serial social climber whose hand he shook, whose back he slapped, whose cash pledges he shoved in his pocket or lodged in his memory vault. The words that tumbled out of his mouth tonight included:

How much money are you worth?

When are you expecting?

Now that you divorced your wife, when are you going to petition for annulment?

An antisocial hat trick. The answers that people, biting their tongue, wanted to give:

None of your business.

What makes you think I'm having a baby?

Why the hell do you care?

His achievement was typical when it came to occasions like that, when the moneyed set descended upon him in force. Nothing wrong with raising money, as far as he was concerned, or with the people from whom he raised it. It all depended on what their money was to be used for. And he had big plans for the money. And noble goals.

No, really, his *were* noble goals. Even unpopular Catholic bishops drowning in their cups can occasionally have them.

This has to stop.

He was referring to the drinking, and by extension his record of sloppy performances in public, but the *This* in *This has to stop* encompassed more than that, what it was that had to stop. He was fooling nobody. If he didn't straighten up, it was only a matter of time before...

"You hear me? What are we doing, Brendan?" he said. "Brendan? *Brendan!*"

Maybe a tow truck was on its way. Damn, he yearned to go home, have a nightcap, get a good night's sleep. On second thought, the nightcap would be overkill. Tomorrow, more meetings with more lawyers tomorrow. These days, lots of hours with lawyers were blocked out on his calendar. And when not with lawyers, then politicians, or project managers, or architects, or consultants. He never grasped what a *consultant* did. He doubted anybody had a clue what had been accomplished when their invoices arrived.

"Damn it, Brendan!"

The driver didn't care that the bishop's famous temper was flaring. The driver wasn't even Brendan.

—

OUTSIDE THE EVENT TONIGHT a couple of dozen placard-carrying protestors shouted at the bishop when he made his studied entrance. The rain seemed to exasperate them and intensify their sense of injured merit and they stood sentry, soaked in indignation. Mackey could hardly miss the signage: STOP SHIELDING PEDOPHILES and SUFFER LITTLE CHILDREN TO COME UNTO ME and JUSTICE FOR SURVIVORS NOW! He was all too familiar with such insolent public reception. He could appreciate they believed he richly deserved hostility. As he customarily did, he approached them open-armed, determined to be humble, civil, transparent. Then again at that point he'd had only one drink, at most two. He assured them that he was doing all he could, that he understood their justifiable fury. His strategy—which was no strategy—invariably backfired. Tonight a white-haired woman spit on him, a first. He flashed, furious, but restrained himself. He wiped the suit front and crucifix with a handkerchief, which he would throw away as soon as he could, and didn't offer a word in self-defense.

He turned and came face-to-face with somebody he recognized.

"Hector," he said.

"Excellence," Alessandro said.

"You sure you should be here?" Mackey would consult with the attorneys to determine whether or not Hector was breaking the terms of his binding agreement.

"Nowhere else I would rather be."

"Peace be with you."

"And with your spirit."

Mackey walked off. He believed that's what Jesus would do. Sometimes he wondered if Jesus, a very good Jew, would have become Catholic. Or a Catholic priest. Of one thing he was certain: Jesus would never have allowed himself to be anointed bishop. Too much paperwork. Too many meetings with those consultants. Jesus would never call upon the services of a driver or a limousine or a damned consultant. And He may have miraculously transformed water into wine for that Cana wedding, but He wouldn't have been sloshed, either.

Some of those malcontents, professional complainers, and bandwagon-jumpers outside the gala were loony tunes, but not all of them, Mackey conceded. If they only had a grasp of nuance, if they only appreciated how difficult everything was. Not that those renegade criminal priests were nuanced in the least. The fact was, the situation was worse than those protestors could have imagined. And if the bishop didn't know better, if he hadn't been on the inside of the whole muddled, sordid process, he might be walking the lines himself, holding up his own protest sign.

This might not be saying much, but he'd put his record up against any bishop in the country when it came to accepting responsibility for the Church's transgressions. Despicable bishops tiptoed around, denied and prevaricated and finessed, and then inserted their pointy mitered heads in the sand. Stanislaus Mackey did nothing of the sort. This in itself was not something to be proud of. He wouldn't want any critic to misconstrue. There was no room for anybody, particularly the pastoral leader of a diocese, to take any credit whatsoever or assume the mantle of respectability, much less innocence. And he wasn't pleading for understanding, not for a second. But the truth was the truth: he had done all that a bishop possibly could in the aftermath. He slashed the red tape, he settled claims even if the statute of limitations had kicked in—and even if it wreaked havoc with the diocese's bottom line, and even if it temporarily hindered the Church's work with the poor and the needy. There existed no statute of limitations, as far as he was concerned, when it came to doing the right thing. And without fanfare and away from the eyes of the press, he personally sat down with victims—whom he learned chose to call themselves survivors—and he apologized and abjectly beseeched their forgiveness, forgiveness he made clear the Church did not remotely deserve. And he resisted the advice of his inner circle who wanted him to broadcast his contrition. To Mackey's way of thinking, these survivors had suffered enough and his hand-wringing would amount to cheap public relations.

He admired the survivors' passion, their willingness to come forward, in some cases many years after the crimes had been perpetrated. He agonized with them. He cooperated with law enforcement. He instructed the bulldoggish diocese lawyers to take the defensive legalistic umbrage down a few notches—and if they wouldn't they could take a hike. He'd seen firsthand the damage those rogue priests had inflicted upon children who trusted them with their souls, and their bodies. He couldn't take away the survivors' pain, but he could acknowledge its reality. He could give them money, too. He could also systematically rid the diocese of the guilty priests—which he did.

In a strange way, his biggest personal challenge lie in managing his own rage, his anger over these reprehensible priests. But fury begets only more fury. Sin, more sin. Hatred, more hatred. How does that help anybody, least of all the victims? Check that. The *survivors*! These criminal priests would pay the price they deserved to pay. In his darkest hours, he tried to forgive them. In honesty, he mostly failed. A better man would do better, Mackey knew.

He also knew he was a lightning rod for the discontented, such as Hector Alessandro, whose dismissal now seemed, upon further reflection, more justified. Alongside the survivors' supporters that night gathered a foolhardy group of enraged teachers, riled over the new provisions introduced last-minute into their employment contract, which he had overseen and which they excoriated as constituting nothing less than a Catholic so-called loyalty oath. If they wanted to keep their jobs, they'd have to sign on the dotted line that they would uphold Catholic doctrine not only in the classroom but also in their private lives. Of course, the teachers coined a new name for Bishop Mackey. Some of their signs derided him as Bishop Joseph McCarthy. Others were less indirect.

STOP WITCH HUNTS ON TEACHERS

It was okay, he could take heat from the teachers, too, because he was doing the right thing, which was never the easiest course to take. That was no damn morality oath. The revised agreement was not essentially changed, he would argue. It *clarified* what it meant to be a Catholic educator of children. If they wanted to teach in a Catholic school, they were required to live up to Church dogma all the time and everywhere. What could be controversial about affirming the truth? The gay "lifestyle" for him was nothing less than, as he put it on the record, "gravely evil."

GRAVELY EVIL TEACHERS UNITED!

GRAND INQUISITOR MACKEY

He had a job to do and he was going to do it. He would run the diocese the right way. He wasn't striving to score points in a popularity contest. His self-confidence and the pure power of his incontestable convictions didn't help. Nothing helped. Why should the truth start helping now?

Well, as much as he would hate admitting, drinking did help, for a little while. If the situation critically deteriorates, for a little while is long enough, and everything about the diocese's situation was infinitely worse than bad enough. Not that this mattered to anyone other than himself, but the bishop hadn't been a serious drinker before he was appointed bishop. Since then he made up for lost time.

—

STAN, YOU'RE A LOSER.

It was a measure of the depths to which he had descended that hardly anyone after his parents died dared call him Stan, except for Stanislaus Mackey when he was talking to and not listening to himself.

If the bishop had lived another life, in another time, he'd be the guy on the squeaky barstool mumbling at the bartender, who also wasn't listening and cared less about the mumbler than about the cocktail glasses he had been wiping with a suspiciously soiled towel slung over his shoulder. In another life, Mackey could also be the bartender.

He formed resolutions to completely cease drinking and, when they failed to achieve traction, resolutions to cut back, and when he couldn't manage that, resolutions to get professional help one day. To get help, to be precise, *one day*. Resolution consultants—there must be such con artists, no? The hypothetical resolution consultants would tell you *one day* is a tomorrow that never dawns. When the house is on fire, who says *one day* I'll call 911?

Members of the bishop's inner circle were beginning to whisper, growing more alarmed. Last thing the scandal-ridden diocese needed was yet another controversy. The Chancery staff didn't use the word *drunk* to refer to the bishop, they said *alcoholic*—obviously not to his face. Why such a clinical distinction made a difference was unclear, but it did. To the bishop, the term *alcoholic* would have amounted to an effort to take everybody off the hook for validating the contempt they felt for somebody who drank the way he did—manically, sportingly, exhaustively, and, all right, *religiously*. All this goes to explain why his staff secreted away his car keys and assigned him a chauffeur. They found the ideal employee, too. As a teenager, Brendan, the new driver, once stayed at Caring Street House and had since served as handyman and custodian in the diocesan schools.

—

THE BISHOP'S BLACK TOWN Car was parked in darkness, lights and engine off. The driver shifted to the side on the front seat and drew down the window separating him from the lone passenger in back. They were on a deserted street in the industrial part of town, where no streetlight shone down on the ill-fated proceedings ordained to pass.

"Brendan, damn it. Let's get the hell out of here. *Brendan?*"

Tonight's serious martini intake explains why only now did it dawn that someone who wasn't his driver was behind the wheel, someone who had pulled the car to the curb on this bleak and desolate street—someone wearing a black ski mask, someone twisting awkwardly from his right shoulder and brandishing a gun in a black-gloved left hand. The bishop achieved instantaneous sobriety. Having a weapon trained on you was not one of the approved twelve steps, but it will sober most people up fast.

"You know," said the driver, "ever notice how some people look like bugs? Big bulging eyes in their pinheads, spindly arms and legs."

"Who are you? Where's Brendan?"

"And some people look like birds, all sharp beak and helium hair."

"What are you talking about?"

"And others look like dogs, all furry and mouthy and wiggly butts."

"Why is there a gun in your hand?"

"Like I was saying, when it comes to you, more I think about it, I say you're a bug."

"What are you doing, my son?"

"Your *son*? You're a sorry excuse for a man, aren't you?"

"Yes, I suppose I am. Who the hell are you?"

The gun was trembling. If it *was* indeed a gun and not the product of the bishop's frenzied, boozy fantasy life. Stanislaus Mackey was almost hoping this was yet another phantasmal visitation on the part of the lugubrious drinking denizens of his occasional delirium. Because the only thing worse than having a gun pointed at you was one being held by an unsteady if hallucinated hand. He was listening as he never had before.

"*Me*? Who the hell do you *think* I am, Excellence? Let's say I'm somebody leading you up to the Lord's gold and bejeweled heavenly throne."

The ignition motor fired up and the engine turned over.

"Where are you taking me?

"Buckle up, Bishop Mackey."

Through his teeth the bishop sucked in all the air he could. It sounded like a fuse had been lit.

Chapter Six
Matty

AMONG THE GALA PROTESTORS was, as it happened, Matty Fitzgerald, a high-profile faculty member at Holy Family High School. He was the kind of teacher HFH graduates nostalgically looked forward to visiting while home on college breaks. That's when they thanked him for all he had done on their behalf, testified he was better than any of their professors, and asked him out to lunch, behaving like the adults they aspired to become one day. Matty's older brother—Father Philip Fitzgerald—had been counseling him to adopt a more measured approach to resistance, or what he called a more *mature* approach. "Mature approach?" echoed Matty, smacking his own forehead with the heel of his hand. "You've always been a condescending son of a bitch." That remark was as foreseeable as it was hurtful, but Philip did his best to reason with him. The bishop was dug in, and not inclined to listen to strident voices or to be intimidated by confrontation. Compromise should be Matty's watchword—well, it was *Philip's* anyway. To that end, he had pleaded with the bishop to meet with his brother one-on-one in private, to talk some sense into him, or at least seek some middle ground, where they could both agree to respectfully disagree. Bishop Mackey might have claimed to be indifferent as to his plunging unpopularity, but Philip was more pragmatic: the protest movement was building a head of steam, and that was not good news for anybody, especially those who wanted to raise capital for a new high school and for the teen runaway center. Philip should have known better. The report he received from both participants was that the meeting was an unmitigated disaster that concluded in short order when the bishop banished whom he considered the self-righteous teacher from his sight. "Sorry, Philip," his brother said. "That's all I got, anger, alternating with rage. How can you tolerate that drunken son of a bitch? How can anybody?" Philip couldn't explain *how* to his brother because he couldn't explain it to himself. "Give me a little time, would you, please? I am doing all I can to undo this mess." "So you *do* agree with me? Thanks, Philip." "Hold your horses, this is convoluted." "It is not that complicated, not really, it is pretty simple. Morality clause is bullshit, and you know it." Philip did know it, but he temporized: "Try to see it from his point of view." "No, thanks. But what a mature approach on your part, congratulations. As always, you're a huge help, big brother." This exchange took place when the last two standing brothers found themselves at the Family Fitzgerald home on a Sunday afternoon a week before the gala. Interested observers of the exchange would be struck by their dissimilarity. Philip in his sharply pressed black clerical suit, lean and athletic and elegant, and the shorter Matty in distressed jeans and red HFH hoodie that rendered him faintly cartoonish, soft around the middle and wild of hair complete with unkempt beard. Engaged in the moment, Matty's head was as usual cocked to the side, as if he were trying to overhear something occurring in another room, and his birdlike features signaled skittishness, and an earnest wish to be anywhere other than wherever he was. Since adulthood, the brothers had been polite to each other, and careful, and they rarely talked at length, unlike that Sunday afternoon. "Well, contracts are due soon, Philip, so the clock is ticking." "What are you going to do?" "Not signing. The blood'll be in the water." Matty and Philip were not particularly close growing up, despite their bedrooms being next door to each other, and certainly enjoyed nothing like the competitive intimacy shared by Philip and Anthony. Matty and Colleen, his sister and the youngest of the four children, both looked on their much older brothers as if they were from another generation or tribe, if not another species, and as rivals for the scattered attention of their aging parents. Sister and brother banded together, unified against their mutual enemy, the rest of the family. They secretly called themselves with sarcastic glee the Afterthoughts, two children born because, well, what else were Fitzgeralds put on earth to do? They made babies. As a result, brother and sister believed they didn't ultimately matter much to their father and mother, who pinned all their hopes on Anthony and Philip, such that the Afterthoughts amounted to walk-on extras in case they were required to play the role of spare, compliant, remotely acceptable child in a pinch. Maybe they were right and maybe the parents were worn out after the two high-drama, high-achieving boys, Anthony and Philip. The older brothers would take the liberty of barging in on Matty and Colleen as they huddled together and talked late into the night under a blanket armed with a flashlight. They resorted to labeling them with a single name—sometimes Catty, sometimes Molleen—which was useful shorthand since the two were rarely seen apart during their formative years. "What are you two brat Molleens always talking about?" Philip would challenge them. "We're conspiring," she said—she was nine, with a good vocabulary. "Yeah, a palace coup," said Matty, ten, a serious reader who was up on imperial takedowns in classical Rome, and he pronounced the word *coop*. "Two idiots," Philip decreed. "Word's pronounced *coo-pay*." Matty followed up, searched for the word, and couldn't determine whether Philip himself didn't know how to pronounce it or if he was teasing him. It might be therefore unsurprising that the first person Colleen came out to was Matty, when she was fifteen, and she felt exhilarated and terrified, but also comforted when Matty hugged her and told her he loved her and asked how she knew, which she said she simply did, and for as long as she could recall. "Now you," she said, prompting him. "Now me, what?" "You ready to come out yet?" It took Matty a minute. "But I'm not really gay, Colly." She smiled knowingly, by her reading intuiting otherwise, but feeling generous enough to allow him the space to discover for himself in time. Nobody, including Philip, had a clue as to the Catty's private agenda or Molleen's. Years later, at the family home on Haymarket Hill that Sunday, Philip was saying, "Jesus in the Jell-O, Matty, Jesus, did you say blood in the water?" This violent image struck Philip as incongruous in the extreme. His brother had previously struck him as being a harmless, world-weary, introverted high school teacher, not some rabble-rouser. As with many teachers, Matty's career choice was made essentially by default, arrived at after undergoing a withering, galling, humiliating process of elimination. He had been a fairly good college student at Saint Monica's, though hardly stellar, but he got accepted off the waitlist into a graduate program in English at the state university, where he planned to pick up his master's or, with luck, a doctorate. He washed out halfway through the second semester, his coursework undistinguished, his papers turned back adorned with scarlet C's. Thus he was not destined to don professorial robes. He loved books but couldn't master the critical lingo or mannered subservience in the department needed to impress the academics running roughshod over the exploited underlings. After his grad student debacle, he stumbled around, disappointing his father and mostly himself. He and Colleen kept in touch, but now years after their nighttime blanket-tented colloquies, it wasn't the same. She had moved on, taking on a conga line of dubious girlfriends, and she didn't bother to share with her brother all the tempestuous dips and turns in her romantic life. Molleen and Catty, once the self-designated Afterthoughts, devolved into afterthoughts to each other, which made them both wistful, but resigned. He himself did not connect romantically with anybody, high school or college, but he was reconciled and usually at peace with that development. Honestly, he wouldn't know what to do with a girlfriend, and besides, nobody was sacrificing herself on the altar of his indifference and volunteering her services, anyway. During this stage of life, he found himself in a state of perennial penury. He was oddly smitten by this quintessentially Dickensian word, *penury*, and by all of the Dickens boy books, where he learned poverty was not a character flaw, the opposite of what his own father ingrained in him. At the same time, he never asked a dime from Paddy, and wouldn't have accepted a handout if he'd been offered—though he did move back for a while into the family home on Haymarket Hill. Uncomfortable as abiding there was, a roof over his head and a bed to sleep in were preferable to homelessness, if on some days by a skimpy margin. He drifted from one dead-end job to another. He sold used cars—but that isn't accurate. He was such an incompetent liar he didn't sell *any*. He ran a barbecue joint brazenly fronting for drug trade, till it burned down one night, in a case of unsolved arson—in which he was, groundlessly and bizarrely, briefly a suspect, set up as the patsy by the shady insurance-scamming dealers. He got work as a pest controller but could not resolve his moral reservations as to euthanizing hapless, trapped skunks and opossums. He did rudimentary landscape work, which he liked more than expected, working in the open air, but the Central Americans demanded he speak Spanish, and he had little capacity for foreign language. In general, he detested all his jobs, and at one point gave up and dropped out of his family's sight for about a year. Using money borrowed from Anthony, which was different in kind from his father's money, he bummed around the capitals of Europe, never calling or writing, except for infrequent communications to Colleen. He was by turns resentful or depressed or inebriated on cheap, delicious-to-him wine. Anthony was always the most generous, the kindest member of the family, and though the two of them never deeply connected, he told his younger brother to forget it, or to pay him back whenever he was able if that was important to Matty though it was immaterial to him. Matty regretted that Anthony did not live long enough for him to be squared up. He missed his brother more and more with each passing year, and the loss settled in his belly like a swallowed stone. Sometime during that subsidized European sojourn, in a bed-buggy hostel, he made the acquaintance of his eventual mate, another American searching for purpose far away from home. The funny thing was, the two of them had grown up within miles of each other, though their paths had never crossed as far as they could determine. "But then I find you halfway around the world, amazing, the love of my life," she said, "and you were there all along while I was growing up. How can you predict anything in life?" "Guess it was destiny," he said. "We *were* fated to be together," she said. He couldn't muster a counterargument. There was a familiarity about her he found reassuring. What a great story, she thought, their European whirlwind romance, which they would someday tell their kids, their grandkids, who would hang on every word. She was no natural beauty, but neither was he, and yet she bodied forth a kind of promise, and a sort of confidence, to set him on a sounder life course. They may have appeared an odd match, those two, she practically a head taller with dark eyes that nobody described as laughing, and he who raised looking askance to a level of art. With her large hands, she possessed workmanlike determination to power both of them, which was attractive to a man who conceded he required a push. After a while, then, marriage seemed to him like a reasonable enough concept, because as he saw it and said to himself, if not marriage now with her, then when with whom? Hard to argue with love, if love it was. He did not bother to drop to one knee to propose because one fairly sober night she announced that of course they were getting married, and he was disinclined to disagree. Accordingly, they hopped on a plane back to the States and were wed before a justice of the peace, why bother to wait, with no troublesome family from either side or any acquaintances in attendance for the brief, stock ceremony. "I can't wait," she said, "to get to know the Fitzgeralds." "Me, too," he said, and she laughed, though he was not joking. Complications inevitably ensued. As for Matty's mother, she swore she would never forgive him for eloping, but that wasn't completely true. She would never forgive *her*. She welcomed him tearfully when he returned with a bride by his side, or really, towering over him. In her remaining years, she would never much care for Claire, who was, to her mind, her son's thin-skinned, prone-to-panic, red-boned, rabbit-faced apparent wife—at least for the time being. Had he been apprised of his mother's dismissal of Claire's character, Matty might have defended her, but he was insensible as to his mom's bill of particulars. At the same time, it was also true that Grace Fitzgerald was also relieved somebody, *somebody*, seemed to have cast her lot with her poor son. Against this background, and once again back on his native soil, possessed of a wife and devoid of realistic job prospects, Matty himself searched for, well, a purpose. It did not take long before he identified one: books. He reaffirmed his love of literature, and seldom did he not have a battered paperback or library-borrowed volume within reach. Unsurprisingly, newly married and awkwardly domiciled with this woman of destiny he barely knew, he began to fantasize about trying his hand at teaching those books in a school. This last-ditch attempt at a career was enthusiastically spurred on by his wife. As for her, she had a well-compensated, apartment-rent-paying position she deplored as an associate dental hygienist, someone for whom tartar and plaque amounted to mortal adversaries, and whose bleeding-gum patients felt post-procedure they had been bested in a wrestling match. She hated her job almost as much as her patients hated her handiwork. So when Philip mentioned in passing at a Fitzgerald family dinner there was an office manager opening at Caring Street, she eagerly applied. At that point, Hector was the executive director, and he and Claire instantly identified with each other as kindred spirits. She demonstrated mad organizational skills and professed an abiding interest in working with kids who were in dire straits. She wouldn't bring home anywhere near the money she made in the dental office, but from the first she unreservedly loved her new job, and loved working with Hector, who was such a good-hearted, inspiring leader. Meanwhile, prospects for Matty's permanent employment as an instructor seemed remote. He dutifully sent out his CV and application letter everywhere and no vice principal in a hundred-mile radius was spared the purpled prose that colored his overwrought application. Then the improbable occurred. He caught on at a tiny struggling private middle school in town when a disgruntled teacher abandoned ship mid-year, and Matty served as a last-minute replacement, a part-time English teacher, three classes a day. The school was treading water financially and could not afford to pay a respectable teacher's wage, but he and Claire were young enough to believe they would make do. On some level, as long as they had a place to live and food on the table, he didn't care about the money. That is because he felt instantly at home, accepted unreservedly by those young children and his new colleagues alike. For the first time, he began to feel that his work, he meant his life, mattered to somebody else—in this case, his young students. Had he stumbled upon his life-affirming calling after all? Colleen believed as much and was thrilled for him. Brother and sister started seeing each other and talking at length again, and he shared with her stories from the trenches and about how every single day he found himself honestly, truly laughing over something his resourceful, impish students said. So when he heard there was a full-time opening at the Catholic high school, Holy Family, which was the alma mater of all Fitzgerald offspring, he asked Philip if he would please put in a good word. Philip said he wasn't in a position to grease the wheels, that outreach on that order was problematic diocesan protocol, and Matty claimed he understood, though he did not. Typical Philip, Claire groused to Matty about his never being there when his brother needed a little help, which wasn't truly the case, and her eyes narrowed in anger as she seethed. Because, in fact, without telling him, Philip did deftly, lightly reach out to the principal and put in a supportive word on Matty's behalf. "At least meet with him, a courtesy interview, I will be indebted to you." He didn't have to draw attention to the political reality that he had a major voice in diocesan budget-making, a far from trivial consideration for the money-pinching administrator. Strangely enough, the principal and Matty actually hit it off, and in due course he was hired. And then, more amazingly, it did not take long before he became nothing less than an authentic star at the high school. Adolescents seemed to constitute his natural audience. Teenagers are temperamentally idealistic and passionate and questing and full of self-doubt and simultaneously full of narcissistic illusion—which summed up Matty to a T—so no wonder he was embraced, being an older version of themselves. Philip watched from afar and never quite grasped how his brother achieved such sudden success. Meanwhile, Matty strictly maintained personal boundaries with students, but despite that, kids were convinced he was the sort of teacher they could confide in, about their own and their family travails. Tough kids fantasized he'd be cool to smoke weed with someday, which he never would, not on his life. In his classes they would consider Shakespeare or Dickens or the Bible or Homer or—really any good poem or play or novel—and students sensed that ultimately they were talking about their own lives, that the stakes were personal and sky-high. They yearned for his approval, they trusted him, they begged for college recommendations, which were worth their weight in gold, they invited him to their games and recitals and homes for dinner. He accepted these invitations whenever he could—increasingly, as it turned out, at the expense of his marriage. His wife began to feel more and more neglected, and her sense of abandonment disintegrated into full-blown jealousy and bitterness, sides of Claire he might have, but had not, foreseen. It wasn't long before their marriage was in jeopardy. "You're fucking those high school girls, aren't you? I know you are, we never have sex anymore, you don't touch me, you don't kiss me, you stay late at school every day, half the time you don't come to bed at night." He had not quite detected the seismic instability in their marriage till then, but he supposed she had half a point. "You wanted babies," she reminded him, gratuitously. Since she thought so, she was probably right. "Well, did you forget where children come from?" This did not qualify as a trick question, but he didn't know what to say. She rued the day she had pushed him into teaching, feeling she had only her controlling self to blame, and consequently threw herself more passionately into her own job at Caring Street. It did not seem to matter that he denied having inappropriate relations with any of those girls, which was truly the farthest thing from his mind. "I must have let you down somehow," she said to him. "No, Claire, the other way around." It often occurred to him to note with dismay the meager compassion Claire expressed for teenagers—at least the ones not hanging on by their fingernails in Caring Street: those were the kinds of kids she championed. Maybe she thought that Holy Family High kids were sheltered and privileged, and therefore unworthy of empathy. Because all right, yes, it was indeed true that teenage girls innocently (and yes, *innocently*) flirted with him, and of course, they were gorgeous, but it was equally true he had standards and integrity, and he kept his disciplined, watchful distance as best he could, which wasn't always easy to maintain. For instance, there were the neediest students, like Terry, the runaway he and Claire would on one occasion, and disastrously, take in for a night. Terry was exceptional in many respects. She was unmanageable, and she insidiously wormed her way into his life. He did his best to be professional with her, which effort was not without complication. But Terry was an extreme case. He wished his wife could appreciate the challenges he faced: to be there for desperate kids who needed him in ways they themselves didn't understand—and desperate kids were everywhere, even in Catholic college prep schools. Finally, the fact was this: he was married, not the most happily married man in the world, nor the most successful of husbands, but he kept commitments. In the lonely hours, when he stayed up late grading papers, his wife sleeping by herself in their bed or watching television, the dull gray drone and hum would permeate the apartment and he began to dimly fear—no, more like wonder if or when—she would inevitably leave him, and there would be nothing he could do or say to stop her—and he could almost make his peace with that. He would never leave her, he was positive of that. While all this was going on, his father had no glimmering of the fabulous turn in Matty's professional fortunes, nor the darker turn in his son's domestic life, because he wasn't curious enough to look that hard, simply thankful instead that his son had a steady paycheck and a community that for some baffling reason apparently took him into their bosom. The day his son produced a grandchild would be a high-water mark in both their lives, and he wished the day would come already. As for Philip, he had no prior inkling of Matty's great, uncommon gift as a teacher. But adolescents crave, more than their idealized versions of sex, more than love itself, being heard and taken seriously—which may be a profound, alternate version of love, and which may be something their own families did not unconditionally offer. As a teacher, Matty had strong views pertaining to pedagogy. He never lectured in class. He conducted his idiosyncratic version of Socratic discussion using leading questions, and he never preached to his students, either, when they shared with him in private the details of risks they were taking in their personal lives, as with drugs or alcohol, or their revelations as to romantic or family dramas. He listened, and he listened some more. Silence never threatened him, which is rare as rainbows for a high school teacher. He was learning something new every day about kids, and about himself, and he had a natural advantage: he felt himself to be, in some sort of absolute sense, an adolescent himself. Someone else—someone like Claire—might say that his psychological and emotional development was arrested. All the same, he worked hard, assiduously preparing for classes, faithfully moderating the school newspaper and the literary magazine, and his colleagues, in a sign of respect in which they held him, elected him president of the faculty senate. He was naturally adept at chairing meetings, his leadership style being warm and receptive, undaunted by conflict, as long as differences were collegially expressed. Despite being largely uninformed as to the essence of Matty's accomplishments and his school standing, Philip was pleased and proud of him. He took no credit for this development, but he was glad to have reached out to the school on his brother's behalf in the first place. More than once the principal pulled Philip to the side at some function and thanked him for referring Matty, who had become his most reliable teacher, his bulwark, a disclosure that fairly stunned him every single time. Nonetheless, Philip could detect in his brother's eyes a depth of self-confidence, at last. All this made Matty's latest turn to political protest so maddening to behold: "Matty, now you're going to throw away this lucky life you've made?" He didn't see it that way. He was standing up for principle. What kind of example would he set for his students if he were intimidated by the exercise of unconscionable authority and rolled over for the sake of keeping a job? "Hottest places in hell are reserved for…" "Shut up, just shut up. You're quoting Dante to me? I'm not in one of your classes." "You need to remember what standing up for something means. You should try it some time." Of course, Philip was worried for his brother. He was taking a stand and he would not survive the self-elected purge. Matty told him that there was a budding movement afoot to put pressure on the bishop, which his brother had of course heard about. "Not to worry about me. I'll keep my dignity." "But not your job." "When I was little and you were my hero big brother, you used to have balls. Philip, what happened to you? But you know what? The bishop'll be out of a job, too." There was an intense, frantic grassroots effort underway all across the community to sign petitions and formally plead with Rome, asking for Mackey to be sacked and replaced by somebody more in keeping with the refreshed spirit of the new papacy. Teachers and families were not the only supporters. Well-established, bold-faced names of Catholic leaders were beginning to sign on—they had had their fill of the bullying bishop, too, and they had stories to tell. Philip laughed his sham melancholy laugh, because if there was one thing he was not, it was jaded. He was beyond cynical. He had too much desire, too many ambitions, too great a need to be admired, to qualify. "Ain't gonna happen. You of all people know that's not the way the Catholic Church works. Mackey's here to stay and you'll piss off the higher-ups and they won't let you get your way." "I don't care, that's their problem, and besides, I'm not Catholic anymore." "Well, big deal, news flash, who *is* anymore?" Matty did not appreciate Philip's derisiveness and disdain, which masked his brother's undetectable, shielded love and authentic concern. "After you're canned, what's the plan, Matty Luther King, going back on skunk patrol? You're so impractical, typical Fitzgerald. And you know what? All those colleagues supposedly lining up behind you, few if any of them will ultimately pull the trigger. They have mortgages to pay and children of their own to feed, and you'll be standing there all alone with your dick in your hand." "At least I won't be dickless, like you." Philip pulled out one more arrow from his quiver: "How can you in good conscience abandon your students? They love you, they need you, Matty." "*I'm* not abandoning them, if anything I'm teaching them my best lesson, and another thing—how can *you* abandon my students?" "Don't do this, Matty, sign the contract, we'll work this out over time, trust me." Saying that, Philip was being sincere. And he also knew, no matter what his brother claimed about no longer being Catholic, as a teacher Matty lived whatever was right and good about being Catholic—and of course he didn't need to sign some ham-handed, ill-conceived loyalty oath to do so. "What makes you think life is black and white? It's never that simple." Matty smiled. "God, you sound like Colleen. She said sign the stupid contract, what the fuck, just do your job, kids need you and you need them." "Colly said that? Listen to your sister. Somebody's finally making sense around here." "Not to me, Philip, not to me. If I have to, I'll go down fighting," he said. "And losing," said Philip. Matty said it depended on how you defined losing. Philip shrugged, deflated, having no more weapons left in his rhetorical arsenal. "Guess you're right, everybody has their own definition of losing." Especially losers, he didn't add. "We'll see whose definition turns out to be right," said Matty. And so they would. That was one thing they could both agree on.

Chapter Seven
Ruth

Don't," THE MAN SAID. He was lying alongside her in bed. There it was, the magic word: *Don't*. That's all it took. Ruth swerved into an apocalyptic mood, like hitting a patch of treacherous black ice on a wintry backcountry road. In her mind, she turned *into* the skid, the way experts counterintuitively advise. She spun out till she corrected, before plowing into the equivalent of a fresh bank of cushioning snow and *oof*ing to a restless resting place.

"Oh, fuck," she said. He was refusing to leave his wife. What made his reluctance all the more galling and heartbreaking was that he did not have one of those to leave.

—

IT WAS MORNING AND her lover stared up at the ceiling. Not that she used the term. Such a fake fake fake word. Who says *lover* with a straight face? Then again, she had limited language resources for him, or for them.

Whatever the word, there was no question she loved him more—or she loved him differently—than she'd ever loved. Nonetheless, the prolonged ceiling gaze was a disheartening sight on a man in bed. As they lay there, she was collecting the fragged pieces of her brain. The pieces didn't click in place, fit where they had fit before. Eminent scientists awarded prizes for groundbreaking research in neurobiology, perception, and consciousness could illuminate the marvelous, complex phenomenon of cognition. So could anybody who had been a teenager.

"What are you looking for up there?"

Another one of those non-question questions she was proficient at. She didn't expect an answer, and, since he read her correctly, he wasn't going to chance offering one. She tugged on the top sheet for cover, turned to the side, and clawed the nightstand surface. She groped for the solace of cigarettes, which she located beside a tall, teetering stack of books. She unsealed the crackling cellophane. It was unfailingly satisfying to open a pack, almost as satisfying, under other circumstances, as opening one of those books. Here in this bed, reading was the remotest of possibilities.

Scuttling for a smoke in the aftermath was a cliché, and she was beginning to consider she had become one herself. For years she had been attempting to renounce the filthy habit, her half-hearted resolution renewed every New Year's Eve before the big ball dropped on Times Square on television. This morning the cigarette between her fingers served as nothing more than a wistful prop.

"Don't," he had said, just like that, "don't." He was lying stock-still, as if posing for a mannered tableau. "I don't want smoke on my clothes." His lips barely moved. His short jet-black hair was beginning to gray and whenever he used to cast his black eyes into hers, she would blink in self-defense. Somebody should hurry and paint a portrait of him—a photograph wouldn't do—like this, in bed with her, to freeze the moment. Even now, she could not get over how handsome he was, and how much he excited her. Excited her? Another fake word in this context. How about: how he annihilated her, how he tore her into pieces, how he pushed her off the emotional ledge—and if he elected, caught her before she landed.

"You're not wearing any clothes."

He pointed at the chair where his disembodied black suit jacket draped sadly as a stylish scarecrow's fashion statement.

"Bless me, Father," she said, reciting from the script for the sacrament of confession, "for I have sinned."

"Think you're clever?"

"You can be such a little prince, Philip."

—

Ruth had not slept with a great number of men, but enough to realize she had plenty to learn—about Philip, about her with him, and about him with her. From the first, sex with him was not the same, it wasn't even a thing, an *it*. Sex could be about relief from hurt, but it could also be about dishing it out. It could be about peopling the loneliness, and it was about being lost and solitary in the dark. It was walking along the springtime shore, it was sprinting into a burning house. It might feel like making love, it might feel like soul searching, it might feel like fun house mirrors—and it might be all in sequence, or simultaneously. Without warning, craving desire might devour her and she might want nothing more than to fuck him hanging off a chandelier. It happened even without chandeliers nearby. She could be swimming, be flying, be skating, be climbing, be falling and falling and falling and never touching down. It might make her feel safe, like being warm at home when the blizzard rages outside, and she might as well be on the moon or under the sea or at summer camp. Not that she as a child went to summer camp, but she had an idea from ads in Sunday papers. Sharing and giving, needing and taking and keeping for herself. She might laugh, she might weep, she might scream, she might leak secrets through the pores of her shivering flesh, in her fingertips, at the tip of her tongue. Humiliated and adored. Denied and discovered. In complete control and at the mercy. Sometimes it was a mistake. Sometimes it was a mistake she couldn't stop making, would never stop making. When it was right, and right in the right way, it could be like oxygen, it could be like water. But when it was very, very wrong, it could also be like her lungs were burning at the top of a mountain, or her throat parched post-trek through the desert. All about herself. All about him. Sex with him made her feel whole before he gently smashed her into pieces. Glad to be alive, wanting to die. For him, for him with her, for her with him.

—

Ruth, with advance warning from her psyche's stormtroopers, had an intuition she was on the verge of the most entangled day of her life. And she would be proved right.

She may have been an esteemed psychotherapist with a many-month waiting list, but she wasn't thinking about any clients, including those she admired and learned from, such as Francesca, people who were committed to what therapists like her called "doing the work." She wouldn't say this in public, or in the privacy of her therapist's office for that matter, but stability, serenity, sobriety—such conditions were not absolute. And who knows, they might be overrated. That inner calm might give testimony to compromise, to missed chances, to fear of taking the right sort of risk. She had not always felt this way. Originally she had gone into therapy longing for such stability, serenity, sobriety for herself and for others. But she had changed. When she opened her practice, a novice having completed her supervised hours, she was savvy and sophisticated enough to acknowledge she didn't have all the right answers. What she didn't know was she had not learned all the right questions.

She was not suffering from sex addiction, a much-contested and often misunderstood diagnosis. But certainly she had metamorphosed into a junky jonesing for the jangled, buzzy, humming, brain-hurricane state she yearned for during hours in bed with the unattainable man with whom she had fallen in love. The sex last night, however, had been, as was true for a while, this side of perfunctory—for her and, she could not help but assume, for him. She had expected otherwise on this occasion. He had called very late, something he had never done before, pleading to see her, sounding needy and distraught, remarkable for somebody normally so masterfully self-composed. She thought that was a good omen for intimacy and rushed over to the apartment. Fireworks did not ensue. She was fast shaping a theory. It was increasingly obvious to her, if not yet to him, why.

—

HER ELASTICIZED MOUTH USED to dazzle and charm, the sight of which automatically urged his own mouth to approximate a smile. And so did her ocean blue-green eyes and her shoulder-length straight blond hair that cascaded down and that he couldn't resist stroking—when they first became involved.

They had had this sort of conversation, if conversation it could be called, more times than she could count. Besides, he hadn't bothered to mention the nicotine patch on her arm, if he had even noticed it, about which application she felt heroic to the point of martyrdom. "I wasn't going to light up. The cigarette is a crutch."

"Like me?"

"Only more reliable."

He'd heard sentiments along those lines before, and not only from her. He did like the luxurious sheets (she had explained the thread count concept, which sounded esoteric and exotic) and the down bedding she provided, which was so different from the domestic appointments he had known as a priest, accustomed as he was to a single bed and wool blankets and a depressed, fatigued pillow for his adult life in one rectory or retreat house or dormitory after another.

"Feeling hormonal?" he said.

She counted to ten. She counted to ten again. "Not sure how much experience you've had with women, but my hunch is you can use some free advice, so here goes: whenever you say something that idiotic to a woman, duck." She had nothing to lose, or she was ready to risk everything, or both. "Been wondering. Have you had other affairs since you became a priest?"

"There you go again, overthinking everything."

"What I said about *feeling hormonal?* Goes double for *overthinking everything.*"

It took a while before he found meager words. "What do you think you're doing?"

"Trying to figure out how special I am." She was going to ambush and smother him with a pillow if he kept staring up at the ceiling.

"If you can't figure out by now…"

"Well, are you sleeping with other…parishioners?"

"Jesus, what is wrong with you today?"

"So you *are?*"

"Ruth, even if I wanted…"

"So you want to sleep with another woman?"

"Even if I wanted, which I don't, how could I possibly manage…"

"You're not answering me."

He turned his head toward her. At last. "No, I'm not," he said honestly. "Can't believe what you're asking. And I have not been with any woman since I became a priest," he said, almost truthfully, because he could answer that either way—it was complicated, depending on the definition of "any woman," and certainly too hard to explain to her in her current frame of mind. "And you and I are not having some affair, either, we're in love. At least I thought we were."

"How come you're not the tiniest bit curious if *I'm* having an affair?"

He wasn't, but he followed her lead: "Okay, Ruth, are you?"

"Am I what?"

"Having an affair!"

"How can you say that to me?"

—

PEOPLE LIKE THESE CONDUCTING a clandestine affair, people who led such separate and disparate lives, arranged their liaisons as they could. She was ten years younger than her bedmate and they were under the sheets that morning in the apartment they had christened their Hernando's Hideaway. The retro name fit with the early, heady, silly, lighter days of their romance, and with their secret, private safe house they wouldn't dare reveal to anybody, and *Love Shack* didn't make the cut. Hotels were a nonstarter: too much risk for a public figure like him. And he had a built-in excuse for whenever he slept away from the diocesan residence; he could always say he was spending the night at his family's home. He was careful not to overuse the deception, and as a result they rarely stayed the whole night together. Their studio was in an upscale neighborhood and it was taken out in her name, and whose bills were paid by her. The refrigerator contained a single quart of orange juice and a few wine bottles, and there was a counter connected to the neglected stovetop where they sat on barstools for their infrequent take-out meals. The residence was aggressively minimalist, except for the kitchen. That was where she symbolically installed a few never-used pots and pans and plates, along with outlet store wine glasses, and an espresso maker, and a music system she was hoping one day would magically spring into action and fill the space with melody—at which point, he would sweep her off her feet and they would dance for pure, crazy joy. Thus far this had not happened.

"We should go into couples counseling," she said.

She received silence for a reply, which she could decode. A) he wasn't sure they were the kind of couple who qualified, and B) forget it, she was out of her mind.

"Therapist humor," she said, though she was more than half serious.

"Not very funny."

"That's why it's called therapist humor."

Admittedly, her domestic instincts were constrained, like her limited penchant for small talk during sessions. For sound reasons, because he was a cleric and had never once visited a Bed Bath & Beyond, his were practically nonexistent. She did purchase a good bed and a good TV. One was put into use regularly and in the past spectacularly, the other not so much. They entertained the idea of acquiring a small couch and at least one standing lamp. The prospect of furniture shopping grew more distant with each passing month, each increasingly rare rendezvous. It had been more than a year since she signed the month-to-month lease. Since they were usually together only one or two mornings or afternoons or evenings a week, most of the neighbors wouldn't have been able to pick either of them out of a police lineup. Which was part of the whole idea. Of course, he had to be cautious, so when entering the building, he adopted oversize jackets and baseball caps and sunglasses. What worked to his advantage—to their advantage—was that he wasn't currently assigned to a parish or to a school. His specialized duties at the Chancery permitted him to fly strategically under the radar.

Father Philip gazed out the bay window toward the boats by the bridge extending across the dark blue waters. The gulls and the hawks wheeled about in the cloudless sky. What had Ruth and Philip gotten themselves into?

"Beautiful day," he said, and would promptly wish he hadn't.

"Yes, indeed, a clear day beckons."

"But we needed that rain badly." Like hitting himself in the head with a hammer.

After a painful lull was allowed to amass, she lanced it. "Great, now we talk about the fucking weather."

"Saving my material for couples counseling."

"That some Irish priest humor?" she said.

"No, but how about this? Irish priest, he runs into a pub with his hair on fire and goes, 'Quick, laddy, a pint of your finest,'" he said, and paused.

"Brogue needs work."

"That's all I got so far."

"Joke needs work, too."

"But you see where I'm going."

"Wish I did." Because in the moment she didn't.

In the throes of falling in love, they had once talked for hours upon hours—philosophy, movies, religion, poetry, politics, family. As far as she was concerned, nearly everything he said constituted foreplay, and more than that: wisdom, tenderness, exhilaration. If he had urged her to rob a bank, count her in as an accomplice. And as far as he was concerned, everything she said had once felt electric. If she had plane tickets to London or Bali or any other distant destination, he couldn't have said no. They confided in each other. His flesh was hers. Hers, his. What had happened? It wasn't that he had exhausted the mystery of her heart and soul. In fact, he believed he knew her less well than before they had begun.

"I have to get going," he said.

It was early on a weekend, prime time for Hernando's, and there was no need to have another fight. They were beyond it. They were like two people stranded on a desert island. There was no longer an external reference point for the involuntary intersection of their lives, and they depended upon themselves to exercise survival skills to maintain their mutual, precarious existence. Spearing fish and climbing coconut trees would have been by comparison a less demanding proposition.

She held tight the unlit cigarette between her two fingers. "I promised myself I would never get involved with a married man."

"Good thing I'm not married."

"That's what therapists learn in graduate school to call a big-ass technicality."

There was no finessing that the illicitness, the peril, the hazards of their relationship were not unrelated to the intensity of their passion—at least at the start. He was not cheating on a spouse, she knew, but he was cheating on something or someone, if not himself. Did it arouse her to think that he was jeopardizing so much—for her? But then again, was he truly putting into jeopardy *anything*—for her? She had explored the mote that separated them from each other a dozen times with her own therapist, never achieving breakthrough. And what was in it for him? Besides the obvious, she meant. But Philip did not lack for the attention of women. He may have been a priest, but he was glamorous and powerful. She didn't believe she had a jealous nature, but men were men. Their drives were plain. Even men who were handsome priests.

"You're the expert on marriage, Ruth. You've been married how many times?"

"Who can keep track? Ten or eleven, ballpark. You know, some of the richest men never buy a new car. They get better value with, I think they're not called used cars anymore, 'previously owned.'"

"Lovely image. *Previously owned*. From the first, you knew our deal."

It was *on* now. She went for it. Nobody ever knows the deal till they do, which they should know from the beginning even if they don't. For instance, when potential clients of Ruth's called to make an appointment for their first session, the entire clinical situation manifested—it was true. In between the lines of their halting, vulnerable disclosures, contained within their hesitations and qualifications and non sequiturs and chatter, as they discussed the proposed day and hour to meet, they revealed to a good therapist what she needed to know about themselves, and opened a map of the path to the treatment that awaited.

"You think I'm crazy?" she said.

"Be more specific."

"You think I'm crazy that I love you?"

"Ruth." He didn't know what to say.

Usually they talked with such intensity only after they were at the bottom of a bottle of wine and they had both finished demanding workdays. But that was the overriding question, and she was in love with Philip, who was a priest, which made him by about any definition the most unavailable male in the world, except for the fact that he seemed to be available to her—sometimes, and in some fashion. But was he really? She was skilled dealing with clients who struggled over similar attachment issues and ambivalence, but her insights were not transferable to herself. If Ruth's clients, who plowed through boxes of tissues in her office, had a clue as to the trials of their therapist's own private life, she was sure they would never take their place on the big settee in her office and spill their guts and weep. They might sue her for malpractice. Ruth was just like them. She had the same problems. Maybe that's why she was a therapist in the first place. Her own failings equipped her better to work with others. It was a theory, a lame one, but a theory nonetheless.

Philip and Ruth looked at each other: they were lovers—there was that word again, that stupid word—who had had the same running conversation for some time now. Maybe they were going to break up, after all.

Philip knew it was his place to speak: "Are you *crazy*? That's what you asked. I ask myself the same thing."

"And what's your answer?"

"Never get very far. Should we break up?" He didn't mean it. He never meant it any time he said as much.

"*Again*? We tried to break up before, remember? We always end up right here in this bed, which is maybe why we try to break up in the first place."

A cell phone rang and she was relieved their conversation would cease, she couldn't take it today, though it was in those hard moments, when conversation was leading people to the most difficult truths, that's when those aha moments clients go into therapy to experience take place—that ordeal is the cost and the gift of therapy. But she wasn't his therapist. She wasn't therapist to herself, either. Most of her therapist friends were in floundering or nonexistent relationships, and they commiserated with each other. Occupational hazard of the therapist's life: confusing their mates with their clients—and vice versa. She should bag her career, start up all over again as, say, a teacher shod in sensible shoes, or a goddamn Uber driver, or a fucking social worker—any other vocation had to be simpler and more satisfying.

"You think you're a good priest?" She came off as half sincere, half perversely curious.

If anybody knew where Philip physically was in this moment, they might have a strong opinion. A strong, ignorant opinion, because how many people understood what it took to live his life, and what it took out of him, what he sacrificed? Yes, his was a double life, fully a man with Ruth, fully a man of the cloth with the parish and the diocese. If he could have lived any other way, he told himself over and over, he would have done so.

"It's not up to me to say if I'm a good priest. But you know, a bad priest can possibly better serve his flock, being another sinner like everybody else. And you? Are you a good therapist?" More argumentative than inquiring.

"Nice, hostile *and* defensive, strong move, which our nonexistent couples counselor would bust you for, but okay, fair question. If I am a bad therapist, maybe I can better serve *my* flock."

"I'm going to be late," he said, and turned his head this way and that as he tried to echolocate the origin of the ring. "Yours or mine?" Their identical phones had the identical ringtone, something they coordinated at a sweeter time, when they were playfully in sync.

It was his. He got out of bed, reached into his coat pocket, took the call and listened. She didn't want to gaze at him standing there, unselfconsciously sure of himself, somehow both more and less than naked. She stared into the middle distance of the next room and listened. He professed to hate talking on the phone, which was one reason Philip and Ruth hardly ever called each other. As usual, his voice on the phone was clipped and tense, his words terse and businesslike, which was utterly unlike him when he was delivering his masterful, moving, and warm homilies from the pulpit, which was how she first fell for him. He had once asked her incredulously, because that was when he wanted to know everything she felt and everything she thought: "It was my voice? My *voice*?"

"Men are dense," she said. "That's also oral sex."

From where she lay, she looked and read his face, anybody could, and what he was hearing was obviously not good news.

"I'll be right there." He inserted the phone back into his jacket pocket.

"That didn't sound like you won the lottery," she said, noticing that he looked reflective, unruffled.

He began to put on his clothes, methodically, wordlessly. She hated when he went stoic. Why did he have to be that way? She hated that it was always up to her to break through the wall erected between them.

"We on a need-to-know basis? Because I need to know."

"The diocese. Something seems to have finally happened to the man."

She had no idea what he was talking about.

"My boss. That man." His face was impassive.

She gasped. "Bishop Mackey's what, dead?"

"You know, for a therapist, you sure project a lot."

"You know, for a priest, you're really not an open book."

"Sorry, shouldn't have said that, sorry. Mackey was wheeled into the ER in the middle of the night, unconscious. They don't know what happened. It's all murky. Somebody might have touched him up a little bit, and he's in the hospital, serious or critical condition, it's all unclear. Seems the tough old son of a bitch'll live."

He powered on the TV remote, and in a second there was the report on local news. He dressed while in the background the beat reporter kept reciting over and over the same scant details. Abandoned limo. Late last night. Reported missing this morning. Located in the hospital. In guarded condition. Brain damage? Stroke? Heart attack? Too early for anything to be ruled out. Next twelve hours crucial. Police were not revealing information, pending their investigation. The diocese had not yet released a statement, and wouldn't do so till Philip reviewed it, but the controversial, beleaguered bishop's formal photo flashed, alternating with images of the cathedral steps and façade and stained glass that kept appearing on screen, as on a loop. It was a magnificent piece of architecture. Clearly, the producer was being what he believed to be crafty, sending an ironic message. The bishop's photo featured a beaming Great Dane-like face and a golden crucifix big as the evening star gleaming on his chest. At least they didn't use his driver's license picture. That is one step away from a mug shot, which some disgruntled members of the flock believed was long overdue.

Next, one of the high school teachers who had been self-sacrificially, frantically leading the protest against the loyalty oath was interviewed on camera, a phalanx of supporters nearby.

"Bishop Mackey and us had our differences—I mean we *have* our differences. He was wrong to give good, dedicated teachers the bum's rush without cause, but we're all going to pray for him, that he makes a complete recovery."

Philip applauded that the teachers decided not to politicize the incident. And what exactly was the incident? Had a crime been committed against the bishop? Who knew? He noticed that one of the supporters standing behind the spokesman, visible on camera, was his brother Matty. He went up to the flat-screen, pointing. "There's my stupid little brother. If there's any shit nearby, he can't help stepping in it." He turned off the TV. Philip couldn't watch anymore. He snapped on his Roman collar and put his arms through the sleeves of his black suit and straightened out the jacket before a full-length mirror.

She lit her cigarette.

"I'll call you when I can, and put that out."

"Promise?"

"I said I will call. I mean it, put it out."

"Love you, Philip." She wished she loved him a little bit less. This wish alternated with her desire that he love her a little bit more.

He put his hand on the apartment doorknob. "Might be a while before we get together again. I don't know how it could, but something tells me this is going to get more challenging."

Then he came back to the bed and kissed her goodbye. It was a disappointing sort of kiss, an impersonal, virtually friendly kiss. She acknowledged he had reason to be distracted, hearing such disturbing news. But somehow that didn't completely account for his remoteness. His stiffened bearing she recognized from a ridiculous episode in her past, when a man she was seeing was carrying on simultaneously and covertly with another woman—a therapist himself sleeping with a therapist colleague of Ruth. She might have felt betrayed, but more than anything she felt offended. That was a rude thing to do. She could never be involved with a man who had such poor taste. All to say, she understood why some people considered therapists certifiably insane. They had a point. She hated herself for making these connections. Not the time to do that. It wasn't all about her. It merely felt that way.

About to get more challenging? About to get more challenging? How could it get any more challenging? And she also thought, madly, incoherently, *Isn't this when you would want to be with me?* But she didn't say anything, and she knew she was forging absurd linkages. Philip had no idea what he was up against. And she didn't tell him what she had decided: this would be her farewell cigarette, although not in order to garner his approval.

Luckily for him, or not, she had missed the opportunity to tell him any of those things, because, not so fortunately for her, he was already out the door. There was also one other thing she had been planning to tell him today, but she never saw the opening. She stamped out the unfinished cigarette, the last one she would touch, and not because he instructed her.

Too bad about the bishop and too bad Philip left so quickly. *Left her so quickly.* She could be losing her mind, she would admit this. She ripped off the nicotine patch. What had she been thinking? This wasn't the time to be absorbing any poisonous chemicals into her body, not now.

Feeling hormonal, Ruth?

She'd missed her period, which normally arrived like clockwork, so she picked up the kits at the drugstore.

Even if the man was cheating on her, which he almost certainly wasn't, but even if he were, he deserved to know. Specifically, he needed to know what at first she couldn't believe, because she hadn't planned this. This is what peeing on the sticks indicated each of the three times she did: Ruth was pregnant.

It was early, she estimated, five or six weeks.

—

WAS SHE CUT OUT to be a mother? She had doubts on that score, because where was the joy? Or was that a stage that hadn't arrived but was imminent? Was she entitled to feel joy? Was she on schedule to feel the miserable way she now felt? Not that she could describe the way she felt that she had never felt before.

She would buy all the books, read obsessively online, do the equivalent of grad school for being pregnant. She'd learn what normal was, she'd track the deviations. If she were indeed five or six weeks, what she read so far said to beware volatile swings. All right, *check*, she had those in spades. What was physically happening to her, inside her, was incredible. The embryo was forming—was the heart really beating? Was it right for somebody like her to bring a baby into the world? Was it right for her to bring a baby into *her* ridiculous world? She could decide otherwise. It was early enough, and this verdict was in her power.

The baby was the size of a bean. She fixated upon that incredible word: *baby*. When would she start thinking about the baby's room, about the baby's toys and furniture and clothes, about the baby's Halloween costumes, about the baby's sex, about the baby's name?

No two women would have the same experience, so the experts said. She'd expect that to be true. Why would anything be different now that she was pregnant?

So Ruth was pregnant. That was a fact. She had the proof. And many decisions to make.

She was having a baby, no question about that. But another, unanswered, possibly bigger question loomed: Were she and Philip having a baby?

Chapter Eight

Philip & Anthony & Francesca & Philip

*H*IGH SCHOOL: THE BEST *four years of your life."*
If that bromide were valid, how messed up is that?

But that is commencement speakers' patented move, which always lands with a splat, DOA.

Consider the hormones, the insecurities, the disappointments, the rejections, the broken hearts, the dermatologists. Cherrypick your poison: secondary school or anesthesia-free surgery? As that reality applied to the two older Fitzgerald brothers, however, maybe not so fast, partly because that was back when Holy Family High had not yet descended into decrepitude, though mainly because high school for each of them was an unapologetic year-to-year victory lap. Certainly nobody arrives at those graduation ceremonies, whereby state and church statute he or she, cap-and-gowned, is urged to follow their passions without hitting a few bumps on the road, and Philip and Anthony were both comparatively lucky—despite a few spectacular, ordinary mashups.

Philip was younger, with all the younger brother attendant crosses to bear and bitch about. Anthony was more socially adept, despite being somewhat introverted, and was regarded the more intellectual of the two—all his grades were As, while Philip's ran the gamut. People were naturally drawn to Anthony. On the other hand, Philip was athletic and extroverted, and people were wary around him, if not intimidated. He was no bully, and he would stand up for a kid being pushed around. His smile could curve into cruelty, and his movie-star good looks could convey generalized, low-level hostility: *You're just not as handsome as me*, he seemed to be communicating with his lowered, penetrating gaze. The brothers were competitive, as dictated by Fitzgerald DNA, but they didn't compete in the same arenas. Girls were attracted to them both almost equally, and there were passionate arguments during slumber parties or in the lunch room as to which brother was more desirable or, as they termed it, cuter. It was a close call, and it was said if you couldn't date one, don't kick the other one out of bed. Anthony was the safe bet, whereas Philip was, if not quite dangerous, moody and unpredictable, quick to hook up and quicker to break up. One night somebody had spray-painted on the gym a warning:

WATCH OUT 4 PHILIP BRO OF
ANTHONY ADORABL FITZGERABL

The custodians scrubbed the wall clean and painted over it, but not before most of the school was entertained reading it. Anthony wondered all day long who did the bonehead deed, and fantasized asking her out soon as he guessed. Meanwhile, Philip laughed it off.

"I know who did it," he told his brother. "This one girl's got a bad case of the Philips. Hate to break it to you, brother. Girls *think* they like the adorable big brother, but they're fooling themselves. They want somebody like me, not that there is anybody else like me."

"Too bad mom dropped you on your head when you were a baby."

"Your fly's open."

There was a facial similarity, but it was less pronounced than might be expected. Anthony was fairer and his features softer, more rounded, resembling his mother. Philip was darker and bigger and stronger, like his father. As a tenth-grader, he was already a starter on varsity basketball. Anthony was a senior and student body president, and therefore theoretically higher up the food chain, though he had never made varsity anything. Well, he did belong to the debate team, which he tried to keep under wraps from his dad and the rest of the family. He knew debate was reserved for pussies, but that didn't stop him.

"I'm trying to study," Anthony said, his desk lamp glowing before a looming pile of books and papers, when Philip barged in.

"I thought I heard you playing your air guitar."

"It's midnight, for Christ's sake, get out."

Philip had been laboring all night over math exercises. "I don't understand this trig shit, and who friggin' needs to know this crap?"

"That's what teachers get paid for, I got to study for a test."

"Brother Anselm, he is a hundred years old and he's got dandruff snowflakes all over his robe and no way he should be allowed in the classroom. Come on, you're good at math, I suck."

Anthony slammed down a fist. "Jesus, Philip, everything comes so easy for you. But when it doesn't and you have to work at something, you're a whiner."

"Easy for you to say, Mr. Student Body President."

"That's debatable."

He had inadvertently given Philip an opening. "Hey, what are you dweebs debating this year? Capital punishment? Nuclear disarmament? Capitalism? Yankees versus Red Sox? Giants versus Dodgers? Don't leave me hanging, brother."

"Funny you ask. It's euthanasia—ethically defensible when it comes to younger brothers? Affirmative or negative?"

"You going out with Pam Friday night?"

"My social life matters to you why?"

"Just asking. Besides, I'm going out with Pam the Bam Saturday night, so she'll feel the full Fitzgerald from me at least."

Anthony shook his head and opened a book, pretending to read. He knew his girlfriend was not going out with his brother, but the trash talk bugged him.

"Fucking with you, Tony."

He always hated *Tony*, as much as his brother hated *Phil*. "Okay, Phil. There's the door, it still works, use it."

"You're not going to help your little brother?"

"Christ wearing a crown of thorns, show me your goddamn book."

"See? I knew it. You're not half the dick everybody says."

Nobody ever said that about Anthony, even after he enlisted in the debate team, which is why Philip took every opportunity to remind his big brother.

—

ONE SPRING AFTERNOON AFTER basketball season had concluded, Philip and Anthony were shooting hoops on the asphalt court in the park, one-on-one, playing H-O-R-S-E. It was a massacre, so one-sided it was not easy for Philip to derive any pleasure. Philip had an array of trick shots and he could shoot from distance with a dead eye. Anthony enjoyed playing but suffered no illusions as to his ability, especially by comparison. Nobody was talking trash—or trig, or Pam, or debate club, for that matter. Anthony was college-bound in a few months, which meant Philip was prepping to have run of the house and to become an upperclassman and lead his team to a state championship, at least so he fantasized. Their exchanges lately seemed freighted with valedictory emotion. Moments like this, playing in the park, they may have hated each other, but they also loved each other. The life of brothers.

They had been shooting around for a while when two guys showed up and challenged them to a game, two on two.

"Okay," said Philip, naturally up for competition, "let's shoot for who's got ball."

"That's okay," said the smaller of the two opponents, "you two Catholic fairies take it out." Their sweatshirts gave away their public-school identity. "You won't hold the ball for long."

"How come midgets like you tag along with big fat guys? Get lonely or something?"

"You're funny, man."

Philip was going to relish giving these jerk-offs the ass-whipping they deserved. "I got the thirty-eight," he told his brother, "you take the fifty-two Stout."

From the jump, a minor miracle. Anthony goes ape, doesn't miss a shot. He had never played half as well. Philip kept feeding him the ball, for the obvious reason that when a guy is hot he's hot, and Anthony was scoring from every angle on the court. Layups and jump shots and scoop shots. He head-faked his man out of his high-tops and drove past him for a pretty bucket. Philip marveled. Did he and his brother magically exchange places? If so, it was the first time, but wouldn't be the last.

The public school kids had some game, too. One—the thirty-eight—was a wizard with the ball: behind-the-back passes, dribbling between his legs, the whole package. The other, the fifty-two, all butt and elbows, was not as talented but consumed space in the key and was a rebound magnet. The game was close, down to the wire, and everybody was sweating and sucking wind and bending down to grab their shorts, catch their breath. The pace was furious and the mood intense. But finally Anthony got past his slower defender and laid it up and in, scoring the winning bucket. Game over, Catholic fairies on top. Another Fitzgerald victory. But now the new and uglier game commenced.

Anthony had taken a path to the hoop that left him exposed as he landed. His man shoved him by the small of his back into the steel backboard stanchion. The sound his skull made was unnatural and stomach-turning, like an off-key rung bell. He dropped to the asphalt, a gash ripped open high up on his forehead. Blood cascaded, flooding his face.

Philip ran over, whipped off his sweatshirt and pressed down on the laceration. Anthony was stunned, but he found he had something to say, because even before the pain had set in, that was in the Fitzgerald code: to talk. "I'll be okay. Really, I'm okay."

"Watch your step, faggot."

Philip walked calmly over. "What?"

He puffed out his big chest and belly. "Homie, I said…"

Philip seized him by the balls, and squeezed with everything he had and the guy was yelping. The little one was pounding him from behind, but Philip was unfazed. That's what adrenaline must be for.

"Hit me again and I will rip this guy's little dick right off. You oughta wear a jock, tough guy with a little dick."

Philip let go, the big guy dropped to his knees, doubled over. At this point, Philip wheel-kicked the fifty-two in the stomach, which sounded like air *oosh*ed out of a tire, and he keeled over. Then he picked up the smaller guy and jammed him headfirst into a smelly garbage can.

Meanwhile, Anthony had barely moved.

"You okay, Philip?"

"You're asking *me*? If *I'm* okay? We're going to the ER, you need stitches for sure. Hope you don't have a concussion. Let's leave these motherfuckers to think about the fairies that kicked their fucking asses."

"Nice game, Philip, huh?" Anthony hadn't felt this happy with his brother for a long time.

"You killed, man, you killed. What the hell got into you? Who turned you into Magic Fucking Johnson?"

—

ANTHONY CAME HOME FROM college, spring break, his sophomore year, Philip's high school senior year. He opened a bottle of stout and offered another to his brother, and they quaffed in fraternal unison. The horizontal scar along the top of his forehead, the legacy of that pickup basketball game, would never go unnoticed by anybody searching his face, and there was a good war story to tell when he wanted to impress a girl. He always left out the next part, how he never played half so well ever again. Funny how brotherly history was so nostalgic and precious to both of them, even, or especially, with the grim stuff. Growing up—and growing up Fitzgerald—is not for the faint of heart.

"Can we talk?" Anthony initiated.

"What you got, brother?" Funny, but his big brother was a lot like girls when it came to talking: it was like a plasma drip.

They were in the gazebo, the sun was beaming, a dazzling afternoon, week before Easter. Their dad didn't mind Philip drinking a beer, he was eighteen after all, but don't let his mother see it as long as he was living under their roof, because she would get upset about her baby.

"Big move, Philip. Very large."

"I know, I know, but all I'm doing is showing up for tryouts at the seminary."

"Don't take this the wrong way. But you haven't been a Holy Joe. I never did see you as a priest."

It had been a long time since they'd had a heart-to-heart, and Philip missed his brother more than he expected and more than he would admit since he went off to college.

"You and me both. This decision will make me be a little less of an asshole."

"That's asking a lot. But come on, you're not really an asshole—all of the time."

"Yeah, I give everybody a break on Sundays. But it's a long way off, becoming a priest. A year in seminary, then college, theology study, then lots of other steps—many years away. Formation—that's what they call it—is drawn out for a reason. So ordination is way out on the horizon—and honestly, who knows if I get all the way to the finish line? I'm going out for Jesus's varsity, see if it's a match, see if I make the cut." He was self-consciously, stupidly belaboring the banal sports analogies.

"Dad's gotta be pissed."

"Just all over the place. When I told him I was praying for him, *that's* when he got super pissed. Lately I been thinking, for all his big hurt feelings, he's not disappointed in the slightest. Could be part of him can't admit he wants a priest in the family, to validate some cornball Irish myth."

"He might think you're poking a finger in his eye. I bet he had plans for you, joining his business."

"Whatever his business is, does anybody really know? Whatever, that ain't gonna happen."

"But wait, go back, how do you explain this miracle?"

Philip theatrically lifted his eyes and extended his beer up to the heavens. "The Blessed Virgin Mary deigned to appear before me in her radiant folds…"

"You're a moron."

"And verily she said unto me, 'Philip, you have been blessed with a calling.'" If he had an objective, it was taking down the emotional intensity a notch, that's all, making it guy talk, brother talk.

"How can you stand yourself?"

"Not counting your ex-girlfriend Pam the Bam, she was the first virgin I'd been around in a long time."

"Really, fuck yourself."

"Pam Pam Thank You Ma'am was no virgin?"

"Double fuck yourself."

"No thanks, but I'll take another brew." Another bottle was opened.

"Come on, talk to me. I don't get it. How you plan to live without, you know, *you know?*"

"You're managing fine without sex, you and Rosey Palm."

He shook his head and he sighed. "Be serious, would you? Talking about you, Philip. How many girlfriends have you had—and still have?"

That was an annoying question, and he swatted it away like a buzzing bee. Truth was, it felt kind of vulgar to keep a running score. "Okay, serious-time, zone-of-truth shit. I don't know how I'm going to deal with that. I know when I am at Mass and the priest's raising the chalice and the host on the altar, or when the priest is making sense during the homily, which is, okay, rare, or when he's there for people in their pain and suffering, when people get sick or die, I want to be that guy. *That* guy. I want to be him. You make sacrifices in life, this'll be mine. I got to know Father Bill and Father Ron, we been talking, and they have helped me settle down, get serious about my life. I admire them, I could see myself being like that to kids like me."

"It's hard to know where life'll take you. The things I know after a couple years of college I never could have imagined. You don't ever want kids, family?"

"Man, now that is *one* thing that totally fries the old man. He harps on the subject, like my vocation is all about him, extending the Family Fitzgerald line's how he puts it. But that's where you come in, once you find Miss Right, hurry and get on the job and give the old Mick some grandkids he can make half as miserable as us. You know what he also told me? He said priests in the old country, they got more tail than he ever did. Then he added, he was exaggerating, nobody ever got more tail than him. I thanked him for putting that image in my head."

"Poverty, chastity, obedience."

"Those are vows some priests take, Anthony. Tinkers to Evans to Chance, another Hall of Fame double play combination." Strictly speaking, that wasn't the case for a diocesan priest. Those three vows were for priests in a religious order, like the Jesuits, like the Dominicans. As a diocesan priest, Philip would take vows of celibacy and obedience—well, again they were *promises*, not vows, but netted out as the same thing. It was also to be expected that he would live modestly, no driving the old man's Maserati around town—which was a long shot under the best of circumstances. If Anthony pressed, he would go into detail. But finally these were fine distinctions without differences.

Although Philip had grown up in the most affluent family in town, living modestly didn't intimidate. In fact, he welcomed the prospect of simplicity. But he wasn't Trappist monk material. If he were honest with himself, he liked the figure a priest cut, in his sharp black suit and clerical collar. How people followed priests with their admiring eyes whenever they crossed the room. That might have indicated how shallow he was, this fantasy of clerical celebrity, but it was true. Obedience would be tough, of course, taking orders from his superiors, because being a Fitzgerald, he never felt he had any of those. But chastity, of course, well, that was the big unknown and he would deal.

"Mom's upset," Philip said. "That bothers me more than Dad."

"When I talked with her, she seemed all right."

"She puts up a good front. Mom's tough, she might be tougher than the old man. She says she's happy for me, that I found my vocation, she's praying for me. She's the only one who goes to church, the old man couldn't be bothered. She was worried about me for a long time, the street fights, the scraps I got into during games, the pot, the booze, the girls in and out of my room. But you know, I've had enough of that. I need to get control of my life and—you're going to laugh when I say the next part."

"Try me."

"I feel like there's a great battle going on inside, for my soul."

"Your *soul.*"

"My soul, yes. I have one, and it's a troubled soul. I feel like if I don't get a handle on my desires and my weaknesses, I am going to end up—I don't know, like the old man."

"Birds of a feather, you two, peas in a pod, Mom said. You look the spitting image."

"People say that kinda shit, but I'm me. I don't want to be like him. I have the will to surmount my temptations. It's all about free will, about choosing a better path and doing some good in this lifetime, which is over in a minute. You know how close I was to buying the farm in that car wreck?" Everybody knew how close, everybody, and the family stumbled around in shock for weeks afterward. "I fell asleep behind the wheel, drunk off my ass on Jack Daniel's, and woke up when the car was in midair, upside down. Actually, in what looked like my last moment on earth, I said a prayer— you know, it might have been the first time I ever prayed, really prayed, in my life. I said to God, get me out of this and I'll fly right from now on. I'm keeping my promise."

"Come-to-Jesus moment. You told me."

"Once I got out of the hospital, I went straight to confession."

"And you been on the high road ever since?"

Philip had to laugh a little. "I'm not pussy boy perfect. I didn't join the debate team like you. I've strayed, I guess, I like the way girls feel, the smell on their necks, their soft hands, so shoot me. I'll still be a man. But I am mostly going in the right direction, mostly, and being a priest is going to help me stay that way. It's not going to be easy, but since when is easy what Fitzgeralds do?"

"Can't argue with you, Father Philip."

"But, hey, I'll marry you and the future Mrs. Anthony Fitzgerald, I'll baptize your little babies, too, friends and family rates."

"You're such a prince."

"No, that's where you're wrong. You're the prince of the family, you always will be."

"And you'll always be my brother, and I will always love you, Philip." Anthony astounded himself saying that, but he wouldn't take it back.

Philip was amazed, too, and moved. "Back at you, Prince Anthony, back at you."

"Before you get any ideas, don't think about hugging."

"You're such a heartbreaker—that's what Pam always said about you."

"And you are a ballbuster."

"Like I said, you always make me think of Pam."

It was getting close to five, the hour when their dad insisted on sitting down to promptly serve up Sunday supper. The brothers stood and—after pretending to hesitate—they *did* hug. Anthony stepped back and looked into Philip's eyes, searching for something he could not identify. If he had to put words to it, it was that he was imagining his baby brother as a priest. It was tough to do. He hoped his brother would be all right. He knew Philip was destined for great, great things, and he probably would become Father Philip. If so, he hoped the priestly life would make him happy, at least happy enough. One thing he felt for certain: the two of them would be there alongside each other forever.

"What?" said Philip.

"Nothing," said Anthony, meaning too much to talk about.

The two of them headed in for dinner, up the hill, along the footpath, past the ever-struggling roses. Philip stopped and looked at one especially dejected bush.

"The old man keeps trying to grow roses, they never take, what's up with that? Must be some Irish thing."

"What's Mom making?" Anthony said.

"Two guesses. All for you, big brother, your favorite."

"Is it corned beef or corned beef?"

"Glad you're home, man." Once, that was something that he wasn't able to honestly say, but he had changed, they had all changed. If the Fitzgeralds didn't surprise, you weren't paying attention.

—

FATHER PHILIP LOOKED OUT across the assemblage. He was positioned before the opened grave, steadying himself for the ceremony of committal, his brother's casket to be lowered into the ground. He stole a glance at his stoical dad. When the man anticipated his son's becoming a priest, he never would have allowed himself to imagine a moment like this. And of course neither could Philip.

Breezes disturbed the branches of canopying trees surrounding the cemetery on this cloudy and cool summer day. He held tight onto his breviary and his black cassock billowed. Faces at the graveside resembled those he had seen a hundred times at funerals, but it struck him as being the first time, because it was. He had never buried his brother before. There was no way in the world he could have prepared himself for this moment. Sorrow and loss may be universal, but not here, not now. His sorrow had nothing to do with anybody else's. Philip was about to inter a part of himself along with the idea of his family.

Francesca, pale and gaunt and shattered, was leaning against her own father, as if the wind threatened to lift her up and carry her off and away, which she could have defensibly been wishing for. Paddy stood rigid, his face immobile, as if he were a tree resisting, refusing to topple. Philip's mother could not stand, had to sit, her body rocked by convulsive weeping, and her two youngest children, his brother and sister, Matty and Colleen, were kneeling by her side, doing what they could to keep her together for the next ten unbearable minutes. Philip wanted to be standing with them, with his family, and not in front of them performing his duties as a priest, but this was his responsibility and he would conform to his obligations. If faith had any meaning, it had to have meaning now, or it never would. His duties were more than religious, or ecclesiastical. They were more serious. They were familial, and, more to the point, they were fraternal.

A hundred people had gathered: colleagues from Anthony's law firm and his loyal associates, too, Francesca's friends and family, and many who were Philip's parishioners, with whom he had shared word of his grief. Philip would not have been able to identify the famous Slip McGrady of Limerick Jewelry & Loan, but Anthony's client was in attendance as well, his brief prison term soon to commence. Paddy's crew was there led by Jonesy O'Dell, on the fringes, their hands clasped before them, heads bowed under fedoras, marshaling their weighty, ceremonial demeanor. They say it is comforting to not be alone in moments of mourning. In the instant, Philip realized all over again that, if others who were here were well-intentioned, their presence did not assuage the sorrow, not in the least. His theological training did its best to kick in. If there were any achievable comfort, perhaps it lay in the notion of an afterlife, and a world beyond this, where Anthony was now safe from future pain and suffering. But that was a matter of belief, of trust in a loving God. How many times had he spoken so confidently on this subject from the pulpit, or to aspiring converts on retreat, or to his grieving parishioners in the rectory, of the mystery that was life and death, of ashes to ashes, dust to dust, which would never be understood till the great reckoning to come, in the beyond? But the small reckoning in the here and now was, whatever it was theologically, inconclusive emotionally. To him, there seemed to be no consolation available. His brother was gone, and that was the truth. Was it fair, was it just? That was not for him to say. That was God's business. But it wasn't fair, it wasn't just—those were the right answers to the wrong questions. It simply *was*. So many tears being shed around him. The human race tapped an infinite reservoir of tears.

"Brothers and sisters, we are gathered here to say farewell to our brother, Anthony. For me to say farewell to my own older brother Anthony. His beloved wife, Francesca, and the rest of his family—my family—thank you for being here in our sad hour. There are no words that can take away or diminish the anguish we all feel. People say that the deceased is in a better place. And though this is hard news to take in, we must believe in a merciful God. It is our only hope to go on from this day forward, without our precious Anthony, inconceivably lucky to have known him for a while, and for me and my family our entire life, and for nowhere near long enough. After all, God so loved the world that he sent his only begotten son to die upon a cross in order to save us—and to save Anthony today and forevermore.

"Last night at the rosary and the wake and today during funeral Mass we heard from so many, many friends and loved ones who stepped up to tell how they were touched by Anthony in his foreshortened lifetime. We heard a dozen beautiful stories of the kindness he extended to everybody—and I bet there are a thousand we did not hear. The Gospel of John, the disciple Jesus said he loved, ends by the evangelist saying: 'There are also many other things that Jesus did; if every one of them were written down, I suppose that the world itself could not contain the books that would be written.' We could say the same thing about Anthony. We heard about how he lived with a pure heart and soul and the way he loved his friends and his family and especially his Francesca, his Frankie. We will never ever forget him, but now we have a sad duty before us. We now must let him go—for now, but only for now, till in the twinkling of an eye we are gathered together on the last day. So let us pray.

"Merciful Lord, you know the anguish of the sorrowful, you are attentive to the prayers of the humble. Hear your people who cry out to you in their need, and strengthen their hope in your lasting goodness. We ask this through Christ our Lord."

Amen.

"Eternal rest grant unto Anthony, O Lord."

And let perpetual light shine upon him.

"May he rest in peace."

Amen.

"May his soul and the souls of all the faithful departed, through the mercy of God, rest in peace."

Amen.

"May almighty God bless you, the Father, and the Son, and the Holy Spirit."

Amen.

—

THE MONTHS PASSED BY, some days like low-flying incoming choppers, some like storm churn rushing down streams and boulevards, others like a muddled trek across the Mojave. Each day was jaggedly different for everyone left behind. Each day, the mind-numbing same.

Francesca and Philip were once again sitting across from each other in her home, which used to be Anthony's home, and which had more in common with the splashy Fitzgeralds' digs than his sparse parish rectory. She had positioned on mahogany shelves beautiful exotic art objects she'd collected around the world, and she hung an array of modernist paintings on the walls. Lately these material things barely registered. She had hardly looked outside herself for a long time.

The two had gotten together regularly, companions in grief, about every other week or so, for dinner, lunch, wine. If they could bear it, they'd go to the occasional movie. They read the same articles and books, exchanged views, and they found themselves usually in accord. Their friendship deepened. It was disappointing when priestly responsibilities obliged him to reschedule one of their dates, because she had come to rely on talking with him—and he felt similarly. Visiting with her, he wasn't performing some clerical duty—or what he had learned during seminary to call "corporal works of mercy." He had come to care more and more for her, feelings she reciprocated. Periodically she would come to hear him celebrate Mass, and he would brighten to spy her in the pew, usually back in the recesses of the church, alone or with her father, who looked out of place, and she'd come up to receive communion from his hand. It was good. It was sad. They helped each other. Nothing helped.

Yes, every now and then she did a double take seeing Anthony in his brother's face, and that was only natural, but Philip was unquestionably his own person. Philip worried about her and prayed for her. Anthony's memory was uniting them, but they had also become friends on their own terms, which they hadn't been before. The two of them would amuse each other, educate each other, illumine each other, but from time to time they would sit there, basking in, subsumed under—there was no other way to put it—the lengthening shadow of Anthony's vanished, but somehow permanent, presence. Occasionally, when her anxiety surged within and got the best of her, she would remind herself to close her eyes and breathe.

The autumn sun was setting out over the water, nights were warmer and shorter, and it was a beautiful sight, not that either of them could see it or, if they bothered to look, care. In recent weeks, she gave signals that she had taken a darker turn. Nobody expects grief to follow a linear course, but she was nonetheless unnerved.

"I've been seeing a new therapist. She's young, so how much can she know? But still, I guess I need to do this, and she is good."

"Good. Good. You have to take care of yourself however you can." In his pastoral role, he was occasionally asked for therapist referrals, so he asked her if she wouldn't mind, would she pass along the therapist's name for future reference. Inside information like that is invaluable.

She would send Ruth's vitals, but wanted to underscore what seemed to her the limits of psychotherapy. "Nobody, not even a therapist as gifted as Ruth, is a miracle worker. If I'm honest, lately nothing's helping a whole hell of a lot. They say the first year is the hardest. Something tells me the second is not going to be Disneyland, either." She had stored a stockpile of mood-altering drugs prescribed by her psychiatrist to address the anxiety, though for the most part she resolved to manage on her own. She discussed this with Ruth, and her therapist counseled her to go slow, and not to be unrealistically demanding of herself.

"Do what you need. Drugs work, Frankie," Ruth said. "When you need them and when they do."

"And when nothing works, they don't work, either. Sometimes pain is nothing but pain, it settles inside your chest for a long winter's night, even if it's in the middle of summer."

—

HER HUSBAND'S PURE *ABSENCE* continually rocked her: the denied expectation of Anthony being there on the other side of the table, or earnestly brushing his teeth in the next sink the way he did, or singing loudly and exuberantly in the shower.

"Hey, Pavarotti," she would say, "don't use up all the hot water."

"Come on in," he'd reply, "if you want to conserve our precious resources, because I have a very precious resource for you right here."

It was stunning, how the ordinariness of daily life no longer shared with him was so gut-wrenching to recall. She'd burst into tears at the store, or at the stoplight, or really, anywhere, when she least anticipated. It was embarrassing, but she couldn't stop herself.

"Philip, you think the pain ever goes away?"

Philip had no idea, but if pressed, he doubted anyone could say anything profound about mourning. Loss is loss is loss. This mantra of his didn't stop him from being put on the spot by people pleading for an ounce of wisdom from him.

"I go on long runs, shoot baskets by myself in the gym at night," he said. "Physical exhaustion almost helps, almost."

"I work out myself, but it doesn't do much for my soul." The real work for her consisted of keeping these memories alive, not in some physical shrine but inside herself. To what end, she could not say, but she suspected it was a sign of her own failure, or weakness, or neurosis—or certainly the once-in-a-lifetime love she felt for him. Every so often she would make another resolution to clear out his closet, dispatch his suits and ties and shoes and jeans and leather jackets to Saint Vincent De Paul, but never followed through.

"I used to pride myself on my capacity for being alone."

In a glib mood he might have answered that life and death happened to her. "What did some wise guy poet say? Only cure for loneliness is solitude."

She blinked. "Empty words, sorry, they don't mean anything. I feel like I'm done. Loneliness is my best friend—along with you."

They had had similar conversations in the past, but it always felt new.

"You are not done, don't say that, you have a long life to live, so much left to learn and accomplish and give to others."

"Again, means nothing, sorry, Philip, I know you mean well. From the first I always felt a connection to you—through your brother, who adored you."

"Let's not get sentimental about us brothers. He and I had our knock-down drag-outs, ask my old man, who had to pull us apart more than a few times before one of us rearranged the other's face. Actually, I was thinking this morning about when he got his bell rung on the basketball court, the gash and stitches on his head. I always wondered if that contributed to what happened, and that's when I feel responsible all over again. They said he'd had a concussion, but do you think he suffered some permanent damage?"

"Anthony told me, it was a huge moment for him. Sounds possible, brain swelling, but the neurosurgeon didn't think so, it happened so long ago—he said it was remotely possible. You know what Anthony mentioned about that fight? Not that that scar was a badge of honor, it was you putting your favorite sweatshirt on his head to stanch the bleeding. He couldn't believe you did that. Your favorite sweatshirt."

Head wounds are the bloodiest. "That's what brothers are for. And also sweatshirts."

"Anyway, an aneurysm like that could happen to you or me right now, sitting here before the stupid gorgeous sunset. Look at that horrible sun. Don't you hate the natural world? It feels like a threat. Like life's one big accident waiting to happen. There's a riptide waiting to take us out when we wade in and least expect. Few times, Anthony would wake up, middle of the night, a bad dream, he'd say it was a dream about you and that car crash you almost didn't walk away from."

"Pretty lucky, I guess, if life has anything to do with luck, and sometimes, seems like a lot."

"How are you, Philip? I never ask, I go on and on about myself."

"That's not true. But me? Lot of work, not complaining, some of it gratifying, some days are wonderful, kind of transcendent, other days pretty lonely—there's that word again—but that is the vocation. I tell the pastor I have a full plate. Know what he says? Get a bigger plate."

"When I look at you, can't help it, I see your brother."

"Makes sense. Your dad there for you?"

"Every single day a phone call or drop-in. Along with my brother, but sure, and yes they are there. But I feel different with you. I feel like you know me in ways I don't know myself. I think I may trust you more than I trust myself. Who did I once used to be?"

"We all love you, Frankie."

It seemed that she had given him his cue to say as much, that she needed to hear she was loved by somebody. She let the words reverberate. But as the silence built, Philip wondered if he had said an inappropriate thing in a delicate transitional moment.

The sun slipped below the horizon, night coming on with the usual complications. Her loneliness was hardest to bear at this hour, to return again at the break of dawn. Moments of transition, that's when she most keenly relived the moment, as if it had happened all over again.

"People try to fix me up, dates, you believe that?"

"Hard to believe, but someday, when you least expect, there'll be some-body." Instantly, he did regret saying that. It sounded canned, dumb, rote.

"Nobody'll replace Anthony."

Over time, well-intentioned friends—nobody half as well-intentioned as Philip—tried their best to soldier up. They covered the gamut of proposed options for her. From dating sites to Ouija boards, séances to speed dating, going back to school to starting a new company, booking a safari to taking up knitting or fly-fishing, something, anything. She heard out her friends, as long as she could stand it, but invariably reached the same conclusion:

whatever they suggested, sorry, she didn't think so. She had good friends, or used to, and nobody of late specifically hinted it was time, past time, *to move on with her life*, thank God. She was reassured nobody ever tossed a *closure* Molotov cocktail across her moat. Only morons subscribe to the concept. Even if it were feasible, Francesca never wished to travel intergalactically to a planet where closure atoms coursed through the atmosphere. That sort of world needed to be smashed into smithereens by an asteroid because it was too tedious to survive in any worthy universe. Part of her couldn't imagine waking up alongside anybody ever again.

And yet, that wasn't exactly the case. Only last week—she couldn't believe she did this, but it was true. Only last week she slept with somebody she once knew professionally before Anthony, a sweet younger man who long ago reported to her and shyly flirted. It proved a disaster, a ridiculous one-night stand, which she knew beforehand was destined for doom. She had been avoiding his calls since, and she hoped he would give up already. She told nobody, not even her therapist, Ruth, and certainly wouldn't tell Philip. Though maybe she should, she should confess right now. She hadn't cheated on Anthony, but she'd cheated. On herself? That sounded so Catholic, but she wasn't Catholic in that way, turned on by guilt and shame. Cheated on his *brother*? That was a bizarre connection, it made no logical sense, but it wasn't completely off. She feared his disapproval. But she didn't need anybody else's disenchantment, she had plenty of her own to work with.

"You want something to drink?" He shrugged, and she said, "Me, either."

"Getting late, I should go, let you get a good night's sleep." He dimly sensed a dramatic turn was coming and half of him wanted to escape before it was executed. Half wanted to stay.

"Don't go, it's early."

He could feel her sadness. Anybody with current brain function could. "Frankie, you all right?"

"I like it when you call me Frankie."

Something shifted in the air. Like strobe lights switched on. Like the temperature elevated. Here was when he should establish a boundary, but where to draw the line? Or here was when he should signal something— but how and what?

"I'm here for you, you know that."

"I know, I know. Would you do something for me?"

"Anything." Those boundaries were slipping, signals registered on high frequency.

"I might ask something of you."

He nodded, waiting.

"This might be crazy." She clearly didn't believe it was crazy, her eyes were fixed on his, steady as a watchmaker's.

Years later, when he recreated this moment, he would convince himself he knew what she was going to say.

She leaned back into her chair. "I would like—it's crazy, and you can say no, but I could use your company tonight."

He responded hastily. "I'm right here." He was winging it. He should shut up. He wished he could rewind.

She would be more explicit. "I need to be held. I need you to hold me. I need to get outside myself. I need to feel different." When she went to bed with her former colleague, that was all she desired, to feel anything but miserable for a minute, and it didn't take long before she realized that she couldn't achieve that objective with that man. It occurred that she might be finally done with sex. But reaching out to Philip was not the same.

So far Francesca and Philip were both inhabiting the realm of plausible deniability. If they were careful and quick, they could walk away unscathed and undisappointed.

He could be sympathetic, but thought better of that: people had sound cause to hate sympathy. She had been going through a tough spell. She would regret saying what she had said, he believed. They would laugh about it in the future, far, far into the future. Philip searched for the gentlest possible words to articulate that what she was proposing wasn't going to happen. "We're old friends, but…"

She would not be patronized. "Please, Philip, please don't make me plead."

As a priest he had been the stunned recipient of any number of bizarre requests. Like the time he was asked—apparently sincerely—to perform an exorcism on a woman's supposedly demon-possessed cat. He didn't bother to remark that he himself found most cats to be diabolical. Or another time, when an embittered and possibly drunken doubter asked him to change water into wine on the spot. He wondered if the man was catering a party. Such inanity had nothing to do with Francesca tonight. He was going to wait for her to come to her senses, though she was giving no sign of that.

"It will never happen again. This isn't about a romantic relationship, we're not going to date, it's not about making love, not about having sex. I need closeness, physical proximity to you."

Unless he was insane, sleeping with her certainly seemed to be about sex. Even if it wasn't about sex, it was about sex, because what wasn't about sex? But then he must have looked mystified.

"We can talk in the dark," she said. "It would be what we all used to call Platonic, and at some point we'll fall asleep, and in the morning, our former lives resume, like nothing ever happened."

Poor Frankie, the pain she must be in. The vulnerability she must feel. The proposition struck him as vaguely incestuous. He had married her to his brother. He had buried her husband. He was her brother-in-law, not to mention a priest, even as her idea seemed fundamentally to have nothing to do with Anthony or with his promise of chastity. He had never allowed himself to feel attracted to her, but should he be giving himself permission now? He was safe as far as she was concerned, was that it? Or was it that she was safe?

"Afterward, we don't have to talk about it. It will be our little secret."

Secrets by virtue of being secrets are never little and secrets never stay secrets forever, he knew that much. "Why do I get the feeling you and I have stepped into some avant-garde French novel?"

She would play, for a minute. "Or Japanese. Or an Irish short story."

He attempted to change the subject, give her an out to laugh it all off. "I was thinking. Should we start a book group?"

"A book group?" she repeated in her smallest voice, which sounded as disconsolate as a little echo of a cough in the church nave. Smart men, men like Philip, can be so utterly clueless. She couldn't grasp how they managed with a woman. Then again, he was a priest, he had never refined the skill as an adult.

"You know, meeting with other like-minded people, interested in…"

She raised her hand, class dismissed. "We're not talking book groups. Not tonight."

So there they were. She was serious. Definitely like a Russian novel. He had not envisioned this step. Should he have envisioned it? Was he blind? What else had he missed? She was asking a lot of him, and she was coming from abject neediness. Fair enough, fair enough, what are friends for? If he acceded to her, he wouldn't be betraying Anthony—it certainly didn't feel like a betrayal of him, and he assumed it didn't feel that way to her. If they had sex, and even if they didn't truly have sex, he would be breaking his sacred promise as a priest, absolutely, which he had never done before. Strictly speaking, he'd never been truly tempted since being ordained, not quite, which almost surprised him when comely women, single and married both, young and middle-aged, encircled and flirted with a fortyish dashing priest gifted with a silver tongue and declaiming from the pulpit.

"A few hours without loneliness. I'm not asking you to leave your vocation, I know you'll always be a priest."

What she was suggesting would only increase her lonesomeness, he rationally considered. Rational considerations did not help.

"Have I made you uncomfortable, Philip?"

He couldn't remember the last time he had had sex.

—

But yes, then he could, and with some lurid precision. It was with the much-discussed Pam, once Anthony went off to college and they had broken up. After regularly jabbing his brother with fake hitting on his girlfriend, while still in high school and well before his decision to go to the seminary, he magically found himself in the back seat of the car with her one night, on a deserted stretch of road, in a clearing near Inspiration Point. They talked. He never got over how girls liked to talk. It was like a drug. He was better at it than most boys, or so he had been informed. She was a lot smarter than he expected. At some point it dawned on him that all the girls he once assumed he understood completely were smarter than he expected, and different. At about the same time, he realized that he was not quite the catch he once thought he was.

"Anthony and I never went all the way, just so you know."

Philip didn't want details of his brother's sex life.

"He didn't believe in premarital you know," she said.

Philip was different from Anthony. Premarital you know was currently the absolute cornerstone of his belief system.

"But since he and I were not going to have any marital you know, I didn't see the problem, right? He did. Anthony, what a guy, I'll always love him to pieces. I just received a letter from him, Mr. College Boy. There's a joint in my bag. Got a light?"

Who didn't love Anthony? It could be tiring to track all the testimonials.

Weed was a good idea, because when was it ever not a good idea? And the predictable transpired inside a fog. She was affectionate—and not inexperienced. What could be wrong with his brother to pass this up?

Of course, it was not long before Pam broke it off. "That was not a good idea, let's be friends, Philip." Saying that, she beat him to the punch. He liked her, more than he wanted to, but he was thankful and relieved. Relieved mainly never to have the conversation about her with his brother.

—

"UNCOMFORTABLE? IT DOESN'T SEEM like the precise word."

Fact: Philip was a priest. He had taken the sacrament of Holy Orders. In that ceremony, he had lain prostrate on the cold altar floor. His hands had been anointed with chrism. Yes, that had happened. But he was troubled. Her reaching out to him seemed more important than keeping a priestly promise, which now felt ghostly and disembodied, and which also described him. He couldn't believe where he was going. He could not refuse her with a clean conscience. He couldn't tell to what degree he was on the verge of rationalizing what was a morally reckless act, descending that slipperiest of slopes. All he could think was that it would be a kindness to her in her desperation. Look, she had trusted him with her vulnerability. And he did love her, if not quite in the way that she was asking—or did he? Did he find her seductive? Of course, he did, but he never once let himself feel the allure. It was happening so fast, perhaps he had been thinking unconsciously along these lines for a long while.

And it would never happen again. Never. She stipulated as much. That had to be the one precondition. And there would be no sex, she said. They would innocently be there in bed alongside each other throughout the night.

After a long spell of complicit silence, she stood up, parting the air as if it were water and she were swimming. To him, it appeared as if that simple act, rising up to her feet, required the strength to lift a mountain, which was her mountain of loneliness. The top three buttons of her chiffon shirt were opened. Had they been unbuttoned all along? She had kicked off her shoes, and the sight of them tipped sideways on the carpet strangely saddened him—and more strangely exhilarated him. Overlapping sadness and exhilaration: he'd been there all his life, just not with Frankie, only this time with her bedroom within reach.

"You can leave now, I'll understand, we'll be friends like before, shut the front door, it will lock behind you. And we'll never discuss what didn't happen. But you can also come to bed. You decide." Those last two words resonated for him, like she was striking a tiny drum.

"Frankie," he said, and lost the rest of what he was supposed to say in the internal din.

She would help. "You don't need to explain one way or the other."

He tracked her as she vacated the room barefoot. After a few minutes, he poured himself a shot at her bar, and then another. She had a bottle of Midleton, like his father. The Irish whiskey itself was evidence of Anthony's presence. And such a cliché, he knew, drinking to work up the courage to act one way or the other. But this situation was no cliché, even if a third party might interpret it that way. Sad randy widow, handsome lascivious priest. But that was bullshit. This was a cross, one cross he had never expected to bear. That was the thing about crosses, you never could expect them in advance, and they never looked like crosses. And this was also a test. Of what, he wasn't sure. But he was sure it was a test of everything he stood for. Only he knew, either way he was going to fail.

He needed to be honest with himself—but it was impossible to be sure he was capable of being honest. He would never have thought he desired her, not in that way, and besides, what was happening now was different. She was different. There would not be sex. He was pretty sure she meant that they would not actually have sex. They could comfort each other, one time, one night. So was that it? He himself needed comforting, too, right? He didn't realize he might have needed such comforting like that till this moment, till she didn't explain, because such things cannot be explained.

He calculated how he could get away with this, whatever *this* would prove to be. Tomorrow morning when he stepped through the rectory door, the dyspeptic pastor would ask why he didn't come home last night and he'd give him the third degree, and Philip would grin and lie that he had a few too many at his family's home and bedded down where he was, sleeping it off in a guest room, in order not to risk being pulled over, driving impaired. Yes, the grouchy pastor would lambaste him for his piss-poor judgment, getting sloshed like that, so irresponsible, but it would blow over. He would volunteer as a peace offering to take the 7:00 a.m. Mass for the next month, or next two months, he would get the parish cars washed, he would paint the dining room, which needed a fresh coat. He loathed himself to plot such a plan.

Loss is loss is loss. He walked down the long hall in the direction Frankie had gone, toward her bedroom, which she had once shared with his brother. Part of him grasped the gravity, namely that in doing what she asked of him, he would sacrifice his friendship with her. And that's when it hit him: that was the true cost of what he was on the verge of doing. Another loss. She might believe that tomorrow they could forget this ever happened, they would never discuss it, their little secret, and it was a one-time indiscretion, though that was not nearly the word, and they could go on as in the past, reading books and meeting for lunch and discussing movies, and he would remain a priest, but she wasn't thinking clearly—which made two of them not thinking clearly. Her grief had taken yet one more serious toll. Was he flattering himself? Had she had reached the point she couldn't be alone, not tonight? What he didn't quite get was that she couldn't be alone tonight without him. Loss is loss is loss. Is loss.

He had consecrated his life. He was a priest. He was also a man. He was more than anything else a friend who loved Frankie, his brother's widow. On one level, he kept thinking, that wasn't a lot to ask. Sometimes life was about—entirely about—getting through another terrible night. People needed what they needed. They didn't have to understand their need. They didn't have to be justified. Mortal existence was the ultimate mystery, but the body was the body. The dilemma of the body-soul dichotomy was no dilemma. Not tonight. He could almost watch himself splitting in half. He was flailing. His lifetime of theology training and countless homilies and Masses and endless scripture study had not prepared him.

And this is when plain truth clicked. He couldn't deny the obvious: that he desired her, and had desired her for a long time. That was when he let himself give over, but that wasn't what was about to drive him. Desire he could sublimate, repress, he'd done it a thousand times. This was different. What he couldn't tamp down was his care for her and what he couldn't deny was what she asked of him.

He would miss her, horribly. He had grown to love her more and more over these last months. Life was about one sacrifice or another. The hour of this great sacrifice was upon him, and upon them. They would never be the same to each other. She would not be grateful, and one day she might despise him for taking advantage of her in her weakness. They would try, he had no doubt, to continue as they were before. And one day, one night, it would come to a halt. Maybe not for her, not that he could say, but it would be over for him. Some turbulent rivers are too dangerous to cross, but there is no other way to reach the other side, which in this case was the dawn, and once crossed there is no conceivable return back to the familiar shore.

He entered through her opened door and stood motionless.

"Frankie," he said, no question mark in his voice.

"Turn off the light, Philip," she said from her bed, her voice even and serene and nothing like seductive, "please."

He would do this for Frankie, whom he loved and who was the love of his brother's life. And he would do this because he wanted to, he couldn't deny that any longer. Hundreds and hundreds of times, he had dispensed the sacrament of confession, or reconciliation, in his capacity as a priest. He didn't know if he would ever be reconciled, ever forgive himself for tonight, or if he would have anything he should confess. This was an experience he had no choice but to live with, the next morning and the rest of his life.

Chapter Nine
Grace

O NE DAY—THIS WAS a couple of years after Anthony's demise—Colleen and her mother were drinking ice tea on the patio, an unseasonably warm, pleasant autumn day on Haymarket Hill. Grace Fitzgerald had something on her mind.

"Why's the sky old?"

"What are you talking about, Mom?"

"Skyline's all honey-colored, olden, golden, is it beautiful?" She pointed toward the water.

"Where'd you hide your sunglasses?"

"You are wearing them."

Grace had been confused a while. She was also having these visions. Not religious visions, either, which she would have savored, being devout. No, these were visions of her husband with devil's horns, visions of the house aflame, visions of olive trees chopped down. So while these were not pleasing visions, she was long-suffering. Till this moment, when she mentioned the disturbing hue of the sky, she had never referenced them to anybody else, and if pressed, she couldn't have explained why she brought them up now.

"You know, being a little girl, I was going to be a nun. I did not have a religious calling, not like my son, who is a priest, a Catholic priest."

"Yes, Philip, and I know priests are Catholic, Mom."

"I prayed for a vocation, but I didn't hear the calling, which you need to become a nun, and now, here I am remembering being a little girl. I would love some ice tea."

Colleen would have done anything to oblige her, but there was a glass of ice tea already in her grasp. Her daughter didn't know what to make of that odd, flat tone in her mother's voice, which was a new development, along with glossiness to her eyes gazing out into the middle distance, where the sky had evidently turned, so she said, gold.

"I saw Anthony yesterday. Did you see him, too?"

Colleen was divided. Call the doctor or Philip, or roll with it?

"Sit with me, young lady, would you please awhile? I won't be long."

This sentiment seemed freighted, mysterious. Colleen decided to roll with it, it was not going to help herself or her mother to convey alarm.

"Have you seen my Anthony? I saw him yesterday. What a lovely man he has become. You know, he's the exact sort of man I think you would like to meet someday. He used to dance with his little sister through the house when she was cranky and wouldn't nap, and she would start laughing, and then we'd all start laughing, till she dropped off. A terrible dancer, I shouldn't tell tales. Like his father, another terrible Irish dancer. Irish tenors sing like songbirds, but the Irish dancing? I don't care what they say, that is beyond them." She laughed and continued: "His father has another woman, you know. Anthony's father. We have stopped fighting about this, men have their needs, needs I don't feel. He tells me I'm the most beautiful woman in the world and gives me strings of pearls—our tenth wedding anniversary must be coming up."

Colleen wasn't going to correct her mother, and she despised her father anew for being the wretch he was.

"There it goes again, the shooting star, so lovely, so lovely. Life is full of surprises, isn't it? I miss my sad little Matty boy, he never comes to visit."

He was preoccupied with his wife and with teaching at Holy Family High, Colleen thought, but he should come by, see his mother. She would suitably berate him.

"I hope Matty finds a girl someday. He gets lonely. A lonely boy. I get lonely, too, I'm glad to see somebody, thank you for sitting with me. Look, do you see that eagle landing on the flagpole? Flagpoles are so silly. Tell me, deary, how are *you* feeling…" She couldn't finish.

Colleen sensed she had misplaced her name. *"Colleen,"* she offered.

"Ah, you have the same name as my daughter! You two should have a playdate. Would you like that?"

—

AFTER COLLEEN LEFT HER in Hilda's care and went home depressed, Philip's mother wrote him a letter, which the friendly mailman…Fred was his name, she recalled, but no, it was Ed…carried away for her the next day. Her grammar school cursive was compliant and clean, and letters were rounded and precise and lines were level, as if she had employed a ruler for guidance. Her fountain pen ink was navy blue, the paper unlined white parchment, and not a word was crossed out, suggesting to Philip as he read it two days later that she had redrafted her missive at least once, but knowing her, more like three or four times. More than anything he was stunned that she, who had never written a letter to him in his life, or at least one he could recall, took to paper at all.

> *Pray for me and for dad Philip Dear Philip*
> *Dear Father Philip*
> *My dear son*
> *I could not decide how to begin so here goes anywho.*
> *I am older now I can begin any which way I pretty please.*
> *The time has come to tell you things.*
> *I should tell you I am proud of you.*
> *I wish I had told Anthony.*
> *Old age is full of regrets I almost wrote egrets which would be funny no.*
> *Whatever you do don't get old full of regrets.*
> *Or egrets either.*
> *Am I worried about you.*

Whenever I see you you seem to be carrying the weight of the world on your shoulders.

When you were ordained I had my doubts—see?

I grow older, and I should speak my mind now or forever hold my tongue.

As I said I had my doubts.

The world does not take kindly to the spectacle of a man of the cloth especially one handsome and smart as you.

People suspect ulterior motives.

They wonder about your darker side.

People they are fools.

I wonder no such thing.

Fitzgeralds know all about the darker side.

I wonder about your lighter side.

I will tell you a secret.

Promise to tell everyone.

When I was a girl I wanted to be a sister.

But I didn't have the nun's calling.

That may be my way of saying that I didn't have the faith or the courage or the intestinal fortitude.

I have no egrets I have chosen the life I have.

It's been a good life I could say that.

But it has not been a good life too.

Being a mother.

Four children.

Being a wife.

Your father is not an easy man to live with.

I say something you of all my children would understand.

Anthony also understands.

Your father and I are getting a divorce.

Did he ever tell you.

I would be surprised he did.

I'm not feeling so well these days.

Not myself.

Paddy didn't want me to tell anybody.

Especially his son the priest.

You.

Don't you worry it will all be for the best somehow

Somehow

Mom

Love

Chapter Ten

Matty & Claire & Terry & Matt

THE NIGHT TERRY RAN off and they salvaged her from the park christened Fitzgerald Green was ten days before the diocesan gala where all the problems were destined to happen before, during, and after. Matty hadn't yet informed Claire about the protest he was planning to be part of. He didn't know if she would try to talk him out of it or not, but he wasn't convinced it was advisable to tell her, either. True, the two of them had been discussing his grim, nonexistent future job prospects and Claire was dutifully, loyally livid on the subject of the high-handed bishop. "That old boozehound," she'd go. "Somebody ought to get to him, force him to see the light. Your brother and your dad—they both have serious juice with the diocese. Why can't they set him straight?" Her husband appreciated that she had his back, so why was he skeptical of her intentions? As for his family, he realized that his father was in elaborate business negotiations with Mackey and that Philip had his own challenges living within the bounds of the Catholic hierarchy, so a part of him issued them both a pass, almost respecting that their hands were tied even if they wanted to help, not that they'd revealed evidence of an inclination to do so. "If I got him to myself, one on one," Claire said, and not for the first time, "I would work my special charms, persuade him to change his tune. Give me five minutes alone, he'll be painting houses next day." She was continually upset about what the diocese was doing to Matty, and she also remained furious about how they had treated Hector, sweet, dedicated, principled, charming Dr. Alessandro. The two had formed a kind of friendship and she still called Hector *Doctor*, she didn't care what bureaucrats thought and transcripts showed. "I can visualize you and your voodoo at work now," said Matty. "You wagging your finger in the bishop's face, poking him in the chest, now that is some kind of image." He laughed. She herself was deadly serious. "I am not a finger-wagger." "You kinda are, dear, but in your own fetching way." And you know, Matty thought, improbable as a face-off between the two of them was, there was a slim chance she could hypothetically influence the bishop, but she would certainly irritate the hell out of the man, as she would any man, if she were given occasion and opportunity. Nonetheless, he doubted any plan of hers or anybody else's to move the man's mind or heart would do the trick. No, the bishop was a stubborn, arrogant man, and it would take an exercise of power, pure power to get under his skin, which is exactly what he and his team were drumming up. It was at this stage of his ruminations that his wife stunned him. "The big diocese gala's coming up. You guys *should* do that demonstration, shock the do-gooder Catholic world." "What did you say?" "Time for public protest..." "How do you know about that?" "I can read your mind." "No, how'd you find out?" "I'm your wife." "Try again." "I don't know, I guess I read the emails." "On *my* computer you read *my* emails?" "They were right there, if you don't want me to read them, you should have said so." "You went on my computer?" "Important point is, you're doing the right thing, I'm proud of you." "So you went on my computer." "All right, if you insist, yes, I did. I'm trying to be a good wife." Matty felt hopeless all over again, but he was resigned. Maybe this *was* what a good wife would do. Then again, there was no question that trouble had been brewing in paradise for a while at home. Since before the beginning of time, since Adam and Eve, paradise has been the default locale for brewing up trouble. A while ago, this husband and wife had drifted into separate sleeping arrangements, almost before they were both conscious of establishing new limits. His imminent joblessness didn't augur well for domestic bliss, that was for sure. "We're going to have to talk about what you did, but not tonight, it's too depressing." "Whatever, Matty. I'm on your side, you know, especially when you do something stupid, like tonight with that student of yours—" "Terry." "Yes, Terry." Because that was indeed the night Terry was consigned to the cramped spare bedroom that had been doubling as Matty's sanctuary, that is, his office. Peace at any price, he rationalized, buying time. Insofar as the girl, his student, had colonized his space, he was relegated to the only other available resting place for the night, the beleaguered couch in the living room, the dejected piece of furniture they had been debating shoving out on the curb along with a FREE sign. Not that he was counting on getting much shut-eye under the lumpy couch-cushioned circumstances that applied to a Dead Husband Walking like himself. Claire supervised accommodations for their guest—not the right term as far as she was concerned, more like *headache*, more like *interloper*. Tonight would take place under her watchful, suspicious, ever-vigilant purview. That was her plan. Somebody around here needed such a thing as a viable plan. One night, and one night only, Claire could stomach this insanity, and tomorrow the vixen could haunt somebody else's domicile. "There's the bathroom, you can brush your teeth, left a spare new brush on the sink, so go clean up now," she adamantly instructed Terry, pointing the way down the hall as if the girl should now proceed to walk the plank. And while she was out of sight, Claire arranged the sheets, the towels, and her own rampant misgivings. She engaged in reconnaissance maneuvers, too, digging into the girl's possessions. What's with all these damn condoms, and what were her designs relative to their use, and her fucking bra, which a proper girl should have been wearing? So all that spoke volumes as to what Terry was about. But then the bombshell. She was startled when she came upon her incredible discovery: "What the hell?" She feared the girl was dangerous, only now she would not be dangerous anymore, Claire would see to that. Matty heard his wife talking to herself as he was slipping on his oversize sleep shirt, and barefoot he hustled back to her across the hardwood floor. He asked what was the matter. "Never you mind, not to worry." "You're not leaving her a towel?" "I will come back with a mint to put on her pillow." Claire repaired to her own bedroom with a towel strangely, awkwardly cradled in both arms, because, as he did not yet realize, she was stealing away with her concealed discovery. Lights systematically were switched off throughout the apartment and Terry came back from the bathroom in the dark and closed the bedroom door behind her without saying a word. To her it felt like it had been forever since she took off from her house, because she should have done this forever ago, though it was only a matter of hours. Sometime in the middle of the night—Matty might have dropped to sleep—he was astounded to find he had a visitant—this was not a dream—who was staring down at him uncomfortably lying there. Terry knew enough to whisper, although Claire seemed to be safely far off in a distant room. "Couldn't sleep," she said. "You?" He struggled to gain his bearings. "You realize..." she began to say. "What?" he said, fearing his bearings weren't to be activated. "You realize," she said again, "I'm not going to school tomorrow, right?" "Oh, yeah, right, I wasn't banking on your doing your normal cameo in class." "If I go to school, my mom might come looking for me with her creepy dildo of a boyfriend," she said, which would have counted as a far-fetched possibility bordering on the miraculous, she supposed, considering her mother wouldn't register for a few blotted-out days that her daughter was missing, unless the slithery, scaly boyfriend clued her in. "So can I stay here, Matt?" It was late and Matty was miserable and he was having difficulty deciphering her intent: she *was* staying here, in his apartment, so what was the question? This was the sort of conversation he had never expected to share with a student—then again, there never had been a complicated student quite like her. "It's the middle of the night." "But we are both awake. So can I?" "What are you talking about?" "Can I stay here for a while, few days, weeks?" That struck Matty as being a formidably terrible idea, even factoring in that Terry showed herself to be in command of a high percentage of appalling ideas. But he should talk. Look at what he did tonight, letting this girl into their apartment in the first place. That move alone earned him an Idiot Medal. "Do you understand what you're asking?" "Sure, I'll read your books, cool library you got, like, homeschool myself, watch TV, wait till you come home from work, I'll cook dinner. I make a wicked..." "Come on, Terry, that's not going to work—for Claire, that's for sure." "Why do you suppose she hates me?" "She doesn't hate you, she doesn't know you." "She *hates* me, I can scope out when somebody hates me, which I'm used to after living with Dash, my mom's squeeze, and she doesn't understand me like you, Matt, you understand me, which's why you invited me over." That didn't seem to describe the current situation in any accurate respect, but what was to be gained by correcting her? "I appreciate you letting me bed down here. I do feel guilty putting you out like this, wish I had someplace else to go. I'll head back to the park, if you want. Just say so." "We can come up with a plan in the morning, remember that teen shelter I was telling you about?" She was sitting on the coffee table within reach of the couch, and this was the first moment he realized the girl was now leaning over in his direction, wearing a white, clingy tank top, extra-large T-shirt, the hem of which she pulled down around her knees, and evidently nothing else. And she confirmed for herself that he took notice. "Forgot to bring my astronaut PJs," she made a face to communicate: dumb joke. "I was kinda in a rush, getting chased down the street and all, you know, girl-in-distress type shit." He looked away toward the kitchen, which seemed like a safer place upon which to rivet his uneasy attention and to expunge the astronaut image. To be clear, it never crossed her mind to tell him her eyes were up here—he wasn't that type of guy, not at all. Saying as much to Matt would have been hostile. And yet, he was thinking, if Claire walked out of her bedroom to get a drink of water or go to the bathroom, this scene was going to initiate World War C. Terry was either impervious to peril or in love with it, he could not tell. He resolved to get rid of this girl before something crazier happened. "You should go back to bed, we'll talk in the morning." "It's already morning." "Terry, let's get clear. I'm your teacher, I'm looking out for you—*tonight*," he stressed. About which commitment he was beginning to regret more and more. "You're more like my friend." To him, she was a kid, just a kid, a troubled kid, with some crazy shit coming down in her life, and nothing untoward was going to happen between them. Wait, there was no *between them*, nothing, whatever she was thinking or doing sitting on the coffee table undressed like that. "I'm a married man, my wife's right here." Okay, that was a leap, and not a logical one, and under these circumstances possibly a simplification if not a distortion. "You don't need to remind me, Claire put that news bulletin up in neon. But you're not sleeping in the same bed with your wife, I see." "I think we should change the subject." "Envious or jealous?" "What the hell?" "Never clear on the diff between the two." "What are you doing?" "I'm asking you to explain the difference. Because you're my teacher, which is what you keep telling me you are, like I got Alzheimer's and can't remember." In the process, she had cast him under her spell, and he realized he was disoriented. Guys, get down to it, they're all the same, *she* thought. She was a teenager, *he* thought, and he knew the limits of their relationship, which was one of those things they didn't have, a *relationship*. An unscrupulous man might take advantage, he would have to acknowledge, and he didn't meet the criteria, now, did he? Did he? No, he did not. He played it out, almost calmly. Envy, he tried to explicate to her in an even tone, envy at its most elementary referred to the soul-crushing desire you have for something of value somebody else possessed, whereas jealousy was the sickening fear, the whiplashing disgust, the drunk-like loathing of being displaced. "So, like, really no difference?" "Big difference, night and day." "Take Claire, she envious or jealous of me?" "Neither." Such an adolescent, such a narcissist, what was Matty thinking bringing her home? "Let me help you out, Matt. She's one or the other, envious or jealous, but she may actually be both." So much for the appeal of pedagogy, and another almost similar-sounding, etymologically related term for a crime the Catholic Church was dealing with on a thousand fronts. At the same time, Terry knew what Joneen might do about now. At least she knew what Joneen, her former friend and perennial pseudo-slut chesty with words, would *say* she would do. Just reach for it, let the guy know you're willing to make him feel good, which is what guys are all about, they're very simple, guys, no matter how old, all they got is an on/off switch, so grab that switch, it's no big deal, it's easy, simple, and two minutes later they're doing whatever you want them to do for you. Gospel According to Joneen. No skin off your nose, it's nothing. But Terry wasn't so sure. She did need Matt's help, and she was desperate, so it was worth a try. "Good night, Terry." "I'm not sleepy, you're not sleepy. Tell you what, had an idea." She was going to go for it, it would be easy, over in a couple of minutes with him in that old man farmer's stupid plaid nightshirt. Why the garment made her summon up "farmer" she could not say, insofar as she had no knowledge firsthand (all right, funny association, that) of agriculture or what farmers wore to bed. But while her brain blitzed, she went in another direction. "What's it like, being rich?" "How would I know? I'm not rich, I'm a high school teacher." "Your dad is rich, which means *you* are rich." "You don't know what you're talking about, it's more involved than that. I work for a living, take nothing from my old man." "But he would help you, say you needed money, say you got in trouble." "That's something we'll never find out, because I'm not asking." "My dad, he stopped paying child support, God knows when, and he and my moms, oil and water, he used to say." Matty felt a reflexive surge of sympathy, which could not be captured in spoken language, and when he sighed she saw his chest rise and fall, which excited her. "Must be cool having all that money," she said. She was on a riotous jag, no braking for her. "I know," she continued, "what *I'd* do with a lot of money." "Yeah?" "Okay, I don't know what I'd do, maybe give it away, give good teachers like you a raise. Or buy a car, new clothes, get a breast reduction, which Joneen says I should." He wasn't going anywhere near that last subject or Joneen, the troublemaker. "Let's stay on the high road." "What does that mean, high road?" "That's the right question, isn't it? I guess I have no idea anymore." "You know, Matt, you oughta be more careful." He supposed that was certainly true, but he waited for her to be specific, and hoped she would pass on the opportunity. "You didn't turn off your computer." Oh, that again? Wait. "You went on my computer, too?" First Claire, now Terry? What was going on? Matty was incompetent technologically, and he had no driving interest in educating himself, it was all a waste of time to him, software, hardware, antisocial media. Owning a cell phone was the extent of his radical and chancy leanings. He was out of step with his own generation in so many respects, and technology was hardly the most glaring example. "And you should clean out your browsing history unless you want somebody finding something you might not like the wrong person finding out, the things they could do to you if they wanted." "You searched my computer, Terry?" He did know about the search history feature. "Don't worry, your secrets are safe with me, and also those emails to the other teachers about the protest you got planned, trust me, I got your back, that bishop's a total dick, obviously." Another thing his wife and his student had in common. "Don't ever do that again." "Anyway, you should be password-protected, nobody ever told you that? Not that I'm judging, a man is like that, I know, no harm no foul. But the things people could see, say she wanted." Matty chose not to illuminate her on the subject of his wife's computer intrusion. "And say if somebody didn't like you, man, they could download pictures and video and shit, or look up X-rated sites, that would get an adult in trouble, put them in lockup, if people had a mind to, like Call Me Tammy taught us, sex ed, is all I'm saying." Terry and Claire—his computer. Test results were now posted on the imaginary comprehensive bulletin board of his mortal existence: Matty Fitzgerald had officially lost control of his life. Lost control of his job, his family, his wife, and his marriage. Not to mention his goddamn fucking computer. How did I get here, on a bed that is not a bed but a miserable excuse for a couch? Miserable excuse: which was appropriate everywhere tonight. "Terry, listen closely to me. I want you to stay off my computer. We clear about that?" "Pretty touchy, Matt." That's the moment—of course it would be dramatically inevitable—when Claire's bedroom door flew open and she sprinted like an unleashed demon down the hall. "What are you two doing, this hour of night, and you, you minx, wearing practically nothing?" "Talking," said Matty. Was that the right term? He doubted it. Claire was this side of hyperventilating, and she addressed him as if she had rehearsed her remarks: "You're like the human sacrifice and they're beating their drums and they're going to dropkick him into the volcano, the guy who's thinking *No way they do this to me*, because listen, Matty, in this jungle tribe your number's up next and this girl's a volcano." He laughed over the outrageous and, when you got down to it, illogical image, which was typical of her when she went off the rails. "You've totally lost me, Claire." "Maybe that's so, but don't you realize what this girl wants? She wants you, she'll do anything she wants with you and to you. She's a little bit desperate, you see that, Matty, say you see that." There she went again, reading minds. "Come on, she's a high school kid." Claire was continually amazed at how naïve her husband was—or if he was simple-minded, or a fabulous liar. "You have no idea how dangerous she is, but I have proof." She glared at Terry. "Physical proof. And she knows I do." "Yeah, right," said Terry, "you off your meds?" Terry was discomfited to take notice that the wife was wearing a farmer nightshirt to match her beleaguered husband's. "Because that's batshit crazy," said Terry. True, she did want to borrow the woman's so-called husband for a minute, to get the help she required. The whole night having blown up, Terry padded back to the room, shut the door. She listened to Claire talking at Matt for a few minutes till the house fell with a thud spooky quiet, and she figured that she kidnapped him back into her bedroom, restaking her claim, poor sad-looking nightshirted thing that she was—they both were. Terry would never wear a nightshirt, long as she lived. She had tuned out the predictable substance of the wifey rant; she'd long ago mastered her survivor's deliberate deafness at home. She determined she would take off first thing in the morning, so she willed herself to stay awake and get an early start. Restless, she repacked her bag, and when she did, she looked and looked for that gun. She wanted to hold it, feel the heft of it, and avoid the trigger, and she would say to herself, *You will come in handy someday.* She had made sure to go back into the park and relocate it before they drove off, but here was the bad news: no gun in her bag. *Fuck. Superfuck. Now what?* She opened the bag of Doritos and binged on the chips, two, three at a time, and when she finished she smacked her fingers free of the orange dust. Claire stole the fucking thing from her bag, or Matt did, sneaky. Now she needed insurance, something to fall back on if necessary, say they were calling the cops right now or in the morning, say they tried to convince somebody the girl had harming herself in mind or somebody else for that matter, and then what would they do to her? Send her back home to the Dash Monster? So she returned to Matt's computer and got to work, entering key words to search, keeping herself busy till the cops barged in or the sun came up, whichever occurred first. Hunting around on the internet on this mission was like rubbing grains of sand in her eyes. The sick fucks you could find online if you waded into the right cyberporn swamps. Sick beasts lurking everywhere for her, and for him. Look at that. And that. And God, *that.* No, thanks. Who are these people? They are not human beings. Man, this is some twisted shit, things people do to each other, to animals, to little kids, what kind of person would do that, what kind of deviant would download the shit and slime and scum and jizz and pus she herself was downloading on his computer, she had no idea. When she couldn't stomach another link, analyze another Petri dish of derangement, she was blasted by the thunderbolt of a new idea. She located Joneen's nude selfie on her phone, which she was glad wasn't deleted, and forwarded it in an email to Matt. People his age use email. There, that was a nice play on her part, just to mess with him, and Happy Trails, Mr. Stay on the High Road. But then another sudden, bright inspiration: she took off her tank top. She leaned into the camera and opened wide her mouth like she saw on those sick sites and snapped a pic. But no, because when she looked she was reminded of some big-mouth bass and then, even more, that hysterical painting of the screamer on the bridge she was shown in Western Syphilis Class (Joneen renamed everything), only not so green and without clothes, so she deleted it. Took another: chin down, head tilted, smiling wryly, eyebrow arched, fakely inviting. This one was definitely better: cheesy *and* sexy, which is what she was going for. She texted it to Joneen, feeling proud of herself and counting on impressing if not electroshocking the girl. Almost immediately, Joneen wrote back, and what was she doing answering texts at this hour? "hmm yowza maybe hold off surgery them's R pretty girls." Then Terry had another idea, why not, she was on a roll. She texted her pic to Matt. If it wasn't so serious, this would be hilarious, wouldn't it? And if they threatened her, she would have ammo to fire back—but fuck, that gun, why'd they have to take it? Or simpler: she'd tell the school, get him fired, which he was already prepared for anyway, seemed like, so she rationalized she might be helping him out by speeding up the whole shitstorm thing. She also should include the pic in an email, too, so that's what she did. She'd call the cops herself; he couldn't lose that image on the school server if he tried. Then and only then she began to worry she'd gone overboard, because *she* would then be on the school server for Tammy the Immaculate, if she ever got her job back, and everybody else potentially to gawk at. She shouldn't have done that to Matt. She imagined that the two of them, Matt and wife, were talking it all out in the bedroom, having makeup sex, a projected image that grossed her out, the two of them in nightshirts pathetically hooking up and united by a common enemy: herself. Same time, he meant well by her, her teacher, she knew that. But should it all unravel for him, she knew he enjoyed the advantages of one enormous get outta jail: his old man would come to the rescue, not sure how, because rich people black ops were beyond her. But she'd finally done everything she could to protect herself. So she pulled out a blank sheet of paper from his desk drawer and composed her note, which she would slip under their bedroom door. But no, she decided to place it on the couch where she last saw him in his pathetic nightshirt and where it couldn't be missed by light of day: "Mister Fitzgerald youre a very bad boy. I dont feel safe in your house anymore. I trusted you. Clair go see for yourself what your husband my teacher is up to on his computer," intentionally screwing up the spelling and punctuation to amuse herself and exploit their stupid pity for who they thought was a stupid girl like her and then she signed it shouting A DISSAPOINTD FORMER STUDENT FORCED ACCOUNT OF YOU AND YOUR WIFE TO LIVE HOMELESS ON THE ST. But then she hesitated, and reconsidered. She crunched up the paper and stowed it away in her bag, the bag with the bra, the bag without the gun. She'd done enough damage for one teenage girl during a single twenty-four-hour period. *See, Matt?* she was saying to herself as she softly closed the front door behind her to leave. *Told you. No diff whatso, envy jealous same same.* It was six o'clock in the morning, and she was never so wide awake as she was now.

Chapter Eleven
Bishop Mackey

STANISLAUS MACKEY HOWLED. LIKE a wolf he howled.

"Shut up back there," shouted the driver.

He'd howl if he wanted, let them do what they will.

No full moon, but this astral detail did not prevent the bishop from howling all over again. If he had known howling was so satisfying, so soulful, he would have unleashed a torrent of howls during his life, a life that was, according to all indications, currently at risk. So many occasions to howl had presented themselves, and he had squandered every opportunity till now: meetings with the disgruntled, arguments with lawyers, dustups with his superiors and his underlings, all the invoicing overweight fat-tie consultants.

Didn't need to have a full moon, either. Though that would be extra inspirational while being kidnapped.

Ah-oooh. Ah-ooh.

Besides, what did he have to lose, howling?

Okay, trick question, he had to admit.

"God, you're still three sheets, shut the fuck up, I said."

But no, he was not drunk anymore, whatever the wolf howl signaled. He had missed a million chances to howl in his life. Time to make up for lost opportunity.

That's when the limousine rolled to a stop at a curious destination. They were at the circular drive entrance of the darkened, boarded-up Saint

Thomas School, which was located on the untamed, farthest reaches of the diocese. Of course, he was familiar with every parcel of church real estate. Such an odd terminus. Why not go all the way, take him someplace completely beyond the pale—Roswell, New Mexico, or Lourdes? To a land of miracles or unidentified flying objects and Martian cadavers? Another bizarre stop—the final stop?—during a strange night's sojourn that began at the gala, where he successfully hauled out wheelbarrows of money, and then followed, not long later, by what he could only describe as, not to put too fine a point on it, his abduction.

He could truthfully say that this was the strangest kidnapping he'd ever experienced, though this kidnapping was, needless to qualify, a first for him. Part of him was terrified, and part of him couldn't take the whole thing seriously. If somebody was looking to take down a load of ransom loot, Stanislaus Mackey was not the candidate with the biggest upside. Given his shaky status with clerics and laypeople alike, he would guess nobody in the diocese was going to hustle up to fill a satchel with unmarked bills and leave it, per instructions, at some remote train station drop-off.

Stars shimmered in skies washed clean by all that rain. The slivered moon loomed so low and close that it was tempting enough to reach out for, like fruit from the spooky tree.

"Definitely werewolf country," the bishop called out to the driver, who was not Brendan, whom he would nevertheless fire if he got out of this mess, and was answered with aggravated silence. No surprise. He was intending to provoke the guy—was it a *guy*? He should have howled instead. Who can resist responding to a howl?

There he was, alone in the back seat, being shuttled for who knows why—although he now knew who knows where. His initial reaction, prompted by the gun's steely appearance, had been mortal apprehension—who wouldn't have felt as much? But his thoughts never ceased churning. He'd been kidnapped—kidnapping was the statutory term, he supposed, not that he was a law enforcement officer or a prosecutor, because how else to describe his unelected, unwilled current circumstances? What script was his kidnapper or kidnappers following? Nobody blindfolded him, or bothered to search him for a cell phone, or cut off a proof-of-life ear or pinky to make a persuasive case for payoff, for which he should be thankful. So avarice wasn't apparently driving him or her or it or them. Mackey had watched too much television, he supposed, or—too late now—not enough.

Whatever was going to happen was beyond his control, and it was only a matter of time before designs became clear. Certainly, the bleak setting that presented itself was perfect for some sort of diabolical half-assed plan to unfold.

This was the part of town where police cruisers wouldn't have bothered to patrol, so whoever was the ringleader was hypothetically proceeding along tactical lines. Mackey was also imagining that whoever this self-assured driver was, he was operating on the footing of privileged information. Everything argued against randomness, therefore, and everything pointed to an inside job of sorts. For starters, the driver had to know enough about Brendan, the bishop's regular driver, and his routines to remove him from the picture. Although, wait a second, unless it was the case that Brendan was himself implicated—but on second thought, this seemed farfetched as it pertained to Brendan, who wouldn't harm a fly, much less a bishop, or so Mackey vainly banked upon.

More than a decade earlier, long before he arrived tonight outside the abandoned school, this was the dead end where suburban growth had once been touted as a can't-miss prospect during a once-in-a-generation updraft in the economy. In all the excitement, city planners had fast-tracked residential housing development and public transportation and soccer fields and parks, and along with freshly paved thoroughfares, stores, restaurants, and shopping malls instantaneously popped up to serve the anticipated population rush. Optimism swelled unchecked: no one in a position of public or private sway doubted that a thriving, budding community would soon be flourishing. New families would flock here, and new families meant new children, all of which translated into new revenues for the diocese. To that end, the church had hastily built from the ground up an elementary school, which at the outset was enrolled beyond capacity. But that was then. The boom failed to sustain, and by the time it petered out, real estate values had cratered. Many, many houses were foreclosed upon or were in mortal decay, run-down and red-tagged and boarded up, unsellable and unsalvageable. Neighborhoods like this took on the character of combat zones. If any part of the economy was vital, it was likely the drug trade, and the gangs ruled the streets and the parks and the vacated shopping centers. It was a bad time. It took a while before the city conceded that it had made a losing bet. And so had the diocese. The school that had opened with abundant hopefulness and fanfare was now shuttered, and the current bishop, still ensconced in the back seat, nurtured no expectation it would ever reopen. As for the diocese: time to cut losses and run from the ruins.

Saint Thomas School was named, with no apparent consciousness of irony, after the saint legendarily called The Doubter, eternally notorious for questioning whether Jesus had in fact risen from the dead. The poor guy was made famous for insisting he wouldn't believe in the Savior until he could place his own hands on the wounds. This moment of show-and-tell was soon to be made available for him, to his drop-to-the-knees edification and mortification. That Gospel story formed the basis of the bishop's favorite homily, which consisted of his simple thesis, which was Jesus's too, namely that Thomas was Everyman. Who didn't really doubt, who didn't ultimately desire confirmation? But that's where faith came in, oh, ye of little faith and no balls. Fortunate are those who have not seen and who nonetheless believe. That was Stanislaus Mackey's story and he, another Everyman, was sticking to it.

Through the rolled-up back seat window, Mackey riveted his attention upon this blighted spectacle. To him, there was nothing sadder, more vanquished, more depressing than an expired school, especially a defunct Catholic school, which represented the ultimate dashing of children's dreams and aspirations.

On a rational level, he knew he should be afraid for his life, but fear vied with curiosity, as in how the hell was this going to turn out? He never kept count of his adversaries, but he had to acknowledge that there were indeed many, many out there who had tangled with him in the past, in this diocese and elsewhere, and they might have been surprised to discover that he hadn't already had the crap beaten out of him—or worse. It seemed altogether simpler: somebody tonight was trying to make a point with him—or to make a point *of* him. How else to explain that this whole affair felt like somebody's conception of bad civic theater? Kidnapping, gun, ravaged wasteland of a town—it was theater of the ridiculous into which he had been cast and he was a leading player. He was as sober as he had been for a year.

"Werewolf country," he reiterated. "Where are the angry townsfolk with their torches when you need them?" And he howled once more.

—

BY THE TIME THE sun would rise, matters would prove to be both much more and much less grave for Stanislaus Mackey. And before too many hours would pass, he would be probed and scanned and prodded and poked and tested and retested in the emergency room of the local hospital. He would be asked over and over again what he recalled of the night. His recollections proved fitful, partial, shadowy, with occasional, unpredictable lightning flashes of crystalline lucidity. Of course, these descriptors would apply to many if not most of his drinking years, but with a difference tonight, a difference that he struggled to decode in the aftermath.

In any event, these are the shards of remembrance, these are the images and the fragments of speech, that he fitfully remembered. When he tried to narrate the events that took place around him, he struggled and struggled. He would have the chance to fill in the spaces left vacant for reasons that were to be made clear—only much, much later.

—

HIS LIMOUSINE DOOR OPENED, and he was ushered out from the back seat by a materializing coconspirator. The gloomy spectacle did not correspondingly improve, and neither did his disposition.

"You howl again and I will smack you."

The night reeked of damp, smoky firewood. Far, far in the distance, pealing car tires and a faint drumbeat, like at some impromptu Caribbean street festival. A siren wailed and stopped, then another picked up.

Walked between two ski-masked people, both equipped with powerful flashlights, along the path to the school door. One man, one woman, he guessed, pure supposition. And the strong intuition dawned that these two had absolutely no fucking idea what they were doing. That meant good news, and that also meant the opposite, if he wasn't very, very careful. People without a plan are the most dangerous people in the world. He grew convinced of this proposition: it was up to him to come up with a plan to survive.

Once inside the deserted main building, passing through the place where doors had been stolen, he sensed that the poor homeless and downtrodden, who were nowhere in sight, had squatted and commandeered the campus. It all amounted to a gigantic fire hazard, or worse, but considering the larger social questions, not an altogether suboptimal use of what was left of the otherwise obsolete school.

Feral creatures abounding, vermin. Stench: sulfuric, vinegary, burnt sugar, worse.

Corkboards dotted with curled-up announcements and obsolescent news, not that he could decipher the words in the gloom—except for the enormous header in enthusiastic, school-cheer bold letters: *Never Doubt! St. Thomas School Rules!*

Stepped over the debris and the refuse (wine bottles, newspaper, wrappers, cartons: the usual) littering the once proud foyer. Incoherent spray paint graffiti.

Never crossed his mind to try to escape, to hightail away, which would have been futile since his hightailing days were used up long ago, or to cry out for help—nobody within hearing distance.

"What circle of hell is this?"

"I'd say this would be your own circle of hell, Excellence."

"*Excellence?* Thank you for the respectful touch."

"Don't push it."

Guided by flashlights, they led him to what seemed to have once been the office of the principal. He heard the furious scurrying of scratchy rodent feet. Inside the spacious room there was an abused conference table and, weirdly, several functional wooden chairs. They sat down in silence.

Stanislaus Mackey broke the quiet and asked them what their next move would be.

"Because it certainly appears you are both clowns and that you have no glimmering as to what trouble you are in, or what objective is motivating you. Why don't we call it a night and agree that nothing ever happened, and we can all go home and forget everything?"

One of them removed the ski mask.

"Bishop Mackey, I'm Claire Fitzgerald."

"Wish I could say it was a pleasure to meet you, young lady. Related to Paddy Fitzgerald and Father Philip, I presume?"

"Father-in law, brother-in-law. And also related to your best teacher, Matty Fitzgerald, my husband, whom you're trying to fire, like you fired my boss at Caring Street, Dr. Alessandro." The other ski mask stayed in place and the wearer remained mute.

"Now that I know who you are, that might constitute very bad news—for all of us. Though most acutely and particularly as it applies to me. You might feel no compunction disposing of me, now that I could identify you to the authorities, who would take seriously, I don't know the legal terminology, your crime spree? You now find yourselves in a position where everything may well spin out of control."

"They won't send out an Amber Alert for you, don't flatter yourself. And no reason to bring law enforcement into the discussion, Excellence. After all, what I would say, if by some chance I were ever interrogated under a swinging light bulb or water-boarded, is that you begged us to take you on a little joy ride after the gala. You wanted us to find an all-night liquor store and pick up a bottle for you."

"Do you think anybody will believe that, Claire Fitzgerald?"

"Oh, small step to believe Bishop Mackey wanted another pop. Besides, it doesn't matter what anybody who isn't here will believe, it's what you will tell as your story, if you're around to tell it. In the meantime, I think you're going to find our input valuable. Thank you for listening as if your life depended upon it. Which it might."

"When it comes to law enforcement, there might be some interest evinced with regard to that weapon that you have trained on me, Claire Fitzgerald."

"That's enough, stop saying my name. We did need to get your undivided attention, true, but as you can see, the gun is now on the table here. And we won't take up a lot of your time, it's late already. We'd like to make a few points for your consideration."

"Hard for me to complain or suggest an alternative, being a captive audience."

The mood changed in the room. Claire lambasted the bishop for his terrible teacher's contract. He was destroying the morale of the whole school community and undercutting the noble efforts of their best teachers, like Matty.

"I agree Matty is a great teacher, or so I have been advised by every Tom, Dick, and Harry."

She instructed him as to what he was going to do now. He was going to drop the whole contract thing, for good. And while she had his undivided attention, she also tore into him about what he had done to Dr. Alessandro, who was obviously the ideal executive director of Caring Street, where the kids loved and respected him. Sure, he made a few tiny, forgivable mistakes of judgment, but his heart was in the right place, caring for the kids.

"Last chance, Bishop Mackey, to clean up these two messes you created. What do you have to say for yourself?"

"You think I owe you an explanation for my life? Nice try. And what makes you think that threatening me with a gun, kidnapping me, is going to further your cause?"

Claire said kidnapping is a complex criminal category, so many gradations apply, she had looked them up, all related to intent. You have false imprisonment, for instance, a much lesser charge. And he was no Lindbergh kid, no Patty Hearst. It hadn't been twelve hours, when the most punitive statutes would kick in—she claimed these were facts. But she was no lawyer, so time for him to listen up for a change. All they were doing was this: righting the wrongs Mackey had committed, and doing what they could by any means necessary.

"Let me stop you right there, young lady. Let me tell you about correcting all the terrible wrongs that afflict this world that you supposedly are on some personal crusade to correct. It falls upon my shoulders, *my* shoulders, to do all I can. I have cleared out the diocese of pedophile priests, I know you agree with me. That was a terrible wrong committed by the Church, a crime and a sin. And I pray every day for those children who have been harmed irredeemably as a result of our irresponsible, unconscionable practices. But Caring Street was a loose operation, and the teachers needed to be put in line, needed to be reminded that they are *Catholic* teachers, ministers, truly, defending, propagating the faith. Thanks to me and our fundraising, Caring Street is going to serve more kids than ever and do a better job of it, and thanks to me, we're going to build a brand-new high school, if your father-in-law comes to his senses, the high school where Matty can teach if he ever wises up and signs the completely well-intentioned contract. There, I've said my piece, blast away if you like."

"I think, deep down, there's a chance you're a good man, or were, Excellence, a good man who made some terrible decisions. You've made your share of good decisions, too, I'll grant you. We're here to help you attend to the better angels of your nature. You have them, don't you, Excellence? The angels? Everybody does. Most everybody, anyway."

"Yes, angels. They look after me. Had a feeling all along, Claire Fitzgerald..."

"Stop using my name, I said."

"...all along that this was about Hector, more than Matty."

The kids need him at Caring Street, she said, and the high school students need teachers who care about them, and who don't walk in lockstep with your out-of-date Church policies. This is your chance to make a course correction, before it's too late.

If you love the least of your brethren, Jesus says, you love Him.

"Help me understand what you want me to do."

"The right thing, that's all, do the right fucking thing for a change. You've been given another chance, could be your last chance."

"You both are risking a great deal in this insane escapade. Hate to admit, but that's impressive. But I also have to add that while you have not succeeded in intimidating me, something is going on. You know, the angels have encouraged me to reconsider. Listen to me, Claire Fitzgerald, you're doing this all wrong, totally wrong. Let me help you."

"Oh, fantastic, look what's happened every time you've helped us all so much."

"If I understand what you've done here tonight, you've risked indictment, conviction, and incarceration in order to *talk* to me? You wanted to *talk*? To persuade me to change my mind? At the point of a gun?

That's the masterminding plan? Why didn't you call my office to make an appointment? True, I wouldn't have given you the time of day, but that's immaterial. But you wanted to *talk*. I have to say this is the dumbest criminal scheme ever hatched. Make room, Ten Most Wanted List."

"Say you'll do the right thing for a change, Excellence, and we'll call it a night."

"Let me put my hands into the wounds."

"How can you still be hammered?"

"I have an idea. Let's the three of us pray together."

"That's your go-to move, Excellence? Prayer?"

"It should be everybody's go-to move, forever. And it should definitely be yours. For one thing, if you ever get out of the shit you have gotten yourself into, you're going to need lots of prayers. Okay, take my hands, both of you, and let..."

—

HE REMEMBERS HE FELL suddenly, strangely ill.

He remembers sensing his left side go numb, heavy, leaden.

He remembers the words he searched for would not cross his lips.

He remembers feeling dizzy, lost.

Swirling. Tilting. Drifting.

He never felt he was about to die. No, the opposite. Take that back. He was Catholic. He was continually conscious of his mortality.

More like, he was being washed over by—no other word for it—grace. He was being held in the gracious palm of divine forces, that of the angels, the angels whose songs and voices filled his heart and his head.

Then, next thing he knew—

He knew nothing.

He was being wheeled through the whooshing automatic glass doors of the ER, and somebody in a white coat scrambled over and read the sign that had been pinned to the front of his black suit, which he later was informed consisted of a single word: STROKE. He had been cast off into the hospital by someone who had fled into darkness. This would count as being a good thing, too, in one key respect. Because whoever it was might be under the illusion they had saved Stanislaus Mackey's life, for what such a miserable life was worth. But over the weeks and months and years to come, the bishop was compelled to conclude something different. He was delivered to safety at the hands of his avenging angels.

Chapter Twelve
Caitlin & Paddy

C AITLIN?"
 In bed afterward, he might mutter unsuppressed syllables of delirious incoherence and sail off into beneath-the-waterfall slumber. Then, upon waking up in the penthouse, he would shower, dress, and go—wherever it was he went in the middle of the night. Sometimes, his functionary Jonesy, the irrepressible Jonesy, would be waiting for him downstairs, probably reading; other times, like tonight, he was flying solo.

She was accustomed to Paddy's postcoital rules of disengagement, and in his wake she convinced herself she preferred to sleep alone and have the penthouse all to herself. She had a college degree's worth of knowledge on the subject of men in their beds, men in her bed. Normally she took pride in being an uncomplicated girl, or at least playing that role. That was what men she had been professionally acquainted with insisted in a girl: uncomplications.

"Caitlin?" he said again when she did not answer the first time.

Basking in her embodied afterglow, hearing him softly call her by name, she shuddered. She detected a confidential almost conspiratorial tone in Paddy's velvety, dropped-octave voice. Her first instinct: he was breaking up with her, but he was going to be tender about it. Second instinct: she had no second. But if she *had* a second instinct it would have been: get it over with already. Her working life taught her she could deal with anything, and she never should have expected anything else.

"Caitlin?" he tried once more. "You okay?"

As ordinary as this question may have seemed, it was a new question on his part. A simple question he may have asked her, but it didn't seem that way. She felt eerily close to him and at the same time she was apprehensive, because almost certainly intimacy beyond the physical was not a formal part of their arrangement. It was as if she were walking down an unlit hallway in an unfamiliar house, wondering if there were trapdoors and feeling her way for loose floorboards.

"Paddy?" She coaxed her voice out from hiding.

"I think I'll call you Caitlin from now on."

How such a breezy-seeming declaration gathered force like the first gust of spring rain.

He wasn't seeking permission, but he didn't do that with anybody. He was signaling, but signaling what? Was it a power play on his part, to update her name, dismissing that ridiculous contrived one, Caitlindee, which he ultimately refused to speak, and pressuring her to take back her own true name, the beautiful one she was born with? Caitlindee was who she was when he met her for their first commercial transactions, and that was precisely who she was not anymore. He did know this much: something *had* indeed changed. He liked her more than he should, and that couldn't be a good thing, unless it was a very good thing, but how could that be, given who he was and who she was? A man his age, a man of his standing shouldn't be entertaining moony notions. The reason a man takes a mistress in the first place was in order *not* to entertain precisely such notions—and also to never say *mistress*. Maybe it was simple: he was an old man, and he was becoming sentimental. God, he used the word *mistress*.

Meanwhile for her, it boiled down to wild hopefulness, optimism that when he said *Caitlin from now on* he was implying that he was going to be with her *from now on*. If she were in a rational state, she would have contested such a sunny interpretation: *Get a grip, get a hold of yourself, this thing you have with him is nothing more than what it is, so enjoy it because it's plenty, it's at least not nothing and probably enough and, face it, when has any man ever treated you half as well?*

"Well, that is my name, Sweets." True, *Caitlindee* had lost whatever freakish appeal it once held. For some reason and possibly against her own self-interest, she felt something strange surge, something like—yes, exactly, intimacy, that was the word, intimacy burgeoning between them. But that couldn't be, could never be. Occasionally Paddy had called her Cait, which warmed her heart. Her own father called her Cait as a child. She had fallen out of touch with him for so long, and had lodged a hateful brief against him for ages. Now the summoned image of him depressed, vanquished her. She calculated, not for the first time, that he and Paddy were roughly the same age. She indulged in no ludicrous fantasy of introducing them. Because they would despise each other. And besides, she was no longer the kind of girl who takes a man home to meet the parents, not that she ever had been.

She threw her arms around his neck and drew herself closer and he received her. Did she and Paddy have, what normal people termed, a *relationship*? They had been together for a couple of months, no, more like three, notwithstanding that she couldn't define *together* or *relationship*. But if she had enjoyed privileged, unrestricted access to his inner life, she would have seen that, like her, he himself was surprised. Paddy Fitzgerald was as transparent as he could be, after all. They were in each other's arms and he called her *Caitlin*, didn't he?

—

HER MOBILE PHONE RANG on the nightstand. "Sorry, meant to turn it off."

He lunged across her body to snatch the phone, his burst of furious energy alarming her.

"Paddy, what are you doing!"

He didn't have to answer to her.

"It's not your phone, Paddy."

"You sure about that?"

"Don't," she said, "please."

"Who's calling you again?"

"It's not important."

"But you keep your phone on anyway."

"I will lose it. Get another number, all right?"

He studied the phone. "I see it's a guy name of Baxter calling. Nice looking, too. Doing business, pedaling your ass on the side?"

"Don't say that, I'm done with since…since you…"

"Sure you are, baby."

"It's nobody, all right? My husband."

—

She hadn't intended to deceive. She also hadn't intended not to. She was reconfiguring her old practices, and it was not easy to do. Nonetheless, her legal marital status was trivial, inconsequential, irrelevant. She and Baxter had split years ago, but never bothered with divorce proceedings, both being busted at the time of the breakup, with no worthwhile possessions to divvy up and no extra cash in the bank for lawyers. They'd lived apart much longer than they had ever lived with each other, and both were all too ready to raise the white flag. Their marriage had been a mistake, pure and simple. It happens, they were sad about it, and they made peace with each other. They kept in touch since, because he wanted, and she had no cause to object—at least until now, with Paddy.

"You're married, and you didn't mention it? What, you think I'd be angry? Don't flatter yourself. Or you think I wouldn't find out? You think that little detail would matter? Why should I care?" His scattershot questions inflicted the damage intended. He would never admit to feeling betrayed, but was he? Why did he care at all? He knew who she was when they hooked up, and what she was, no use being romantic about it. "I should have known better," he said. "We all learn from our mistakes and move on." So that's where he was going: moving on.

She sat straight up in bed. "Nothing's happening, him and me. And give me back my phone."

"Nothing's happening between you and your husband."

"Give it back."

He was fascinated by her assertiveness, and he handed it over, curious as to what would be her next move, and his.

"Look, we broke up years and years ago. I'm not going to start explaining my past to you. You know better than anyone, my past." Yet she had to acknowledge that her not turning off the phone as Paddy insisted might have indicated some unconscious, inscrutable motivation.

"But he's trying to reconcile, right?"

How could he possibly know this? "Who knows what he's thinking?" She'd better tell the truth, having nothing to lose.

"And you're talking to him?"

"Yes, a little, time to time, but I love you, there I said it, and I don't love him. He's weak, he's desperate, he's lonely, he's the opposite of you." To the extent she was aware of what she was doing with Baxter, she would have said she pitied the guy. They had memories, yes, but they were uniformly terrible. The shared losses of their ill-considered marriage were all that remained to tenuously connect them.

"Sure is the opposite of me. One thing, he's married to you."

"And I don't ever expect I will ever walk down the aisle in a white dress the rest of my life. Look, I will hire a lawyer, finish this off."

"An ex can be hard to call off, especially if somebody has feelings."

"I said it's over." That was the absolute truth, perhaps. But she had to say more. "I gave him a few bucks, he's broke, can't afford rent."

"You gave him money, which would be my money."

"I wanted him the fuck out of my hair. Couldn't figure out another way. He got a job parking cars at some dumpy hotel. It's on the way to the gym, and he saw me passing by one day, I wish he hadn't, I thought I'd never see him again."

"That a hotel you use?"

"Paddy, stop, please. You know better."

"Not so sure. But then you gave him some of my money."

"Okay, yes, right. It was a mistake, I'm sorry, I was wrong. I was trying to get rid of him once and for all."

"How much?"

"Two hundred."

"But it wasn't enough, was it?"

"All right, *five* hundred and you're right and I'm sorry."

"Any other surprises? Like say you have a family, kids with him?"

After a long moment, she burst into tears. She wished that the floodgates had not opened.

Sympathy for her was not forthcoming. "It's a yes–no question, it's got to have an answer." Was Paddy negotiating? Did Caitlin have more power than she had a right to have?

"Not yes–no in this case."

"I don't understand, but I don't need to, maybe you have other secrets." He was losing his hold on the situation. "I don't know in my business I can afford to be with somebody I can't trust."

"I'm not a part of your fucking business empire. And what, you're disappointed in me? Take a number, Paddy, heard that shit all my life, and it used to be true, but not now. You are different. But you just said you didn't care. Only now you sound like you care. Which the fuck is it?"

"I'm waiting, answer the question, family, kids, yes–no."

What did he say? That he was *with* her? "I don't want to talk about that, not yet."

"When, then?"

Then she did something feral crazy. She shot out of bed and stood looking down on him, which she half-sensed was risky, striking a pose of dominance she shouldn't have dared with a man like him. She was dependent upon him. Only she was about to be summarily dismissed. In the instant, she also felt liberated, maybe free of him, maybe free of some idea of herself. She didn't care about the penthouse or if he would throw her out on the street, she didn't care about the diamond earrings, the silver bracelet, she didn't care about the cash he stuck every week inside the fancy French and Italian purses he bought for her. All she cared about was saying what was on her mind, let the chips fall where they may.

"When? When, you want to know when. I'll tell you exactly *when*, Paddy. Like exactly when you fucking say one time you care about me, which you fucking should because I care about you, and you know what? You can lie when you say it, it doesn't matter. See, I don't have a lot of requirements, I'm not high maintenance, then I'll tell you everything. Do whatever you want to me, but I'm nobody's property, not anymore, I'm done with this bullshit. Another thing. Never touch my fucking phone again. Got it?"

When she hastened into the bathroom and closed the door, Paddy Fitzgerald felt as distraught as he had felt in a long time—strangely enough, and this was another shocker, since Anthony. Maybe it was true, maybe it was the Irish in him, and maybe types of grief and loss reanimate and unfathomably interconnect across time. He heard water running hard in the sink, he wondered what she was doing, what she was waiting for. All he knew was that she was doing something to him that he would not have expected. She'd pitched a kind of scene, but now he was no longer angry, which also surprised him. He had to admit that her standing up for something, and against him, took a kind of courage he admired. Either that or a kind of stupidity. The two conditions could be tough to tell apart. He wasn't practiced in not controlling expectations—others' expectations as well as his own. He'd have to do something about that. And he wouldn't hesitate. He could start by getting rid of her, or by hiring her a lawyer. Or both, and maybe not in that order.

For him as for her, time excruciatingly passed. She was wasting a lot of water. He searched for a clock on her nightstand, but it was not to be found. He would have to get her one of those. Because what kind of nightstand doesn't have a clock? And what kind of person doesn't need a clock near the bed?

"Come back," he finally said, experimentally, tentatively. And then he called out again, louder, with conviction and without a question mark. "Please, Caitlin."

She'd never heard him use that word, *please*. The tap squealed and the water flow ceased. "Anything else on my phone disturb the great Sweets Fitzgerald?" Her voice from the other side of the closed door was clipped and clear.

Looking at her phone again would show weakness, so that never occurred. "Don't women want to talk after a fight?"

She flung open the door and defiantly stood there dressed in jeans and a pullover sweater, prepared to exit the penthouse, her slightly pigeon-toed feet bare, the designer sneakers he bought her held in her right hand.

"I may not know the first thing about women, but near as I can tell, you and me, we just had a *fight*, didn't we?" That would have been a first, a fight between them, and unimaginable previously.

If that were true and they did, she wasn't sure who won. Was it possible she had won? She had better wait to find out.

"Going somewhere, Caitlin?"

"Assume you've had enough of me, so what do you care?" She couldn't believe anybody had ever spoken to him the way she did and part of her couldn't believe she had said what she said, not that she wanted to take back a single word.

"What happened to the clock by the bed?"

"There's my phone, go ahead, I don't care, you need to know the time."

"You made your point. Your clock, didn't you used to have one right here?"

"I guess I did when I had to wake up and go somewhere, and maybe I don't have to anymore. Maybe I never did have a good reason to be anywhere but where I was. Why I need a clock? I gotta be somewhere? All you gotta do is snap your fingers, Paddy."

"Nice watch." He was referring to the sparkly, black, eighteen-karat white gold and diamond-studded Piaget on her slender wrist, which he had given her, a special-edition numbered timepiece, as he once detailed to her while she almost keeled over, mesmerized with joy.

"Yeah, I had this rich boyfriend who gave it to me when he once liked me. So. You want your fancy watch back, Paddy? Here. Take it." She extended her hand. "I said take it. You can have it. I'll swing my trusty old hundred-buck Swatch back into action, which is more like me anyway."

"Stop, come back to bed, it's late, we're both tired, Caitlin."

—

THEY WOULDN'T ADDRESS IN SO many words the subject of their fight, their anger with each other, anger over each other, because neither knew what to say, but after a while she did undress and did return to bed, and soon she was lying there, taking her place, her back to him in the darkened bedroom with blackout drapes. They would spend hours separately wondering what it was that had transpired between them—if it was something between them. Neither was unafraid of what the clarifying morning light would reveal.

Sometime during the night, when they could not sleep despite being so tired, she did speak in a hushed voice. She addressed the wall. "I was nineteen. We had a baby. Boy we named Ben. He never got out of the hospital, twenty-two hours and he was gone. I can't have any more kids. That what you wanted to know? Because that's all I got."

She turned over to face him and they held tight onto each other till they waded into sleep as if it were a river flowing down from snow-capped mountains.

—

NEXT MORNING, WHEN SHE rubbed the sleep from her eyes, she thought she might be dreaming, but no, she could see Paddy was there, lying next to her. For an instant, she was frightened he would be upset. But the apprehension dissipated when he woke up, sighing. It was a fact that he had spent the night with her, which was of course a first. As momentous as that may have been, she was still trying to come to terms with the night. Whatever the fight had been about they may never understand, she thought, or ever discuss.

That's when he proposed the incredible. The two of them had never had breakfast together, he said. Going out for an ordinary morning meal after a night in bed—that's what lovers do, don't they?

She said, "There's a good omelet shop downstairs, near the..."

"Great, but I had another idea," he said. "How about breakfast at my house?"

"What did you say?"

Chapter Thirteen
Big Mimmo

THE BLEEDING FIREBALL SUN was starting its descent over the rooftops as Francesca's father, Dominic Scalino, aka Big Mimmo, drove into his driveway. He noticed a coyote on the nearby hillside, sly and feigning nonchalance while being on the hunt. Coyotes were becoming more and more of a nuisance in the neighborhood, and at odd times of the day, too. They kept down the rodent population, so they had half an excuse to live. Their mating screams startling, waking him up in the middle of the night were one thing. But now to judge by the handbills on the telephone poles, cats were going missing, toy dogs disappeared, and people were growing militant. If a coyote entered his property, Mimmo'd have to do something about it.

He walked into his house through the garage. The big dog thudded over to him, expecting a head rub, which he deserved and which he got, along with an insanely desirable liver treat for good measure. Who would win a battle between this dog and a coyote, Mimmo wondered. Problem was, when a fight broke out with a coyote, it was a good chance there was never a single coyote, and that they schemed to be chased by the dog—all the way into the pack of coyotes gathered in ambush. It's a violent world here in the suburbs.

He was taking care of his daughter's dog because she and Tommy went out of town for a few days, in the name of stabilizing their shaky relationship. Dickens was a very good dog, a chocolate brown pit bull mix with a sweet disposition, and the dog felt at home here in this house with a man who was evidently in possession of a limitless supply of liver treats.

Big Mimmo had returned from his doctor's appointment, which had not gone well, as could have been predicted. The man didn't trust the medical profession in general, but he figured he had to take a little bit seriously the results of the latest series of distressing tests, or at least pretend to.

"If you want to hang around in the world for a while, you need to start making some serious changes in your life," the doc had said. "Lose thirty pounds. Give up the damn cigars. One glass of red wine a day, tops. You're not a young man anymore, Dominic."

"You're not telling me to walk a half hour every day, like you usually do."

"Because I give up, why waste my breath, but you should definitely do that, too."

Big Mimmo, who had been gratuitously, rudely reminded he was not a young man anymore, opened up a fine bottle of so-called Super Tuscan Tignanello, and poured some into a goblet. It needed some air but it tasted wonderful accompanied by a chunk of Parmigiano he slivered off the wheel of Reggiano on the kitchen counter. Then he clipped the end of a Dominican gran robusto and lit it. Living alone, he could smoke in his house anytime he liked. Not as before, before his wife went into assisted living, which was required, given her needs and maladies. Way back when she put her foot down about smoking in the house, and that was an argument he was never going to win. Things had changed, largely not for the better. He took the wine and the cigar outside and sat in an Adirondack chair and settled in to watch what was left of the fading sun's show.

Dickens sidled up to him for another pat and with any luck another cube of freeze-dried liver. The man didn't have any doggie treats at hand outside, but he did have some of the tantalizing cheese, and he slipped the dog a piece. To judge by his eagerness, that had to taste better than freeze-dried liver.

He liked to talk to the dog, who seemed to understand him perfectly. "We're both misunderstood species, *daverro.*" The dog signaled agreeableness as he relaxed on his haunches and appeared content to be looking out in the same direction as Big Mimmo, each of them claiming territory, the whole sky, for his own. He poured himself a second glass. The wine was coming around even if, according to his grim reaper of a doc, he wasn't anymore.

He heard the front door open, and Dickens scampered happily in that direction. What was Mikey, his son, doing, coming over? He only came over when he needed some money or a shoulder to cry on. But Big Mimmo was wrong.

"Papá," Francesca said, opening the glass door to the patio, while the dog seemed thrilled he had her again. "I'm back."

"I can see that, *tesoro*. Tommy with you?"

She and Dickens had a bond that was obvious. Tommy? He was not with her.

"You two were going away to spend quality time together? Never understood that, *quality time*, like is there any other kind?"

"What are you drinking?"

He showed her the label on the bottle and she went back inside for a glass and poured herself one.

"*Come va*? You gonna tell me what's up, *carissima*?" It was a week after the gala, a lot had happened that night. None of it pleasant to her mind. First Mackey, second the fight between her and the cop. Ex-detective, she would have corrected him.

She sipped and sipped again. "Nothing went according to plan. We couldn't decide whether to break up or get serious."

"I know what you mean, I remember..."

"So, Papá, we decided to do both."

He wasn't following his daughter, who was smarter than he was, which he was smart enough to understand.

"What I mean is, we're going to get married..."

She flashed a new diamond on her finger. "Tommy wants to make an honest woman out of me. Somebody had to."

At first he thought she was joking. She wasn't.

"Your mama would have been happy."

She let his remark linger, because her mother was not going to register that development, or any other developments.

"How did the doctor go?"

"Aces, Francesca, *carissima*, aces. I put a bet in, I'm going to outlive the guy."

"That's great. You happy for me, Papá?"

"I been happy for you since the day you were born."

"Think I'm doing the right thing?"

What could he say? He took her hand in his.

She knew, as he did, Tommy was no Anthony. Anthony himself was no longer *Anthony*. He had been transformed into an image, a towering memory, an unattainable ideal. This was not fair to Tommy. It wasn't even fair to Anthony. But the dead always get the last word.

"But life, life is for the living, tesoro."

"You always say that. I don't know what it means."

"*Va bene*, okay. You will when you need to."

Chapter Fourteen
Paddy & Philip

THE REVEREND PHILIP FITZGERALD was meeting his father at their traditional lunch spot, the venerable expansive eatery known as Noah's Boat House. Lunch or dinner, it was usually hard to get in, unless you were a Fitzgerald, in which case: "Lovely to see you again, we have your table, please come this way."

Jonesy O'Dell escorted Paddy into the marine blue dining room—nautical lanterns, anchors, harpoons, wooden steering wheels, propped oars, lobster crates, nets stretched across ceilings, and one unlucky marlin mounted above the fireplace, that sort of establishment. Fortunately, the fare was better than the hackneyed décor promised. Jonesy pulled back a chair for his boss. He would not be invited to join them at table, where Philip, who had arrived early, was already seated.

"I'll call," said Paddy. "Don't wander off on one your fishing expeditions, see if you find out about that thing we talked about."

"Of course, that thing, thank you, sir," he said, and fixed his direct attention upon the man's son, saying, with singsong languor, drawing out and inserting a breath between the two syllables, sounding vaguely prosecutorial: "Father?"

"Mr. O'Dell." Jonesy did not have a glass eye, but to look at him, it felt as if he had two. Whenever Philip did look closely, he met steely, inexpressive resistance. Jonesy trained his sights on Philip, as if he were sizing him up all over again. That was Jonesy O'Dell. Philip did not blink.

"Enjoy a pleasant lunch, Mr. Fitzgerald," the man said, pausing before pointedly adding with a lilt of doubtfulness, "with your son." He walked off, parting the air in his engulfing wake.

That was Paddy's cue. "Philip, why you gotta bust my man's balls like that?" A complaint but also a genuine question.

His son would not take the bait, because there was nothing to be gained sharing his contemptuous views, which his father would never endorse, and that was that for now.

"Cup of chowder, Dad, the usual?"

"Not feeling it."

Despite the reassurances implied by its name and seafaring design, Noah's wasn't located near a respectable or even a negligible body of water, and nobody of Biblical pedigree had recently been sighted on the floor or at the bar. Whatever colorful, dramatic tales related to the restaurant's historical origins had all been carried off by the tides of time.

Paddy was unclear about something, or maybe he understood every-thing perfectly, and so on this occasion, he launched. He had attended, of course, that infamous fundraiser that was sensationally covered wall-to-wall after the fact by the local media on account of what happened to the bishop—even if what it was that happened to the man was far from clear. Whatever it was, it didn't appear to be auspicious. He feared that whatever it all meant, it was connected to a bigger picture of rampant disorder. The world had irretrievably changed around Paddy. About that, he was growing by the day increasingly convinced. The town wasn't what it used to be. Same with family. Why, his son the priest might be in peril, and he might not know it. Was there some lunatic on the loose who was randomly assaulting bishops—which was the public's suspicion? Or was some more sinister and calculating principle—and nefarious agency—at work?

"Jumping to conclusions, Dad. They never established Mackey was assaulted, only that he somehow found his way to a hospital, thereafter shuttling in and out of consciousness. What makes you think a mastermind had mayhem in mind?"

Paddy wanted his son to understand his paternal unease, because to his way of thinking, the appeals of mayhem, if not the product of ingrained disposition, often crossed most people's minds. "I'm concerned. That's what fathers feel for sons, you know. They haven't found who pushed Mackey's button."

"Again, assuming there *was* somebody and a button was in fact pushed."

"Explain the car then, the driver."

Philip couldn't, or why the car was abandoned and the driver AWOL. So yes, that was dicey. And there seemed to be no reason not to think that Mackey hadn't been traumatized by whatever had taken place to him, or around him, or because of him.

"Things must be crazy for you guys in the Chancery. Funny word, *Chancery*."

Philip had his hands full with the aftermath, and he and his father hadn't gotten together since the gala. "You have no idea."

"So it's open season on the Roman collars?"

Philip didn't think so, though everybody was more vigilant, if not more paranoid.

"You want me to assign my guys to you? They can keep a low profile, nobody'd hardly know they were around."

Philip found that prospect amusing in a sick way—*he* would know they were around. That's all he needed, enforcers tailing him, keeping tabs. "Oh, I'd love to have O'Dell on the job, and he'd love it too, in his parade of sharkskin suits."

"My guys don't wear the sharkskin, that's for my swarthy Italian brethren."

Philip reminded his dad that a priest of his stature, with a reputation like his, and a priest with his particular last name dare not risk bodyguards. Having protection conveyed fearfulness, but more important, it ran counter to his role as a priest: a man consecrated, a man existentially prepared to sacrifice himself if called upon. That's precisely what a father doesn't like to hear, especially one who, like Paddy Fitzgerald, has the reach and the clout to thwart perils and perpetrate a few of his own.

"You mean well, Dad, I guess—but let's change the subject, I'm hungry."

Then father reminded son that he had pledged his normal six figures at the event that night, which Philip knew already, and which his father knew that he knew.

"You've always been generous."

"All because of you, boyo."

His son's mood turned testy, which happened whenever his father was patting himself on the back. "I'm sure there are other benefits besides alleviating your guilt, but honestly, thanks."

His son might be a superstar in the diocese, but his father didn't appreciate the snide tone and cheap implication. "Innocent until proven."

His father was justified. "Sorry, Dad, I'm out of line. Not sleeping well these days." That had more to do with Ruth than with the bishop, but he saw no percentage in calling that out.

"I'd be knackered, too, if I were you guys. I grant you absolution, *Father*, you're welcome." Paddy missed no opportunity to hit on the square that *Father*, like a physician with that rubber-head mallet employed to check reflexes. Calling one's own son *Father* never failed to echo bizarrely—to both of them. Yet this all went to the man's contentious Church dealings. Considering Paddy's notorious career, he might have been the sort of man who reasonably calculated he should hedge bets against the grim prospects of the afterlife by giving generously to the Church. Paddy was to be confused with no such mortal. The afterlife, if there existed such an eventuality, was in and of itself not an interesting problem to ponder. That was because, by definition, it was something out of his control. Up until the Great Divide, Paddy would exert some of his own influence. Besides, there was nothing wrong with giving to the Catholics, as far as he was concerned. Deductions are deductions, and Paddy paid income taxes—at least his accountants certainly filed the paperwork and dispatched the justifiable amounts of money. And the diocese, even after taking serious direct as well as indirect financial hits as a consequence of the pedophile lawsuits, remained in a position to do business with a man like Paddy Fitzgerald. If he himself had gone to Catholic school as his own kids had, he allowed that he might have turned out different. Though really, probably not.

"I am gobsmacked, what happened to Mackey," said his father, who couldn't let it go. The way the bishop was touched up—close quarters—and the limo, the disrespectful disposition of the man's beleaguered body, in the goddamned ER. "It was overkill, message he got sent, and it was definitely personal, what somebody did. What's the latest on his condition?"

"Well, there you go again, making unsubstantiated assumptions. What are you, a conspiracy nut? Hey, he's going to live, but he's no spring chicken, so he's not firing on all cylinders—which I'm not sure he himself understands. Sight's shot in one eye, likely temporarily, his hand shakes, and he's having memory challenges. Still, the doctors are amazed at how well he's doing, relatively speaking. He actually goes into the office now a couple of hours a day, but he doesn't get out much except to say Mass in his private chapel. Word is, he's cut back on the sauce, too—which counts as a miracle." Philip wondered what the difference between kill and overkill could possibly mean. "Wait, what kind of message do you think, and are you saying there are impersonal messages?"

Of course there were impersonal messages. Sometimes business dictated that course of action, when you needed to get your point across, with subtle but effective emphasis.

"You close, you and Mackey?"

Philip concluded that changing the subject was becoming an increasingly remote possibility. "He is my superior, the spiritual leader of the diocese."

"So you're saying you don't like the guy."

"He's the boss."

"Man, you really don't like him."

"Excellence had been drinking way too much lately, even by his standards, and he donned no velvet glove when he executed decisions. He had to shove some bad priests out of their pulpits. It got messy, a few times. He's got the finesse of a pastry chef with a chainsaw. He also fired the Caring Street House director, a popular guy the outcast kids respected and who kept the place going on the juice of his charisma. The guy made a few stupid mistakes, so Mackey might have had justification, but he went about it the wrong way. Then, for some reason he goes and takes on the teachers with that ridiculous loyalty oath slash morality clause—which I tried to talk him out of. He wouldn't call it that, he'd call it clarification of Catholic principles, but make no bones about it, that's what it is. I asked him, and he was not pleased, I asked him what problem was he trying to solve. Teachers! The most dedicated people in the world, teachers. I shouldn't be telling you all that, but same time, if I look at it from his perspective, he wasn't on the job to make friends, he was there to save the diocese from imminent financial ruination. Big-league stuff."

"Guy likes to pick fights, like every other jelly-armed thirty-eight or forty."

"You think he's a thirty-eight suit coat? Maybe," said Philip. "You could be right, but he looks more like a plus-forty short and stout to me."

"And with a zero drop at his forty-inch waist. Shaped like a melting stick of butter."

As for fights, Matty Fitzgerald himself was in the thick of the political battle around the bishop's imposition of the morality clause, which identified teachers as ministers and implied weightier moral obligations, according to the bishop. The teachers' cause had been gathering momentum prior to the incident, and now a few weeks afterward, while Mackey's health was on the slow upswing, the movement appeared to be accelerating all over again. Philip was proud of Matty for standing up, not that he would tell him so, but he was also concerned. As a matter of principle, his brother had consistently rejected financial assistance from his father, but if he were one day unceremoniously thrown to the gutter, that resolve might be tested. The bishop probed a bit with Philip, but he wasn't foolish enough to pressure the priest to use his influence to call off his rabble-rousing brother. Mackey may not have been a rocket scientist, but he knew people like the Fitzgeralds were not easy to manage. As for Matty, when he had been subjected to Philip's withering questions, he only stiffened his spine, one thing a Fitzgerald was equipped to do since birth, if not before.

"Mackey ever come after you?"

"No, not really, no. We have our differences, nothing I can't work through."

"Or work *around*?"

Sweets Fitzgerald was supposedly well-known by that moniker—at least that's how reporters referred to him in their articles on rising crime and corruption in the city. In reality, few dared use the name to his face. You had to be stupid or sleeping with him, like Caitlin, who fell into the latter category and who, as Paddy was discovering with each passing day, was much smarter than he initially presumed. The name Sweets was allegedly attributed to the man's legendarily amiable, charming, disarming Irish temperament. The handle was nothing but ironic, which journalists missed, as some invariably do with such subtleties. Like when a guy big as a baby grand is called "Tiny," or the eighth-grade dropout "Genius." Paddy Fitzgerald was only affable up to the point he was provoked, and then left no doubt he was anything but sweet.

When the waiter approached, father and son were holding menus they were pretending to peruse. They needn't have bothered, as they knew the offerings by heart. The entrées and waiters' blue-trimmed white jackets hadn't been updated since before people carried around phones.

"Father? Mr. Fitzgerald?" said the watery-eyed waiter by way of familiarly greeting them. "Ready, gentlemen?"

"Give us a few, would you, Seany?" said Paddy.

The waiter shuffled off arthritically, and Philip wondered what they were waiting for. They always ordered the same dishes. It wouldn't take long before he realized his father had a lot more on his mind.

"You left early from the big bash," said his dad. "Have a secret rendezvous?"

"You're very amusing, Dad. Anybody ever tell you?"

"Actually, no, nobody ever has, they know better."

"Feeling under the weather that night. I think it was food poisoning from lunch at the Thai place, went to bed soon as I could."

"Back to the gala. That Bishop Mackey, what a right idiot, he was like three fucking sheets that night. And that was a noisy demonstration outside. Which was rude. I wanted to tell the peckers all nice to shut the fuck up, show some fucking respect. But I didn't, and you know why. You saw Matty out there, didn't you? I did, too."

"He yelled louder. Free country."

"Anyway, ask me, Mackey'd been two inches from getting whacked for a long time. Jesus, what a piss artist."

"Whenever you slip into your Irish when we're at Noah's, I half-expect a brogue. Even so I wouldn't know about getting whacked, Dad. By the way, how many ways can you Irish say *drunk*?"

"*You Irish*? You forget you're Irish too, Father Fitzgerald, and who's a wiseass now? Look, you can't piss off forever the crazy kind of people he pissed off all day long, I don't care if you're in a Roman collar and wear the funny hat..."

"The mitre."

"And carry the big stick."

"They call it the crozier. Shepherds and bishops use croziers, though sheep don't get herded into churches these days."

"Yeah, and good thing. There are grizzly bears in the pews."

What Paddy knew about inflicting pain upon a man would not be something he would elucidate for anybody else's benefit, including his own son's, but this much was plain: it was a lot harder to do than movies and TV made it appear—not that he was admitting anything because if you took your chances and asked him a direct question, he had nothing to admit. The toughest of tough guys often paid a high price for taking somebody out, no matter how much somebody richly deserved being whacked and how much they got paid to do the honors. Even those most conscienceless of guys would revisit the moment in their nightmares. Or so Paddy Fitzgerald watched dramatized in the movies, which sometimes, rarely, got it right.

Father Philip had learned how to live down—and simultaneously to capitalize upon—the family reputation. In fact, having a supposed mobster boss for a dad seemed to invest him with an air of faintly menacing authority not customarily reserved for a diocesan priest. It worked like a charm getting a table at Noah's, that was for sure. He wasn't a monsignor yet, though that seemed a foregone conclusion, but he had ascended the ranks in the hierarchy, moving from one post to another, from education to communications to, currently, outreach to troubled and runaway youth. Professionally, he had no ceiling. The interim position he now held at Caring Street might have constituted a demotion for the typical priest, but not for Father Philip—he would have campaigned for the job. He was often offered and often declined pastorship of the most affluent and sunny suburban parishes, but since his last parish assignment, which is where he had met Ruth, he had come to prefer other assignments and opportunities, and to revel in his status in the Chancery.

"For the record, we don't go after men of the cloth, even if they're douches, and some of them are, so call me reasonable. I got my own problems."

"Especially when you and the diocese are in bed together, excuse the expression."

"I can do business with anybody, wise guy, long as they're sensible and fair."

"Like when the diocese is thinking about building a new hundred-million-dollar high school on the land you'd like to sell them—"

"At a bargain price. You know how this works. You got price and you got terms. Terms and cash. I was willing to give him terrific terms—take your time paying, I told him."

"And agree to hire your construction company."

"We'd put in a competitive bid, of course, and keep our fingers crossed. Technically, you know, it's not my company, I'm an investor in a privately held corporation. You gotta admit, Philip, it's a beautiful piece of property, nice level land zoned right, and my guys are the best Teamster shop around. Everybody'll be happy, you'll see. The diocese gets good value and nobody's any the worse for wear if I wet my beak, like Italians say."

"They'll likely want to name the institution after you. I can see it now: Saint Paddy's Catholic High School."

"Has a ring. The mascot should be the Irish, like Notre Dame, right? Or what do they call the Saint Monica's, where you went to college?"

"Runnin' Whippets."

"Pretty little dogs, them whippets. And what about where you went after college, what were they called? Great basketball team I made a bundle on back when."

"Georgetown Hoyas, a name nobody understands. It's Greek for…"

"I'm not saying it's gonna be easier raising the rest of the money and building a first-class high school if Mackey was out of the picture."

"But it *is* going to be easier for you with the bishop functioning not quite a hundred percent in the picture."

"Like you and him, him and me, we had our differences. Must be something about us Fitzgeralds."

"As I understand it, His Excellence wants to build on one site, and you want to build on another."

"Hold on, stop right there. He was trying to play me, pretending he liked the other site, which anybody not blind could see was nowhere good as mine. Like I say, minor differences. I'm feeling like the petrale sole almondine, how about you?"

"The site Mackey said he wanted to build on—stop me if I'm wrong— the other site he might have wanted to build on was not a property you happened to own."

"Man, my parcel's a beauty, you're right. Twenty-five acres, pristine, stable earth, pretty much totally out of the flood plain, what's not to like?"

"I hear he preferred the other site, good value. The sole is always good, but it's salmon season, that's what I'm thinking, pesto on the side."

"Like I say, Mackey was negotiating. Trying to, anyway, and good luck, see you in Tipperary. So fucking obvious, excuse my shanty Irish for your delicate ears. He wanted my land, only he wanted to steal it. Pesto's too Italian for my blood, no thanks. You always had a taste for the Italian. Mackey's so-called preference, eight acres, twenty-five-year flood plain, an old public school building that needed major renovation, nothing but headaches. You'd have to rent fields for football and soccer and baseball, and it would take years to get the plan out of zoning—if it ever did. They'd make the diocese build a new highway off-ramp, too, and put in two new stoplights. You know how much all that costs, how long that takes working with the city, county, and state?"

"But it was still a whole lot cheaper up front. Word is you and Mackey went at it behind closed doors. He wasn't going to budge is what I hear."

"He had his own ideas, God bless the bishop, not that he is resting in peace. Some were good ideas, others, not so much. He is stubborn, some might say difficult. Bottom line: you get what you pay for, Philip. Don't the Catholic kids deserve the best? You always liked pesto with the salmon, not my thing, little too bitter, you hanging out with Italians? But take Anthony's wife, I always liked that Francesca, even if she was Italian. She knew how money and cars and the ponies worked, nothing wrong with that."

"Frankie always was terrific."

"Her old man, Mimmo, piece of work. He was a good book back in the day—he took my action, anyway, and paid up on schedule. Word is, he lost the feeling."

Hearing her name gave Philip pause. "You remember I introduced her to Anthony. She preferred him to me—maybe because of that little complication: me about to become a priest. But hell, that's not true. Everybody preferred Anthony. He was a better man than all the rest of us could ever be. She and I fell out of touch, it happens, I didn't take it personally. Now she seems to have a boyfriend she's semi-serious about. You see her at the gala? She's very generous, and she seems to have plenty to invest. Tell the truth, I have missed her, maybe we'll be friends again. She's been getting involved with Caring Street lately, so that'll be good for us."

"You and her have some falling out?"

"Wouldn't say that exactly, life throws unexpected changes your way. I'll always care for her."

"You trying to tell me something?"

"I am. I'm taking a pass on the sole almondine, having the salmon with pesto."

Paddy executed a sharp turn, leaving Philip wondering where this line would lead them both. "Fathers and sons," he announced.

"Irish writers, singing an old song, they cannot get enough of fathers and sons."

"Not that I would know anything about any kind of literature."

"Your dad, my grandfather, you never talk about him. He must cross your mind."

"Not once. Every day. Same thing."

Philip had long ago given up hope of hearing his father wax elegiac about his own father. If there were charming anecdotes about the man, they never ushered forth. "I used to wonder what he must have looked like."

"Like a man tending the furnace in hell or prodding the eternally damned with a pitchfork. Count yourself lucky I burned all the photographs. He made me who I am, son of a bitch that he was." Paddy fell silent, and without further provocation, his mood darkened, a lunar eclipse. "You have no idea what it's like, losing a son you loved." He had blurted the words before he could reconsider. Before he could imagine how they might be heard. But he wouldn't have cared one way or the other.

Philip lunged forward on the table, as if he had been shoved in the back, which in a sense he had been. "That's right, I may never have a son. And you have no idea what it's like to lose a brother you loved." He had sympathy for his father when he wasn't angry with him, or he had both feelings at the same time, like now.

Paddy surged back in his chair, as if he had been slapped, and deserved it, then recovered. "Don't know what came over me, I get ambushed."

"Three years."

"Like yesterday."

—

ABRUPTLY AND WITH LITTLE fanfare, the week after whatever happened with the bishop, the owner of the smaller site pulled his property off the market and the path seemed clear for the diocese to purchase Paddy Fitzgerald's twenty-five pristine acres. Philip's father believed the deal made more sense than ever. Win-win. Negotiations could in theory start up again whenever the bishop was up and running.

"It's a free country, Philip, and the gentleman who owned the pitiable site had a change of heart, so I wish him a long and prosperous life. And I gave the diocese a bargain price, too. Shaved twenty percent off my original asking, though I didn't need to, I had him by the balls. Like the lawyers say at over a thousand bucks an hour, it's all moot now. They should be drawing up a letter of intent, case Mackey ever sees the light in this lifetime."

"Land you've owned since forever, and your original asking price represented, what, a five hundred percent profit?"

"That's what accountants are for. I always liked that piece of property. I enjoyed going there, being by myself, nobody around."

"Should we get some wine?"

"Who knew real estate was going to skyrocket like it has? One day I was going to get polo ponies, wear those funny boots with the tucked-in pants."

"Jodhpurs."

"Look, Philip, they call it real estate. Real. Estate. Like I always say, they don't make too much of that stuff anymore."

It was an old line, but Philip laughed, couldn't help himself. "Yeah, Mackey told me you said that. Which totally pissed him off. That's the generous kind of guy you are, Dad."

"Thanks, *Father*. Besides, you'd think the old bastard would have remembered how I made music for him."

—

BECAUSE HE DID. BEFORE the bishop and Paddy Fitzgerald tangled on the real estate, the diocese never seemed worried in the slightest about the family ties between a mobster—critical to note, an unarrested, unindicted, unconvicted, alleged mobster—and one of the diocese's insider, glamorous priests. Mackey, if anything, was pleased and charmed. Soon after being installed with tremendous fanfare in the cathedral, for instance, the bishop tugged on the sleeve of Philip's father.

"Mind if I call you Paddy?"

"Knock yourself out, Bishop."

"May sound stuffy, Paddy, but bishops are addressed *Excellence*."

"No kidding? No offense, *Excellency*. Say, that was a nice ceremony in the cathedral for you, very spiritually uplifting."

"*Excellence*, and it was, it was indeed. I was moved. It was missing the one thing every great cathedral in a great diocese like ours positively needs. You can help."

Mackey spelled out what that need was: a new pipe organ. The old one was sad and often out of commission, for all practical purposes on its last legs. Paddy Fitzgerald would indeed help. Twenty-four hours and a pledge of a half-million dollars later, the bishop's—His Excellence's—prayer was answered, with the divine intercession of a Fitzgerald.

Philip wasn't that concerned about the affiliation, either. He was untainted, at least when it came to his connections to the family business. At the same time, he was wondering if and when the other shoe would drop—if there was another shoe—and who was wearing it.

—

"DAD, ABOUT THE PROPOSED high school site, you're not concerned about appearances?"

"We had the property assessed, good price I offered, like I said. I gotta work, so no wine for me, but order a glass if you want."

"Could be seen as an insider deal."

"Tell me one good deal that isn't an insider deal. If you don't have a conflict, you're not worth doing business with in the first place. You of all people should know that. And appearances, least of my problems. Me, I got the DA up my ass all day long for twenty years, I ain't worried about nothing, my big Irish nose is clean. And my Jewish lawyers like to steal the Mick Catholic prosecutors' lunch. How come district attorneys are all Irish Catholic in this town, can you tell me that? God, I'm glad Anthony never tried out for the wrong team, the prosecutors." The reality was Paddy Fitzgerald had over the years summarily taken care of all his rivals, encouraging them to engage in other enterprises, someplace far away. One by one they departed, never to be heard from again. Nothing the Irish Catholic DA could pin on him, of course.

"All this news comes as great big relief for your son, who is a simple man of the cloth."

"Where did I go wrong? One son a priest, another an egghead teacher, a daughter who likes girls, lives I think on a farm, calls herself vegan. I always thought you'd be the lawyer in the family, every Irish family needs to have one, and not Anthony. If anything, he should've been the priest, not you."

Philip didn't argue, it made sense, not that he had ever consciously conceived of such a vocation for Anthony, which in and of itself surprised him. Because Father Anthony seemed eminently plausible. Only after a few seconds did he register the knife his father had inserted in his back. Expert assassins deliver the fatal blow the way Paddy had, before the mark sees it coming.

Philip took mental notes of this moment, and this whole lunch, and he knew why. It was for the purposes of ultimately crafting the old man's eulogy he would someday deliver at his funeral high Mass, where that magnificent pipe organ would enrapture the cathedral up to the rafters. That would have sounded heartless had it been expressed out loud, but it didn't make it less true.

"And the Colleen vegan thing, which, what does that mean anyway?"

"For starters, like Mom found out, rest in peace, it means you can forget Hilda cooking corned beef for Sunday supper."

"Like Colleen'd ever come to the Family Fitzgerald house to eat dinner, she's so busy protesting against police brutality—which, have to say, makes her old man proud. But Philip. Tell me something. When you going to be a bishop? I mean, Mackey moseys on down the primrose lane and there's an opening. And that big petition that's circulating, to give him the boot, does the trick."

That wasn't how it worked. "First, the Church won't respond to public pressure or protests about Mackey. Or if they are so inclined to shuttle him off, they'll make sure nobody knows it. Second, the pope personally appoints bishops. Third, they don't place new bishops in their hometown. And fourth, I won't ever be a bishop—I'm not their kind of guy." Philip may have been largely correct. Yes, the pope made the final call from Rome, but in practice, he relied upon a country's cardinals and archbishops for input. No bishop would be appointed without their going to bat for a candidate. As a result, the process was more Byzantine, and political, than the Holy See's on-high administration, and that meant bishops were beholden to somebody else besides the pontiff on his throne in the Vatican. "Funny thing, Dad, Mackey himself the other day made some offhand crack about my being a bishop someday."

"See what I'm talking about? A groundswell of support for you builds. And he's thinking you would protect and extend the piss artist's legacy."

"Yeah, well, that's not gonna happen."

"I'll have my associates at the Vatican Bank put in a good word. They can be persuasive."

"I'm sure they can, but no thanks, and if you have incriminating information having to do with the Vatican and all the scandals, I don't want to hear about it."

"Fair enough, boyo. I have a question. You happy, Philip?" His dad was making breathtaking transitions, swinging for the fences today.

Philip was struck dumb. His father had never exhibited such curiosity before.

"Happy. I asked if you were happy. That such a strange question?"

When he found his voice again, he said, "From you, kind of."

"Put it this way. Ever want a pretty wife, kids, your own brood, my grandkids?"

"Moving fast, you're making me dizzy, Pops. First I'm a wheeling dealing bishop, then a dad taking his kids to the park."

"I'm not getting any younger, could use some Fitzgerald rug rats. I'm so old, I say whatever I want whenever I want."

"Like that's a new development? Okay, what the heck, I'll play along. Sure, the notion occurs, not so much as it used to when I was a young man in the seminary. But that train left the station a long, long time ago, not long after you and mom dropped me off at the seminary."

"Never forget, your mother of sainted memory cried all the way home. Stayed in bed a week."

Philip was genuinely sorry to be reminded.

"Your sister, she fancies the girls. I hear lesbians can somehow have babies now, but she seems to have one new girlfriend after another. Guess the only one who's got a real chance of giving me grandkids to spoil someday is your egghead brother, Little Matty. If his ball-busting wife ever lets him take his dick out to play."

Philip grimaced and leaned across the table to embody his unease. "Dad, we're in public. People see I'm a priest. But yeah, Little Matty is thirty-nine and in no evident haste to reproduce, continue the family line. Don't forget his wife is still early thirties." He didn't mention that he heard Matty and Claire were on the outs, that it looked like they might split up. "Not tracking all your switches, Dad, but I love Matty and Colleen, you love Matty and Colleen if not Claire. Where you going with this?"

"You I understand, Philip. You're just like me. Matty talks like a high school teacher."

"Which he is, so that's kind of to be expected. But how am I like you?"

"It's obvious. And then Colleen. I've always treated Colly right, with respect, haven't I? I have an open mind. I got guys in my crew—it's not like the old days—I got guys who, you know, swing that way. I got my black Irish crew chief. They perform, lissename, hotshot, I got no problem."

"This is a first. You want to ask me if I'm gay and if I have some sort of sex life, Pops, excuse the expression?"

"Excusing a lot of expressions today, Philip. You want to tell me?"

"Because I took a vow of celibacy doesn't mean I'm gay. And in case you missed this, I am a Roman Catholic priest, and until the Church changes the rules, which they won't in our lifetime, there'll be no married clergy in America—though married priests are all over the landscape in Italy and South America, and the Church looks the other way."

"Not talking about marriage."

"Very sophisticated distinction, Dad, you know that? You can be heterosexual or homosexual or bisexual, for that matter, if there is such a thing as bisexual, which some malpracticing evangelist psychologizer somewhere may doubt, but you're forbidden to act on those desires."

"So you have those type desires?"

"You're not going to let this go, are you?"

"You're still young enough. And you take after your mother, which might account for you being the best-looking padre in town. It's not too late to begin a family, Philip."

"You have no idea."

"I know more than you think I do."

"Speaking of—what did you call it, such *desires*? You socializing with anybody these days?"

"You're being coy. You implying you want to know if I am seeing somebody?"

"No, I was asking you straight up. Don't expect you to tell me."

"Nobody'll ever take your mother of sainted memory's place. My age, I don't need a ball and chain."

"Matty thinks you're dating."

"That's because your puffin brother bumped into me outside a restaurant one night with a pretty skirt, nothing but an acquaintance of the female persuasion."

"She's a dish, he said, and—how old is she?"

"I'll have to look at her baptismal certificate someday. Man, your brother has some kind of fantasy life. Me, I don't operate under no illusions."

"Tell me something I don't know. Nobody ever called you dumb."

"They never called me Sweets either, unless I was okay with that, which basically I ain't. So lemme ask. You got an idea? Who you think busted up the bishop?"

"If Mackey was assaulted, *if*, cops don't have any suspects, at least any they want to talk about. And Mackey doesn't clearly remember that night, so he's no help. Of course, he could also come around someday and remember everything. For the cops, in an investigation like this, the person they always like first is somebody connected to the spouse, or is the spouse."

"Yeah, being that the guy was kind of married to the Church, that means there's a lot of suspects."

"Who do *you* think? Who would want to hurt the guy and why?"

"First of all, whoever did it was no pro, a professional would've finished him off, instead of leaving him like that, all fucked up..."

"Damn, Pops, again? We're in public. *I'm* in public."

"And maybe leaving a potential witness, too. Of course, the guy might have thought he had killed him because the guy was possibly also a dumb mook."

"So not a pro, then who?"

"Or he was a pro and wanted to leave the impression he wasn't. Maybe he was pretty cute. Mackey brought a shitstorm down on those priests who were guilty, and he may have covered up for some of those molester fucking priests, for reasons we'll never know. Then again, those molester sons of bitches who are hiding in the woodwork might feel a little bit vulnerable themselves. And Mackey kicked the skunk when he rammed that contract down the teachers' throats like a fucking Teamster boss. Saint Paddy's High School should have the best teachers, like your brother Matty. I don't care what teachers do in their fucking private lives, how about you?"

"You can't curb your tongue, can you? Well, those are the places where I imagine the cops are going in their investigation. But you know, for the record, Mackey has plenty of faults, but he was fair when it came to financial settlements with survivors in the lawsuits."

"Exactly, another thing. All that money flying out the window to pay off lawsuits, including some of my hard-earned cash. In my book, it all adds up to him being a problem for some nasty son of a bitch. Problem men naturally get what they got coming."

"Good bet, but don't all enforcers feel that way?"

"Yeah, and you know what else? Even the ones they take out of their misery. It's a big relief when they turn out the lights, the party's over."

"That's beautiful, Pops. Touching up somebody as a public service."

"You sure you know what you want?"

Philip hesitated, irritated that he had heard yet another crazy question about his personal life, but his father filled in.

"To eat, Philip. What do you want to eat? Seany's got Maine Lobster on special."

"I'll stick with salmon."

"Me, too, sole. Two peas in a pod, both set in our ways, aren't we?"

"Hope you're not right, fuck."

"We're in public, Father Philip, watch your tongue, you're a priest for Christ's sake. Hey, another thing, you know if Matty's going to keep his job? Did he sign that contract?"

"He didn't sign, he was adamant. Matty's got some big balls but he'll be adamantly unemployed with his principled testicles. I admire his integrity, but I tried to talk him into signing, just go along for now, let it all play out."

"Unless you can talk some sense into Mackey and take care of your little brother, who's going to give me a grandson?"

"If Mackey is ever lucid again, I will give it a shot. After all, one day they might name the place Bishop Mackey High School."

"Fat chance that, if I have any clout. I'd like my boy to teach at Saint Paddy's Catholic, a name which I am liking more all the time. Now that I think about it, I won't sell the diocese the land after all—unless Mackey drops the teacher contract demands. If Mackey wants the new school, he needs to pick his battles and get his shit together."

"You wouldn't hold up a sale, and turn down all those bucks, would you, Pops?"

"Try me. Matty's my boy, and it's my land, and now that I think about it, I'll shave the price a little bit more, maybe a lot more, to whet his appetite.

It's only money. I'm too old to be fucking around and way too old to be fucked with by a too-big-for-his-britches cleric. He needs me more than he knows. Listen and learn, Father Philip, that's the key to forging a good deal. When you know something the buyer doesn't: that he needs you more than he is willing to admit to himself." Paddy wasn't too proud to acknowledge to himself that he was working his own son.

Philip saw through him, as usual. He was processing the new information. He would have something to negotiate with the bishop, after all. It would have to be done subtly, he couldn't strong-arm Mackey, especially Mackey in a somewhat debilitated state. The bishop would have to think this was his bright, peacemaking idea, and his father would have to think he got one over on the diocese. This would require the fullest application of Philip's artfulness. It might possibly bring him back into conversation with Frankie, too, which he sorely missed. Evidently, the first thing Mackey did upon coming back into his office was call her. She was ready to head the capital campaign, and she and Philip could talk again—in theory at least.

"Coming up with a new plan always makes me hungry," said Paddy, "let's eat."

—

SEANY LUMBERED OFF WITH the lunch order into the back kitchen, and a moment later, as if he were lying in the weeds, Jonesy O'Dell turned up. That doesn't capture his mode of reincarnation. His was the sort of presence that purely materialized, displacing the air, as if he never quite arrived, but was already there before you were conscious of him, like a bird on the windowsill, like a migraine after you found yourself, blackout shades pulled down, in bed. He had worked for Paddy for as long as Philip could remember, and he was there to reinforce Paddy's positions, to underscore his preferences. He was also there to drive the car and accompany and assist him in whatever way deemed necessary, before Paddy was conscious of what he needed. Therefore, indispensable as he was, he might have been called his right-hand man, except that the term could have registered off-key, considering that his right hand was mangled, bent back at the wrist, fingers permanently curled. No transfixing backstory related to the appendage was spun pertaining, say, to a tragic industrial mishap or to a heroic deed in military combat, at least one Philip ever heard. Maybe Paddy knew the facts, or the condition was congenital, and if O'Dell had information to impart, he did not have any Facebook friends with whom to share it. O'Dell's disfigured hand frightened small children who unhappily crossed his path, and among adults he was infamous for his downbeat demeanor and ferocious eloquence and natty suits, which never appeared susceptible to the threat of a wrinkle. Notwithstanding his appearance, he never considered himself disabled, and no one regarded him that way, because he wasn't limited in any domestic or professional regard. He had no difficulty doing whatever was physically required—pouring the Irish on the zinc bar, driving the getaway car, lifting boulders out of the way, physically encouraging someone to come to Jesus or, if not to Jesus, to Jonesy. His boyish face made him look twenty years younger than he was and he looked immune to breaking a sweat, and so he appeared despite the detectible limp, allegedly the byproduct of a disagreement that could not be settled by means that were civil. He stood out among Paddy's crew, which he ruthlessly captained, because none dressed half as elegantly as he, and all the rest of them were white. O'Dell leaned down to whisper in his boss's ear.

"It was like roller skating in the ice rink to track his slippery derrière," Philip overheard Jonesy.

"You're very good," said Paddy, clearly pleased to praise.

"Mr. Fitzgerald, that's nothing other than scurrilous buzz talk advanced by diverse louts and roustabouts regarding this humble and obedient servant, yours truly."

"When I'm done having lunch with my son, then," Paddy told O'Dell, and that was it, leaving out precisely how the matter, whatever it may have been, was something that they would take care of in due course.

His man nodded and addressed Paddy's son with his characteristic sham deference.

"Father Fitzgerald, how are you this fine day?" he said, as if it were his regrettable duty and distasteful obligation to say as much, and for all intents and purposes, it was.

"Thank you for inquiring, Jonesy." The priest sipped ice water and did not answer the question. Here he made direct eye contact with O'Dell and didn't bother to fake deference.

But Jonesy relished every chance to poke the priest's puffed-out chest—passive aggressively, as he was well aware of his ranking in Fitzgerald social hierarchy. "This Sunday's Gospel reading's a favorite of mine, Father."

"I never see you at Mass, Jonesy, but miraculously, you're always up on the Scriptures."

"Matthew 22, as you may remember. Many are called, few are chosen. Jesus, he speaks in parables."

"Yes, verse twelve," Philip noted.

"Verse fourteen, you mean, and the parable concerns a man who tries to crash a wedding party, and that's where the many-are-called-few-are-chosen wisecrack comes into play, though it's sometimes made an object of fun by iconoclasts and pissant doubters, as in *Many are cold, few are frozen*. In any case, that's when the king, who is hosting the wedding party, regally and righteously denies admission into the big bash to somebody who was undeserving. Some guests are unworthy, don't you know. You see, it is what we humble Irish students of the Bible call a parable, Father Fitzgerald."

"I've noticed you yourself often attempt to speak in parables, Jonesy. Like Jesus Himself."

"Our Lord and Savior died on a cross that we all might live, a rumor you may have heard. And I'm sure you agree that Semitic Jesus was black. Just like me."

"He was certainly blacker than somebody white like me. But black like you? Biblical scholars, with the exception of Jonesy O'Dell, might regard that notion with skepticism."

"So you're agreeing with me, he's more along my spectrum, Black Irish." And then he turned to Paddy and deferentially declared, "With your permission, I think my work here is done, Mr. Fitzgerald."

Jonesy and Father Philip didn't shake left hands marking their farewells to each other, and they wordlessly communicated they wouldn't wish to do so if the ceremonial last-ditch prospect presented itself on an otherwise deserted island to which they had both been exiled. Philip didn't trust the man and didn't approve the access to his father, and the sentiment was reciprocated. It was a matter of chemistry, which made everything possible. Chemistry accounts for falling in love and for cooking a great meal. And also for bombs.

—

PADDY HAD A POKER face, and was proud of it, too proud. Perhaps another man couldn't tell if his father was rocking four aces or bluffing with nothing but pig slop in his hand, but his son had the sense that he was on the make for the only card necessary to achieve an inside straight. Hard to earn a living banking on a draw like that. As everybody knows, you have to play the cards you've been dealt. Anybody can play a royal flush. It takes a poker player to make something out of nothing. That is, Philip suspected Jonesy had highlighted for his dad a complex if not challenging opportunity, one which he had not quite anticipated. If so, that would have been a surefire way to stimulate his appetite, and to enhance the prospect of petrale sole for a man for whom disappointment was never on any day's menu. Unpredictable opportunities, if not problems, seemed to be presenting themselves for all men named Fitzgerald.

Once O'Dell dematerialized, they returned their attention to the wine list, where Philip identified what he declared to be an excellent Sancerre. It would perfectly complement their entrees.

In a minute, Seany popped the bottle and poured the chilled, straw-colored wine. Paddy was not overly fond of the grape, and certainly not the white varieties in general, but how could he not graciously accede to the wishes of his son? And yet, he also wondered how he managed to raise a boy who actually ordered white wine. Such inclination exhibited in others, that is, non-Fitzgeralds, amounted to a character flaw. Where else had he gone wrong with his boys?

"*Sláinte*, Father Philip." They clinked glasses.

"Your health, too, Pops."

Chapter Fifteen
Brendan

GALA NIGHT, WHILE THE bishop was slapping backs and shaking hands and tugging sleeves and sipping the last martinis he would ever have in his life, his driver slipped into The Emerald Green for a couple of pops. This was not a first for him. He routinely repaired to a bar when he had a long wait ahead and hours to kill. Perched on a barstool, he would await the call to return and pick up His Excellence and drive him home at the end of the festivities—and until then he would tune his own internal strings. Brendan was proud of his ability to hold his liquor, and if he was slightly impaired, legally speaking, it never showed. The bishop's suspicions never arose for obvious reasons: blind driving the blind. A couple of hours into this evening, in the general swell of humanity, while the party raged in full swing across town, Brendan headed into the tavern's men's room. He did not walk out.

Fast forward several hours.

Around closing time, a patron reported to the bartender that something was amiss: a man was unconscious and sprawled on the floor inside a bathroom stall. That was Brendan, and soon he was being jostled awake, afflicted by the biggest, acidy-toilet-disinfectant-laced headache he'd ever known, with no recollection of what had happened. He looked for a clock, nonexistent in the men's room, and realized that he had certainly lost his job—as well as his watch. Along with his cell phone, and his wallet, and the cash in his money clip—and the limo keys. When he got to his feet and rushed outside, the car was nowhere in sight. He called the police on the Emerald Green's phone, and they arrived a casual hour later. The uniform wanted to know if he needed a hospital, but Brendan said no. The cop was considerate enough to drive him to his apartment, where he took to his bed. Of course, he had no idea of what had transpired with the bishop. He had to assume that Mackey got home somehow, and that he would get fired first thing in the morning.

"The bar was crowded," Brendan told the detectives the next afternoon in the interrogation room. "Don't remember much." He had dressed in coat and tie for the interview today, he couldn't tell you what prompted him to do so, but it may have seemed right, respectful. He was the sort of man whose clothes seem to have been borrowed from somebody else, in his case borrowed from a larger man, a roommate and off-and-on partner. Being nervous about what awaited him at the police station, Brendan had shaved a little too energetically and his neck was nicked. If pressed, he might have said he wanted to present himself in the most flattering light possible for the authorities.

"How many drinks you throw down?"

"One or two."

"One or two?"

"Or three." Brendan had to figure the detectives knew how many. He certainly didn't.

"Drinking with anybody special?"

"So many people, you know the Green is packed every night, college kids to truck-drivers to lawyers—to cops. But I drink by myself, watch the game. No use bringing anybody else down."

"Who won?"

"Won what?"

"Game you were watching. Who won?"

"I don't recall. Yes, I do, it was the Cubs and somebody else, so Cubbies won."

"Good game?"

"I don't follow baseball, I'm a baskets guy, the Bulls."

"You from Chi town?"

"From lots of towns."

"How long you been off the wagon?"

"Not long. I'm not proud of it, but there it is. Sobriety and me didn't mix."

"You were going to lose your job if the diocese found out you're drinking, correct?"

"Not that Mackey would ever notice, being, you know, himself."

"Sounds like you may have hard feelings about the bishop."

"I don't expect I have a job anymore, if that's what you're asking."

"You have any issues with His Holiness?"

"His Holiness means the pope. His Excellence is Mackey, and not really."

"I'll remember when I'm at Saint Peter's Cathedral, thanks. But you and Mackey, you had issues?"

"Tough man to please, to tell the truth. Time to time, he barked about one thing or another, driving too slow, driving too fast, you know. Hard job, I guess, being the bishop. Man, I can't believe what happened to the old guy."

"What happened to him?"

"What I read in the morning paper."

"You didn't call to check on the bishop."

"Way I figured it, nobody'd take my call. Am I right?"

"Got any plans to take a trip?"

"Not that I'm aware of."

"If you win a vacation, turn it down. We'll talk again."

"That it?"

"What're you expecting? A blue ribbon?"

"What about me? You looking for the guy who did this to me?"

"It's a guy?"

"I don't know who he is, but he could have killed me. You got a suspect?"

"Don't wander off, Brendan. One last thing. You like boys?"

"I don't have kids."

"I know that. I'm asking you if you like boys."

"Where's this coming from?"

"So I guess we should assume you like younger boys."

"Wait a second. You talking about that kinda shit? Hold on. No way, not me."

"But you're curious, right?"

"The fuck that have to do with child molesting?"

"Your anger issues, Brendan. You working on that?"

"You gonna arrest me for getting beat up? And if you're not, I gotta go and look for another job."

"Let us know if you need a reference."

—

"You worked that night behind the bar, Kenny?" The bartender was next in line for the interrogation room.

"Yes, sir."

"You always serve underage kids?"

Kenny did not, not intentionally he would have said, though he didn't card as strictly as he should have, so silence was probably his best refuge.

"On the video we can see somebody looks pretty much like a teenager who doesn't shave with a shot glass." He showed Kenny a photo and asked if he knew him.

He did, unfortunately. What he didn't know was that the Emerald Green surveillance cameras were in operation that night, only because the new manager was sucking up to ownership, something the former manager failed to do, which is why he was the former manager. They had installed the cameras in the first place on account of all the bar fights, and because the bartenders had adopted a cavalier attitude with regard to collecting for every single drink.

"Oh, that's the kid they hire time to time, cleanup, but I didn't see him that night. Somebody else must've served him. Street kid, I think, forget his name. Comes and goes, shows when he needs some cash, I guess."

"Kid set up shop, doing business in the men's room?"

"Wrong type bar for that, wrong part of town."

"What type bar is it?"

"What, you from Mars? Kind of place people drink like it's their profession."

"Emerald Green, original name. How long they take to come up with that? Sweets Fitzgerald, he's the owner, right?"

"Man, I seen that dude's picture in the paper, once or twice, and I wouldn't fuck with him no way, but he ain't the boss."

"Sure about that?"

"He don't sign my payroll checks."

They showed him a picture of Brendan, the driver.

"Wild Turkey, beer back, so-so tip, not a big yapper. Except on his cell phone a lot. Turned around and he was gone. We found him closing time in the head, at first looking like he was stupidly sleeping one off there, but then, well, you know better than me."

"Tell us about the street kid." It was somebody with shoulder-length thick blond hair, lots of metal in his ears, nose, and mouth, ink up and down his arms. They tracked him on camera easily because he stood out, being so young, and obviously out of place, as he came through the front door, stood behind Brendan for a minute and tapped him on the shoulder. A minute later Brendan headed for the men's room, and was followed by the street kid. Twenty minutes later, they believed they could make out Metallica boy leaving the bar through the front door, but he was hard to pinpoint in the inebriated crush at the Emerald Green. "Anything else you remember, Kenny?"

"I remember the guy we found in the john met up earlier with somebody else, seemed like friends."

"This guy?" They showed him a photo of somebody who would turn out to be Hector Alessandro.

"That's the guy. I think something went south between those two, because the Brendan guy and the other guy went at it pretty good, somebody got all worked up, and then the other guy huffed and puffed out and Brendan stayed, to do some serious crying in his beer. If I didn't know better, somebody got broken up with. Not that it's any of a man's business."

Chapter Sixteen
Baxter

After the lengthy, alternately leisurely and combative Fitzgerald father-*Father* lunch at Noah's Boat House, Jonesy O'Dell chauffeured his boss up the once-upon-a-time fabled circular drive entrance of the now-faded glory that was the Delsey so-called Grand Hotel. Paddy was regretting his son's French wine, though it was not too bad, he supposed, but he couldn't drink the way he once could and not pay a price, and certainly not midday. Still, the wine intake maybe powered him into the right receptive frame of mind to pay a visit at the old ghost town of a hotel. Equipped with Jonesy's intel, he should finish what had been started with Caitlin. His personal motto—he had no personal motto, but if he did: When tough decisions beckon, take the pain now. Or dish some out.

The Old Dell, as it was nostalgically nicknamed, used to be the premier social destination in town, but it had seen much, much better days, long, long ago. A lot like me, Paddy thought, almost amusing himself. The façade cried out for restoration, and the parched plants along the driveway strip begged for irrigation. The hotel insignia banner on the flagpole looked flustered if not distraught, fluttering somewhere between full- and half-staff, as if they were in officially noncommittal mourning. And somebody should wash the windows for Christ's sake, what a terrible first appearance for prospective clientele. Paddy wondered when they were finally going to put the joint up for sale, or throw in the towel and transform the whole place into high-priced condos. The chains were slaughtering the standalone hotels, here and everywhere. If he ever bought the place, he would import a tony restaurant, add a club to bring in the kids, then revitalize the spa to attract the moneyed, trust-fund-baby, Botoxed set. It would take a serious investment, but he had a hunch the hospitality industry had a future in town if somebody knew how to update a washed-out boutique operation like the Dell. Not that he truly cared to save the business; he was merely indulging himself in a thought exercise.

"Mr. Fitzgerald, if I may. What kind of farcical stage name is that," said Jonesy. "*Baxter*? I am already predisposed not to countenance the mope."

"You're not going camping with him or sharing a toothbrush, so not to worry your pretty little head. And I don't know what kind of name, it's the guy's name," said Paddy, not defending the mope. "Everybody gets one, Jonesy, a name, and you yourself have two of them." He was relieved that Jonesy O'Dell wasn't yet making immaterial associations between his own last name and the Old Dell Not So Grand and going off on one of his extended riffs.

Yes, the second glass of Sancerre might have been ill-advised.

"That the mystery guest of honor over there?" Jonesy asked and Paddy in the back seat confirmed it might be. "I'm guessing he's a forty suit coat, you agree?"

"Forty, looks like forty-two tops, but yes."

There was only one parking valet working, so business must be lagging. Paddy slumped, repairing himself out of sight behind smoky tinted windows, in the back seat of the Mercedes S. Circumstances did not demand anyone assume a dignified posture. When the car came to a halt, Baxter lazily circled around and approached the driver's retracted window and leaned down close enough for Jonesy to be offended by the guy's drugstore cologne.

"Hey, sport, nice wheels, welcome to the Delsey Grand, staying with us?" A handsome blond, slim-shouldered fellow was Baxter: chiseled features, unfortunate ponytail, big white teeth—someone who effortlessly conveyed the impression he was only temporarily parking cars while counting the hours till the higher-ups realized the potential of a man like him and snapped him up, bless him with a new suit and an office and a fat expense account so he and his hundred-buck haircut could strut their stuff.

"Wish we could accept the offer of hospitality, but this will be a quick little come to Jesus. *Sport.*"

Baxter was confused by that weird statement, and more confused when Jonesy hopped out and looked him up and down. Engine running, the valet got behind the wheel. The valet was startled when Jonesy reentered the car on the passenger side.

"Shut the fuck up, and drive, got it, *sport?*"

Baxter obeyed when Jonesy flashed the gun holstered inside his suit coat. Then he realized there was a passenger who raised his head in the back.

"Don't do anything stupid, Baxter," said Paddy. "Though stupid wouldn't be a first, according to the reputation that precedes you."

"Do I know you, sport? I don't think so."

"Drive, Forty," said Jonesy.

"What's that mean, *forty?*"

"Suit jacket size, moron."

"Shows how much you know, thinking I got a suit."

"Fucking drive."

The Forty guided the car into an alley a few blocks away. You could almost see the wheels turning in Baxter's head as he contemplated drastic but doomed escape maneuvers.

"Switch off the engine and keep looking straight ahead."

"They're going to miss me, I'm gone too long."

"Nobody'll ever miss you, you're dreaming. They'll think you stole a car." Jonesy was irritated but curious, too. "Hey, Forty, what kind of fruitcake name is Baxter?"

"I don't know, never crossed my mind, it's my goddamn name, blame my parents, I do all the time. What's your name?"

"Captain Hook, laddie boy Baxter, with your shoulders small and slight."

Paddy occasionally forgot Hook was the ring name his man boxed under before being recruited into his crew. So signing up with Paddy was a natural career transition for a southpaw heavyweight scrapper whose right arm was not once raised in victory by a referee. When Jonesy took to the ring, Paddy was impressed by the man's capacity to take a punch and his willingness to go toe to toe with his opponent despite not being in possession of sophisticated pugilistic skills, what with one maimed hand jammed in his twisted left glove.

"Okay, I know what this is about. I'm gonna square you guys up soon."

Paddy spoke up. "Who am I, you think?"

Jonesy tried to help: "It's the number one philosophical question, Baxter, *who am I?* The ontological first question, right before *why shouldn't we commit suicide, get it all over with?* That's what the French philosopher Camus wanted to know, something all of us at some point, especially somebody like you"—he turned toward Baxter to dramatize the point—"are inevitably invited to contemplate."

Paddy liked it when Jonesy rhapsodized like that, usually anyway. "I had some good French wine with lunch, tasty stuff. I wish I had passed."

Baxter was not faring so well. "Is it my turn to speak?"

"I must insist," said Paddy.

"Just guessing who you are. You're my broker."

"Oh, he favors the cutey boy," said Jonesy, who proceeded to backhand smack him in the face, not easy to do considering the contortions called for in order to deliver the left-fisted blow. "Don't look at me or him again."

Baxter spit up a little blood onto his shirt. "You hit like a fucking billy club, okay okay okay? What the fuck you want?"

"How much you owe?" asked Paddy.

"A nickel."

Another punch, courtesy of Jonesy.

"Jesus Christ, stop, okay! What the fuck happened to your hand, Captain Hook?"

"What are we, mates? Shark bite. Dead shark. Start spilling, *sport.*"

"A dime, okay? A fucking grand, and stop punching me. Bears should have covered against the Niners and I wouldn't owe nobody nothing."

"Let me help you out," said Paddy, and he peeled off twenty hundred-dollar bills and tossed them over Baxter's shoulder, where they fluttered down onto his lap.

"Who I gotta kill?"

"Fucking comedian," said Jonesy, putting him on what was intended to be final notice. "Never forget for a minute, nobody likes comedians."

"Oh, you? You're not killing nobody today," said Paddy, "but I tell you what you're going to do. First, give my gentleman associate your cell phone."

"What gentleman associate? All I see is this prick over here."

Jonesy laughed. "Good one, Baxter—which is a wanker's name."

But then he did hand over the phone and Jonesy slipped it into his jacket pocket.

"What's your password?"

"Ready? Let me spell it out. F-U-C-K-Y-O-U-two. That's the number two."

Jonesy was amused again. "Funny man, we'll put that on your tombstone."

"You lost your phone privileges," Paddy said, "but tell you what. Here's a few more bucks, buy yourself a new phone and get a new number, 'cause you misplaced your phone. We'll know right away if you keep your old number, and you won't be happy. And another thing." He peeled off twenty more hundreds. "You got a plane to catch, I don't care where, as long as you get on board one today."

Jonesy weighed in: "A land far, far away, like one where you can hop on a dromedary or camel and travel far into the distance, so consider the vast desert climes of the exotic Middle East."

Baxter was muddled. "The fuck's a dromedary?"

"One hump," said Jonesy, "camel's got two. Could be the other way around, I forget. But the hump and/or humps contain tremendous stores of fat that enable the spitfire beast of burden to go for practically forever without watery sustenance. There are no Irish dromedaries, in case you were wondering. As it goes in Jeremiah 2, 'You are a swift dromedary traversing her swift ways.' One hump should do the trick for you. Unless, of course, you require two."

"What kinda guy don't like a good hump now and then," he said, amusing himself.

"What'd I say about comedians?" said Jonesy after punching him.

Baxter didn't know how this could be remotely possible, but he remarked that he was now even more confused.

"Confusion's a good point of debarkation for you," said Paddy, "but my associate does produce that destabilizing effect. So leave your valet jacket and start walking away from the hotel, and your whole brainless life here. Because you see, it's your lucky day, I'm feeling generous." Another thousand bucks. "Here's what you're not going to do ever again. You're going to not call Caitlin, am I being clear? Which would be hard anyway, since her number's changed already."

Jonesy added. "All is changed, changed utterly, a terrible Baxter is born, to quote the great Irish bard, Yeats. And I will smite you, says the Lord, with my mighty hand."

"I'm going to regret asking. You will *what* me?"

For Baxter, a first: he was correct. Jonesy was happy to demonstrate what *smite* meant: a quick backhand snap to the bridge of the nose. Then he handed him a beautiful linen pocket square from his jacket, which in swift order turned crimson. "Tilt your head back, chin up," he recommended; no point staining the car seat.

Paddy resumed, getting back on track: "But if by some chance you should find yourself a mysterious stranger in town once again, trust me, I will hear about it, and you will find yourself extremely disoriented. And if by some miracle you should ever pass her by on some street in some other part of the world, you will keep walking—better yet, start sprinting in the opposite direction."

"Shoulda known, you're the new guy."

Jonesy punched him twice, *thwack thwack*, in the rib cage. In case in all the excitement the man had forgotten who was sitting there and what was the nature of his predicament.

"I think you broke a fucking rib."

"Yes, the new guy, which means," Paddy said, "you should know you'd be the unhappy former guy."

"Got it, sir." He couldn't endure one more punch. It's like the cartoons depict. You really do see stars.

"That's better. Any questions?"

"She's a good girl," said Baxter, "so you know, never meant any harm, just needed the bucks."

"That's not a question, keep talking, might make you disappear, to be sure."

"Don't worry about me."

"I don't worry, that's what other people do around me. Let us help you out. New plan. Drive to the airport."

"You going to whack me?"

"I gave you money, what sense would it make if I killed you? That would be cruel, right? And Captain Hook will underline the point, if necessary. But if you keep talking, might seem like the right thing to do. Drive. And don't make me regret not killing you. As I say, play your cards right, this could be your lucky day, think of it that way."

"You know, always wanted to go to California."

"Nice weather."

"But no dromedaries, I'm guessing, whatever the fuck they are. Where should I go, you think?"

Jonesy said to Mr. Fitzgerald, "Now he thinks I'm the nearly departed's travel agent—sir, are there still travel agents?"

—

BAXTER DROVE TO THE airport, the car silent as a funeral cortege. He did pipe up at one point. He had to get something off his chest.

"Just so you know, Cait's a good girl."

Jonesy reminded him if he didn't shut the fuck up he was going to really hurt him.

"No, that's all right," said Paddy. "Talk, Baxter, it's all right, it'll be good for your mortal soul. Only look straight ahead, not in the rearview mirror."

"She deserves somebody to treat her good. You better be good to her, go ahead smack me around, if you want, I don't fucking care, you'd have killed me already if you were planning. She actually told me she loved you. I hope she's right because she deserves somebody loving her back. Me taking off means zippo because me staying here meant nada to her. She's too smart for me, might be too smart for you, I don't care who you are."

Paddy thought that, for an idiot, the man was making some sense.

Jonesy noted the remarkable change in the unfortunately named former valet. "I feared he was about to swoon, and swooning and driving, not a good formulary."

"That's a funny term, *swoon*," said Paddy, enjoying giving voice to it.

"Yes, it's my OED word of the day, to *swoon*. Fascinating etymology, much favored by poets, you know, Keats and Tennyson and Yeats and the rest of the frilly-shirtfront brood."

"Swoon," mouthed Paddy pleasurably once more. "Very Irish, sounds like."

"Maybe so. *Still, still to hear her tender-taken breath, and so live ever or else swoon to death.* That would be Keats, or that's Yeats, camel or dromedary, if you will. If you're going to barrel off into the sunset, swooning's as good a way as any."

It took a while, but they reached the airport departures terminal drop-off.

"Any other last words of advice for your legacy keepers?" Paddy asked Baxter.

"Yes," said Jonesy, "we'll put your wisdom at the base of your memorial monument."

The man slumped, his rash hopefulness deflated, a popped balloon. He'd overplayed his hand. It wouldn't have been the first time for somebody like him, but it might be the last.

"You're not worth killing permanently, don't worry," said Jonesy. "But thanks for all the heads-up, I see we have reached our destination. Step lightly, boyo."

Baxter started to climb out before Jonesy changed his mind but not before Paddy threw at him an envelope with more cash. He did have something else to say. "I would've skipped town if she ever asked me."

"No, you wouldn't have."

Baxter slowly nodded, doing *his* best version of philosophical. "Yeah, I suppose you may be right. She's a tough girl for a guy to shake. You'll find out if you don't already know."

"Have a nice trip and stay there." Jonesy took the opportunity to punch him once again, this time near his armpit.

"I think," said Paddy, "you have a preview what'll happen if I ever see you again. Here's a clue: don't count on getting a cake with your name on it."

Caitlin's husband, the once and future ex, was catching his breath, face battered and holding his bruised, aching side and listing along as he drifted toward the crowd of fellow travelers, pockets bulging with money he'd soon be, if his lifelong record were predictive, pissing away at craps or the track. He couldn't resist a valedictory gesture, so he flipped them the middle finger, back turned to the car's occupants, underscoring whatever minute residue of self-respect he had remaining, before blending in with all the other nomads and tourists and fading gradually from view.

"That went well," said Paddy, adding in a burst of generosity: "Not the altogether worst mook in the world." The wine wasn't talking. He didn't think it was. Then again, it didn't take much these days to affect him, not like before. He wouldn't tell Jonesy, but all he wanted was to close his eyes for a few.

Jonesy was respectfully skeptical of Paddy's relatively optimistic assessment. He assumed the driver's seat, channeling all his frustrations into his iron grip on the wheel as they drove away. "You might have allowed me to do what one day will need to be done, Mr. Fitzgerald, if I may say so with all due deference."

"You'll get your chance. But Jonesy, Jonesy, Jonesy, we can't eliminate all the mopes and snakes and mud rats, can we?"

Jonesy wrestled his mouth into an upside-down smile and cocked his head to the side, reflecting on the not entirely unpleasant prospect. "We can certainly take our best shot, sir."

"*Swoon*," said Paddy feelingly, "swoon is quite a word. You're kind of a maniac, aren't you?"

"All for you, Mr. Fitzgerald, all for you."

Chapter Seventeen

Tommy & Francesca

"N o, thanks," said Tommy, and he picked up a moving box in one corner of the mostly empty office and put it down in the opposite. That didn't feel like progress, but it was at least an action. Moving into his new digs might have been stressful and he was making it up as he went along in the spare space he had leased. Stressful was not his resting state.

"Come on, honey," said Francesca, "let me help you set up your base of operations."

"I have a base of operations? Sounds impressive. You do realize it's me, the dog, and nothing on my appointment calendar for as far as the eye can see."

"Let me help, would you?"

How did it come to pass that pleading, imploring, auditioning was becoming her default mode of communication with him? She had never adopted such poses in her entrepreneurial ventures or with Anthony or even as a child with her mom and dad. At her age she didn't expect to grow accustomed to it. Relationships evolve over time, proceeding naturally if not logically through stages, she supposed, and it was unfair and foolish to compare the past to the present, or Tommy to anyone else. And yet, was she needy with regard to him or was he resistant with regard to her, or was it a little bit of both? Bookmark this topic for the next session with her therapist, she thought.

"I don't think I can afford your pay grade."

And without further ado, there it was again: the money subject.

"Hey, the price is right. I'll do it pro bono, Mr. Ex-Detective Man, sir."

She reminded him—wasn't this obvious to him as it was for everybody else?—she was gifted when it came to selecting furniture, hanging pictures, painting, all the design choices, the personal stamp touches that make a space come to life. Nice little office that this potentially was, five hundred square feet, it would pose no great challenge for her. She could follow through on punch lists like nobody else. Take paint, for instance. To her, paint was magical, how swiftly and dramatically it could transform the mood and tone, and she enjoyed the process, from mixing colors to drop cloths to donning a dapper painter's cap. She was going to push back on his *no, thanks* as gently as she could. He didn't mean to brush her off. She had to believe that.

His attention was snagged by the painter image. "Wait, you paint, like, rooms?"

"Wise ass, and yes, I can handle a brush."

"Wonders never cease with you, Frankie."

"Yeah, and don't forget it, buddy." So much for *gentle* pushback.

She was thinking modern, fresh, clean. Like that. He was thinking dark, old, shadowy. Dark green lampshades. Heavy crimson drapes. Like that.

"Tommy, let me put *your* personal stamp on the place."

He cocked his head, a gesture he would never resort to during an interrogation, which was when he was low-key and blank. "Frankie, let me get this straight. *You* want to put *my* personal stamp on my place?"

"Okay, that sounds weird, but you know what I mean. Let's look at this pragmatically: this is how you will present yourself to a prospective client. Light and transparent, or shady and brooding? Door Number One, Door Number Two? For somebody in trouble, what does she need from you to instill confidence and trust?"

"Why do you say *she*?"

"Good question, don't know why. You busted me." He did that more often than she could have expected.

"Is this your idea of an intelligence test?"

"Stop it, would you?" Because it pretty much was kind of a test.

"Put it that way, Frankie, I'd say he or she would feel more confident dealing with somebody used to the dark, which is where all the bad news lurks, under the stairwell, in the attic, down in the basement. How about that for my personal stamp?"

He was making a good point. They were standing in a sixth-floor office in the dismal, dark echoing hallways of a building downtown, an edifice that came complete with a groaning, quaking elevator. All the hallways were missing was a haunted house pipe organ. His business address was gloomily ideal, and gloomy was perfect for a PI's digs—or so he presumed. Corporate sparkle and gleam probably wasn't high on the must-have list for some hypothetical client of Tommy's who was desperate for investigative services. As for the current state of emptiness of his office proper, there were two boxes and two dining room chairs Tommy appropriated from his apartment and positioned on the parched bare wood floor, which virtually grumbled for sanding and polishing or at the very least for coverage. A beat-up wooden desk with one drawer was left behind by the previous tenant, and it was where he expected to park himself. He'd need a file cabinet, as soon as he had any files to file. Frankie had the right Persian in storage and that would hit the sweet spot between unexpected artistic statement and seriously moody self-assurance bordering on the upside of arrogance.

"I am happy for you, Tommy."

"I know you are, Frankie."

Their dog had a prominent, prospective role to play, too. A private investigator might benefit from the presence of a large, sweet dog, which Dickens was, lying there under the windowsill on his dog divan, because sleeping was his preferred mode of being. Well, that and gobbling up treats and playing with a ball, any ball, anytime, anywhere. A double message of a sweet dog, one who also looked like he was not to be toyed with—unless you had some freeze-dried liver to distribute, in which case you two could commune.

If Tommy and Francesca were formally engaged to be married, wearing rings to advertise the future, they were hardly swept up in frantic wedding stage panic. Wedding planning was, to both of them at their age, the essence of overdetermined. Destination nuptials in Mexico or Italy? That would be a long shot. Maybe they should elope, Hawaii or Vegas, be done with it all by getting down to the real business of making a life together, till, you know, as the traditional wedding vows stipulated, time and mortality did with them what they will. It seemed like they had recovered mostly from their fight at the gala, if it was a fight, and it seemed that it was. It was certainly not *not* a fight.

Such a bizarre night all the way around, the gala, from risky tux to risky Philip to the upsetting aftermath in the strange unconfirmed, vague news involving Bishop Mackey. As a matter of fact, Philip had called Francesca a couple of days after the gala to make a lunch date, and she accepted. She was surprised to hear from him, and to hear him say he could use with talking to a friend, things were strange in the diocese. She had not mentioned this social development to Tommy, not yet. And Philip had not mentioned it to Ruth, either. Perhaps because it didn't qualify as a social development and because she was waiting for the right uncharged moment to do full disclosure. And this moment, as Francesca and Tommy discussed setting up shop, didn't appear to qualify.

Frankie tried to change the mood by making what she hoped was a lighthearted suggestion. "Let's get a graphic artist to stencil a big eyeball on the door right over *Tommy Thomas Private Investigator*, you know, like in the movies."

"Eyeball's nice. You and your movies. I don't miss those black-and-white old warhorses. But I was thinking *Saint Jude Investigations. Lost Causes Our Specialty.*"

She was thrilled for one reason in particular. The *our* in "our specialty" seemed hopeful for the two of them. She was reading too much into what he said. She had a tendency to do that. But she wouldn't hit that hopeful note yet, too premature.

"It's certainly got a ring. Kind of Catholic-sounding, no? You good with that? While I'm thinking about it, you also need a big old desk and a bookcase and some lamps and a couch and a few real chairs and this cool little wet bar I saw in a catalogue. Stock a few bottles of bourbon, you'll be all good to go."

"I gotta get better on the computer and that tech stuff."

"Your landline is hooked up—do we need to hire you a secretary?"

There she was, getting ahead of herself, but she meant well, he figured. "Let's wait till the phone's ringing off the hook, give it, I don't know, a day or two."

"With your reputation in town, you'll be swamped by clients in no time, you wait and see."

"Cheating wives and embezzling bookkeepers, missing cats and persons, the disappeared last will and testament—the sad sack human race is full of opportunities. You got child custody cases and insurance fraud cases and restaurant employees carting rib eyes out the back door…"

"And you can do surveillance and conduct interviews, investigate corporate defalcation, all the good stuff, and you'll be great at this. And I can help however you need. Spreadsheets are my life. And think what fun we could have doing stakeouts." She couldn't control herself.

"No one ever had fun on a stakeout, trust me. No one."

He pulled out an envelope from his coat pocket. He was proud to show her what it contained. His state license to legally conduct business as a private investigator had arrived.

"When did you get this?"

"Not long, couple weeks."

"You didn't think to tell me?"

"The letter came in, like I said, the other day. In fact, I just told you."

This brought up a host of questions for her, being Francesca. "You going to carry a gun?"

"No."

"No?"

"Not all the time, unless I need it."

"So you are going to carry."

"I got a concealed carry permit, so sure, when appropriate."

"And you don't want me involved?"

"I don't get involved in *your* business."

New argument. "Never was informed you wanted to be."

"Always nice to be asked."

"Okay," she said, moving fast, sensing this was an opening she needed to take at this delicate point in their relationship. "I'm asking you to get involved in my business, someday, when the time is right." How much did she need to spell out? If she offered too much she'd sound desperate. If she offered not enough she'd sound like an ice queen.

"Someday, Frankie?" They both knew what that meant: the indeterminate future, which is exactly what she was not interested in anymore.

"You know what I mean." Desperate or ice queen. Both lousy options. Tommy had another valid point. She had one, too.

"Someday I'll think about it." To him, sometimes it already felt like it was too late.

"Why do I get the feeling we continually come to some sort of crossroads every other day, Tommy?"

"Crossroads, man. Let's not get dramatic."

"You know how I love hearing that word, *dramatic*. Do you love me?" Escalation seemed on the docket.

"Talk about being dramatic. Of course, I do, of course." Too fast, his response, reflecting his positioning, not his resolute, felt commitment.

Maybe she was too old to get serious about Tommy, maybe she'd been through too much. Could she give her heart to anybody again—as in any man in the world? And even if they were engaged, maybe he was too far along in his life, too fixed in his ways, to get serious about a woman like her.

"Do you want to know if I love you, Tommy?"

"It'd be good to be reminded from time to time."

She believed she reminded him every single day, by word and by deed, to invoke the language of her Catholic catechism that instructed her in grade school, faith and works, faith and fucking works. "Consider yourself reminded."

"Of what?"

Here is when somebody like him needs assurances. Here is when somebody like her needs self-assurance.

She changed subjects: that might get them through this. "You do your Italian homework for tomorrow night?" They took a weekly class together at the community college: Intro to Italian Conversation 101. Once a week was not enough for anyone to get adept at a language, and not advanced enough for her to formally review all the grammar she took for granted.

Once a week, however, was enough for them to put a stake in the ground of doing something together.

"Forgot."

"You want some help, work together on the assignments?"

"Nope."

"Italian's harder than people think. They think because you can do some stupid Italian accent, it must be an easy tongue to master. And you know what? They have two past tenses. You'd think one would suffice. And then there's the subjunctive, the *congiuntivo*, it's giving me, even me, trouble, all over again. I suspect the hypothetical and contrary-to-fact grammar would give you trouble."

"So you're implying I am not comfortable with the hypothetical, the contrary-to-fact, the contingent, the prospective, what you said. As if I were ever able to do that with you, Frankie."

This was going nowhere. "I'm going to take off now, meetings. You're going to be great at this private eye biz. See you for dinner?"

"You tell me."

"I say yes," she said, firmly.

"I'll pick up something for dinner. You feel like fish?"

Her shoulders slumped.

"Salmon's in season," he said, "saw some line-caught in the Mulvaney's case…"

She straightened up. "Don't, okay? Just don't, all right?"

Her weird, unprovoked, as far as he could ascertain, intensity ensnared him. "You all right?"

She couldn't explain herself. "I don't want you to get any fucking fish. Do I have to explain everything?"

No, but it would be good if she could explain *something*. "I got it," he said. "Okay. Chicken?"

She couldn't tell him that she didn't want to take any chances anymore, not with the fish. She changed direction again. "I do think you could use a rug in your office."

He studied anew the potential layout of the room. He concluded that her judgment was astute, he *could* use a rug, even an expensive Persian like hers, which would likely cost, knowing her, more than a year's detective's salary. He got his point across by a shift in his shoulders, by a tilt of his head.

They were getting somewhere after all. Because she didn't respond to his tacit acceptance of the rug, either. Her business career had taught her if you have to talk through everything, walk through every step of your thinking, process each and every shading and nuance, you are effectively in retreat, and you have nothing worth negotiating in the first place. Every great deal is a leap of faith, on both sides.

"Frankie, don't take this the wrong way, but you think like a guy. You can't help trying to fix shit." He meant that in a good way, mostly, he would swear, but didn't.

In a sense, he may have been largely correct, that she did think like a guy, because for one thing she didn't press him to say more about what thinking like a guy meant. If she pushed back, she might have said it was only around him where she thought like a guy. If Tommy brought out aspects of herself she was previously unaware of, that might qualify as a good thing, no? Her beleaguered therapist might breathe a sigh of relief if her client astonished by ceasing to process every single jot and tittle, the imaginary, the projected, the mental scraps, minutiae—the subjunctive of life.

"What if I said you think like a woman?" This might have been entertaining, under other circumstances, specifically not those involving her and him. They had a chance if they could get through moments like this.

"That's what great detectives do, think like a woman, or even average detectives like me."

"I think you're selling yourself short. You're slightly above average in the gumshoe department."

"Detectives ask follow-up questions to follow-up questions, you assume nothing in evidence, you probe and you prod and you poke around some more, till you get to the truth of the crime, the facts, the guilt and the innocence. The obvious never is. If it were, there wouldn't be a need for a detective. The art of detection would be irrelevant if there were no artists of concealment. Criminals and detectors of criminality or innocence— joined at the hip." He was having fun, too. Moments like these, he had no question that they had a chance.

"Didn't know you were so good at talking dirty, Tommy."

"Stick around, baby."

"That's the whole plan."

They both had a lot to learn about each other, and she caught herself wondering if they would.

—

THAT AFTERNOON, LONG AFTER Francesca went home with Dickens the dog, Tommy had a meeting with somebody he wasn't expecting who knocked on the green smoked-glass door. Once inside, the conversation got off to a fast start. Tommy didn't have a great deal of practice or patience with the red tape of small talk. The man introduced himself.

"Forgive appearances, setting up shop." He sat behind the battered desk, and the potential client took a dining room chair in front. "Lot of Fitzgeralds in town," he said, not that that was news to him, or anybody within a hundred-mile radius.

"Tell me about it," said Matty.

"I'm pleased to meet Paddy Fitzgerald's son and Father Philip's brother."

"That a problem for you, Mr. Thomas?"

"Tommy, and not at all. Francesca referred you?" He didn't mention that she left a while ago, or that she was planning to come back someday with a rug he could never have afforded to buy.

"My sister-in-law Frankie said you might be able to help, whatever I had going on, not that I gave her details."

Funny thing, she didn't mention. Tommy concealed his bewilderment. His bewilderment reserves were severely diminished after all his years on the job. He believed he had seen, well, everything.

"You heard Frankie and I got engaged, right? Is *that* a problem with you or the Family Fitzgerald?" He had asked her father for his approval, and came away from the meeting almost certain he had received it. Big Mimmo was a hard read, but Francesca said that was the Full Scalino: large-scale, lockdown, plausible deniability. The most he ever gave anybody.

"None of us'll ever get over Anthony, but Frankie is entitled to her own life, and if she's okay with you, which she obviously is, you're okay by me."

They got down to business. Matty was a high school teacher and he was being effectively dismissed as a result of his refusal to sign the bishop's strong-arm contract. He was one of twenty or so teachers who wanted to put up a fight.

"I heard about Mackey. Sounds like you need a labor lawyer, not a PI."

"Probably. Only right now, I need information." He and his colleagues wanted the dirt on the bishop and on the business affairs of the diocese.

"Talking hardball? You think Mackey's shady? You heard he's pretty dinged up, right?" To Tommy, Matty's proposal sounded harebrained, impractical, and pointless, but he was going to be polite to his future relation—though what that relation technically was, he had no idea. Sort of a brother-in-law?

"But he's making decisions."

"Not drawn naturally to the soiled laundry, but let's keep talking."

Matty was ready to comply.

"Tell me again, how did my name come up with Francesca?"

"I wrote her an email asking if she knew anybody like you, investigations. I didn't tell her much."

"This conversation will be between us, then, as in confidential."

"There's another thing, too. Totally different thing, since you don't seem to be all that interested in helping me with the bishop."

"I want to help, but don't see how snooping into the bishop's private life is going to be useful for you, or me."

"And who knows, this other thing could be a little more serious. Somebody downloaded some nasty stuff onto my computer."

"Everybody watches porn, so I'm told, not my thing. Nothing to be ashamed of, and I don't think you can get fired from a Catholic school for that—at least for now."

"You don't get it, it's not mine. I didn't download it. Someone got access to my computer. Which I can explain. And it's not that kind of porn, it's the really bad kind. I deleted it all, but nothing is ever permanently deleted, so I hear, and tech is over my head. There's one more thing, too." Matty told Tommy about the selfie Terry sent him.

"You got a lot going on there, my friend. About this Terry? She a colleague? Your wife find out about her? I don't sit in judgment of anybody. You know, if you need marriage counseling…"

"You've got this all wrong, she's a student."

"So she's not an adult?"

"She's in high school, or was in high school." Matty reached for his phone. "Do you want to see it?"

"You didn't trash it?"

"Is that the right thing to do?"

"Put your phone down. I absolutely do not want to look. In fact, all you've told me is that a student of unknown age sent you a selfie that you considered to be, let's call it inappropriate. But you didn't give me any more detail than that, okay? You're certainly not offering to distribute to me a photo of a child, a selfie whose content may or may not be a concern, am I clear?"

Tommy asked for more background, and when Matty finished providing it, the PI wished he hadn't and that Frankie had never encouraged her oddball, troublemaking brother-in-law to walk into his unfinished office. He loved the work she once told him he was born to do, but this was going to be a test. Of what, as of yet undetermined.

"Matty, upon reflection, the men's room is right down the hall."

"Good to know. What are you talking about?"

"The men's room is right down the hall, turn right out the door, easy to find. Go find it. If you wish, you can enter in your password and leave the phone on the desk while you're gone let's say for the next ten minutes."

When Matty returned, in ten minutes, Tommy had come up with a few ideas and a lot more questions.

Chapter Eighteen
Ruth & Philip

T HEIR ROMANTIC HISTORY DATES from one Sunday at church after the eleven o'clock Mass. Like many a storied romance, or even an untold one like theirs, it didn't begin with valentines, chocolate, and pink bubbly. Their introduction, such as it was, took place a couple of years ago, and it was innocent and it was accidental both. Meet-cute? On the spectrum. To be specific, they met when and where the two of them physically collided with each other in the vestibule, the quaint term for the intermediate space between the church entrance doors and the church proper, where congregants worshipped in pews before the altar and where Father Philip consecrated the Eucharist and delivered masterful homilies from the looming hand-carved pulpit.

Not long before that fated Sunday noon, she had dragged herself back into the fold. That turn of phrase did charm her: *fold*. Short for sheepfold— she looked it up. Was she a petite *baa baa* black sheep seeking shelter in her little enclosure? Hardly. To review her religious history, she had been a devout child, then a doubting teenager, and later a couldn't-be-bothered-with-God adult. A typical odyssey, she supposed, for someone of her generation. So it wasn't nostalgia over her lost or misplaced meaningfulness now animating her. No, instead she was surprised she heard within herself a voice calling out to her to *return*—though hers would amount to being a return to a place where she had never quite been before. Come to think of it, that fairly describes most worthwhile odysseys since Homer got the nostalgia ball rolling. She'd seen something like this phenomenon—of returning to the past that was now the future—play out over and over again with clients who came to her for counseling.

She could rationalize that this move back on her part had something to do with the understated, beautiful, soaring church architecture, or the music, and true, the architectural confines were conducive to spirituality or meditation, and the choir was first-rate, their voices uplifting. She fleetingly contemplated auditioning for a spot on the risers up in the loft. She had been first soprano in her high school chorale, and to this day she enjoyed belting out the old show tunes from *West Side Story* and *Oliver* and *My Fair Lady* and *Man of La Mancha* in the shower, and the occasional classical piece like *Carmina Burana*, which was demanding but very satisfying to sing, and at Christmastime, of course, *The Messiah*. *For unto us a child is born. Unto us a child given. Unto us…* Since high school she had restricted her performing to private venues like her shower, where she was the star, but she was publicly timid these days—or perhaps it was that she wasn't in the mood to chance being rejected by anybody or anything, not even the choirmaster, who regularly sent out calls in the church bulletin for volunteers: "You don't have to be Leontyne Price or Luciano Pavarotti, but if you can carry a tune, and can spare a couple of hours on Thursday nights for rehearsal, we want YOU!"

All that does not explain how it was that she started going to Mass on Sundays. Living alone, she went to church by herself. It had been a while since she had divorced her untrustworthy husband of four of the longest, most futile, torpid, desolate years. He had a wandering eye and she didn't harbor the willpower or the faith to hang with him or with the marriage vows. People make mistakes. Her whole career as a therapist was predicated on that truism; it all depends upon being resilient in the face of one's disappointments and blunders and crises. What therapy does—what therapy *should* do—is help clients learn from loss and act from resilience. The corollary truism: both partners in a failed marriage are almost always complicit. She acknowledged as much. She had a bookcase dedicated to self-help and brain research, a seemingly awkward match, but she found it a torrid hookup. Where therapists went wrong was in prompting clients to endlessly revisit the past, their childhoods, for understanding and for determining a future path. As if causation mattered, or as if it were comprehensible. How many times with a babbling, self-involved client she came this close to a tirade like this: "Guess what, Samantha / Hillary / Justin / Antoine. Life makes no fucking sense. *Your* history makes no fucking sense. We're never going to straighten things out with your mom and your stepdad and your dad and your stepmom. They don't matter anymore, they're dead and gone. You yourself matter more than ever. How do I know that? I'll tell you. Because you're sitting here with me, your fucking fifty-minute-hour therapist. Why don't we come up with a better story for today and tomorrow?" Which was a point of view that, when she summoned it up in those terms, shed some refracted light upon her return to the sheepfold.

Painful as this was to admit, Ruth's marriage breakup was lackluster, boring. It was not the stuff of *Wuthering Heights* or romance novels, that was for sure. Since then, she had experienced zero interest in dating, especially after signing up briefly with online matchmakers, the whole meat market aspect of which depressed her. But one good thing about being unattached, maybe one of the best things besides watching what she wanted on TV and not negotiating around the remote control, is that she didn't have to persuade some skeptical man to attend Mass with her, or to explain herself to anybody else, or to defend Catholicism—all tedious occupations, especially because she didn't care to be called out. Honestly, she couldn't defend lots of the Church's outdated, sex-obsessed positions. In any case, it was not only the church ambience that drew her. She liked the scriptural readings and the ritual, certainly, though she was dismayed by Church politics and dogma, which often seemed offensive, if not transparently dumb. When her friends and colleagues found out, especially other therapists, they made gentle fun of this new Catholic phase in her life, but she pushed back, saying their lack of understanding what she was doing was not an argument, and certainly no reason for her not to go there. In fact, she didn't understand, either. Catholics have long loved mystery. A mystery, theologians say, is a truth we cannot understand. Bingo. And that was a sentiment any therapist could subscribe to—but only under threat of torture, because therapists were all about understanding the mysterious, all about making the unknown known, dredging up repressed material to the surface and articulating it. At the same time, Ruth had witnessed at close range the limits of therapy in her own life. She had begun to question her life's calling.

—

WHILE ALL THAT WAS in play for her, the unfathomably handsome priest named Father Philip surfaced. He had been assigned to her newfound parish, and she was held spellbound by his presence on the altar. They locked eyes a few times after services and smiled. And one day after the eleven o'clock she turned a corner leaving the church and next thing she knew, being distracted and flustered thinking about him, she plowed right into him. They both laughed as they reached out to each other to keep from falling.

"I am such a klutz, sorry," he said. "You okay?"

Looking up into his black eyes, she was more than okay. And she felt nothing so much as stunned to be in close physical proximity.

"No harm, no foul. I don't understand that expression, do you? How are you?" Her mouth was cottony.

"It's from basketball, and I will survive. *Philip*," he introduced himself, not Father Philip.

"I think I know who you are, Father."

"I noticed you in the back pew."

"I thought I was keeping a low profile, so there goes my top-secret CIA clearance."

"Yes, your espionage cover is now blown." He reached out and held onto her hand again. She did appear unsteady on her feet.

"Ruth," she managed to utter.

"I love that name, Ruth."

"They ought to name a book in the Bible after me."

"What a brilliant idea. But you know, I think they did already."

"Something about corn, right?" She was playing dumb for some reason. She knew the book well, one of the shortest in the Bible, and a moving story about loss, fractured families, and new marriages with enormous implications. A therapist like her could use such storytelling material to her advantage.

"Oh, you're a scriptural scholar." He was impressed, raising his eyebrows.

She told him no, she was no scholar of any stripe, she was a psychotherapist, thereby shocking herself. She couldn't believe she gave up this information so freely, for this was the type of disclosure she normally withheld indefinitely, because that sort of professional identification never failed to intimidate people, when they didn't find it a social or romantic deal-breaker. And by all means, never divulge as much to a seatmate on an airplane; you would never hear the end of family pathologies from takeoff to touchdown. And few men feel comfortable around a shrink, or look forward to the prospect of being routinely shuttled under the psychological microscope (as they might imagine) by somebody who was supposed to perform such analysis for a living. So when she realized she had impetuously made this admission, she realized that her curiosity with regard to Father Philip had been unconsciously mushrooming, and that her interest in him might transcend the pastoral. Wait, he had introduced himself as Philip, not Father Philip, and what did that mean?

"That's fascinating," he said, though she lost the conversational linkage to the extent that she forgot what his *fascinating* applied to. Then she recovered the connection, to her momentary relief. He had been through therapy and around therapists before, she would have guessed, because everybody with intellectual substance seemed to have been, and she would have been wrong.

"Some people think therapy is a kind of religion." She couldn't finish that off with a "Philip."

"And some people see religion as a kind of therapy."

It registered somewhere in the deep recesses of his recollecting mind that Ruth was also the name of Francesca's therapist. What a coincidence. This was not a big city, but it wasn't a hamlet, either. There had to be a lot of Ruths who were therapists. He wouldn't probe, not for a while.

"See you next Sunday," he said. "I promise I won't knock you over next time."

That was kind of him, but it was too late for such nicety: she was already floored.

—

She did not go back to church for the next two months. She knew going there was a bad idea, but she was not quite sure why, or what the idea was. Then, one Sunday, she appeared once again at the eleven o'clock. Father Philip happened not to be the celebrant, and as a consequence, she felt both relieved and disappointed. And this revealed everything to her. If psychotherapists understand anything, it's ambivalence. Ambivalence is abundant and essential as water. It doesn't mean you kind of want X and kind of want Y, it means you really want X and you really want Y. When she left Mass, she felt like she had attended a wake.

"Hi, stranger," Father Philip said to her outside, standing near enough to the door that she could not exit without facing him. He was wearing his black clerical suit. "Where have you been keeping yourself?"

"Oh, been on the road a lot," she lied.

"Some exciting destination, I hope."

No destination on the planet seemed more exotic than the vestibule. "You didn't say Mass today."

"Sharp observer."

"Yes, I've been told I am the master of the obvious."

"The obvious is where all depths lie."

She caught herself smiling at him, feeling certifiably insane, really wanting X, really wanting Y.

"Cup of tea?"

Was this a trick question?

He tried again. "I'd love a cup of tea, care to join me?"

In the moment, she would have agreed to anything.

—

They had tea in the rectory that day, and talked for a couple of hours, and from then on she never missed Sunday Mass. Everything began to speed up for her. It was as if the world had concocted a devious plan. They would cross paths with each other at the movies, at restaurants, at cafés, at art exhibits—and of course at church. She couldn't escape. They were subconsciously circling each other—if it was indeed subconsciously.

One day they found themselves at the wine store, where they caught themselves looking over the offerings, and she said to him, with a smile, "Are you following me?"

"I was about to ask you the same thing."

"What are you looking for?" She was referring to all the racks of red wines that were lined up near them. She was ambiguous enough in her phrasing to accomplish what she did not at first realize she wanted to accomplish.

The suave and polished priest took a minute to find the words, and he studied her face. "Ruth, honestly, I have no idea."

"You know, what I find useful when I am at a loss is, Philip, I go on a long hike."

—

THE BIRDS WERE SCREAMING and darting about, and it was a sweltering spring midweek day in the regional park, and Ruth and Philip had no human company on the paths. They were both vainly trim, wearing shorts, tennis shoes, T-shirts, sunglasses, and baseball caps.

"Is it true," she said, looking up the road and not into his eyes, "the rumor?"

"Yes, I am a fabulous dancer, might as well break it to you now before you catch me on *Dancing with the Clergy*."

"No, everybody knows about your secret dance career. I was referring to the rumor about your being reassigned."

"Oh, that, yes, it's true. Parish work is great, and I will miss it. That's where I get to serve real people in genuine need."

"Did you rob a bank or something?" She was being playful, but then she realized she might have struck the wrong note. "Sorry, dumb, I shouldn't pry, none of my business."

It was fine, he assured her, but no, he wasn't in trouble, at least as far as he knew, he qualified. He had asked to be transferred away from parish assignments. It was time for change, new challenges, was all. So now he was going to oversee a whole range of diocesan programs: outreach, education, public relations, the whole gamut. He told her a little bit about what he hoped to do someday in the future, working with runaway teenagers, abandoned or abused kids plucked from the streets. As a rule, she didn't specialize in adolescence, but she was curious, she hoped to hear more. And he filled her in on this dream job fantasy of his.

"You'd be a natural, Philip, these kids need somebody like you."

"Well, if the day ever comes when I get assigned to a post like that, I hope I can count on you for professional advice. In the meantime, they've stuck me in the Chancery, doing admin, personal assistant to the bishop, moving chess pieces on the diocesan board."

"Philip, I can't help but say it's weird. I finally meet a priest I feel a personal connection to, and he slips away."

"I'm not slipping away."

Was that true, what he said? And what did he mean? She wouldn't see him at church on Sundays, yes, but that could be all right. He wasn't moving to the moon.

And they walked and walked.

At the top of the steep incline, which caused their breath to labor and where she had led him along, she realized they had said practically nothing for the past ten minutes or so. Their silence could have been a result of their being physically taxed, but she doubted that. From this vantage, they could spy in all directions, all of them devoid of other hikers and observers.

Without word or warning, Ruth stepped off the path, headed off into the shade of a clearing, and leaned her back against a massive trunk of a tree. Philip stood away, a few paces, for a while. She motioned him toward her. Also without a word, he closed the gap. When they stood next to each other, beneath the canopy of the pines, they took each other's hands.

"I'd like to kiss you," she said. "No, that's not it. I would like you to kiss me."

"I'd like that, too, but that would be wrong."

She kissed him gently. When he pulled himself away, she drew him back towards her.

"It doesn't seem right," he said, "that this should be wrong."

"Which means it isn't." She wanted X.

Then he kissed her harder than she had ever been kissed before. She felt as if he was suctioning all her breath. He tasted of mint and eucalyptus. She felt his sweaty shirt and his hands upon her damp back. Up close like this, he smelled faintly of incense. She sensed the exploratory thrust between her legs.

"What if somebody..." he started. Her index finger lightly crossed his lips.

"There's nobody but us," she said, thereby voicing the universal fantasy of all new lovers.

Chapter Nineteen
Philip & Francesca

FATHER PHILIP WAS BEHIND the outreach vehicle wheel, Francesca riding shotgun in the passenger's seat. "Music?" he suggested. "Hip-hop, country, classical, pop, Broadway show tunes, opera, Springsteen, Frank Sinatra? Bet I can find a spa station, too, which I really, truly hope you don't like. *Find your center. Breathe deeply. Be kind to yourself. Namaste.* There's an Italian channel, too. *Ritorna me...*" he sang, and he wasn't bad, either, as far as he was concerned.

Her unresponsiveness as to listening options he construed as indifference, and her failure to be impressed by his Dean Martin baritone was not something to which he could take exception, either. The air was thick enough, he supposed, what with all the unspoken conversations they were intent on not having.

Every few days, it was his practice to drive around, never solo for obvious reasons (legal exposure, logistical support), accompanied by a staff member or, occasionally, a board member, as Francesca had recently become. Here they were on the prowl for troubled, desperate, endangered kids who had taken to the street, more than likely disappointed in their search for such refuge that is not available out here. Around Caring Street, they referred to combing the town as *fishing*. As in what Jesus did, according to the Gospels, fishing for those hungry for loaves and fishes, or in need of a savior or salvation, or any other sort of viable miracle. For Francesca's idiosyncratic and guarded and private and, she would readily concede, phobic reasons, she recoiled from the image, but kept this information to herself. She never told anyone Anthony's last words, and never would.

Today marked the occasion of Frankie's first expedition. Being alongside Philip in such purpose-driven activity felt fairly normal, felt almost all right. It had been such a long time since the two of them were engaged in close proximity with each other, and she thought it was worth a shot.

—

UNDER THE HIGHWAY OVERPASS, on the dirt incline, above which a cavalcade of cars and trucks droned nonstop overhead, was a slump-shouldered teenage girl in T-shirt, felt vest, and shorts, sitting on the ground, skid-marked knees drawn in toward her chest, backpack close by, smoking, and smoking with a determination bordering on vengeance. He hit the brakes.

"Seen her before?" Francesca asked.

"Fresh one."

Twenty feet away, he had stopped the white van that featured on the door a dove symbol done in electric blue along with the bold scripted logo:

CARING STREET

The girl with chopped-up, psycho bird's-nest hair and zombie-blue lipstick and eye black to supply a football team stared in the direction of the van, as if she were a coyote or wolf and the van a doe—or the other way around. Kids had to be tough or at least appear tough to survive out here, so it was difficult for Frankie and Philip to read her with assurance. Having done this sort of reconnaissance for a while, Philip gave up assuming anything about kids who took to the streets. They could emanate from any part of town or from anywhere out of town, they could be destitute, they could be middle-class, they could be from affluent homes. They could have parents who abused them, parents who gave them fancy cars, parents who never ate dinner with them, parents who hung like fog over their lives. Kids with parents who plastered their pictures everywhere, from telephone poles to signboards to cyberspace. They could also be bereft of parents or any family. They once might have been foster family rejects, or victims. Kids on drugs, kids who were kicking the habit, kids who were parents themselves. Kids who took off when they conceived no alternative. Street kids defied stereotypes. That's what made the work heartbreaking—but also, when it was successful, humbling. And what constituted success for Caring Street—well, that was always a big subject for staff discussion. But one definition underlay all their efforts: success meant survival for one child at least, at least for today, at least for the time being.

Philip and Francesca got out of the van and the girl jumped up and conveyed readiness to bolt.

"You guys the Moron Church of the Whatever Saints?"

"Nope," said Philip, reluctantly amused.

"Oh, wait, I get it. You guys are them fucking Catholics. I know about you Catholics, I went to your school. I hate Catholic shit. Perverts."

Philip asked his running mate if he was that transparent. She confirmed he sort of was obviously Catholic, even dressed, as he was, in jeans, baseball cap, and denim jacket.

"What're you, trying to get me to look for your lost puppy, then throw me in your child abduction van? You guys are sick. You ain't gonna turn me into an Amber Alert."

"That's not it, not at all," said Philip, quickly realizing this was not going to be an easy one to land. It wouldn't be the first time for that experience.

The girl screamed, "Do-gooders, leave me the fuck alone! I got a knife."

"Just trying to help," said Frankie, though for some reason she didn't believe there was a knife and she chastised herself for using the word "help," the last thing a girl like that would admit to wanting. "It's not about Catholic *shit*, though sure, there is some of that going around, and, okay, I am Catholic. We both are." Her entire statement must have sounded insane to the girl and it would need to be unpacked for a few hours in order to be intelligible to anybody else. She was new to this work, and she would improve, but she let it stand for now.

Philip swung a brown paper bag side to side over his head so she could see there was nothing up his sleeve, trying to ease her mind, the prospect of which didn't appear promising. "Got you a sandwich here, a banana, juice. I can leave it right here on the sidewalk, if you want."

"I ain't taking the bait, I don't need your handouts. I can take care of myself. I will cut you, I said, if you throw a net over my head."

"It's food, honest. Nothing else."

She was starving, and had no choice. "What kind of sandwich?"

He told her what was on today's menu.

"Okay, put down the bag and fuck the fuck off."

"Will do, we're fresh out of nets," said Frankie.

"We'll circle back in a while," said Philip, "and if you're here, we'll show you where you can get a cooked meal, hot shower, and a place to sleep, as long as you need. Up to you."

"Go on now, molest some other kid."

They'd heard similar things before and they expressed willingness to comply with her wishes.

"And don't be sending no cops."

"Okay, what's your name?"

"Mother Theresa."

Francesca and Philip walked back to the van.

"I like her," she said.

"What's not to like?" he said.

If that girl was new to the streets, which was how she certainly looked, she had about forty-eight hours before she was confronted with some fundamental, brutal decisions: sex for food, sex for money. Francesca said, "She wants us to come back. She wants help. But on her terms." They both could respect that.

—

For going on a decade, Caring Street House sheltered runaway and abused teenagers. Hector Alessandro, as founding director, put the House on the map. Despite his sterling record of achievement, he had been summarily dismissed by the bishop, and he was replaced by Father Philip, who now oversaw operations, consulting with and managing the staff. He knew he had a lot to learn in order to do a good job.

Francesca had taken her seat on the Caring Street board and consulted pro bono on finance and administration. Philip had pitched her to join up when they met for coffee a few days after that gala. That was when they spent a peaceful hour plus at the café, and a pleasant time it was, too, light and affirming. They were careful. Neither of them came close to revisiting the intense episodes of their shared past. If there was one other thing they had in common, it was they both had vast capacities for psychological compartmentalization. Philip never reflected on that character trait of his, and when Francesca did so, she feared it was a marker of personal failure. As far as he was concerned, what happened happened, nothing would undo the past. As far as she was concerned, what happened indeed happened, of course, but the past was present to her and it happened all over again in her heart when she remembered.

As for Bishop Mackey, as he was recuperating and slowly improving, he was absorbing withering heat with regard to axing Hector, the never-ending pedophilia lawsuits, and the controversial teacher loyalty contract. Philip knew something about the bishop that people outside the Chancery forgot or refused to acknowledge, that Mackey was a dedicated, committed supporter of the House. He may have been pilloried in the community and in the courts, but when it came to Caring Street donors, his commitment was cherished. He quietly raised serious money and he did all he could to satisfy the shelter's budgetary requirements. And as important as anything else he did, he also assigned his most talented, charismatic priest to supervise the agency, Father Philip Fitzgerald. As for Philip, Caring Street was—and this did not surprise him—the most rewarding service of his priest vocation. This, *this* was the type of work he was meant to do.

Francesca had an entrepreneurial temperament and she always enjoyed getting involved in projects new to her such as Caring Street. Now that Tommy had made it clear that he wanted to run his new private eye business pretty much without her, which was a blow, she had precious time to invest. Her reputation in the community proved immediately beneficial, and she felt good about her contribution. Caring Street was so different from chairing board meetings at the college or doing lunch with somebody or other. She was no lady who lunched, stupidest meal of the day, in her estimation, a waste of time set off by self-consciously healthy portions of, these days, relentlessly fashionable food like quinoa. Not that such lunching ladies were bad people, not at all, and there was nothing wrong with quinoa either, even if she badly yearned for a burger afterward. Often these philanthropically inclined women were good, productive citizens with good hearts. It took so much effort to get affluent people to think hard, and in revitalized ways, about the truths of their lives and the dreams that had turned into ash in their post-middle-aged grasp. Here, working for and with at-risk teenagers, life felt more intense, the stakes higher, the risks more serious. Frankie would orchestrate emergency referrals for therapy and medical doctors and envision ways to reconcile kids with their families, if at all possible, and if not always successfully. There were always those kids with families that simply failed. Whatever the Catholic Church's or the diocese's or Bishop Mackey's shortcomings may be, and they were copious, this organization generously served needy kids, wherever they came from, wherever they were going. If a teenager was homeless or abused or in danger and found a way to Caring Street, they were given a hand, no questions asked. True, a small percentage of kids might be, in her unprofessional opinion, sociopaths, and most of them were suffering from deep wounds, but a few of them were brilliant, compassionate, misunderstood children in bodies that made them appear to be adults, which they weren't. Which takes us back to the child at the underpass.

—

PHILIP AND FRANCESCA HAD driven to a nearby park, where they sat in the van, telling Fitzgerald tales, and providing the girl time to mull over her prospects. Then they headed back to her. When they drove up, they found that she had come down from the incline and was standing on the sidewalk, the crumpled-up paper bag down by her frayed tennis shoes.

She put her hand up and had a stipulation to make: "Don't get out of the van."

Francesca rolled down the window.

"Tuna fish sucked, too much mayo."

"I'll inform the chef," said Philip.

"I ain't drinking the Kool-Aid," the girl said.

"Good, we're not serving any."

"You gonna tie me up, take me back to my stupid house with my junkie mother and her creepy boyfriend in his boxers cleaning his guns?"

"We're not doing anything you don't want, and nothing that'll put you in danger, promise."

"You got any sickos at your place?"

"You'll be safe."

"Why the fuck should I trust you?" Both Philip and Francesca heard, instead of "trust you," trust *anybody*. That was always the issue on the table with these kids.

"That's more or less the right question, Mother Theresa."

The girl grudgingly came close to smiling.

"We have to earn your trust," said Francesca, stepping in. "All you have to do is give us a chance."

"Gotta do better, I heard that before."

"Not from us."

But she was exhausted. "I gotta get some sleep tonight, haven't slept for two days, and I need a shower, and this is the best I can do, I guess."

"Why don't you hop in, Theresa?"

"How'd you know my name?"

"Lucky guess."

"Wait a second, what's this place called, Caring Street? Fuck a duck, that's where my crushable teacher, Matt, was trying to take me."

Philip's head snapped back. "Matty Fitzgerald's your crushable teacher?"

"Was. What's it to you?"

"Nothing. He's my brother."

"Some kinda small world. I stayed with him a little while when I first ran off."

That sounded bizarre to Philip, and he said so, and Terry picked up the sly insinuation conveyed by the priest's uneasy body language.

"Jesus, not like that, man. Matt's not that way, come on."

"You call Matty *Matt*? And we're still talking about Mr. Fitzgerald, your teacher at Holy Family?"

"*Was* my teacher at Holy Family, but I'm not there anymore. And that's his name, right, what he wanted me to call him. He's a very cool teacher."

Philip was thrown off, not that he should have imagined his little brother capable for a moment of inappropriate, or criminal, behavior with an underage girl. Almost certainly not, anyway. Whatever the case, he'd reach out to Matty as soon as possible, get more information.

This exchange convinced Terry she had done the right thing with Matt's computer and with the sext she sent him, because now he wouldn't fuck with her, not if he knew better. Being on her own as she was, she had to look out for herself, because nobody else would. And that meant other people, sorry, had to get thrown under the bus.

"Piece of work, Matt's wife is," said Terry. "First, I was thinking she was some kinda wacked-out bitch on wheels, thinking sick shit about him and me, like you did, but then I realized, she loved her husband, and was looking out for him. She's okay, pretty much. Little problem. When I crashed at their place, she also stole my mom's boyfriend's gun, hard to explain."

Philip was having trouble following—and crediting—what she was saying. "You got a gun on you?"

"You deaf? I told you, Matt's wife stole it, after I stole it, which I did steal it to get it out of my mom's house, so he wouldn't shoot her, the crankhead. Maybe what's her name…"

"We still talking about Claire?"

"Maybe Claire was trying to help me or some shit like that. Do I look like I need anybody's help? I mean except for a bed and shower and some real food that ain't tuna fish."

Francesca and Philip looked at each other and wondered what they had gotten into. The immediate issue on the horizon was that Claire, Matty's wife, worked intake at Caring Street.

Philip told her to hand over the knife.

"The what?"

"No knives allowed at Caring Street."

"Oh, right. Good plan, but I don't have one. I'm not as tough as I look. No, I'm tougher, I don't need a knife. I talk to people who want to give me trouble, they decide they all of a sudden got better things to do. So drive, Uber man. You can tell from where you're sitting, I could use that shower."

Francesca looked at Philip as if to communicate that was one thing she was right about.

Terry hopped into the back, and she could hardly fail to detect what she considered the chemistry sparking in the front seat between those two Caring Street lifers. "You know, you guys look like the perfect couple. Don't take it as a compliment. I hate perfect couples."

"This is Father Philip," said Francesca. "He's a priest."

"I knew that, priests are kinda obvious. Like his brother, he's not so bad-looking."

—

Philip left Francesca and Terry in the van and went inside to consult with Claire.

"We got a girl we fished out from the street, but I wanted to talk to you first before we came in."

"Give her something to eat?"

"Sandwich she devoured, but hear me. She says she knows you—and Matty."

Claire had handled intake duties for a while, but that was a new one to her.

"She said you and Matty took her in one night, seems she used to be a student of his. She also says you stole a gun she herself stole…Weird story, seems like."

"That's Terry all right, big imagination. Yeah, that's quite a story about a gun. Troubled kid, no question."

"Is she right for us?"

"She's what Caring Street is all about, Philip. I did have some trouble with her, I'll be honest, but I blame myself, I should have trusted Matty's judgment. Your brother's got such a big heart, and the kids all love him, like Terry. So, sure, bring her in, she and I'll work it out. People change, and my gut tells me she's been through a lot. If we don't take her in, where else is a girl like her going to go?"

"What's she talking about, you stealing her gun?"

"Come on, Father, does she look like the type to be carrying a weapon? And you know me better than that."

Chapter Twenty
Philip & Ruth

G LASS OF WINE?" PHILIP invited Ruth, opened bottle in hand, both sitting on barstools in their hideaway apartment that afternoon. They had talked on the phone over the past few weeks, but had not been physically together since the morning after the gala and whatever it was that had happened to Bishop Mackey. He had been busy managing the aftermath and doing all he could to accomplish the everyday work of the diocese, all the while trying to do his work at Caring Street. "I got your fave Sauvignon Blanc."

"No, thanks." The idea of wine made her sick to her stomach.

He poured himself a shot of tequila, unsure if he had her permission, or if he wanted it.

"What's with tequila? That's a new thing for you."

It *was* a new thing for Philip, but he had nothing revealing to add. The silence stretched along the counter where they sat at opposite ends and the quiet sludged up the air between them like invisible grease. Same time, he intended to appear jovial, cheerful, positive. He wasn't adept at faking that. He could *almost* tell she wanted him to appear anything but, which only increased his commitment to keeping things light. He sensed escalating intensity, but unless that was attributable to their temporary separation from each other as a result of forces beyond their control, he couldn't put his finger on the cause.

"You smoking these days?" For a change, he didn't use an accusatory tone.

She shook her head.

"Proud of you. Not easy, giving up."

She let his unconsciously provocative words hang, suspended on the tightrope between them, accumulating greater mass. But she couldn't tolerate the tension, and she commenced the journey down her mental slalom...

Ruth possessed the therapist's essential knack for highlighting, or underscoring, those extraordinary disclosures that are cloaked in the mundane. (Classic moment on this score she remembered hearing in her office: "Nice weather we're having." "What do you mean by that wisecrack?") She never saw a pulled curtain she didn't try to draw open. When she accomplished that feat, and it was no small thing, light could flood the room, although sometimes darkness pooled. Either result could be something she could work with. And when psychic walls popped up between her and her client, as was hardly uncommon, she wouldn't use a battering ram. No, she looked for a door, she and her client, a search party heading off into the darkness. In her experience, there usually was a door, often hidden or small, occasionally constructed in an unexpected place. The door could be sealed shut, of course, but that's what a talented therapist learns how to do: To encourage subtly, artfully the client to open wide the door they discovered to let them both come inside. But what if that turns out to be an elevator door? Going up, going down? That is the question, isn't it? She once had a lighthearted former flower child, rage-against-the-machine ex-hippie who became, as a result of an unexpected and mind-boggling inheritance from a stepfather she hardly knew, an unfathomably rich (and depressed) client who suffered from debilitating vertigo as well as continual motion sickness. For her, elevators would have amounted to a nonstarter, at least without proper meds. Poor Delphine, wonder whatever happened to her after she bought that tiny Greek island—last she ever heard of her. But for most people, anything but going sideways produces therapeutic dividends. But it's come to that now? Talking dividends, therapy? How could Ruth feel simultaneously exhausted and wired up? She'd gone cold turkey with the coffee, too.

That is how long it took her to respond to his saying he was proud of her for stopping smoking:

"Yes, I mean no, because there are people who are always just around the corner from giving up, thank you," she said, admittedly nonsensically.

Passive-aggressive is a specialized faculty, one she lacked. When she came upon its manifestations with clients during a session in her office, her first barely resistible inclination was to go all World Wrestling Federation upon them. It was among the most insidious syndromes to address. That's partly why working with adolescents, who can be masters of passive-aggressive, can be so exasperating. Philip and she, she began to realize, were going to have to endure this new awkwardness until one of them decided to blow it up. Ready, set…

Philip never for a moment aspired to being a therapist or to undergoing therapy, for that matter. At the outset, her profession thrilled him as much as his thrilled her. When things were going well between them, he regarded her vocation as glamorous and fascinating. When they weren't going so well, he would feel alternately amused and annoyed by therapy-speak. But he never condescended. No, he was smitten and he felt lucky to know her. At the same time, he might have some clue to the nature of the world Ruth inhabited, from his exposure to those unconscious or deflected disclosures that took place in the rarefied tiny enclosure known as the confessional box. That's where he listened as supplicants for forgiveness owned up to their faults and failings, their treacheries and infidelities, which unfailingly moved him. The longer he was a priest, the surer he was that there were those who didn't completely give up and divulge the ultimately sordid unfiltered, unmediated truths about their lives—and they were wise to do so. They held back some guiltiness in reserve, feeling there were some sins they were not ready to own up to, or that they were unworthy of forgiveness for some unnamed sin. He himself shared that feeling. But if he'd had the chance he would have advised them that there was nothing—absolutely nothing—he had not already heard before, and he would assure them he was acquainted with much greater sinners than they were, whoever they may be. He shared that experience, too. Nonetheless, some indeed felt they were healed in the confessional process—and that was not a suboptimal result. As far as they were concerned, that might have qualified as a transcendent experience. In a way, it might have been simpler for someone to speak in the darkness to somebody else in darkness on the other side of the screen. These days, you could also opt for face-to-face confession, which could strike somebody as the equivalent of surgery in the battlefield triage tent. Non-Catholics have been known to cynically deride the entire concept. You commit *your depravities and you go dump the news on some invisible priest on the other side of the screen and you automatically receive a free pass, a clean bill of psychic health? Come on. That's mumbo jumbo and a whitewash of your conscience. Philip agreed that the critics had half of a point, but they missed the essence. Unconcealing oneself, even partially, was never simple, and coming to terms with one's own culpability required fortitude and faith in a forgiving Divinity. In this way, the priest functioned as nothing less than the conduit of God's love for a sinner pleading forgiveness for transgressions, including the sins they dare not articulate. A priest might be riddled with guilt himself, might conceivably be a son of a bitch, but he could help other sinners come to terms with what they had done by being present with them in their naked moment of admission. In this age of relentless self-absorption, loving oneself and forgiving oneself were deemed virtues and sufficient. Father Philip begged to differ. And he had firsthand the rock-solid proof: himself. Given the high stakes of the confessional encounter, it was no wonder people didn't seek out the sacrament as often as they used to. And that was an understatement. Confession had practically collapsed as a religious practice, though it had been modernized during his lifetime, rechristened the Sacrament of Reconciliation. Philip preferred the old-school terminology. Remarkably, and this is something he kept private, he himself hadn't taken that sacrament for a long time—he had not confessed and he was not reconciled, either. Early in Philip's priesthood, confession went for hours on Saturdays for people willing to tell what they did that they regretted and beseech pardon. These days, confessional hours were abbreviated and pews were mostly empty on Saturday, unlike when he was growing up and churches were buzzing and people stood patiently in wait for the onslaught of grace. In many parishes, confession was available now only by appointment. These days in some parishes the confessional box was the default repository for hymnals and custodial equipment. What had happened? Philip was sure people sinned as often as they ever did, but they felt less of a need to unburden themselves and receive the grace that flowed. Maybe therapy was their preferred recourse to self-deliverance. Or assuming one's own guilt had fallen out of fashion. Or people did their confessing on Twitter or Facebook or Instagram or somewhere bloodless and fleshless online, prophylactically and anonymously. When you confessed you were hidden in shadows behind a closed door, but you were not anonymous—just the opposite. He was always amused to recall a story told by an old priest. "Lady of a certain age takes a knee in the creaky confessional box, Philip, and she goes, 'Bless me, Father, for I have sinned. It has been thirty years since my last confession.' I say to her, 'Thirty years? Just the highlights, my child.'"*

He didn't like where Ruth's line of thinking, and the silence gathered between them, was leading him.

"Something on your mind? You look distracted," she said.

"We haven't seen each other for a while."

"You look burned out, too."

"Thanks a lot." But he guessed that was how he must appear. He had been putting in longer than ever hours and it was grueling working closely with Bishop Mackey, who was struggling to recover full function. All the same, the bishop was also doing unexpected, extraordinary, remarkable things now, on a regular basis. "One thing is, Mackey, he's driving me crazy—but in a great way, hard to explain."

Whatever happened after the gala that night just might have altered the bishop's perspective on his life and his faith. Philip would concede the possibility. Take the matter of Patricia, who had once been a good nun for over twenty years. Her case presented a sticky challenge. Patricia left her religious order almost fifteen years ago, at age forty-four, and took up with her partner, with whom she had fallen in love. She and Gina were happy together, and in their hearts remained Catholics, despite the church's not recognizing their union or the sanctity of their love. Then Gina's cancer got the best of her and she died an agonizing, protracted death in hospice. After a year of living alone, or so Patricia told Bishop Mackey and Philip, she heard a calling to return to the order and resume her vows, and she humbly pleaded with the sisters for readmission. She wasn't motivated by loneliness or financial considerations either, because Patricia had a loving family and Gina left her enough inherited money to live in her accustomed ways, if that was her preference. But it wasn't. Patricia yearned once again for the communal life and heard a calling to return to her vocation as a schoolteacher. Her superiors put her through the paces, and after a lot of hard talk and harder prayer, they took her back with approval from the Vatican, embracing her wholeheartedly—the prodigal nun parable, they may have called it. Superiors established no conditions, but Patricia donated every cent of her financial assets to the order anyway. She had no need for money anymore, but the order did, and a life of willed poverty felt more meaningful than ever to her. But then there was a complication. When Mackey first caught wind of the sisters' decision to put her back in the classroom, he was adamant: she was not the kind of nun he would permit working in his diocese schools. She had made her choices, had lived in mortal sin, or as he put it, in a gravely evil state. Sister Patricia's order was infuriated, but powerless before Mackey's authority, and assigned her to administrative duties with the order, placing her nowhere with access to children, as the bishop insisted.

"But then, here comes the truly crazy part. You won't believe this, Ruth, last week Mackey—out of the blue, Mackey said he'd had a change of heart as to Sister Patricia. I had no clue she was still on his radar. But then he goes and tells me, notify the sisters that Sister Patricia would be welcomed back into the classroom. Everybody is entitled to make a mistake, even a major one like hers, he told me, but she deserved a second chance. And get this. He wanted to be clear about something else with the nuns. He was sorry for what he had put Sister Patricia and them through, and he asked me to convey his apologies, and to ask for their forgiveness. Believe that?"

"That's a great and weird story. Something must have rearranged his brain, and his soul. Now that his heart might have been pried open, you think there's a chance he's going to drop the morality clause from teachers' contracts? That is such a crackpot idea: calling them ministers."

"Yeah, I know, I know, I'm working on that, too."

"I hope you're trying to convince him to do the right thing."

"And I'm not done. He also said we should check back in with Hector Alessandro, remember him from Caring Street? He wants to meet with him again. He is wondering if he'd made a mistake there, too. My head hasn't stopped spinning. I'm no neurosurgeon, but I guess amazing turnarounds and happy endings can happen when you least expect them."

That's what he said, to which she replied, "Hope you're right about that." She knew he was about to spin out more.

—

"You okay, Ruth?" She didn't look it.

"Why should I be?"

So that's where they were going.

"You want me to leave?"

"The opposite. I want you to stay."

"Not going anywhere, Ruth."

"I want you to stay. I want you to stay, and to marry me."

The old argument had taken a decidedly unfeasible turn, and if she was determined to raise the stakes, he was prepared to call. "Maybe this is wrong, what we are doing, and what we have become. Maybe it's time we stop. We had something wonderful, which I will always treasure, but maybe our time is up."

"Patronizing asshole. Why don't you treasure *that*?" She refused to weep.

Philip threw down another tequila shot. They were going to have that conversation again—except that here she proposed the impossible marriage idea. He understood why they would talk about this and why they should. He asked her again if she would like a glass of wine, because that helped her mood in moments like this, but she refused, and then at long last explained to him why she wasn't drinking.

"I am pregnant, you idiot." She rushed off into the bathroom, where she could be sick by herself if it came to that, and stayed there for a long time till she gathered herself.

—

"How'd that happen?"

"What, they don't teach biology in the seminary?"

"We took precautions."

"You mean *I* took precautions, and shut up." Gloves were now off.

He was at a loss for words.

"Restrain yourself being overly concerned for the woman you supposedly love."

"What are you going to do?"

"What am I going to do? What am *I* going to do? Are you serious?"

"The priesthood, it's my life."

"That's your problem, not mine—and not ours. We have a baby on the way. Ten weeks, says the OB. Not an embryo anymore. Know what a fetus looks like at ten weeks? You should go online and look up what your child is doing. Ten weeks, nervous system, fingers and toes."

"Jesus."

"Look around. Jesus is not helping you or me. What'd you say a minute ago? Amazing turnarounds can happen? Got one up your sleeve?"

"Okay, Ruth, what are we going to do?"

"I can show you the sonar."

Not now, not yet ready to look.

"Wait a second," she said. "You think there are *options*? You really want to go there?"

"I'm going to take care of you, if you let me. But I don't know what that means."

"This is the biggest moment of your life, isn't it? Guess what? Me too, me too."

"It's not how I expected it all to end."

"Son of a bitch."

"What I mean is, this is not how I expected my life would go."

She almost said he should have thought about that before, but she herself should have thought about that, too. "When are you going to come over to me?"

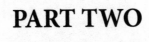

PART TWO

Chapter Twenty-One
Francesca & Paddy

THE THROATY SYMPHONY OF Maserati tailpipes heralded Paddy's arrival that early afternoon. He stepped out of his beloved vintage car, the effort to do so not as smooth nor as uncomplicated as it used to be, what with the hitch in his hips and the arthritis in his creaky knees that the quarterly cortisone shots alleviated but only temporarily and to a limited degree. The subject of knee replacements had come up with the orthopedist. And while she had her patient's attention, hip replacement, too.

"I'm not saying surgical intervention is inevitable, Paddy, but it is foreseeable," she said.

"Foreseeable maybe by you, deary," he said.

The patient himself was not interested, no matter what the MRIs showed. He didn't need joint replacement, he needed doc replacement. In the meantime, he resolved to live with the discomfort, or outlive it. Ah, the golden years. The stage of life that was all about, you might say, general contracting. If it wasn't about his body's electrical or mechanical repairs, it was about the damn plumbing. Don't get him started about stumbling out of bed four or five times a night. As he once confided to Jonesy in an unguarded moment, "Some days my whole mortal existence consists of one constant effort to piss, interrupted periodically by dinner or buying baubles for Caitlin—not to complain," he complained.

Jonesy said, with emphasis, "I can relate, and no man is a hero to his valet, the one exception being you, sir."

"You're very adorable, aren't you?"

"The things people say about me, I would blush."

Such considerations notwithstanding, brightly smiling Paddy hobbled over to arms-akimbo Francesca, waiting smiling for him near the one tiny, ramshackle structure left standing on his property, the land that could be the site of the new high school, if negotiations bore fruit. "Am I late, Frankie darling?" he asked, though he knew he wasn't.

"No no no, right on the button, Paddy."

She was the sort of businesswoman who made it a priority to evince respect for peers by arriving early for an appointment, something that would impress a man like Paddy Fitzgerald, and it did. On the other hand, Italians—like her own father—seemed willfully incapable of being on time. Just because it was a cliché didn't mean it wasn't true. To Big Mimmo, people waited if you were important enough, thereby showing *you* respect. Again, she subscribed to the opposite. On one level, today she was conspicuously signaling deference for her negotiating partner (and father-in-law); on another level, it was an easy method of gaining a slightly subtle upper hand.

Nonetheless, Paddy was hardly a candidate to be played. Same time, he realized he was spinning in the eddy of uncharted waters: about to conduct a business negotiation with his dearest daughter-in-law, who was here representing the diocese and Bishop Mackey—and who herself had arrived early, too. If this connection, this family history, granted him any leverage, it was going to be tough to revel in it—though the prospect was enticing enough to possibly exploit. Of course, he imagined, she might feel the counter position, that it was *she* who had the unarticulated, unacknowledged leverage over him. Paddy had no fear of conflicts; as he informed his son Philip, no potential conflict? Don't bother talking. Family and business: most people say mix them at your own peril. Maybe they were right, too. Yet some of these obvious people don't know enough to bet on the winning horse if they got past-posted race results inside information.

Paddy genuinely liked the girl. Well, he should correct himself: the *woman*, a woman who was probably as wealthy as he was, if not wealthier.

She had been and continued to be in his own heart his daughter-in-law, the love of his eldest son's brutally foreshortened life. They hugged: a frank, warm embrace.

She gestured with feeling toward the Maserati, the White Lady. "Special occasion, Paddy?" She recalled that he drove the car for such times deemed *special*.

"Could be, Frankie, could be, you'll have to tell me." He couldn't resist turning tables. And he also couldn't resist acknowledging to himself that he might have outlived the purpose of having the Maz. This was a young man's car, not the car of the old man he had become.

"Haven't seen your gorgeous wheels for a long time."

He could cite exactly how long it had been, if pressed, to the day. "No point not driving it, not getting any younger. I was hoping the bishop would be joining us, heard he's feeling his oats again."

"Word is, he's feeling a little better, day by day, thanks. I'll pass along your regards, he asked me to represent."

This negotiation had been going on for far too long, everyone could agree. They weren't building the Panama Canal, said Paddy, and not for the first time, so he went for it. "You have authority, do you?"

"We're talking, you and I, see if we can move the ball down the field."

"This is a simple real estate deal, and I was hoping Mackey would finally get serious."

"I don't know about *simple*. But the diocese is serious, that's why I'm here, and I wouldn't be, and I wouldn't waste your time or mine, if the diocese wasn't."

"Life being brief as it is, how about we do a deal, Frankie?" He'd heard the diocese counters in the past, which he dismissed as semi-ridiculous if not in bad faith, so he wasn't in the mood to play softball. They had exhausted his patience. When he was a younger man, he would have walked away already, not before telling them where to go with the horse they rode in on. It was different now. For one thing, Mackey had roped in Francesca, so he was shrewder than Paddy counted on. In any case, he said to her, and pleasantly enough, "What the fuck." Even if it was Francesca he was dealing with, he found it proved useful to throw out a *fuck* or a *shit* as soon as possible in the lead-up conversation, to make the proceedings sound gritty, real, because that's what a good deal is, gritty and real. And then surprisingly, preemptively, and without setup, he tossed out a number, a big round number, but materially smaller than his previous big round number. Based on his past, he would never have done that; you let the other party show their hand first.

"You have done the due diligence, so you know, you of all people, Frankie, that's a very good price I just quoted you."

She shouldn't have been totally surprised that Paddy jump-started the conversation, and she wasn't, so she was careful, mindful of not revealing too hastily *her* cards.

"This whole thing has been going on forever, Frankie, time for Mackey to shit or get off the pot, somebody might crassly say." So he had gotten the *fuck* and the *shit* out of the way now.

"Let's say," she said, "for the sake of discussion, we can ultimately work with something in the neighborhood of that number. For the proverbial sake of discussion."

He was in no mood to slow-play anymore. Her presence had both complicated and simplified matters, which he appreciated that the bishop slickly and accurately presumed would do the trick.

"Paddy, I have a feeling I know what you need."

He tilted his head, sensing she was about to make a bold move.

"*Merende?*" she said. By which she meant snacks. She said it used to be thought by linguists that Eskimos have lots of variations of words referring to snow, which sounded fascinating enough, but it turned out not to be so. But Italians do in fact have several alternative terms, subtly differentiable, for snacks—and sleeping, for that matter. She digressed, which was the point. Digression is also an indispensable tool of the artful negotiator.

"Sounds serious."

"It's *very* serious. It's *food*."

"You Italians, does it always come back to eating?"

"Oh, for us it's often about money as well, and occasionally God."

"All the same, then."

—

ARRIVING IN ADVANCE OF their meeting, she arranged a little table and a couple of lawn chairs on the other side of the building in the shade afforded by two sturdy, spreading Japanese maple trees, and that's where she guided him. She had laid out a beautiful white linen tablecloth, upon which were set out cheeses, sardines, salami, flatbread with dark pink, thinly sliced prosciutto, beautiful green olives and capers, and two gorgeous sliced-up peaches that glowed. It was pure Francesca: do something unexpected and surprising, disarm somebody participating in a difficult set of circumstances, create an atmosphere of openness and generosity, all via the miraculous ministrations of delicious food.

"We're having a picnic, Frankie dear?"

"On such a beautiful site, where we're going to build a beautiful new school someday, doesn't that sound like a nice idea?"

Celebrating seemed the essence of premature to him, but what could be the harm? "And look at this." He picked up the impressively labeled bottle she had opened next to the two country goblets.

"Anthony's favorite Brunello, 1997, a great vintage in Tuscany. Seemed like the perfect opportunity to open it—I mean, what are we all waiting for?" Thereby planting a seed. And thereby allowing Paddy to realize she was attempting to plant a seed.

"I was surprised when my boy took an interest in wine, figured him to stay a beer and Jameson guy. Though nothing wrong with the red Italian wine."

She was thinking how much Anthony had changed over the course of their marriage. "My dad and Anthony constantly talked wine, went shopping for the best vintages and visited wineries when we traveled to Napa and Italia. French and California are great, but—surprise—my dad turned up his Italian *naso*. He enjoyed educating Anthony, because, as he said, my husband knew everything else in the world worth knowing so it was about time he learned Italian wine: Sangiovese, Barolo, Barbaresco, Valpolicella. Not to mention, according to my dad, he was smart enough to marry, well, me. And Anthony had a good palate, he said, and Mimmo didn't blow smoke, unless it was true, or unless he was getting good odds."

"What I know about wine wouldn't pack a leprechaun's pouch, so Big Mimmo can one day teach me, too."

"You kidding? He would love that."

They sat down and Francesca poured the ruby red wine. It should have been decanted, as it would have been had it been served in her and Anthony's favorite Florence restaurant, the hilariously overpriced but fabulous Enoteca Pinchiorri. Yet with enough air in the swirling goblet, the wine would only get better and better the deeper they went into the bottle, which, with any luck, they would achieve forthwith.

"Try the focaccia, that will make the wine pop."

And he did and it was true. To his untutored palate it was gorgeous. He was appreciating the velvety drink as he had never appreciated wine before. Older he got, no use putting off learning new tricks. He had a lot to learn about other things, too, if Caitlin proved to be a keeper—and the image of her face surfaced in his mind.

After a few minutes of silent wine-drenched pleasure, they both simultaneously cast their eyes across the beautiful expanse of land. Paddy had initiated the preliminary surveying, but even if he hadn't, he was aware of the boundless promise of this property—and so was she. Here, he was thinking, right here where they were sitting, with the rolling hills in the distance, this would be the perfect spot for the main school building. He dared not venture such a notion out loud, certainly not at this stage of the conversation, though Frankie would have been moved to hear exactly what he was imagining— which was one reason he would not mention that. Problem was, united in love for Anthony and his memory as they may have been, they were also two people with individual drivers in a commercial negotiation. In a typical negotiation there was a winner and there was a loser. In a good negotiation, there were two winners—both parties got and gave value they could live with. Individual interests push them into each other's arms.

He was curious about something else. "You and Philip friends again?"

"Dear Philip. We were never not friends. But we're spending some time together again these days. He tells me he's happy big things are going on for you."

"He's happy, is he? That would be news, him being happy. And Philip, my Philip, he's curious about what he thinks is my romantic life. What about you, Frankie, seeing anybody?"

"Yes, I am, but I don't know. I don't know for sure. Sometimes it feels right, sometimes it feels beside the point."

"You know in your heart if the man's a keeper or not."

"Anyway, Philip says your *amore* is quite beautiful."

"An Irish lassie amore. Might be too young for me, or I might be too old for her."

"Where'd you two meet?"

"Oh, I don't know, the usual, let's say the opera house?"

She laughed. And he did, too. He wasn't going to give up that information, and that was fine, it was unimportant. "Philip says Caitlin seems to have a very good heart, and you two might be serious."

"One glass of fine wine into our conversation, I can say yes, that's all true about her, she's a good girl. But serious? We'll see, we'll see. I did ask her to move into Haymarket with me. God, doesn't that sound like college kid stuff? Living together? One day she'll make an honest man out of me."

"That's wonderful, Paddy. I'm thrilled to hear, and I can't wait to meet her. *Cent'anni*," she announced with a flourish. "A hundred years. That's a good-luck toast." She raised her goblet of Brunello.

"Oh, good, I guess, because I can always use some good luck. But I won't be around if we wait a century to do a deal."

Frankie and Paddy clinked glasses, and they proceeded to get into it as never before.

—

"We're not having a fire sale, sweetheart, that figure's a bargain, and you know it."

"I can see why you think so."

"That's the spirit, Frankie."

"What kind of terms can you give us?"

"Bank money's dirt cheap these days, they're practically giving it away, why you want me to finance the deal?"

"Not saying we do. Just talking, considering all the options."

"I can work with you on the terms, the timing, all depending."

"On what?"

A fair contest, then: they both had done lots of complex negotiations. She found it interesting that he was moving forthrightly into the higher weeds. When it came to deal-making, every bit as important as the specifics, you needed to figure out what the other party wanted. Amateurs think it's about cash, but that proves why they are amateurs. Cash pushes deals only to a point, and then the real interests kick in. It was usually a version of respect, or fear, or some preciously held preconception, usually about family or financial security or ego. Beyond all that you need to ask: Why were the parties engaged *now?* Figure out the timing, assess the urgency, everything else should fall into place.

"Depending, I don't know, like let's say naming rights, here and there," he said.

"That's certainly on the table for us."

"Construction contract…"

She poured them both more wine. She wasn't prepared to give away the store yet. "Let's not get ahead of ourselves, but we would of course entertain a sound, competitive bid from you—or any first-rate GC. A construction deal with the seller might strike people as monkey business, but we could see our way around working with that." Actually, she didn't have a problem at all with that, and she could artfully structure the deal so as to make sure the diocese was meeting the burden of honoring its fiduciary duties.

Piece of cake, he was thinking, he didn't expect she would give in so readily, or at least not resist forcefully. "And let's not forget the dumb loyalty oath. We gotta deep-six that bullshit right now."

That was a heave from out of right field. She didn't see that one coming, but she should have. She rallied. "Don't give me up to Mackey, but you and Philip and I all agree on that one. That was a crackbrain idea the bishop had." She was holding back something. What she didn't add was that the bishop, though he hadn't announced this, had been thinking about flipping on the issue, thanks to, she had every reason to believe, Philip's good influence behind the scenes. She would keep that concession in her pocket for the time being, waiting until the crucial moment when she could gain maximum leverage.

"If that should happen, then we're halfway home to popping the champagne, Frankie—or another bottle of what is this again? Brunello, right?"

"And if you throw in the Maz…"

"I'll never give up that buggy. So dream on. When Irish eyes are smiling…" But then his eyes darkened, and his head felt weighted down on his neck, and he was not comprehending why—until, that is, he caught himself remembering there was a time long ago when he was prepared to give that car to her and Anthony on some big occasion in their lives, like a major anniversary, or the birth of their child. Infinite and unending seemed the disappointments life had handed him—and, he would have to admit, life had handed her, too.

She picked up on his shaken state of mind but couldn't intuit the precise emotion roiling the air. "Can't fault a girl for asking. It's a beauty, that car of yours."

He steered himself back into control. "And another thing. If Matty kept his job at the school, I could be even more flexible."

"I don't think we are going to go down that road, micromanaging staffing decisions."

"As my wife of sainted memory would say, Jesus, Mary, and Joseph. Sure you can, and you want to."

At this juncture of a fast-moving conversation, she should signal that she—meaning the bishop and the school—could maybe work with that. She wouldn't tip her hand; she might have her work cut out with the bishop. "Everybody knows Matty's a great teacher, and I'm sure the bishop naturally wants the best for the kids." Taking the middle course seemed prudent here, and saving that concession for when they verged on cinching the agreement.

"Pretty smart, old Mackey, dinged up as he is, getting my cherished daughter-in-law involved." Because Paddy *was* indeed impressed. But then, he had to move in for the deal. You can play hardball or you can flatter your way into wresting an agreement. Paddy preferred to do both, simultaneously.

Time for the head fake. "I don't know about that, but I did tell His Excellence not to get his hopes up too high for my meeting with you today," she said. "For the Fitzgeralds, money is money. And also is money."

"You don't believe that for a second, Frankie. And I wouldn't be talking in the first place if it were true."

"Good talk, Paddy. I'll get back to you right away, once I draft the letter of intent."

"Finally! And I know you will. Of course, your LOI will be very clean. And so we're clear, I've been patient enough and my generosity wears off in, let's say, forty-eight hours." He had softened her up with the reduced price, but he needed to drive home that he was in charge. "Nothing personal, my dear, but we need to get to a binding agreement in the next couple of days or this deal is dead, and not ever rising from the dead like Lazarus."

"What did you say? *Nothing personal?* You know what Anthony would say. Everything's personal."

Paddy smiled his saddest smile. "I can hear my boy saying that."

The two of them shared the silence, and they reflected on the loss, and the remembered joy, they also shared.

"That's my beloved father-in-law."

"You know you'll always be a Fitzgerald. You're a lifer, hell or high water."

She never required being reminded. She knew all about hell and all about high water. Beyond that incontrovertible truth, they both knew they had cinched the deal.

Chapter Twenty-Two
Colleen & Caitlin & Paddy

"M IGRAINE OR YOU WANT to ask me something?" said Paddy to his daughter. "You got that squinty look going."

Her withering migraines dated from long, long ago, for which reprieve she was beyond grateful. And nobody would want to summon up the memory of such icepick pain.

"I do not squint," she squinted. "Do I?"

"See, right there, I can almost hear your face squeak. You sure no migraine?"

"Matter of fact I do have a question for you, so here comes *your* migraine. Let me inquire indelicately. You out of your damn mind, Dad?" Colleen knew that he knew what she was asking about. "I'm curious."

"You've always been that way with your squinting curiosity, Colly. Let me know once you figure out my mental state."

A talkative and confrontational child—her mother called her mouthy— since she exited mewling from the birth canal, she always enjoyed greater latitude with her father than her brothers did, and she capitalized upon that advantage.

"Fine, then, this just in: You *are* out of your mind."

—

THAT EXCHANGE, SUCH AS it was, took place the day before Caitlin moved into the Family Fitzgerald home on Haymarket Hill. It might be easy to appreciate why a grown daughter would be less than thrilled to welcome with open arms her ageing widower father's lover. Full stop: the very notion of his *lover* was too much, practically instilling vertigo as she contemplated the grotesque prospect. But still, her father indeed had his whatever-was-the-term for this new relationship, and this woman—all right, fine, *his* woman—was about to take up residence in the family home. At the same time, it may not be so easy to explain why, given who Colleen was, independent and freewheeling and open-minded, why she herself cared. To her, being judgmental was a mortal sin, not that she subscribed to the concept of sin, mortal, venial, or class B felony. Her mother of sainted memory continued to cast her long shadow in the psychic hallways of every Fitzgerald alive—with the possible exception, she was beginning to think, and she would be wrong about this, of Paddy Fitzgerald himself.

Her father wasn't to be on the premises, but Colleen herself was, when Caitlin showed up with her dozen or so boxes of belongings and three beaten-down plaid suitcases, everything toted inside by Jonesy O'Dell and the bemused crew. According to the prearranged plan, she claimed the spacious sunlit bedroom adjoining Paddy's master suite on the top floor, a tall-windowed room that compared favorably to the master. The sight of her bedraggled luggage made Colleen feel something like sympathy—and bafflement as well: as in how come her dad hadn't bought new bags for her? This seemed like a missed stitch. Another missed stitch in addition to his not being present for the move-in. He explained he didn't want to get in the way—but when did he ever *not* want to? Was he counting on his squinting daughter to represent the Fitzgerald welcoming delegation?

—

As SHE BUSTLED ABOUT in her lime-green tennis shoes and shorts, hair pulled back with a lime-green scrunchie, Caitlin's demeanor appeared hardly triumphant or festive—more like electroshock therapy aftermath. She was not orchestrating activities; she seemed content to be following others' leads.

Jonesy was transporting a very large box in which Caitlin had packed her shoes. He peeked inside: must have been twenty pairs. He did have a job as a young man selling women's shoes in a department store. One thing he learned on the display floor was that a woman whose feet were to him too large or too wide, no matter how pretty her face, how graceful her personal style, was not a keeper, at least in terms of what some might label his misogynistic or possibly fetishistic bias. The sight of her bodily misfortune was too sad to bear. On this score, he wouldn't wish for Miss Caitlin to misunderstand, or question his probity and decorum, or to think he was being in the slightest bit inappropriate, so he would never breathe a word along these lines to her, but he did believe the pretty girl was possessed of supremely gorgeous feet. He'd never been berated as sexist by any of his many, many lady friends, but that revealed more about his social circles than anything else. More to the point, he knew better than to share his podiatric, or shoe salesman's, point of view, most especially around the spirited Miss Colleen, who was always walking point along the women's objectification trail.

"Where shall I put these ravishing shoes of yours?" he said.

Caitlin had no idea, and said put them anywhere he'd like, but she must have been weary or rendered uninhibited by the stresses of the move because she added: "You like them? I don't think they're your size."

"Yes, I do admire them. And no, Miss Caitlin, they are most definitely not."

"You yourself always wear beautiful shoes, Mr. O'Dell, like Paddy."

"Mr. Fitzgerald is my role model in all matters."

"You and me got that in common as well, then."

"*And did those feet in ancient time walk upon England's mountain green and was the holy lamb of God on England's pleasant pastures seen.* Or thus sings the bardic poet."

"It sounded a lot like poetry."

"Except for the wretched jingle, the England pleasant pastures part— bloody tyrants, the Brits. Please excuse the coarse language, Miss."

"Thanks for your help, Mr. O'Dell. And the poetry."

"Pleasure, Miss Caitlin."

Paddy's daughter observed doings from a distance. No doubt, Caitlin was taking an enormous leap. How could she possibly know what journey she had embarked upon? And then, how could the family know what was about to happen to them? She didn't strike Colleen as the type of woman who blended into the furniture and wallpaper, and Fitzgeralds didn't resemble potted plants. So high stakes were on the table everywhere, if not fireworks in the sky above Haymarket, the way Paddy Fitzgerald would have it. And so yes, indeed, she thought, solid chance her father was out of his mind.

But what's that supposed to mean, Colleen asked herself, not moving into Dad's bedroom? At the same time, she didn't wish to visualize the stark domestic alternative.

—

COLLEEN EXPRESSED HER MEAGER enthusiasm to Matty this way: "On the plus side, now we know at least somebody can stand the son of a bitch enough to move in with him." Her brother was also skeptical of Caitlin, and critical of the minx, as he labeled her, but he ultimately didn't care a great deal one way or the other about his dad's love life, the very nomenclature of which was unfathomable. Matty had his own problems, which he would share with anybody, provided an opening, which Colleen wasn't of a mind to furnish—she had other matters pressing upon her.

Colleen followed up with Philip on the phone. "You didn't know he was planning this?"

"It's a respectful passage of time, I suppose, four years since mom, considering the man's advancing age."

"Pretty dramatic, don't you think? You mean, he didn't give you a heads-up?"

"And why would he, at this stage of his life, start telling me anything?"

"Matty calls her the minx. Red hair, stiletto heels, micro minis, like that."

"Really, Colleen? Matty's take on women, or any other subject, is automatically suspect. Why sound like a mean girl, why not give her a chance?"

"Easy for you to say, living in the security and safety of the Chancery, not here on the hill."

He said that was a first; nobody ever put *safety* and *Chancery* in the same sentence. "Appearances can be deceiving. And maybe the two of them really love each other. Stranger things have happened."

"Name three."

"Okay, fair point, but love doesn't come around every day."

"Profound, Swami Fitzgeraldananda."

"Actually, it *is* profound, Colly. Now, maybe he should have thrown in with someone more age-appropriate, but it's his life, and hers. She just might be okay. Longer I'm a priest, the less surprised I am by the human race."

"So you would hitch them up, Reverend?"

"Haven't been approached, but canonically, priests cannot quote marry unquote anybody, that's a sacrament performed by the couple themselves."

"Blah blah Baltimore Catechism, you drunk?"

"Not yet, but after our charming conversation, that's an increasingly attractive option. I'll come by, welcome her to Haymarket, show her around where Paddy buried all the bodies…"

"Wait, stop, what?"

"And you and I can slip away and conspire about God only knows what."

Philip could understand why his father didn't alert him in advance of Caitlin's move-in, but despite what he said to his sister, he remained perplexed by his father's romantic turn. Not as much as he was perplexed about his own romantic developments, of course, and romantic was not the ideal word choice. Everything was happening so fast for him on every front. But if the old man had his few moments of joy late in life, more power to him. Was his dad actually going to marry the girl? Nobody knew or, if they did, was saying, and he should stop saying *girl* right now and start saying *woman*. It might be a tough habit to break, given the way his father referred to her: as a girl. He doubted the happy couple themselves knew what their future held in store. He had concerns about a woman described by his sister in the way she did, concerns he kept to himself, but of course he didn't know her. The only important question was, how well did his father know her? But if he understood anything about his father, Paddy Fitzgerald's prenup would be airtight.

EVERYBODY WAS COMING TO terms with the new realities of the reconstituted Family Fitzgerald. For one thing, in no time, Colleen had to admit that, whoever Caitlin was, she didn't come across as a gold digger. Of course, she could be too clever to show her conniving hand off the top. Yet the truth was, something about Caitlin fascinated Colleen. She was complex: elegant and awkward, self-assured and uncertain, silly and serious. She was certainly temperamentally different from every Fitzgerald, adding some fresh spice to the Irish stew, and that could be in and of itself a good thing. Maybe it was the case that Caitlin was warmly approachable around Colleen and affectionate to her father, but not in a syrupy, prepossessing way, and he seemed—what he wasn't with his own kids—completely at ease with her.

It didn't bother Colleen that if her father remarried, her "stepmother" would be ten years younger than she. She'd had all the mothering she ever needed, and all the mothering she didn't need. She also wasn't the type to be obsessed about financial ramifications, if, say, they ever married and Paddy passed into the Great Hibernia in the sky—would Caitlin inherit everything? Nothing? Colleen wasn't greedy, and money mattered less to her than she supposed it should have, but that was a function of her being raised in affluence and therefore feeling entitled and moneyed by birth. The nearest she got to embracing the altered family dynamic was when she reminded herself that her father would not be dissuaded from doing what he wanted with his riches, and besides, why would he write off his own flesh and blood at this late date? Besides, the whole estate subject made her feel dirty and disloyal, so she resolved to put it out of her mind.

Originally, and more intensely, Colleen had questioned if she would ever tolerate the pretty pretty girly girl with a transparently sketchy past and a wacky wardrobe half out of Saks and half out of Victoria's Secret, full of flashy bustiers and tight miniskirts and skinny jeans. But she liked to think that she was tolerant and had her own challenges to deal with and therefore wouldn't write off another young woman wending her way however she could. To her way of thinking, women universally had a tough time making it in a patriarchal world.

But then, look what transpired. Before too long, to their mutual amazement, the two of them, Caitlin and Colleen, were hanging out together in the kitchen or in the gardens, talking and cooking alongside Hilda, or heading outside to tend to the olive trees and flower beds and to weed and to feed the plants, side by side with the serenading, happy gardeners. This was all part of a full-scale reappraisal of her whole life. For instance, not so long ago Colleen had renounced her vegan experiment—it wasn't her, although she wasn't completely sold on the corned beef concept, either.

"Vegetarian, I get, I guess," said Caitlin, being diplomatic and measured, "but vegan sounds like work. Is eating supposed to be a job?"

"Thing is," Colleen told her, "I was always hungry, like if I had the chance I could devour raw steak with my bare hands. My skin turned beige and blotchy. Boiled meat I could live without. Life without pepperoni pizza or burgers? It ain't worth living. I'm not going to talk about the gas and the crime scene investigations unit bad breath, leave that to your imagination."

"Thank you for sparing the colorful details," said Caitlin, in a tone that initially startled and then amused Colleen, which transition perfectly summed up her increasingly nuanced, growing sense of Caitlin.

Paddy liked seeing his daughter visiting back home on Haymarket Hill, and liked it more that she had evidently taken a liking to Caitlin.

"It's good, you coming around more. You happy where you're living?" he asked her.

"What's not to like about my apartment? It's like a frat house for deviants—that could describe frat houses, period, I suppose. My downstairs neighbors are into whips and chains and leather, I can hear the creaks and snaps, and my upstairs neighbors are Jehovah's Witnesses. I'm not converting to either."

"That's the sort of domestic account your loving da loves to hear. There's plenty of room here in your home if you want a change of scenery."

She was rendered speechless a moment. True, she did still regard it as her home.

So he was explicit. "You can move back, if you like, for as long as you want."

There had to be a catch, and he read her mind.

"It would be nice to have you back home, if you'd like to be here, a squint-free zone."

"Okay," she said, surprising herself.

"Okay?"

"Okay."

"Okay, then."

"One, Dad, you gotta let up with the squinting thing, and two, what's the tariff?"

"Tariff? Oh, Colly, Colly. Your money's no good with me."

She was out of work, and therefore broke again and had no money good or bad, and the next week she moved into the guest house. It felt like she had never left. And that was both good news and the opposite.

—

COLLEEN TOOK CAITLIN UNDER her wing, turning into her personal reclamation project. It wasn't long before she began to present her books to read, suggested movies and TV shows, and the young woman seemed receptive. So far Collen hadn't broached the fashion challenges she posed or offered to go shopping with her to update the clothes, or to see what she could do to take down the bordello look a few notches. Could Colleen characterize her feelings as sisterly? Growing up, she felt close to Matty, but she had always fantasized about having a female sibling.

Colleen had moved around from job to job, school to school, never landing on a career, much less a vocation. She dabbled in marketing, in sales, in human resources. Her résumé would have appeared incoherent, had she composed one. But she herself wasn't incoherent, so she always found some employer willing to give a smart, appealing young woman like her a chance, often in positions that proved to be over her head. Invariably she would lose interest in the work and then her boss's confidence, and finally her job.

One day Caitlin and Colleen found themselves midday with nothing to do.

"Movie?" proposed Caitlin.

"Not in the mood. Lunch out? That Greek place with the fab hummus?"

"Think I need to check myself, taking in too many calories. I should hit the gym today. Want to come with?"

"Teach me to work the speed bag?"

Caitlin would, and also show her how to skip rope the right way.

"You know, a punching bag sounds like the ticket."

"It is fun, let me tell you, you get all the frustrations out of your system."

—

THAT WAS THE FIRST time they worked out together. Colleen was impressed, and acquired a few tricks and learned a new, taxing exercise routine. Afterward, in the tony gym café under soft track lighting, they sipped on their kelp and kale smoothies. Colleen had a question about this concoction: "People don't die from drinking this?"

"Weren't you the vegan? You get used to it." She rattled off the replenishing nutrient bonanza in their cups. "After a while, it almost tastes pretty good."

"Have to trust you on that one."

Then their conversation, and their connection, took a precarious turn.

"What's the plan, Caitlin?" Vintage Colleen move.

Caitlin bristled, bracing herself for that unexpected broadside she should have expected—people were like that with her, they made assumptions, they thought she required refinement, tutelage. "Plan about what?"

"About your own life."

"I think I'll meet you back at the…"

"Wait, wait, let me start over." That was Colleen being Colleen, being direct, but it didn't work this time, not with Caitlin.

"You do that a lot, I hear, starting over, how's *that* plan working for you?" Best defense was a good offense, according to Caitlin's default survivor's mechanism.

"All right, fair enough, and point taken, but I wasn't going there, really, Caitlin, really."

"I'm nobody's trophy, in case you're wondering. Paddy—your dad and I, we have a bond, which I get it, that might not be understood by his family, or anybody. It's too late to start caring about what other people think, which is what I learned from his example. I told him, day ever comes, which it might never come, knowing Paddy like I do, I'll sign a prenup to nuke all prenups, so don't worry about losing anything to me, Colleen. You think I'm in it for his money? Must be a rare talent, reading other people's minds."

"We're getting off on the wrong foot, my fault. Let's take a deep breath." The way Caitlin went off, with so little provocation, might have signaled that she was protesting too much, but Colleen didn't conclude as much. Caitlin was a hard girl to figure, or Colleen was working too hard, or both.

Caitlin nodded, signaling reluctant, and limited, willingness to listen—a minute more.

"I was asking what you—a smart young woman with…"

"Nobody's ever called me smart, so stop."

"Well, I just did 'cause it's true, so what do you like doing?"

"I barely finished high school."

"Education has nothing to do with smarts. You have an intelligent way of dealing with people, people are attracted to you."

"'Cause I dress like I do, I guess."

"If anything, the opposite." She came this close to talking about the fashion choices, but it was bad timing. "You have so much to offer, Cait."

Caitlin was taken aback, but decided she would tell the truth. "I like cooking, and I like reading the books you give me. I don't always understand them, but I like them—because you want me to like them."

"Well, you like them on your own terms, not because of me."

"You know, your dad said something a little bit similar. He wants me to try new things, on my own. But I think he means it in a good way. One thing I like, I like food."

"I cannot believe how you enjoy your food, you eat like a football player and you're still what? A size zero? I gotta watch myself, but you can eat burritos and guacamole and chips and don't put on a single pound."

"Good genes. And working out like a crazy person."

"Yeah, I noticed that, and I am gonna sleep well tonight, thanks to your kick-ass workout."

"Anyway, your dad, he said why don't I open a little café?"

"Ever worked in a restaurant? I have, and you either have restaurant in your blood or you don't, and sweet cakes, unless you live and love restaurants twenty-four seven, you don't. So what else?"

"Like I said, books, the ones you give me. I have read more in the past few months than I have my whole life."

She looked to have been struck by lightning. "Hey, you know what? I saw the ratty old bookshop on the edge of town is closing up. Dodgy neighborhood, but that's okay, that's opportunity. The old man will buy it for you."

"Wouldn't that be kind of—what you said—patriarch-ish?"

"Yes, it could be patriarchal, but in your case not." Colleen spun out the fantasy awhile—books, authors, customers milling about, touching covers, asking questions and offering opinions and being at the center of interesting discussions all day long. To envision all that was a sweet indulgence.

"You really think, Colly?" But she was simultaneously considering: talk about impractical Colleen's pie in the sky.

"Listen, I want to thank you for making my dad happy. He hasn't always been that way, after Mom, I mean."

"Paddy was so devoted to her, I'll never take her place, I know that, and I wouldn't try."

"Men and women, an unending mystery to me." Her own parents had not paved the way to the palace of marital wisdom.

Caitlin raised her eyebrows, lowered her perfect chin, her skin flawless and aglow post-workout, and she looked knowingly across the table and said not a word, to which Colleen responded:

"Okay, I see what you're doing there, but maybe I'm not gay. I mean, I *was* gay, and I could be gay again, but I'm not now. And I'm not saying men in the abstract interest me, though men in the abstract obviously have advantages over the other kind, taking my wacky brothers as samples of the species. And by the way, it's not gay anymore, the word's *queer*."

Caitlin tried hard to keep up with the rapid pace of social change, and feared she, as young as she was, would never catch up. Colleen kept moving fast.

"Yes, I wanted to sleep with the women I slept with, the women I cared about. That doesn't make me queer."

"It doesn't not make you not gay, I mean *queer*, right?" She was unsure if she said what she meant, or if she understood what it was she meant.

Colleen smiled. "Good point, people love who they love, men or women." She sensed an opportunity to make a big statement, and she seized it with both hands. "You got that last thing right. I reject the entire patriarchal ethos of heteronormative."

Caitlin liked the sparkly new words Colleen taught her, like patriarcish and heronormal, even if she was mostly unclear about them. "Me, too, Colly."

Well, she did or she didn't get what she was saying, but in either case, it was all right with Colleen. "Wait, if you did go into the bookstore biz, what do you imagine that would be like?"

She didn't know. She had her doubts, she supposed. "Like the restaurant biz, isn't it supposed to be in your blood?"

"I would help you, I would love that. Seems to me, you'd be a natural, because a bookstore isn't about selling books so much as serving people who love their books, who live for their books. You're a people person, which nobody ever accused me of being."

"The personal touch, I get that, so it's like any kind of business."

"A little bit, seems like."

Colleen had a radical proposal. "*Floozy's*—you like that name? Edgy, no? It's a bookstore for everybody, not just floozies, not just women who are floozies at heart, because you know what?" She was knocked back by the thunderbolt of insight. "When you get down to it, we're all proud floozies."

Caitlin felt dizzy after having one too many—of ideas. "You're amazing, Colly."

"I know, right?"

Caitlin sipped the sea-green smoothie and wrinkled her nose, having had her fill of the healthy potion. "Let's get out of here, grab some beers, keep talking."

"About time, girlfriend."

—

THAT NIGHT THE TWO women, after three pints apiece not quite sober but nowhere near legitimately hammered, rushed back into the house together, talking over each other. Immediately and excitably they raised the whole entrepreneurial topic with Paddy. He endeavored to take them seriously, and he listened when Colleen rolled out the concept, obviously devoid of specifics as to capital and liquidity and burn rates and sunk costs, all without spreadsheets and projections or accountants to reinforce her case.

"So we're talking hypothetically, blue-skying then," he said. "So let's concede nobody makes money selling books in brick-and-mortar establishments. Do I have that right? Because I heard this rumor making money's the whole purpose of doing business."

They did agree they weren't going to get rich hawking books, or break even. "At least off the bat," Colleen said. And she made an attempt at worst-case scenarios, which had to do with competition from deep discounting of units online, so as to show off her tenuous grasp of the realities. She had already learned that publishers don't sell books, they sell "units."

"I should have bought stock in Amazon when I had the chance." He often lamented his missed opportunities.

"Hey," said Colleen, "Amazon doesn't make money selling books."

"Really?" said Caitlin. "No shit?" This didn't sound heartening.

Here was the thing Colleen wanted her dad to understand. This store would be unlike any other store in town, it would be a warm, welcoming, inviting place for people to gather and to talk books and...

"And to *buy* books?" said Paddy.

"Yes, of course to buy books," said Colleen.

"What Colly said," said Caitlin, trying to further the discussion.

"Caitlin, you want this, a bookshop?"

"Yes, sweetheart, I think I do." That might have been the beer talking, but she cast a look toward Colleen that amounted to *Don't I?*

"And Colly, you're all in, ready to work hard?"

"Absolutely, Dad."

"Here's the thing I want both you businesswomen to think through, and it's a tough question. That old bookstore failed, so what's your magical formula for making yours succeed instead?"

The two women searched each other's eyes and wordlessly interrogated themselves until they arrived at the best possible answer they could come up with.

"Because it will be *our* bookstore," said Colleen, "a Fitzgerald bookstore, that's why, and we Fitzgeralds never fail." She knew that wasn't truly the case, that failure was also a Fitzgerald marker, but that didn't make it the wrong thing to *say*.

Caitlin fell silent, and she was shaken to realize she had witnessed something monumental taking place. Somehow before she was conscious of this fact, she had become a Fitzgerald, too.

Now, to a businessman like him, that commercial concept sounded heartbreakingly naïve and nowhere near bankable, but he also knew that enthusiasm and confidence were indispensable starters—and unquantifiable. In and of itself, that factor did not mean the plan was unviable. "Whole thing sounds a little dicey, but you know what? I have a weakness for risky, and for my two favorite girls, so let's keep talking."

—

THE TWO WOMEN GOT to work. They camped out in the bookstore neighborhood, they read everything they could find about starting a bookstore, they roughly sketched out projections and forecasts and budgets. They also had a great good time entertaining several excellent alternative candidates for the store name: Searchers Books, Chancer Books (as in, take a chance reading a good book), What's the Story Books (as in Irish greetings), Bender Books (which sounded like a kick, a bit on the boozy side), but then how about going all in for it, as in Boozy Books? Upon further consideration, no, not unless they acquired a liquor license. Gobsmacked Books? No, but they were getting closer now.

"I got it," said Caitlin, "I got it…Bang On Books. You like?"

"Fuck, yeah, I do. Bang On Books, we got a winner, baby. Bang On Books, love it." Colleen was elated, and also impressed by her new partner in crime.

"But you know, gotta say, Floozy's Books, I keep coming back to that. I might like it a little bit more." She rolled around the word on her tongue. Floozy's. Had she come back full circle to their initial idea?

"Well," said Colleen, "the first idea can often be the best idea."

"I know, I know, life's like that," she said, and wondered if that were true.

"So you make a good point—for a floozy." It was a fun word to enunciate. "And that's what we are, after all, a coupla floozies."

Before they knew it, they had settled on it, and Floozy's Books, should it ever come into existence, was destined to be its name.

Unlike the agonizingly prolonged land deal with the diocese, this contract came together quickly. Almost too quickly, Paddy sensed as he dug into the details, intuiting that the owners of the old bookshop, cash-strapped as they were, were too worn-out to go on negotiating with him, they had had their fill. But he left some money on the table, no reason to humiliate people in their bleak hour of financial resignation. And they certainly were upstanding human beings, not an everyday sight in his world, naïve as hippies, well-meaning in their tie-dyes and Birkenstocks, and, as he could tell, absolutely ill-equipped by temperament to run a business. Paddy would bring his acumen to the store once the girls took over. He did the due diligence, semi-diligently. This deal hardly constituted a major cash outlay. Financial exposure wasn't his main concern, and he wasn't sweating the details as he normally did. The capital investment in Caitlin and in his daughter, too—*that* was what he was making, and *that* was the risk he was taking and *that* was well worth making. Were he honest with himself, he wanted to please Caitlin, not that there was anything simple about his designs. That's what happens when somebody like Paddy Fitzgerald falls in love, and he couldn't deny anymore that, crazy as it seemed, unexpected as this development was, he was in love with the girl. *Woman*, he meant to say, knowing Colly would correct him if she were reading his mind, which was a talent that she, along with her mother, possessed in spades. He would get this, and everything else, straight eventually.

—

PADDY TIPTOED INTO CAITLIN's bedroom and whispered, "Good morning, sunshine. You awake?"

It took an excruciating moment for her to reboot her brain. "No." She sat up in bed groggy, as he retracted the crimson velvet curtains, opening her bedroom onto an ostentatiously clear blue sky. She winced to rein in the unbridled assault of daylight. "Now I am."

"Meet me in the garage, baby." He could barely conceal his exuberance.

She could barely conceal her puzzlement. Garage at this hour, why? Sleep was important to her. She'd been reading up about its restorative powers, about how as we age we need more not less sleep, all of which sounded instinctively right. She herself usually slept like a teenager and privately treasured the jewel of her bustling dream life, not that she could always reliably reconstruct upon waking the narratives and images that had cinematically dazzled her when her eyes closed. She heard that people apparently reclined on a psychiatrist's couch and described in great detail their dreams, which apparently held some mysterious, unconscious key to their waking life. She supposed dreams must have some sort of deep significance, but for her the deepest significance was that her dreams constituted an alternate world she inhabited, traveled, and negotiated, as if she were a tourist of herself. Much like her so-called real life, her dream life instilled inside her questions and problems, too—but different ones. As for sleep, eight hours was fine, nine or ten much better. People used to call such a regimen "beauty sleep," but she hadn't heard that old-fashioned phrase lately. Would she have to cut back on her sleep quotient once she immersed herself in the book biz? She suspected that was inevitable. She seized the alarm clock Paddy had given her as if by this gesture she could freeze time's relentless momentum. "It's eight o'clock, Paddy."

"I know, I know, I got up at six, so I overslept, too. Come out there when you're ready, no hurry, fresh coffee'll be waiting for you in the kitchen."

For someone as graceful as she, whose body in fluid motion was normally blue-ribbon saluki graceful, she moved deliberately but in no way ponderously in the mornings, so it was almost nine when she appeared in the garage in her white bathrobe and fur-lined pink Gucci mules, coffee cup steady in her hand. Paddy was delicately dusting the hood of the Maserati as if he were tending to a high-strung animate creature.

She wondered what could possibly be so urgent. "What, you want me to help clean your car?" She looked incredulous, verging on slightly annoyed.

"You like the Maz?"

They'd had this kind of exchange a few times before. It seemed crucial for her to acknowledge every so often this proud possession, so that is what she dutifully did.

"It's a beauty, always like when you take me out for a drive."

"Good, very good, glad to hear. You can squire me around someday. Because, tell you what, Caitlin. Been thinking. The car's yours."

Speechless, she tried to let that piece of nonsense settle in. But she couldn't achieve that result. "No, it's your precious car."

"Only now it is yours, because I just gave it to you."

"No."

"Yes, and please, here are the keys."

—

PADDY FITZGERALD, ALMOST BEFORE being conscious of this development, had rumbled onto the phase in his existence when mortality was no longer an abstraction but loomed an everyday yet inexorably invigorating fact of, well, life. The grim reaper richly deserved his reputation, he conceded, and was worthy to be dreaded, so Paddy was not blithely looking forward to the inevitable thunk and thump of the scythe on his door. He suffered no illusions as to the promises of the afterlife, or banked on his eligibility to cash in on them if they were ever to be made available. But he wasn't on the cusp of becoming a Buddhist monk, either. It was nonetheless the case that with each passing day having possessions and generating wealth and wielding power mattered less and less, when for a once-upon-a-time impoverished Irish American kid, acquiring all that, reasonably enough, used to be an all-consuming enterprise. He would grudgingly admit there was a time when he first put Caitlin up in that penthouse that she herself was a type of gorgeous, prized possession. Here and now when it came to her and the Maz, however, he was being pragmatic. It wasn't solely a matter of acknowledging the obvious, that he could not take it all with him. What sort of moron doesn't grasp that first principle? Losing his son and later his wife underscored the limits of time in a devastating way. All the same, he felt baffled as to how, ever since Cait moved in, he caught himself thinking more and more about his late wife, Grace, but with a resonating difference, a difference he was struggling over. It wasn't as if he were comparing the two women. Grace's image was molten in his memory. Sometimes she was his new bride on the honeymoon, sometimes the mother of his children pressing cold cloths on their fevered brows, sometimes an old woman knitting and knitting deep into the night, or finally dying in a hospital bed, her warm hand going cold in his. Sometimes, somehow, all his images of her were superimposed upon each other, like a deck of playing cards. He missed her, of course he did. Not that he regretted Caitlin's moving in. But it was almost as if he were only now beginning to understand Grace and to understand what their marriage had been and, if he dared admit this, what it still was. Which made no rational sense. But that's what death does, he supposed: the incomprehensibility of it crushed everybody and everything in its path.

Meanwhile some other principle was now at work inside. Take the car as an example. Owning and driving the Maz once gave him deep and abundant pleasure, it was true, but the prospect of handing over the car to her—to *Caitlin*—gave him much, much more. He was relieved to have survived long enough to recalibrate his values—and happier to have found Caitlin in the first place. Because that was the truth: he *was* happier. Not happy necessarily in some absolute sense, but most certainly happier. Only in retrospect, that's when we understand all there is to be understood. He now lived in the perpetual early gloaming of retrospect: the bright blazing fireworks on the horizon before the swoop into the black night. But what did that insight portend for him and his connection to Caitlin? Would it never be understood by him until he wasn't around to understand it? And what did he mean by understanding anyway? Maybe it was crazy, maybe he was crazy, but he loved her. No, this wasn't crazy. Unless it was crazy to love her, because that was the simple truth, that he loved her, even if it wasn't simple at all.

—

"But your Maz is only for special occasions, you said."

Caitlin was continually updating her self-conception and struggling to understand who she had become, but she knew that she had changed, she knew that for certain. She couldn't erase the memory of the former life she renounced, and couldn't dismiss it, either. As uneasy as her purchase was on the past, she was a woman "with a history": that's precisely how her mother would have euphemistically framed the idea of her daughter's so-called career had the woman been around and had she ever given a flying fuck. *Woman with a history,* meaning a woman with a type of past that wasn't a subject for polite conversation, whatever the hell that was, *polite* conversation, which was one thing Caitlin was unsure she had ever been party to. If it weren't for that history of hers, she wouldn't have ever known Paddy in the first place, so there was that element to factor in. Not that he and she explicitly discussed and broke down the sequencing. It was the truth, but the truth can be overrated, she believed, insofar as the truth was not ever obviously or absolutely factual, much like her, for whom truth was changing, for whom facts were mutable or perpetually slipping in and out of focus. Sometimes she stood in conflict with her own history, which made no sense, except for her it did. The closest she got to understanding how Paddy had come to terms with her and her past was that her past no longer mattered anymore, but if it did matter it only mattered insofar as that was purely and simply how he met her, under circumstances that were not so pure and not so simple: an instance of circular logic, she might have framed the thought, had she been familiar with that intellectual construct, and she wasn't. Had Paddy resolutely, willfully, wishfully, magically wiped clean her slate, assuming her past life was none of his business and irrelevant to their relationship now? The Baxter business muddled the situation, and Ben, too, poor little baby Ben, and how Paddy reprocessed those fragments of her past. And when she revealed that part of her life, that was the morning when he changed toward her: he took her home for breakfast, and now it had become her home. Colleen might have characterized this possessiveness of his, if that was the term, as being predicated upon his essentially patriarchal predisposition, but Caitlin then could have countered: well, there's an upside to everything. Then throw in this fact: time jumpstarted all over again when she and Paddy fell in love. A woman with a history suddenly had a new history, and a future. They both were now free, radically liberated from all the facts that had preceded them. And that stipulation had a benefit for him, too: the record of his own past was now, as far as she was concerned, wiped clean, too. Lovers routinely indulged themselves in the illusion they are starting over. That may be the central lure of the idea of falling in love again. Not that her memories pre-Paddy were fairy-tale cherished, hardly, but some of them indeed were in the ballpark—masochism gave her no thrill. Truth was, there was always darkness at the edge of town. She did what she had indeed done, she was who she had certainly been—only *whoosh*, not anymore. Then again, she never could expunge the recollection of one night when the goal consisted of making it to see sunlight again. Anybody who did the work she did had a story on that order to tell. She always assumed she possessed a first-class bullshit detector, and trusted her sixth sense about clients, not to mention trusted the madam who doled out her assignments, but this was the time when she learned she was naïve. The john tied her up, which was not part of the deal, and he unfolded his plan. She was his now, and he got off on her humiliation, and more than that, her terror. Before that night, she would have affirmed it was nothing but a job, it did not reach into her soul, her heart. But this guy had conceived a big buildup to his crowning moment. At her lowest ebb, he instructed her to tell him that she loved him. Nothing she could do about it. Make me believe you, he insisted. So she did tell him that, and did all she could to make him believe her. That was the night when her work did slither into her heart and soul. She couldn't take a shot at him when she had the opportunity and the desire, once he'd untied her: he turned his back when he evidently had confidence he had broken her down to his satisfaction, and there was the fireplace poker within reach, but some primitive rationality kicked in: if she killed him, he would be with her forever. When he had his fill, he let her go and she was never quite the same. And he paid her, too, and disgustingly added an extra hundred and thanked her, the dirtiest money that ever crossed her hands. None of these images occurred to her this morning in the garage as Paddy extended her the car keys. That past life of hers taught her about the nature of a gift that is hardly ever a gift, that is, freely given, freely accepted, no strings attached. Instead, to her, a gift used to be a dangerous thing to accept, which is what she had gleaned from all the gifts many men had given her in the past, like that kimono she had worn around Paddy till she had to lie about and one day she threw away. A gift is a kind of contract, a kind of pledge. In her former life, she knew the transactional terms of any gift that came her way. She realized what she was giving up by accepting something given to her: she was giving up a part of herself in exchange. Almost since the first day she moved in with Paddy, a part of her worried this actualized fantasy would all come crashing down, that it was nothing other than a transaction, that this whole new life she had walked into was a dream from which she one day would be rudely awakened, that she would disappoint him, that she couldn't possibly live up to the idea of her he had cultivated in his fantasies.

You know what she woke up this morning not thinking about? Money, that's what. Until she thought about not thinking about money, that's when she was thinking about money all over again. Once, and not so long ago, she used to think about money all day long, which goes a long way toward explaining her life choices, when she didn't have much of it. The best thing about where she found herself now is that she never had to think about money in the same way as before. Sure, she had done things for money, and at some point who doesn't? Name any people not canonized. But she had standards, she wasn't walking the street, not that once or twice she didn't come close when the pressure intensified, and not that she couldn't empathize with those who made other choices—which were not choices at all. This line of reasoning caused her to wonder if she were trading in one sort of commercial transaction with men for a different kind of commercial transaction with a man named Paddy Fitzgerald. That's when she felt her stomach spin-cycle so fast she had to hold on to the Maserati *Dama Bianca* to brace herself. But then the world slowed down and she said to herself, before she could say it to him out loud, that she loved him. Love was not supposed to be in the cards for her, only then it was. Incredible as it sounded, she did love him. But it was more than that. They did love each other.

—

BECAUSE THEN, BECAUSE THEN, because then, what Paddy said next crystalized everything.

"Special occasion?" said Paddy. "Special occasion," he repeated. "What's a special occasion anymore? For me, waking up in the morning is a special occasion these days. And waking up in the morning having you here in Haymarket, that's a ridiculously special occasion. So that's why you can drive the Maz whenever and wherever you want, it's all yours. Because *you* are the special occasion.".

Falling in love: At some point in their renounced past lives they'd both given up on the idea. Until this moment, that is, when they were not so sure they were sure about that.

"It's too much, Paddy," she said, glistening teardrops rolling down from her gleaming green eyes.

"So are you. God, sometimes you make me swoon. Love that word, *swoon.*"

"I don't deserve you," she said and she believed.

"You're right about that, Caitlin dear, you deserve much better."

He wished he could give her more, much more than a priceless car, and that's precisely what he would see to for the duration of all the years stretching out before the two of them.

Chapter Twenty-Three
Dear Aunt Charlie,

H<small>I</small>! I <small>HOPE YOU'RE</small> doing good. My counselor, her name's Claire, she encouraged me to write you. Yes, I have a counselor because I've been staying awhile at this place Caring Street the Catholics run. I know you and Catholics don't get along (I can relate!), but I gotta say, they've been alright to me. Couldn't stay at home now that mom is, you know, pretty fucked up, sorry but it's the right expression, and I can't stand her boyfriend, who's a creep who scares me (a little). They use all day long. I don't want to whine, I'm a big girl, I can deal. But then I couldn't so I took off. The saga of the traveling pants, the Terry sequel, this time it's personal ha ha.

Anyway. Next week is my 18th birthday. You probably don't remember that's OK. Here they are going to give me a little party and a cake, I think.

They're also giving me the old heave ho. But in a nice way, and I'm no ho. Sorry bad joke. Been here too long is all. 18 is kinda the cutoff point expiration date on my milk carton, I guess. This priest here, Father Philip, he's been pretty good to me too. Turns out he's the big brother of my old English teacher at HFH, Mr. Matt Fitzgerald. Small world huh? But I'd hate to paint it! ☺ Don't tell anybody, but I kinda had a tiny little crush on him, the teacher not the priest, and not that he's that way, he isn't, not at all. And he wouldn't do anything bad, he's OK. Even his wife's OK, who's Claire, who works here—oh, I just wrote that a minute ago. She's a little bit of a do-gooder but that's not her whole story. She's funny too which I didn't catch at first. She said she knew Matt and me had a kind of <u>soulmate</u> connection, but she didn't mind. <u>Soulmate?</u>—she was an ex-hippie, I think. Not that there's anything wrong with it because you were too. Anyway girls in class were always falling for the guy (which was very true, I can testify). Hey, <u>she</u> fell for him, so she understood. As she said, nothing could get in the way of their marriage. She's right too I bet.

Funny to be writing a real letter on paper with a pen. I'd send you an email, but I don't have your email address sorry and I could find your snail mail address on my phone lucky for me. Guess this is my first letter ever to you. Except for thank you notes when you sent me presents which were always cool and generous.

So I was thinking about your offer, you know, to live with you a little while? Remember when you said? Would that be OK now? For a little while like I say? I got a job lined up at a bookstore (Matt's sister has a bookstore), and I'll be going to community college after I finish up at McKinley Central continuation. Too bad I never did graduate from Holy Family, nothing wrong with the place, but I can't go back "in every sense of the term" to quote my Eng teacher.

I promise to keep my room clean, to do any chores you want even the kitty litter box (how are those tabbies of yours?), cook dinner (as long as it's spaghetti, I mean, but you can teach me, you're such a great cook), and mostly stay out of your hair.

Claire said I should tell you the simple truth hold nothing back. So you have the whole picture, she said. You see I had a bad year, last year. Did some stupid things. Had some stupid friends. Made some mistakes I regret. But mostly I regret how I couldn't help mom. I worry about her every single minute of every day. I'm not blaming her honest I have my own issues.

Matt's friend, this guy he showed up at Caring Street, he spoke to me about how to make things right with my life. The guy used to be a cop, a detective, I think, but he was pretty OK to talk to. I hope this doesn't ruin things for you and me to live together, but here goes. I told him about how I sent a selfie to Matt I shouldn't of. I can tell you more if it matters, but this was all on me not my teacher. I was having a bad night. And the selfie was a bad thing, if you know what I mean. And no, I wasn't drinking. I wasn't thinking either. I'll tell you more if it matters to you like I say but you know what I'm talking about use your imagination. I also messed around with Matt's computer and downloaded bad things on it. Reason I'm telling you this, and I would tell anybody is that I don't want Matt to get in any kinda trouble like I told the ex-cop and it's all on me and I'm sorry.

Because and this is true I promise I will try to do the right thing from now on.

So would you think about it please, me living with you for awhile? I can pay rent if you want of course, soon as I figure out how much I'm gonna get paid.

I want to be a better person. I want to be a good woman someday. I'll never forget it if you can see your way clear to helping your niece. I promise to do my best. I wont let you down

Lots of love to you Auntie Charlene

T: your loving niece

Chapter Twenty-Four
Floozies

TWO MONTHS AFTER THE business deal finalized and the lease was signed and sealed, the bookstore, freshly painted and deep-cleaned and reorganized, opened for business. Floozy's inaugural night party was festive and luminous, with piped-in music and delicious catered small bites and better-than-expected wine, thanks to Francesca's dad's contribution. Caitlin herself looked radiant as she presided. Over time, guided by Colleen's subtle counsel, she had toned down her fashion choices. Tonight, for instance, she was wearing blue jeans and a red silk vest over a white shirt—Paddy's oversized white French cuff shirt, worn for good luck, sleeves rolled up, indicating both stylishness and industriousness. Colleen endorsed her appearance, saying that that was how a hip bookseller should look, and Caitlin was pleased with herself—and pleased she had pleased Colly.

"You're looking très academic chic," Colleen said. "With a little bit of pluck thrown in, if you don't mind my saying so."

"Lots of pluck to both of us!"

"I'll overlook the clunker, and I'm not plucking around, either."

"Colly, isn't this a great turnout?" she said, and it was. "I know now how big our demographic is—people like me, who are getting into books for the first time, and all the lifers, too, like you." *Demographic* was a fun word to say, and another new term for Caitlin. "Because you are so perfect, guiding people to their choices. Hand-selling, that's what you call it? We are going to have so much fun."

"Yes, we're Floozies and these are our books, sister. Here's to you," she said, lifting a glass.

"No, to us, Colly, to us."

Everyone they expected showed, and some they didn't.

—

"FATHER PHILIP," SAID CAITLIN, "what a nice surprise."

He was not in his dress blacks, opting instead for his casual civvies: sweatshirt, black jeans, baseball cap, tennis shoes. But notoriously, Catholics can pick out a priest at fifty paces, no matter what he's wearing.

"Congratulations, Caitlin, what a wonderful night. When you get a chance, recommend a few books for an honorary floozy like me?" He didn't need such advice, but he wanted to signal acceptance of her, and his wholesale approval of the enterprise.

"Your sis is your go-to resource." A few minutes of happy talk later, she wandered off to greet the newcomers to the party.

Philip gravitated toward his sister. "Where's your dad?"

"My dad," she said, "is supposedly on his way, any minute. He's keeping company with your dad."

"Recommending some reading material for him?"

"I was thinking some bedtime reading, the Kama Sutra."

"You're going there?"

"Cait's okay, by the way, otherwise I wouldn't be here."

Francesca and Tommy were there, too. They looked the typical couple wandering into a bookshop after dinner down the street, either the popular Mexican or the Thai place. The store location guaranteed serious foot traffic, day and night, which was a factor the previous owners hadn't capitalized on. They had closed their store too early, and Floozy's was going to stay open late, six or seven days of the week.

Terry was helping with the food and wine, alongside Claire. Colleen hired her on Matty's recommendation, and she had panned out well, so far. Matty himself was elated to see her employed, and he popped a deviled egg into his mouth as she poured him some mineral water and made not a single snarky remark. He could tell that she was thinking snark the whole time, but holding off, trying to take on a new persona. He was hoping the new persona would work better than the old one ever did. And one day she'd leave her aunt's home and head off to college after finishing up at the public high school. Matty would see she'd get into the right place by writing killer recs.

Ruth's office was located a few doors down, and she herself ambled in after work when she caught sight of the festivities. Nearby the Mysteries section, Philip was chatting with his sister when Ruth and his eyes locked, and they held their glance long enough for Francesca, across the way, to notice. But what was it that she noticed? She couldn't be sure. She guessed she shouldn't initiate conversation in public with her therapist, because maybe it was against the Law of Therapy, but she wanted to. The topic promised to come up when they met for their regular session tomorrow. Her therapist was wearing something she hadn't seen her wear before: an untucked shirt. Unless Frankie were mistaken, and there was no chance she was, Ruth was comfortable to be seen showing in public.

Chapter Twenty-Five
Francesca & Ruth

"NICE SURPRISE BUMPING INTO you last night," said Ruth to Francesca as they settled into the matching red leather easy chairs facing each other, assuming their customary places in her office. The psychotherapist subtly maneuvered the little clock on the side table an inch so as to be able to discreetly track time.

"Nice? I felt pretty self-conscious, like I showed up for my final exam in a two-piece."

"You're funny, but all good, no worries." The two of them had come so far over the years, was Francesca unconsciously implying at this late date that for her, therapy was a type of test? Ruth should pick up on this theme—but no, she determined, just move along. A cigar was sometimes just a cigar. She missed her cigarettes, but hated cigar smoke.

"Same here then," said Francesca. "But I didn't know how to relate to you in social circumstances. You know, like when you run into your high school teacher at the grocery store, and you analyze what's in her basket—the milk, the bread, the six bottles of vodka. Awkward!" Nothing but a banal little joke, but Ruth was interested that school was being connected yet again to her therapy—a not insignificant connection for somebody like Francesca, who excelled as a student all the while feeling that she, the outsider, never belonged, was never truly worthy. Ruth was thinking now she would look for an opening to circle back to this subject. This particular cigar wasn't just any old cigar.

"It would have been fine to chat, two people being civil, friendly at a bookstore opening. And what a wonderful job they did updating the store. Such a great addition to the neighborhood, people need a place like that after the old one shuttered."

"My whole clan was there—well, Anthony's clan, who are my people still. Colleen and Matty, whom we've talked about a lot. And the recent addition named Caitlin, my father-in-law's new inamorata—that's her store. She's a sparkler, isn't she? Pretty young, too. Anyway, the mighty Family Fitzgerald in full force in the house, except for Paddy, the patriarch, who showed up with his bodyguard, Jonesy, after you sneaked out."

Bodyguard? That's interesting. But Ruth would keep her touch light, not taking the bait after being accused of slipping away stealthily. "Stayed as long as I could remain on my feet. Five months along, as everyone can see. I get worn out before I know it." That was true last evening, and today had been particularly taxing as well: six sessions, which was too many, but she was trying to fit in everybody for at least one session or two before she took her leave.

"Had you met them before? The Fitzgeralds?"

That could have been a borderline inappropriate query, but Ruth chose to ignore the possibly subterranean intention. "They have a huge reputation in town, of course. It feels like everybody knows them."

"Father Philip was there, too. Anthony's brother, who married us. Did you get a chance to meet and talk with him last night?"

Okay, antennae were now up. That might have been unremarkable with somebody else, but Francesca had never opened a session with so many directed, personal questions; Ruth would need to get this under control forthwith. "Can't say I did have a conversation with him." More to the point, and not surprisingly, when Philip's name entered the conversation, a sense of heightened risk crept up on Ruth. Maybe this had to do with her being pregnant, but she had the premonition that unless she kept her emotional balance, she could lose her footing on the slick psychic ice.

"He's so handsome, Philip, don't you think?" said Francesca. "He and Anthony were close as can be, and of course Philip took his passing as hard as you can imagine."

Ruth listened carefully and let the words settle into the middle of the room. Frankie seemed to be referencing something important and charged, something as of yet unspecified that would come out, if she were given a chance. "Let's talk about you. How's Frankie doing these days? Anything on your agenda?" *Agenda*: odd, atypical word choice for Ruth. Her hormones raging, she needed to take a break from work soon.

"Correct me if I'm wrong, and I'm probably projecting like crazy, but I had this glimpse that you and Philip seemed to have some chemistry across the room. Maybe I am being out of bounds, and he's your client, or was."

Certain clients indeed spring a trap like that, again perhaps unconsciously, crossing boundaries with their therapists; any good, professional, seasoned therapist—and Ruth certainly qualified—knew her way around the treacherous pathways of therapeutic transference. "Well, *projection* is an interesting concept. I don't need to tell you it would be out of bounds for me to respond to that question. So my question for you is: Why do you ask?" If Francesca answered that last question honestly, Ruth would hope to run with it.

"I'm not sure. Philip—Father Philip—and I once were very close, too."

What did *too* mean and to whom did it refer? Time for the therapist to shut up and wait and listen hard, and so she did.

"He and I became very close in the year after Anthony, but we drifted apart for strange reasons, and you know, maybe not so strange in the end. We're trying to find our footing again, it's been a while, and I have missed his company terribly, there, I said it."

But what exactly did she *mean*? Ruth had to jump in. "He's important to you, I get it, and this is the first I'm hearing about him—and your relationship." Ruth castigated herself for saying something so inane, and with critical undertones. And critical of whom? Frankie? Philip? Herself? She needed to manage this potentially fraught moment much more carefully. She also had to ask herself how it was that Philip never once mentioned Frankie, not once. Amazing how the mention of Philip's name in somebody else's mouth could disarm her so swiftly. In addition, she worried she was talking too much, hardly ever a good thing for a therapist; better to sit with the unspoken, better to be patient for the client to point the way.

"There was a time, and maybe there'll be a time again, I don't know, when we'll be close again. That would be—I don't know the word for what it would be. Affirming, hopeful, comforting? Have you ever cared for somebody so much that you made mistakes, mistakes out of caring for them?"

As the silence gathered, and as Ruth elected not to answer yet another question, Francesca sensed a transformation in Ruth. She believed she was seeing into her therapist all over again. Before she was cognizant of hazarding this hunch, she could intuit that Philip had a place in her therapist's life as a cherished client, or so she was speculating. She wouldn't have ever guessed that Philip ever saw a therapist, not till this moment. That was a healthy sign, for him to go to therapy, because who doesn't need therapy at some point, and Ruth was terrific for her for so long, so good for him. Francesca decided to risk telling the truth, and she knew this might be a mistake but she couldn't avoid it.

"Might as well tell you this, Ruth. It's been on my mind all over again, and I've never told anybody before, till right this minute." She took an audible, deep breath, which struck her therapist as quasi-theatrical. "Philip and I had an affair, a brief affair. It happened, I can't undo the past. I have never forgiven myself, on one level, and on another I needed him as much as he needed me, so maybe I haven't forgiven him." And then Francesca recalled a telling connection, which she decided to share. "You know, if he did become your client, patient, whatever, could be it was because of me."

Ruth's eyes widened and waited for Francesca to say more—and wished she wouldn't.

"I remembered, the first night he and I slept together, I let on I was working with you, and how much I appreciated you, and he asked for your name, you know, for parishioner referrals. Of course, I'm not asking again if he's your client."

Ruth had been summarily presented a serious problem, an ethical conflict. But that was not the most serious aspect of this revelation. The feeling of being betrayed was building and building. Betrayal by Philip, betrayal by Frankie, a double betrayal of her. And yet rationally, she knew it was not a betrayal of her, and yet, irrationally, and convincingly, it was nothing but a betrayal. Things not said, experiences not referenced, could be every bit as wrenching, and jolting, as things that were spoken. It didn't require a therapist to highlight that. Or a priest, for that matter. It took all Ruth's powers to shove into the emotional background, for now, her feelings about Philip. She and he would need to talk this through, but then again, how to broach the subject? She could hardly raise the issue with him without breaking a confidence, not to mention without implicitly accusing him of bad faith. It was all too much for her to process in the moment, so as hard as it was to do, and this may have been the single most difficult moment in her therapist life, she willed her attention in the direction of dealing with the client seated across from her—for the next—she looked at the clock—for the next thirty-nine minutes.

Why hadn't Francesca mentioned before now that what she was clearly signaling constituted such a major experience—and the corollary, every bit as significant, what else of major import had she not disclosed? Ruth felt nothing so much as deceived. Surely, she might have brought up this affair at some point, an affair with her own brother-in-law. She had previously talked through so much of psychological and emotional consequence: her one-night stands, her professional struggles, her widowed depression, her troubles with regard to Catholicism, her unresolved relationship with her underworld-associated father, her internal conflicts about her wealth, her mixed feelings about her own success, her questions about Tommy and their future, her free-floating anxiety, her high school boyfriends and her fear of dogs. Had her client been operating in bad faith all along? Exactly as Philip was? Even if the two of them were not exactly conspiring to withhold information from her? So what else was she keeping to herself? Ruth would be tempted to believe Francesca was being strategic, that she had deliberately decided not to tell her about Philip till today, but to what end? Because more important, yet again, why was she telling her *now*? But then beyond all that, more pragmatically, how could she, given her own relationship with Philip, continue to treat Francesca a minute more? She had no confidence she wouldn't be affected by this intimate new revelation regarding Philip. She was a practiced clinician, true, but clinical had limits. She would have to take up this subject with her own therapist, to determine if she could ethically relate to her client, and to figure out if she could manage the risks of counter-transference. She was pretty certain the verdict would be either no or hell no. But in the meantime, she went here, buying time, and simultaneously wishing not to discover the truth: "What was it like for you, being sexually involved with your late husband's brother?" She came this close to retracting the brutal, harshly phrased question, which made it almost sound like she was accusing Francesca of incest, but couldn't, and she let the question stand.

"I only know I will never deny its importance."

No one had ever asked her to deny its importance, because she had testified she had never told anybody else, unless she was referring to denying the significance to herself. Ruth was an expert in conducting her own internal dialogue while at the same time discussing matters with a client, proceeding along parallel tracks, but this moment posed an altogether tougher, more complex, in a sense triangulating challenge, so maybe it would be advisable to shut down the session immediately. Of course, if she did that, it might be injurious to her client, and theoretically irresponsible to Francesca, who would feel plausibly bewildered and rejected.

"Let's back up a second," said Ruth. "Why do you suppose you have you been probing me for information about him?" She knew it was not the perfect launch point, but couldn't resist.

There was heat in the room. "Am I? *Probing* you? Why do you say that?" Frankie wasn't probing into Ruth, she felt, she was probing into herself, and if anybody else, Philip.

"You seem quite concerned as to whether or not Father Philip and I know each other. What would be the difference one way or the other— what would be the difference to you in your therapy, I mean?" Of course, that was also the issue she was grappling with herself.

"Honestly, I'm not sure what's going on, Ruth, right now between you and me."

The moment of truth loomed on the horizon. "Are you jealous I have other clients I care for?" She started to correct herself, but didn't: *Whom I care about.* "And I'm not declaring he is my client."

"But if he were your client, he might have mentioned…I don't know, me."

"Again, confidential." Secrets were multiplying, the way they have a tendency to do once one secret sharer blunders into the clearing.

"But Ruth, you would have to imagine that that information would be noteworthy to me. And even if you couldn't tell me, then you would know something about me that I didn't know you knew about me, which seems like dirty pool on your part."

To Frankie, that perfectly captured the irrationality she was embracing, and wishing she wasn't. To Ruth, Frankie was describing her therapist's soul, and wishing she wasn't.

"Bad faith? Are you accusing me of betraying you, Frankie?" A real question on the swept-off table.

Francesca shot forward in her chair. "Don't put words in my mouth."

She was justified to push back, but Ruth continued on this tack. "Let's try again. If such information is crucial to you, what is stopping you from reaching out to him, to Philip, to discuss whatever you find important… like his therapy or his possible association with me and including whatever happened between you two, about which I could not possibly know anything?" With that last loaded utterance, she said too much, she realized.

"He's a priest, for one, and that means there is no possibility of a long-term romantic relationship."

"He was a priest then as well—I presume." Ruth asked herself how she could lift herself out of this conversational tar pit. "Not to mention the family complications with the Fitzgeralds."

"It's simple. I was in mourning, and I was out of my mind."

"Matters of the heart and loss can be inscrutable. But are you suggesting he took advantage of you in a vulnerable state?" Saying that, Ruth crossed another line. For one thing, she was aware that in this session she had spoken more than she ever had with Frankie. For another, she was now investing her imagination in Philip and his relationship with Frankie, and not Frankie and her relationship with Philip. It was all over now for Ruth as Frankie's therapist. Her mood darkened further. She helplessly imagined Frankie in bed with Philip. She could see it, she could see her, she could see him, she could see them. Much as she hated to do so, she saw Frankie in a new light—and Philip, as well. She ought to run out of her office right now, let her client lock up.

"If anything, the other way around, I took advantage of him, I used him."

She lifted up both her hands as if it were redundant to state the words: "Meaning what?"

"Meaning under other circumstances we might have had a chance, if I could have opened my heart to him, because he was available to me, the way I wished to be available to him. I know this must sound crazy to you, and dangerous, and absolutely irresponsible on my part, I know that, don't remind me. I can hear what you are thinking, Ruth. Not my finest hour."

This observation took Ruth's breath away for a second, she wished she had never heard it. But she had to respond. "Are you asking if we, you and I, can help shape a new conversation with Philip? *Father* Philip?"

"You know, I think you have already." The sadness overwhelmed Francesca. She was thinking of all she had lost, all she had left behind, all that had been taken away from her. While she would admit to feeling sorry for herself, another revelation loomed and she would soon have to act on it.

"How have I helped?" said Ruth, doubtful such a thing were possible.

"By making clear to me that your and my relationship is drawing to a close. We had another session scheduled for next week, I realize, but who knows, I mean..." She didn't bother to finish the thought.

What Francesca did unmistakably convey to Ruth was her crisply enunciated anger, which stunned her, but after her stomach stopped churning, two solid minutes of silence later, she felt relieved, too. And that antagonism directed toward her therapist was deserved, even if she couldn't pin down what her therapist was doing. A strong woman like Francesca, who had survived personally and professionally through turmoil, could grasp that Ruth was in some imprecise way not wholly on her side.

At the same time, within Ruth it also felt like a blow to her ego, as it always did when a client walked away, leaving her to feel as if she had failed—not only in her healing task but somehow in her entire life. But the matter before her was simpler and much murkier: she desired to know more, too, about Frankie and Philip. It wasn't a matter of voyeurism or jealousy, either. Not exclusively, not entirely. It was richer and stranger than that. And more than anything, that signaled to her that she was now categorically out of her depth. Ruth had reached the point where Francesca's life was not uppermost in her mind, as it should be; instead, it was Ruth's own relationship with Philip. If she were not superhumanly vigilant, she would continue to exploit her for her own purposes—and this would amount to her most depressing hour as a therapist—and as a woman.

Francesca defended herself against what she construed to be the unspoken charge buried in her therapist's extended silence. "I need to fix what I broke in the past and come to terms with the people in my past, talking about Philip, in order for me to have a chance to move into the present. All that staying-in-the-moment bullshit. And of course you're going on leave soon to have your baby with your husband, and you'll need to be with him and your baby, so the timing is right for me, for us, to make this change."

The subject of the therapist's supposedly married state had never come up before, but Ruth could sense that, as she herself was doing, Francesca was wandering around in a dark wood that was bizarre to her.

"This is abrupt. You upset with me, Frankie?"

"Yes, but I shouldn't be. Are you disappointed in *me*, Ruth?"

"No, of course not, nothing discussed in therapy is disappointing." Ruth was not truly speaking her mind, but she couldn't defend herself, either.

As far as Francesca could sense, Ruth knew much more than she was willing to let on, but she revealed an inner disquiet and refusal she wasn't going to describe, if she could, which she obviously couldn't.

"We should stop, Ruth. You were a good therapist to me. I will have loving thoughts for you and your new family. I don't see any baby pictures or any other family pictures in your office, which I never quite registered before, so I gather this is your first baby."

At this juncture, with a different client and under far different circumstances, Ruth might have picked up on the rich subject of family pictures—rich because Francesca was seemingly invested in their absence—but all that seemed utterly moot. Here was one profound subject therapist and client had never specifically addressed: Frankie's childlessness. Was this a concern she repressed, or was this a crucial issue indirectly expressed by her, which Ruth missed? It was reasonable to wonder whether or not Ruth's pregnancy and her maternal leave had sideswiped Frankie. But Ruth had to ask herself whether or not framing it that way—as Frankie's *childlessness*—said more about her than it did about her client. Were pregnant Ruth's hormones getting the best of her? Solid chance, yes. She'd had clients who terminated pregnancies, clients who miscarried, and one client who recently gave birth to a stillborn child. It would be impossible, not to mention irresponsible, to generalize about the emotional state of these women, so various, so multidimensional in their pain.

What would it be like for Ruth to be a therapist after having a child herself? Would she be better, wiser, more grounded, smarter? Or would she be distracted, milk-stained, sleep-deprived? The only thing she knew was that she would be one day a mother herself. Some female clients of hers were physically unable to have children, for one reason or another. And not all women wanted to be mothers, and some of those who did should have never been. Some women struggled to get pregnant. And some adopted or decided against that option. But for all them, for each and every one of them, it was a subject somewhere top of mind, and heart, at some stage in their lives.

But these concerns did not seem to affect Francesca. For her, either the questions didn't occur, or if they did, she had no answers nor any desire to pursue them. Or perhaps this was not a subject for her to take up with her therapist. But if so, then, would it be taken up with anybody else? Was it ever taken up with herself, and how could it not be?

And Ruth was now more upset than ever about her client. She didn't know Frankie at all. She was in dangerous territory; she was this close to sitting in judgment of her.

"You're welcome back, whenever you want to resume the work." Ruth was holding on, wishing never to see Francesca again and simultaneously desperate to hear more about her relationship with Philip. She wondered if she would have the courage not to mention Frankie to Philip. She could cleverly frame the disclosure, if she chose, so as not to forfeit her ethical obligations, but she was fooling herself—she was already in breach, both with her client and with the father of the child she was carrying. But she was also thankful and almost impressed that her client was behaving more ethically, more consciously, than her therapist.

"But I have to say what I am thinking. Something tells me that you know Philip very well."

"Big jump, that *very well*, and let's say that's the case, why or how or to whom would that matter anyway?" If Frankie only knew.

"You're not denying it."

"Which I could not do even if I wanted to. I mean, even if it were true. And you're angry with...? Whom? Me? Somebody, *Philip*, who you think I may know very well? More than anyone, angry with yourself?"

"You're sounding glib, like Philip used to sound."

"But you went to bed with that man, whom you loved, glib as he is. Or was. A man and a relationship you never mentioned before to me." Ruth's own therapist—she could visualize the outrage painted on her face as Ruth narrated what had taken place—Ruth's own therapist listening to the report would be scathing.

"I never said I was in love with him, but you're perceptive, as usual. And when he was around me, he was never glib, and what we had together no other two people ever shared with each other."

To Ruth, Frankie sounded like a spurned adolescent lover. "If you were to stick around, or if you were to start up with another therapist, that's where the real conversation would begin, with a lot more transparency on your part, with that recognition of loss, and disappointment, because that's where you and I began, years ago. But you're right, under the current conditions I may not be in the best position to treat you." Finally, she was telling something akin to the truth.

This told Francesca everything—about Ruth, Philip, and herself.

"Goodbye, Ruth, and thank you."

"Goodbye, and thank you, too."

"You don't mean that."

Ruth had never seen that side of Francesca: the hurt, the anger. With another client, or in another lifetime, that would have amounted to a breakthrough. But it was nonetheless true what Francesca said, that Ruth did not mean to express gratitude. There was nothing to be gained by calling her out. "Our time seems to be up."

"That's true, Ruth. I may never get over Anthony, and that probably says more about me than it does about him, or our marriage. Truth is like death, which never seems to end, and it smacks you in the face over and over again when you least expect, don't you find?"

Ruth leaned back heavily in her chair, exhausted, joined her hands across her belly, obeying some primal instinct to shield her baby—from what or whom, she could not say. Then she said, "That's as good a note to end on as any. You take care, Francesca."

"*Francesca?* So formal, Ruth, after so long. But fine, I get it. So you take care, too."

Francesca would not let Ruth have the last word. If this counted as a victory, it was one not worth achieving. What neither of them knew at the time was they were not quite finished with each other.

Chapter Twenty-Six
Caitlin & Company

A GREAT BOOKSTORE—IT WAS Caitlin's dream and Colleen's plan to create nothing less. They also wanted a *good* bookstore. But what was a great bookstore? Was greatness to be conceived strictly in financial terms? The attainment of a positive-cash-flowing, bottom-lining going concern? Of course, that was the goal, of course it was; they were not babes in the woods. And that would not be easy, or simple. For one thing, they had to factor into their success equation strategy that their tiny business's commercial objectives were affected by macroeconomic forces, local and national, the grand-scale buying and technology trends out of their control. Since neither woman held a master's degree in business administration, the subject quickly paled once they invoked the term *discretionary income*. They knew their business depended on that stuff. So yes, bookselling was a tough go, and they didn't need schooling from *The Wall Street Journal*. To the WSJ they did not subscribe, though to Paddy Fitzgerald they did.

As for a *good* bookstore, now—that was different. That was something in their power to achieve from the instant they opened their doors, irrespective of whether the economy was booming or in recession. Paddy might not thrill to the concept, but a good bookstore was more than a profit-generating enterprise. To put it another way, profit indeed took the form of cash, and that was the store's lifeblood and certainly beautiful, but there was also a kind of yield not tangible enough to register on P&Ls and Cash Flows and

Income Statement spreadsheets. A *good* bookstore demands sound book-loving and book-talking people on the floor and in the back. It requires an extensive enough inventory of perennial favorites along with hot current books to hand-sell, as well as putting systems in place with reliable distributors to speed up special orders of units not in stock. All that may seem thunderously obvious. Though not to everybody. Alternative logic might go this way: Who can compete with online megabeast booksellers, with their virtually limitless inventory? Therefore, some bookstore owners adopt specialized themes, like architecture, or design, or feminism, or LGBTQ, or social justice, or politics, or crime and mysteries, or food, or whatever. Other courageous stores curate their offerings, geared to local tastes, prejudices, and demographics. Anything could work, depending.

In other words, these two entrepreneurs were feeling their way along, and for now Barnes & Noble, Amazon, Powell's, Indiebound, and the rest need not feel threatened—*for now*. Colleen speculated there was probably a kooky bookshop in some nook of the book universe offering for sale one book at a time and one book only: "But man, it is a fantastic book that keeps flying off the singular shelf." Then Colleen quickly circled back, with grimmest determination: "Forget that. The scientologists already opened that kind of bookshop. And look how that worked out."

Caitlin blinked, unsure what such scientists were doing with their business, and also unsure how seriously to take her business partner or if she needed a new one.

So, most definitely feeling their way along.

Whatever the business model, when it comes to *good* bookstore ambience, warm, welcoming lighting artfully situated never fails to appeal to customers, and so does reliable air-conditioning to fend off high summer's depredations. Of course, when there's a steaming heat wave outside, people don't automatically gravitate to a bookstore, they head for the pool or the beach—but they hoped they might do so equipped with one of those notorious summer beach reads. ("Beach read" was a term Caitlin struggled to understand because she would have hated to read at the beach, one of her favorite places to go when younger. She loved swimming and being burnished by a deep bronze tan, which happened in a flash for the milk-skinned girl.) And when it's chilly outside—well, there's nothing that compares to curling up with a book before a real or imaginary fireplace. Some bookstores opt for background music, which involves a little bit of risk insofar as individual tastes make for tricky complications. One customer's Gregorian chant is another's Eminem or Grateful Dead. Others opt for library reading room or monastic silence—either may work beautifully, again, always again, depending. A coffee bar can be excellent, too, if the baristas are hip and stylish and captivatingly inked, and if quality control is vigilantly monitored. And if a license is affordable, a wine bar. It's hard to imagine a bookstore that doesn't feature readings, and sure, they can be a chore to organize and authors can be prickly prima donnas, but the payoff is enormous: readers see and hear favorite writers in the flesh and in action—and with any luck (it's by no means a sure thing) they buy their books and have them signed. The down-homey touch can be a winner as well. To that end, Hilda would daily bake a fresh big batch of cookies, either her world-renowned chocolate chip or oatmeal raisin, and Colleen would enticingly set them out near the cash register, where the aroma would transport the spirits of customers who craved them like they were designer drugs.

Not so well-known or valued is that the coolness factor of a good bookstore ratchets up by having a nonhuman creature with a sweet personality on the premises. Cats in a cross-species venue might be problematic, being that they are, as everyone knows, noncompliant cats; and a parrot, stunning and impressive to behold as well as entertaining, can also be annoying and possessive and loud and, well, repetitive. Baby goats are absolutely adorable at the petting zoo, but fair warning: they eat paperbacks (and everything else).

As for Floozy's, everything fell into place when they borrowed Francesca's pooch, an arrangement that worked out all the way around. The dog care permitted her to attend to her frenetic capital campaign fundraising. And her sociable dog was a natural draw. He romped free-range, and for an eighty-plus-pound, athletic, protective and muscular dog, he was unfailingly gentle and affectionate and curious and showoffy—an equal-opportunity nuzzler and pawer of children and adults. So it came to be that Caitlin and Colleen and the staff had a loyal, furry, four-legged staff member to keep watchful company over them and their customers. The only unfortunate adjustment was to insist Hilda not furnish her chocolate chip cookies anymore, because Dickens was rascally enough to pinch one— and as any vet would caution, scarfed chocolate usually leads to doggy ER, if not calamity.

Caitlin and Colleen agreed: it was fortunate fun for Floozy's to have the dog. But that spurred Caitlin's suspicion. "Something's off, Frankie's working all the time, I get that, we all are these days. But then she leaves Dickens with us, whom I love, and not with Tommy."

"I know," said Colleen. "First she says Tommy's traveling a lot these days, which is good for his business, and which means she's got the dog solo. Then she reports Tommy said that Dickens scared off a client, which called into question the dog concept in his office. But she said Tommy actually liked when Dickens growled at the guy, whom he didn't want to work for anyway, a scumbucket two-timing husband trying to conceal assets in a divorce. So I'm confused."

"Two explanations mean..."

Colleen finished: "No explanation."

"Both explanations can be true."

"Or both false."

"You got a feeling about Tommy?" asked Caitlin, feeling brazen enough to pry.

"Yeah, no, I don't know, maybe. Basically, once a cop..."

"Which is what Paddy says."

"I can see," said Colleen, "how it might have started between those two, what drew opposites together."

"You can see that, Colly? I don't know if I get it. I do know sometimes things start up with people, and then they change, and it's weird and it's right, and one day they wake up and they don't recognize themselves. Sometimes totally for the better, and they can't believe how lucky they are. You know what I mean?"

Colleen understood perfectly. She'd seen in her own home and with her own eyes that very thing happen.

CAITLIN WAS PLEASED, NOT only about the tail-wagging presence, but about everything. Floozy's was her baby, and Paddy was 100 percent behind her. She was feeling the love all around. It was as she had fantasized since the night after the gym when she and Colleen first cooked up this idea. There was so much to do all day and night long, almost all of it absorbing and new. She and school had never gotten along, so in a way this bookstore was her full-throttle foray into self-education.

She stood nearby the hot new releases on the display tables and let it all sink in, allowing herself a moment—a moment to revel in what she had accomplished. She looked around. She had no previous conception that walls and tables of books—*her* bookcases, *her* stock—could look so beautiful, so substantial, each book promising to tell a story that would make a difference to somebody as soon as it was opened and read. Colleen had proven prescient, too. Caitlin *did* have a natural gift working with customers—with her *people*, as she would call them. Several book clubs carried over from the former store, and she was looking forward to getting to know and serve them better, and to furnish books she would recommend. And working with Colleen was an unadulterated joy; she was her rock, her sidekick, her sisterly muse.

Sure, there were mundane matters and chores—vacuuming, dusting, refreshing the bathroom, keeping the storefront windows sparkling, helping the homeless drifting in and out by handing out sandwiches and the more than occasional few dollars. Updating daily the slick website that Colleen had put up. Arranging point-of-sale merchandise: pens and cards and gadgets and key chains and novelties of every sort—pure profit and kicky, too. And attending to the banking and the credit card companies and keeping in the loop the bookkeeper and the accountant. And about those bills, of course: that stack of invoices on her desk demanded continual attention. And what seemed like a never-ending stream of communications from publishers and marketers and distributors, as well as emails and phone calls from publicists for poets and novelists and memoirists asking for a forum. Soon she would be attending conferences and sales meetings, where she would acquire the fine points of bookselling. She was humble, because she knew she had a long way to go. She was particularly looking forward to meeting best-selling authors as they passed through town on tours, so full of hope and anxiety over the books they put before the public. Caitlin would make them feel at home.

For a few delectable moments, she gave herself over to the meditative reverie. They had created a *good* bookstore, yes, they had. She had no premonition this satisfying feeling would be fleeting.

—

FLOOZY'S WAS CLOSING THAT night, devoid of customers. It was after ten o'clock, where did the hours go? Terry was filing stock, organizing materials, straightening out the shelves, making up signs, industrious alongside her bosses. They'd had a strong week of sales, and the first month proved better than they might have predicted. Paddy would review the numbers and be encouraged, Caitlin hoped, and the store would find its legs sooner rather than later.

The store landline phone rang and her incandescent mood instantly darkened.

"Floozy's," she said.

"Hey, you."

Stunned, she walked outside with the phone. "Are you fucking kidding me? Never call me again, never."

"Wanted to hear your voice one last time."

"You heard my voice, Baxter, so now go, but wait, how'd you find me?"

"Call it dumb luck. You don't have your cell phone anymore. And we're not Facebook friends anymore, so thanks for the diss, but everything's online, so I saw the puff piece about the store opening. Congrats. Good picture of you. I like your new hair."

She was relieved that Paddy had not actually killed him, as she had feared when her husband—soon to be ex-husband once her attorney filed the proper papers—seemed to have evaporated, at least until he made his preposterous presence felt tonight on the phone.

"Where are you?"

"Don't worry. Under a rock."

"Look, you have to never call me again. You will ruin everything if you don't get us both killed first."

"I'm not going to hit you up anymore, sorry about that. But don't you want to see me, one last time, promise? I'm on my way to Alaska, to work a rig, which with my luck will go kablooey."

"Work a rig, right, I can see that right now. You're such a lying piece-of-crap drama queen. We don't have a future, you get that, Baxter, right?"

"But we had a pretty good past, didn't we?"

"No, we didn't, are you high?"

"You're looking gorgeous tonight. You always do. How long have you had that haircut?"

Furiously, she scanned the whole street, up and down. "Where are you? You stalking me? You are out of your mind. You have no idea what you are dealing with. I'm gonna go, never call me again, now go vanish for both of our sakes, please."

And she hung up and headed back into the store, trying to look upbeat and feign that nothing was amiss.

That's the moment a new customer walked in, directly on her heels, and she turned to face him with a practiced shop-owner smile. It was normally welcome to behold such an apparition because new customers are any fledgling concern's lifeblood, but everybody on the floor was dragging after a long day, and they were hungry for a late dinner. She should take them down the street for those excellent burritos—yes, that was a good plan. This new prospective customer was male, in itself a good thing for owners stretching beyond the target female *Floozy* market, but it was too late.

"Sorry, sir," said exhausted but courteous Caitlin, "we're closing, open again in the morning. Please come back."

"This'll be quick," he said. "Just need Terry one minuto."

That sounded peculiar, and now that she took a closer look, the scruffy man—battered baseball cap, scabbed-up face, soiled oversize sweatshirt, flip-flops on life support—didn't resemble someone looking for a beach read today, or ever. "Who shall I say is asking for her?"

"Not asking. Told you, lady, I'ma need Terry." Tone antagonistic, bordering on ominous, and then he raised his voice, dispelling doubts as to whether or not he had been dubbed a knight in shining armor. "Terry, where you at, bitch? Don't be sneaking out the back," he hollered across the store. "Time you get your ass home, your moms and me."

"Fuck me," Terry said as she sauntered from the storeroom. "I don't think so, Dash, you loser. Why don't you drag your own ass outta here, take it back on the street, where you belong?"

"What's up, Terry?" Colleen closed space, protectively big-shouldering, prepared to assert herself.

"This jerk-off is the lowlife scum boyfriend of my mom."

"Sweetheart, is that anyway to speak to your loving stepdad?"

"No, but I'm talking to you."

"Fuck if I know why, but your moms misses you."

"I miss her, too, ever since you heaved her off the deep end."

Colleen said she was going to call the cops if he didn't leave right now.

"Good idea," said Terry, puffing up.

"Got a bone to pick, bitch. Where's my fucking gun?" he said.

"All right," said Caitlin, "we're done, get out."

"You got it?"

"You're so fucking high."

"Not high enough. But hey, looky here, whaddaya know, I happen to got another gun," which he pulled out from the back of his waist and waved around, theatrically, and nervously. "You're coming with me, bitch."

His eyelids appeared superglued wide open, his eyeballs popped out like a cartoon character's.

"What, now you going to shoot me? You're so fucked up, you'd probably blow off your own head first, which would be an uptick."

"You're right, second thought, I don't want you back in my house. Been so nice without you. Who needs you bitching and moaning? Always with the *Nothing to eat*," he whined sing-song, "*Turn down the TV. Wash your filthy clothes*. What are you, the queen of fucking England? You think we're all put on earth to feed you food or something?"

"How the fuck you find me?"

"That flat-chested Joneen, pretty cute despite, she came by sniffing around, and she told us where you'd be. I tracked your ass to the teenager rat hole you been staying. But then you weren't there anymore. Now you're living with your slutty aunt who ripped off the inheritance money from your moms, who needs the money because she owes me. I'll get that money one way or another. You should also close your curtains when you go to bed. Just sayin'."

"A speed-freak Sherlock Holmes."

"Never heard, but 'bout time we all go Plan B. I wasn't planning to when I came in, but I think I'll have to borrow what's in the cash register, so pretty redhead girl, hand it all over right now."

"I don't think so, mastermind, we can identify you to the cops." Instantly Caitlin wished she hadn't shared the all-points bulletin with a jacked-up man wielding a gun.

"Give him the money," said Colleen, increasingly wary. There stood no chance reasoning with a meth head.

"Yeah, just do it," said Terry. "He's out of his tree."

"Yes, I am. So get out the way." He pointed the gun at the women, backed them off. Behind the counter he scooped up the cash receipts in the register. He was pissed with the paltry haul. "Ninety-some bucks? You running a soup kitchen? There's no fucking cash."

"Man," said Colleen, "two words, 'credit cards,' ever had one? You are a regular Bonnie and Clyde, minus Bonnie and minus Clyde. Going for what everybody knows is a fat score—a bookstore."

"Plan C. Everybody, wallets, purses, backpacks, whatever. And another thing, now I think about it, let's have some fun, party time, take off your clothes, now, strip. Case you got any ideas coming after me. Plus, the bitch's moms can use some new shit to wear, Christmas is coming up someday, next year."

The women were defiant, resisting, a moment.

"Hurry up, bitches, I could get upset."

Colleen said, "Sick fuck."

"All right all right all right," said Caitlin. "Everything'll be cool now."

"Hey, Red, gimme that flashy little watch you wearing, too, fake diamonds and all. Fancy-looking, man, my old lady'll wear it to the movies. Give it up, bitch. Now."

Caitlin handed it over, and he shoved it into his pants pocket. She was going to miss the Piaget. And she was going to dread telling Paddy what happened to it. She was so stupid to wear it at the store.

"Second thought, sell it, make a couple hundred bucks."

Colleen couldn't stop herself: "I've lost count, all the ways you're an idiot."

"Thank you very nice for the watch, pretty girl. So now it's showtime, bitches. You, too, Terry, for old time sake, everybody peel. *My eyes are up here…* Fuck you, Terry, always saying that to me, *My eyes are up here, My eyes are up here*, had my fill ah you. And you're pretty foxy, Red. Bet your bush is all nice and trimmed, the way a man likes it. Lemme see."

"Must be a long time since you seen one," said Terry.

"You sweaty cunt."

"You're disgusting."

"All my life been told."

Colleen weighed in: "Something tells me that won't be a problem much longer." She would be proven prophetic.

Whatever the nature of the master plan conceptualized by Dash in advance—a plan of his devising being in and of itself a long shot, given who he was and his defective executive function—it was imminently destined to be foiled by a cross-species team working in tandem.

"Oh, fuck," said Dash, though not, as might be surmised, to any of the women he was in the middle of humiliating. That's because an amped-up, scatterbrained intruder like him couldn't miss the brawny dog named Dickens bowling headlong from the back of the store and rushing straight for him, rumbling with a menacing growl deep within his barrel chest. The man lifted the wobbly gun and struggled to take aim at the snarling dog, but he couldn't gain a purchase and soon regretted it was too late for shooting range practice, so he clambered for safety and the exit. Dickens vocalized ferociously and lunged and assumed a viselike grip of his ankle. The man screamed in agony, wildly waving the gun around, unable to master it, but he did accidentally manage to squeeze off a round. The gun boomed and blasted the mirror behind the cash register, which shattered in a thousand pieces, as the women dove for cover.

It was at this juncture that the gun was dislodged from his hand, Dash and weapon both knocked onto the floor—by an unexpectedly materializing new arrival, a man rushing inside to take him out at the knees. Writhing as Dash was, and repeatedly punching his adversary in the face at the same time, summoning every frantic ounce of his speed-freaky enhanced strength, he also kicked Dickens in the balls with his other foot, getting the dog off him. Then he scrambled from the store, leaving behind his flip-flops and most of the loot, dragging his chewed-on left foot into the night.

The women might have chased him down the block, now that he was disarmed and disabled and barefoot, but what a tableau of bodies presented itself, adjacent to the Recently Released Books table, like roadside triage after a mash-up. The gun on the floor that had menaced them was now unthreatening. The Floozy denizens were mostly alarmed and concerned about poor Dickens, flat out on his side, whimpering, gasping—as Caitlin got down on the floor and cradled the dog's massive head and petted him. At the same time, Colleen and Terry were also wildly curious, as they stood over the mystery man who was bleeding from his mouth, and who was strangely smiling a skewed, self-satisfied smile.

"That went pretty good, didn't it?" the man struggled to say. "I think I got a loose tooth."

"You motherfucking son of a bitch," Caitlin said.

He staunched the blood leaking from his nose with the torn sleeve of his shirt, a shirt she herself recognized from a weak moment a lifetime ago. What was wrong with her to summon up such a trivial detail, a sad reminder of her poor choices in the past?

"But we have to stop meeting like this," he said.

"Damn straight," she said.

"Wait," said Colleen, "you know this guy?"

"You want to know if I *know* this guy? Colly, nobody knows this motherfucker. This asshole doesn't even know himself." She was referring to disappointment incarnate, sprawled and beaming on the floor, her ex, Baxter.

Colleen didn't know what she was supposed to do with perplexing information like that, and awaited her cue and further illumination. "At least," she said, "all the asshole got away with was a few bucks."

In the moment, Caitlin didn't correct her, but he also took her watch.

Chapter Twenty-Seven
Father Philip & The Bishop

IT WAS MIDMORNING AFTER a fitful, restless night, nowhere near the hour Philip started drinking. There was destined to be nothing remotely normal about today. Lately he had begun drinking more than he ever had, and with something of a purpose, a purpose whose origins he didn't comprehend. He didn't think his drinking was a problem, but if it was, it was a manageable one, nothing but a temporary, passing phase. And he wouldn't call it a diversion, and he would certainly not locate himself on the alcoholic spectrum. On balance, no big deal, he considered. Look, he drank a bit, all right, sometimes more than was prudent, he supposed.

He was standing there, fully dressed, vaguely at attention in the middle of his spare quarters, *spare* as in monkish. Personal touches were negligible. One bookcase, a pretty Navajo rug he impulsively picked up on vacation years ago in Santa Fe, unadorned walls. A rack of five black suits on wooden hangers in the armoire. A reading chair, where he never read. He read instead at the little wood desk in the corner, where he also worked on his laptop, underneath a bronze banker's lamp that had been abandoned here by a long-forgotten somebody. The second-floor room did have a pleasant garden view worth studying down below, if he were in such a mood, and he wasn't. More than anything, his bedroom often made him feel as if he were passing through on a business trip, staying in an off-the-grid, understated hotel. To this day, he felt more at home at his family's on Haymarket Hill, and much more so at his and Ruth's hideaway. Speaking of which: their shared living arrangements were about to change, radically and soon. All of which directly went to the issue before him today.

He threw back a shot of rare sipping tequila. To be clear, marketing types called this a *sipping* tequila, but he did not personally exercise such a sipping delivery system. Its heroic glow electrified him, right on schedule, speeding from his tongue to his belly to the tips of all ten fingers. His simple objective was to steel his nerves before venturing across the grounds and formally initiating conversation he had put off for too long. He rehearsed his lines once more and swallowed another, second shot, which was more sustaining and bracing. Now he felt something like brilliantly gleaming, along the lines of lit-up neon.

At first he may have landed on tequila because of what it wasn't; that is, it wasn't Jameson's Irish or his dad's go-to Midleton's. If he ever reflected on the subject, he might conclude that he didn't wish to brand himself with the Irish stereotype, as if that mattered when he wanted to tie one on. He was a private drinker, unlike the bishop, but to be fair, unlike the way the bishop *used to be* when he got routinely, embarrassingly gassed in public. Philip had to ask himself why it made some kind of difference, and to whom, that he only drank by himself, or alone with Ruth, and never in social settings, especially any Church-related occasion, where he drank mineral water exclusively. Clearly and altogether consciously, he set high value on being perceived as abstemious.

His drinking, such as it was, did not constitute a joyful activity. His father had been when younger an inveterate joyless drinker himself, and Philip wondered about genetic predisposition. These cheerless associations were real, but he deemed them irrelevant. In the dimmest recesses of his childhood past, he acquired the information that his grandfather, his father's father, whom he never met, was legendarily an out-of-control lifelong stinking drunk. Paddy Fitzgerald never belabored his own father's story, or any other aspect of his personal, family history. Such material seemed to be screened off, out of bounds for discussion or amplification. Paddy conveyed in myriad, relentless ways that he would never for a second let it be said he was the victim of anything or anybody else. To tell the truth, that was a singular character trait of his dad that Philip envied.

Thanks to tequila's ministrations, as he headed across the grounds he didn't feel the ground under his shoes, and in a few minutes he was rapping on the bishop's office door. When granted permission, he entered, prepared to tell Stanislaus Mackey what he had determined about his future life as a priest—figuring it was well past time to be forthcoming. He wasn't quite looking forward to the moment, but then again, he could not justify to himself, or anybody, and especially Ruth, deferring any longer. The leaden mass of his covert life seemed to be pressing down upon him, occasionally making it hard for him to breathe without effort. He wasn't going to be able to hide much longer. A third shot would have pushed it, but then again, no risk, no reward. That thought was followed by a recognition that two had been already one too many.

—

PHILIP HADN'T INQUIRED, BUT the bishop volunteered an update on his health. TIA, transient ischemic attack: that was what he had endured and been recovering from since. "Well, that's one way of looking at what happened, I suppose." If Mackey wanted to indicate that such a medical diagnosis was ultimately an incomplete if not a misleading explanation, he succeeded—and puzzled Philip accordingly.

"You mean a mini-stroke?" asked Philip, although any terminology containing *stroke* sounded ominous. Some type of neurological impairment of the bishop seemed clear to him and every other observer of Chancery business, so not quite a news bulletin. The diagnostic confirmation was significant, even if it wasn't, the bishop seemed to be intimating, settled business.

"Evidently they don't call it a mini-stroke anymore, but that's the idea." Specialists would be monitoring him closely, having been prescribed new meds, including a modest daily baby aspirin, along with physical therapy twice a week. Considering his age, the man was progressing under the circumstances. But what *were* the underlying circumstances?

"You do seem to be doing much better, Excellence." He did notice that the left side of the man's face appeared subtly, almost imperceptibly, rigidified, palsied—or was he imagining that?

Mackey said in fact he *was* feeling better, thanks. Recovery was a long road to take.

"I don't think I ever told you, I got to know your sister-in-law."

Obviously, the bishop had known Francesca well, but that's not whom he was referring to.

"Your brother's wife." As if Philip needed assistance defining sister-in-law.

Information snapped into place. "Oh, you're talking about *Claire*?" The look of horror would have shocked Mackey had he been searching for corroboration.

"She and I had an important conversation—important to me, and definitely to her."

As far as Philip was concerned, an important conversation with that difficult woman would have constituted historic occurrence.

"Yes," added the bishop, "on the night of the gala."

"I didn't notice her in attendance."

"That's because she wasn't."

Philip was now concerned, as the bishop was not making sense. "Excellence, sorry, I'm lost." Not to mention, why was he relating this information to him?

"I was lost at first, too, but there it is. She wanted me to understand Matty's point of view about the contract, and also Hector Alessandro's situation."

"You discussed Caring Street. You and Claire." Statements, not interrogatories.

"We did, yes, we did."

"When, where?"

Those probative queries may have been borderline intrusive, and they didn't interest Mackey, evidently, so he swatted them away. "She opened my eyes as to the human cost of my decisions. I know you did your utmost to alert me in advance, and I'm sorry I failed to heed your counsel, only I heard things in a new way when she opened her heart to me."

Again, more news to Philip. "Claire *has* a heart?"

"You are being unkind, Father, and wrong, too. Claire might have played a big role in saving my life."

"Excellence, I'm lost."

"That much is obvious. Have you been drinking this morning?"

—

THEY TOOK THEIR PLACES on opposite ends of the black leather couch, and Philip was hoping he could ultimately gain some information if not insight, and address the mystery as to what happened on gala night. Maybe the bishop would be forthcoming at last.

"I understand the allure of drinking if anybody does," said the bishop, philosophically, "so I'm not going to wag my finger. All I'll say is, be careful, Father. Next thing you know, you wake up one day, gaze into your bathroom mirror, and twenty years have passed you by. It's a common curse of the priestly class, as we're all aware."

"Some things were weighing on my mind this morning, Excellence." Philip didn't have a drinking problem, he almost defended himself, this was Mackey's pure projection. But he wasn't going to protest, not now, not after considering the agenda that loomed before them. "I wanted to take the edge off a little."

"I understand the urge. Before we get into that, Father, I need to catch you up on a few things. I've decided to put Hector back on the job as executive director at Caring Street. I know after your own fashion you cautioned me before I fired him, but back then I was still riding up on my high horse, and like you, I was wobbly in the saddle, and for the same reason. Which means you're out as the administrator, but not because you did a poor job. You did all right, but Hector is unquestionably the best man for the job, and I hope you take this in the right spirit, but you yourself aren't, Father, it's not in your wheelhouse. You have other, more valuable skills."

He couldn't disagree with the assessment of his performance, but he was wounded, what with the unceremonious dismissal. He opted for *gracious*. "Thank you for granting me the opportunity to serve, Excellence."

"Been meaning to ask, what's the latest on Sister Patricia? She's thriving in the classroom now, I hope."

"Kids adore her, I'm told, and she is fitting into the convent as before—a fantastic, seamless transition back to her former life."

"Arrange a classroom visit for me, would you?"

What Philip was thinking was: *What the fuck is going on with him?* What he said was: "I will see that it's put on your calendar."

"And about the teacher's contract, Father. Been thinking. Let's go back to where we were before I conceived of my not-so-dazzling plan. The old standard contract is plenty good enough. As you told me more than once, and which I systematically ignored, no point fixing what isn't broken. I'd hate to push out excellent teachers like your brother Matty at Holy Family when we open the new campus. We've suffered enough collateral damage in the Church the past few years. Please let him know we are counting on him to be teaching brilliantly at HFH for a long, long time."

"Excellence, that's great. I also hear, the word on the street is, the capital campaign is building up a head of steam."

"It is indeed, and Francesca is rapidly leading the way to accomplishing our fundraising goals. Thanks to her, Caring Street will soon be securely in the black, and will stay there, and the high school property—oh, wait, I have some more good news for you, Father. I signed the formal Letter of Intent on the real estate deal last night with someone you perhaps know, a certain Padraic Fitzgerald." Mackey told him the number that had been struck, thanks to artful, deft, creative Francesca. It was roughly two-thirds the number Philip and everyone else on the inside had expected and he was stunned all over again. This was turning out to be some kind of morning. Perhaps he had thrown down the right amount of tequila after all.

"My father *agreed* to that deal?"

"I'm sure you played a role with him, being the good son and good priest you are. Thank you, Father. He gave us a damn good run for our money, didn't he? And it took some frank conversation and Francesca's incredible, persuasive ways, but yes, he did finally agree. Paul on the road to conversion and Damascus kind of thing, don't you know. The communications people will send out a press release first thing."

Philip shook his head in wonderment. "Should we have a toast? I have some nice tequila in my room."

Bishop Mackey sighed and said with mournful emphasis: "Father, I don't think so—*Father.*"

All right, that was an inappropriate suggestion, especially to somebody like the bishop, but that rare reposado would have come in handy—for Philip.

"That's quite an amazing development, Excellence. As is Sister Patricia. And Hector. And the teacher contract. And the new school campus. And my little brother Matty back in the school. I count six miracles attributable to you, Excellence, many more than the three strictly required by Rome for beatification." Philip reared back, fearing he'd crossed a line, making light of sacred ecclesiastical matters. But he had misread Mackey's frame of mind yet again.

"And my being on the wagon, don't forget that one, so I count seven. I pity the poor devil's advocate arguing against my all but inevitable beatification. Yes, all Saint Stanislaus Mackey is missing is his stigmata." He held up both palms to confirm that he wasn't bleeding in the places where Christ's wounds were when he was nailed to the cross. "Then again, it's too early to tell for sure. Which is always the case. Everybody's got their own cross to carry, don't they, Father? Philip? Philip, are you feeling all right?"

"Me? Never felt...." And his voice trailed off. He couldn't finish off enunciating the falsehood that he never felt better. Father Philip Fitzgerald had been rehearsing for days—months and months, more accurately—what he was about to tell the bishop, about the renunciation of his vocation as a celibate priest, and there was no point in delaying any longer.

"Excellence, if I may, there's something I should tell you."

The next sentence out of his mouth would mark the beginning of the end of his vocation. There are indeed such dramatic moments in life, he imagined, when one approaches a turning point from which there is no return, a definitive leap from the known to the unknown, or possibly from one unknown to a greater, more unknowable unknown. A warrior feels this keenly, the instant combat commences, and the bullets start to fly. Or an athlete, at a crucial stage in a game, a race, a match. Or a mother giving birth and then nursing her infant, or a father holding his child in his arms for the first time. People on the altar, exchanging wedding vows. A person burying a friend, a parent, a loved one. A man prostrate on the cold, marbled cathedral floor, being ordained. This is when you say to yourself, from this point forward I will never be the same as I was. All the routine and enormous moments that punctuate and demarcate everyone's ordinary life, in other words. Turning points existed everywhere and always, if you permitted yourself to be conscious of them.

"Before you speak, Monsignor."

Mackey must have been confused again, and Philip was derailed, being called *Monsignor*. The man was losing it in real time.

"Before you say another word, there is one other news item to share, which is about to be made public."

Philip feared the bishop sussed out everything about his life with Ruth, so he waited submissively, fearfully.

"Father," said Stanislaus Mackey, "I now need to address you Reverend *Monsignor* Philip Fitzgerald."

Philip countered: there must be some mistake.

"I don't think so, Monsignor." Mackey peered over his bifocals beneficently.

Beyond everything, Philip also picked up the bishop's anything-but-subtle signal. And maybe the bishop was right, now was not his time to unpack his story. Or maybe Father Philip had not quite reached his turning point yet. *Monsignor* Philip.

—

"Forgive me, Excellence, I'm reeling. I did not see this coming. *Monsignor*."

"You should have. You should have long since been a monsignor, but alas, the wheels of Church politics grind agonizingly slow. My first months in, I recommended you, but the Holy See takes its sweet, divine time."

"What's important is that this is a marvelous day for the diocese, for Holy Family High School, for Caring Street. Because I don't know what to say about *Monsignor* Fitzgerald."

As the bishop rose to his feet, Philip was growing more and more certain Mackey knew everything that Philip was planning to tell him. Mackey glanced around as if he were searching for something he had lost track of. He stepped to the bevel-edge leadlight window outside of which spectacular red roses were blooming. He looked and looked and then said, "Oh, my God, there they are again."

Philip asked what he was referring to—the roses?

That wasn't it at all. "The angels, there they are again. There they are, and they're everywhere, if you're listening for their intonations and if you're receptive to their voices."

The priest was not of a mind to engage in a theological discussion with his superior and spiritual mentor. But he didn't think he should let that bizarre remark stand without responding.

"Excellence, would you like some rest? You've been through a lot."

The bishop smiled. "Monsignor, I feel I've been half asleep my whole life, I don't need any more rest. You know, I have to give thanks to your sister-in-law."

"Frankie, I'm sure, knows how much you value her. We all do."

"Certainly, I think the world of Francesca, but no, I keep telling you—*Claire*. She's the one who helped me attend to what the angels were telling me. I doubt that was her explicit plan, I doubt she even believes, but that's all right, she is a vessel, and you are a vessel, and I am increasingly convinced I am nothing more than a vessel, an old and battered vessel on turbulent high seas."

"*Who* is telling you *what*?"

"The angels, I just said that, aren't you listening?"

"The angels." Again, a statement, not an interrogatory.

"Unfortunately, you are skeptical."

"Not in the slightest," Philip lied.

"Yes, you are, Philip. But the seraphim and cherubim and archangels, thrones and dominations, powers and principalities, all nine choirs of angels—the whole spinning world is a-swim, is swarming, is buzzing with them. How many stars are there in the universe? There are even more angels. They are messengers, which is what I had forgotten, pickled as I was with booze. Angel also means messenger, and priests and church elders are called angels in the Scriptures. So now I attend to their clarion calling. That's their act of mystical intercession."

"And their message is?"

Mackey shook his head, not angrily, but powerfully, assertively. "I see what you're doing there, Philip, I sense you're concerned about my mental, my emotional stability. I cannot fault you, I suppose, and I am a little bit touched by your ratcheted-up concern, or is it unbridled suspicion? At least you're not being your typical condescending self—for a change. But when you ask me to tell you what their message is, I know you're not asking in the proper spirit, Philip, not yet, otherwise I would tell you, if I had the words. And their message is not like some silly epigram contained inside a cracked-open fortune cookie. It's not like the I Ching, it's not astrology or numerology, or any of the base gnostic systems of divination. It's a message you'll hear someday when you're prepared to hear it, and you'll know you're ready when you hear the message loud and clear, Monsignor."

"I see." Which he didn't, but that seemed to be what the occasion required.

"You recall what we learned in seminary, Philip. How a priest has two angels, one guardian angel assigned at birth, as it is for everyone, and one specially assigned when you are ordained. My God, given what struggles we priests have, I think we could keep on their toes a dozen, if not our very own legion of angels. Because when those pure spirits in the infinite recesses of a time before time began were given the chance to serve God or Satan, to become angel or devil, they had the singular opportunity to say Yes. And that's what they did, they said Yes. We mortals spend our life pitching left and right, backward and forward, up and down, off target or on, right or wrong, but the angels? They are the Yes in our lives. I'll tell you a secret, Philip. Not so long after I came back, after the hospital, I woke up in the middle of the night, restless, and then I screamed, or tried to. If I did, I don't think anybody heard me. You see, there was an angel sitting on my bed, calm and reassuring. I myself located a well of inner peace after a while, and the angel made me to understand, and without words, all over again the big Yes I needed to affirm. You want to call my doctor, don't you, ring the alarm bell, right?"

The bishop didn't need a supernatural messenger to figure that one out, but it was true, that's what Philip was contemplating doing as soon as he could liberate himself from this wild conversation.

"Excellence, would you tell me what happened to you the night of the gala?"

"Someday, I might, if I can find the words or remember. And if I determine you are ready to listen."

"It would help me a great deal if you would."

"I'm sure it would, but in the meantime, you will do what you will do, Philip. I want you to know, I have never felt saner, clearer, more attuned. And you, Philip? How troubled, how vexed are you?"

"More than I can say."

"You will do the right thing, Monsignor, when the time comes, when you tell me what it is you wanted to tell me, and when you're ready for the eternal Yes. In the meantime, listen, and listen very, very hard, and you may be blessed to hear the angels—including your priestly angel. That's the secret that is no secret. *Now* is the other word for eternity."

Philip took stock, which was hard to do what with his mental inventory shifting and jostling, crashing down. Mackey was insane or deluded, or Mackey was now a holy man, and what could be the difference in the end, because perhaps there wasn't a difference. Frankie was working magic on Mackey and everybody, and evidently Claire was, too. His brother Matty still had a job. His father had done something unexpected, which Philip should have long ago learned to expect. In all the tumult and misdirection, one thing felt sure, and one thing only: Ruth was about to give birth to his son—to give birth to *their* son. This counted as a miracle of the first order, too. That was some kind of Yes. He wouldn't tell Mackey or anybody that he had no time for angels. But then again the bishop probably already knew. And if you care, you angels, thought Philip, and if you have some grace to spare, grant some to Ruth and to the baby, and, while you're at it, me.

Philip agreed that now and eternity indeed meant the same thing. And he would do the right thing by Ruth and their little boy, if there was any way he possibly could.

Chapter Twenty-Eight
Paddy

H OW FARES THE NOBLE beast?" Paddy asked Caitlin.

"Frankie said he'll be all right, lion that he is. No internal injuries, according to the vet, but he'll be way sore, so he's on heavy-duty painkillers. Not as sore as that guy. He'll be lucky to walk a straight line again, if he ever could."

There was commotion in the kitchen downstairs. Hilda was banging pans, rattled about what had taken place tonight, distraught not only for poor Dickens but for the girls, what they went through.

"Hilda's frying up a steak for Dickens," he said.

"He'll love that, and I don't know what would have happened without him. Frankie's going to spend the night here with him. She's trading shots of Irish with Colly right now, we better have a spare bottle."

"You know what would have happened, and so do I, and I told you not to open your store in that rat-infested part of town. Jesus, Caitlin, Jesus."

"I don't think you did, and for the record, I've never seen a rat anywhere near the store."

"Some people, they're rats."

"And I'm going back, and nobody, and no way that freak, is going to intimidate me." She had been hitting the Midleton hard herself. "I gotta go to bed."

"It's your new girl's stepfather?"

"Let's call the cops, Paddy."

What a quaint concept, the police. "This is not a job for John Law. Nobody will ever hurt you again."

"Nobody should promise that. That's not the way life works."

"Especially with the Great Blue Line—they protect nobody. Me, I will take care of you. I'm not Baxter, either, and speaking of him, the young man and I seem to officially have a new problem. He doesn't take instruction well, which is unfortunate. I know I'm supposed to be thankful for what he did, but it's going to be hard. For him."

"Baxter may be a fool, but he was the one running into the burning house, he was putting himself between me and a loaded gun. Damn it, Paddy, he should get a pass, risking his life."

"I will consider options available to him, man-to-man, and I give him credit, partial credit for tonight. In any case, I got my guys coming to the bookstore tomorrow, from now on."

"My customers will feel so secure."

"I'm just beginning. My people'll sit on the store from outside, that better?"

"You're scaring me, Paddy."

"You never need to be scared of me, never. Everybody else? Different story."

"What are you going to do to him?"

"Who?"

"Stop, really, stop."

"Why do you care?"

"I don't care if I ever see him again, but you can't eliminate everybody who gets in your way."

"Caitlin, darling, not so sure about that. But I'm more concerned about you. You should take something, get some sleep. The watch, not important. I'll get you another one just like it. What matters is you're okay."

When he hugged her tight, she trembled, fatigued, and allowed him to hold her up, which underscored for him he had work left to do.

—

"SORRY TO DISTURB YOU, Mr. Fitzgerald." That was Slip McGrady the following morning, calling from the sanctuary of his Limerick Jewelry & Loan back room. "A man of extravagantly sketchy disposition has befouled my establishment, offering an extraordinary watch, a timepiece I could never have forgotten—and that could never have been legitimately in his possession. The ignorant loon begs four hundred dollars in exchange, if you can feature that. I thought you should be promptly advised."

"This would be the beautiful Piaget that originated with you."

"May I be of assistance, sir?"

"I appreciate your alert concern, Mr. McGrady. Would you please stall till my associate Jonesy arrives to address this nuisance?"

"Always a pleasure to see Mr. O'Dell, so I eagerly look forward to his imminent arrival. Because, Mr. Fitzgerald, I don't care to boast, but I can be, when called upon, a world-class procrastinator. On that score, if I may also respectfully add, sir, I will never forget the artful delaying tactics practiced to my advantage in court by your dear son Anthony, whose loss I still keenly feel and will always lament. And so with your permission, I will discuss the vagaries and intricacies of our unpredictable weather patterns with this most dubious specimen of the human race for as long as required. For it indeed appears he is unaware a nasty storm is on his horizon."

"That does seem to be in the forecast, and you are a prince, sir."

"You're too kind, Mr. Fitzgerald."

—

PADDY'S CONSTRUCTION COMPANY, AFTER the deal had been struck months earlier, had swung into action with a fury borne of a tight building timeframe. A few short hours from now, around sunrise, his crew would be laying down rebar for the main school building foundation, and Paddy was supervising a different sort of job here in the darkest predawn hours. The steel supports were laid nearby, grid readied for installation, after which, at some point, cement would be poured. Timing couldn't have been more fortunate for structural purposes, though not for Dash's.

Jonesy illuminated the situation for the ultimate edification of the barefoot, limping speed freak: "If we had world enough and time, this dumbness, bitches, were no crime, etcetera and so on. Be brave, man up, it'll be over before you know it because world enough and time, my man, world enough and time." They stood next to the deep pit that had been dug. Three others in Jonesy's crew held Dash, and one was loudly complaining the guy fucking reeks of horse piss, could they get this over with already before we hurl?

"It's organic physiological processes at work," explained Jonesy, "for the man is fearful, the body has its own logic and demands." In his gloved hand he held the man's weapon, retrieved from the store's floor that night.

In addition to Paddy and Jonesy and those reining Dash, there were crew members on either side of another man on the scene, one who appeared similarly distressed but in his case rendered incapable of speech, for a change: Baxter.

Jonesy and company had picked up Dash at the pawnshop, reclaiming the watch in the process. They had dragged him outside by his greasy hair and thrown him in the trunk.

"As Jesus promises us sinners," fulsomely intoned Jonesy in his baritone, "the last shall be first and the first last. Luke Chapter 13, your lucky number. And we are all sinners, but no one more sinning than you. So look at it this way, boyo. You are indeed a sinner. And you're certainly finishing way back of the pack, far out of the money, so this could be a big opportunity for you if you play your cards right." Jonesy found mixing his metaphors to be one of the hallmarks of his creativity.

Arrayed before the pit was when and where the man tried to apologize, but he stammered and stuttered, so it was hard to determine ultimate intent. They did catch a mumbled, aggrieved complaint about the infection he believed was swiftly coursing up his leg from the rabid dog bite.

"Now you're insulting that dear old beast? Bad mistake, we love that magnificent canine, who doesn't have rabies, though you probably do and might have infected him. Tell me, what is your suit size? I'm saying you're a fifty, fifty-two."

"What the fuck?"

"Suit size, not a trick question. What is it?"

"Never owned a suit."

"But if in your forsaken existence you ever owned a suit, I'm going with fifty-two."

"Whatever you say, motherfucker." Then Dash addressed Paddy: "Said I'm sorry, sir, whoever you are. I'll never do that again."

"I know, man, I know," Paddy said, "but some things cannot be papered over. Besides, your exit won't be tearing a hole in the fabric of the universe, and nobody's going to miss your presence. Look at the bright side, you won't be chasing your next fix, either, and your foot won't be causing you further discomfort."

"Then you can fuck the fuck off, too."

"Now, now. Be careful, we could spare the bullet, so what would you like, your choice, last choice you'll ever make. You can scream if you need to get it out of your system, nobody within a mile can hear."

"Told you, I didn't know what I was doing, high as a fucking kite."

"So you're ready to turn over a new leaf, that what you're telling me?"

"Yes, I am, I really am, and I'm fucking goddamn sorry."

"I know, I know. But I'm not a big speculator in the rehabilitation business and besides, you and I both know that you won't turn over a new leaf, right?"

"I didn't know what I was doing. I feel like shit, what I put those women through."

"Taking responsibility is a pure bitch, isn't it? But it's okay, you'll feel better soon enough. Question: Did you get off on humiliating, terrifying my girls like that?"

"I was wrong, said I'm sorry, give me a chance, would you?"

"That would be considerate on my part, you're right. Let me think about it."

"I won't let you down no more."

Paddy paced awhile in a circle and returned to where he had been. "Well, let me alleviate the suspense. I've given you all the consideration you're ever going to get, and more than you gave the girls."

"But I didn't kill nobody!"

"That's what I call a technicality, because you could have and they indeed feared you might."

Paddy turned on his heels and headed off toward the waiting car, calling out to Jonesy to do whatever he determined advisable, because he was finished with this little problem. But Paddy did have some brief last words for Baxter: "Next time, have a nice trip and stay there."

"Mr. Fitzgerald..." he tried.

"You've said and done enough," said Paddy.

That's when they both heard Jonesy reminding Dash: "Troublemakers? They all inherit the wind. Book of Proverbs, man, reflect on Holy Writ while you can."

But Paddy was pondering nothing less than the purpose of his life as he slowly walked back to his car, down the hill, beside a stand of trees that would soon be cut down. What was he accomplishing here tonight? Because the fact was, by taking this course of action he wasn't being true to himself. He had no dread of being caught, because nobody was going to miss the guy, and he had zero apprehension about the body ever surfacing once construction was underway. But even so, this was retaliation, a disproportionate administration of justice or, when you got down to it, nothing but unalloyed revenge. The loser made a legitimate case, it was true. He didn't deserve to pay with his life because he had not taken a life—though he had taken the watch Caitlin loved, and which he was looking forward to returning to her once Mr. McGrady professionally cleaned and polished it, good as new. Nonetheless, Paddy had hopped on the road to reckoning and couldn't take the off-ramp toward forgiveness, and not because he was concerned Jonesy and the others might privately begin to question his resolve, which was something he wasn't worried about. He himself was questioning his own judgment. Paddy took no delight in this circular self-interrogation. He knew that Caitlin would be horrified if she found out, not that she would, because that's the sort of soft-hearted person she was, but she was both at the center of his response and irrelevant. That pathetic junkie had violated Caitlin and Colleen and the girl who worked there, whose name he forgot. But he also violated Paddy, challenged his power, not that the guy specifically intended this, but that was also immaterial. When a man like Paddy reaches this intersection in his life, he cannot double back. Paddy wanted blood. He earned blood. He would shed blood. When a man rationally decides to take a life, the way Paddy did, rationality is the secondary victim.

When he was a much younger man, he knew what he would have done. Employing his fists and a billy, he would have personally caused the man to bleed all over himself, to hear a few bones being crunched, to spit out a couple of teeth—and in order to make a point, he would keep him alive, so that the guy would survive to always remember who it was who put the beatdown on him. That association led him to deciding what Baxter deserved, which was different from what Dash deserved, perhaps harsher.

Over the next couple of days, the foundation of the new Holy Family High School main building would be laid and the cement poured and probably nobody would remember Dash ever again, except, that is, for Paddy in the years he had left to live on earth.

Pop pop pop. He heard the reports in the near distance. He was not startled.

Matters needed to be addressed swiftly, directly, even when strictly speaking there was no absolute need, and not while there existed no genuine future threat that needed to be eliminated. And yet there was a kind of need he felt inside that would never be quenched. He would waste no opportunity to exercise his power, not as long as he could, and he would because he could, and because he could, it was right, or right enough.

It was remarkable that Jonesy chose to put a few of the man's own rounds in him first. Kindness was always a matter of context, a relative, contingent proposition.

—

JONESY RETURNED TO THE car, near where Paddy was standing, and he was both downcast and upbeat, as he always ambivalently felt after he completed such a task. Taking a life was taking a life, however miserable and worthless and dangerous that life had been. He had left the crew to finish up at the site, and he had not returned alone. He had Baxter in tow.

"So," Paddy said, "this has been a busy, busy night, and we've all been through a great deal. But Baxter, we have arrived at your moment of truth now. Now, man up, no need for tears, hear me out, young man."

"Mr. Fitzgerald, I saved Caitlin, don't that count for nothing?"

"Shut the fuck up, you whimpering dribble dick," said Jonesy. "You disobeyed a direct command never to return to town or have anything to do with Miss Caitlin."

"Where was I? Oh, yes. You have a choice, Baxter. You can take Door Number One, and you watched for yourself where that leads. Or you can choose instead Door Number Two."

Baxter trembled, shook his head, side to side, up and down. He'd witnessed a murder, and could easily pick out from a police lineup the henchmen, if it came to that. But that's what gave him greatest pause: that was at the heart of Paddy Fitzgerald's plan, to have him see everything with his own eyes, so he would have no doubts about what was in store for him tonight—not that he had a doubt. But why psychologically torture before killing him, what was the point? Why didn't they throw him in the pit with that idiot who robbed and shot up the store?

Paddy allowed Baxter a few minutes to ruminate before resuming. "You curious as to Door Number Two? Let me help. Door Number Two: from now on you work for me. You'll get paid when and whatever your boss, Mr. O'Dell, feels like paying you. You do what he tells you to do for as long as we need you, and you won't ask any questions or free-lance or make any quote helpful unquote suggestions. And if Miss Caitlin ever hears from you, or if you ever so much as utter her name and I hear you, or if the day should come when you enter a room where she and I both may be and your eyes meet for a second—for a split second—that's when we will escort you to Door Number One."

"Too good of a deal," said Jonesy, "if you ask me, for a wankster sport like you."

"I do have to acknowledge it took some bravery to risk your life in the bookstore, or maybe I'm feeling generous. What do you say, Baxter? Sport? It's getting late, I want to go home. To my Caitlin."

Baxter had no option, of course, but he could imagine the sick pleasure Paddy would enjoy, seeing him in bondage, twisting anxiously whenever Caitlin—whenever *Miss* Caitlin was nearby, whose name he would never speak again. What was both impressive and perverse to him was that

Fitzgerald had no concern over Baxter's ever flipping. It was purer than that. The man wanted him to witness for himself the type of fate that he could visualize awaited him should he disobey him again or rat him out. A case could be made that he was an accomplice to the murder. And yet it was more intricate than that. He had new employment, doing exactly what, no idea, except he could make a few educated guesses. In his life he'd held dozens of jobs, none for long or with anything resembling distinction, but nothing like this. He would be enslaved to serve the man who had taken his wife, his ex-wife, he should qualify. It seemed to him more than a little bit vile—and more than a little bit brilliant on the part of Paddy Fitzgerald. This was a means of killing him every single day without putting a bullet in his head. He begrudgingly admired this plan. So there Baxter was again, as ever, in his default life stance: walking a fine line, servile between stupidity and big balls. Which was all along what Paddy counted on.

A smile must have flickered because Paddy asked what he found amusing.

"Can't believe I'm saying this to you, Mr. Fitzgerald, but," and he took a deep breath, "when do I start?"

"Right now. Go back to the site and grab a shovel, so you can never forget where you can locate Door Number One."

Once he was out of earshot, Jonesy said, "Let me know when you want to be done with him once and for all, Mr. Fitzgerald."

"Patience is a great virtue of yours."

"Yet another scurrilous, baseless rumor, sir."

Chapter Twenty-Nine
Another Family Fitzgerald

Back in Ruth's apartment, now their apartment, Philip was softly singing a *rock-a-bye baby don't you cry* lullaby. Based on the available evidence, the boy, gently, securely in his arms, was buying it. His eyelids were fluttering and he was breathing deeply against his father's chest. They were standing out on the deck, the sun was setting gaudily, and a refreshing autumn chill filtered through the air. Ruth told him he had promise when it came to putting down the baby for a nap, even if that was only good for an hour or two before feeding the ravenous boy again. Her labor had been protracted but finally medically uncomplicated. That's why they use the word *labor*, she reminded him, and if she hadn't quite forgotten the experience, she also would not willingly bring it top of mind—though that epidural was a game-changer. Besides, look what her labors produced: a perfect baby boy, ten fingers, ten toes, eyes of steely, transfixing blue.

"You upset, Philip?"

He told himself not to cry in front of a woman who just gave birth.

She didn't wish to explore his emotional state. It was fairly obvious, and she loved him for it.

"I'm really not," he said, and turned his back to her as she sat exhausted at the table and sipped tea. "A boy needs his mom *and* his dad," he said, to himself, but it was all right for Ruth to overhear.

He does, she communicated without saying a word, he really does.

"How can we do this, Ruth, and how can we possibly *not* do this?"

She stopped herself from slipping into therapist mode—she was done with that chapter of her life, at least as far as her relationship with Philip was concerned, but what was the new chapter to open in their mutual book? "All new families have challenges. We have ours, and they're doozies."

"We are a new family." Fifty-percent question, fifty-percent declaration, one hundred-percent Philip Fitzgerald.

"We should give it a good shot." It was worth trying, worth trying for their baby.

"Worth trying for all three of us."

So there was a *three* of them.

"I am still a priest."

"Yes, that's right, a priest who is the father of a beautiful baby boy."

"And a man who is in love with a woman named Ruth."

"Who's in love with you."

"That makes it sound simple."

"Who says there's anything simple about love and family?"

"You think we should get married?"

"Are you about to take a knee?"

"I think I might, and if I did, would you say yes?"

"That depends on what you ask."

"They are expecting me back at the diocese."

She conceded that was likely the case.

"I don't think I am going. I think I am staying here."

She could tell he was caught in the crossfire of conflicting forces, but articulating them was the forerunner of actions, decisions. And yet, they had to be realistic. It would be a while before they could work out domestic arrangements, and it certainly would not be easy. There could be a while when he would be living in two places. But they knew that going in. And someday, so they hoped, they would put it all together. One home, one family, now and forever.

"I honestly don't know if I can be a good father and husband. My track record is spotty."

The therapist Ruth once used to be, and might be again, knew what she was supposed to do, to probe for meaning in his words, but she was not his therapist, never was, never would be. He was a man with secrets of his own, and flaws, some similar to hers, but she could live with them—and, she was hopeful, with *him*.

"You're a good bet," she said.

"Now you're sounding like Frankie's gambling dad."

"Why do you mention her name?" There was some intensity to her words.

Philip never did answer her question, but for Ruth it had been a while since she reviewed in her mind that last session with Francesca, though in the immediate aftermath she replayed the memory of it over and over and over again. If she had not discontinued Frankie's treatment, her own supervisor, to whom she had disclosed everything, would have put her foot down. But again, this was a long time ago, four months. Sixteen weeks is long enough to change the world, and since then, her world would never be the same. The day would come when Ruth and Francesca would revisit their individual relationships with Philip, and it would be an important day because the subject by then would have been rendered utterly irrelevant.

"Well," Ruth said, "I have to imagine Frankie probably thinks you would be a great dad."

"On the other hand, I could end up like my old man."

"Well, I am clear on that one. You are definitely not Paddy Fitzgerald, Philip."

"I'd probably be the last to know if I was."

"You're not, honey."

"I want us to make a beautiful family."

"Then we will, Philip, we will. When are we going to tell yours? The boy's a Fitzgerald, after all."

"Okay, about that," he began.

—

Philip met Colleen the week before Ruth's contractions began and her water broke as she stood in the shower, and after a speed-limit-violating race to the hospital, fifty miles away, twenty hours later, a baby.

He had taken his sister out for coffee, and at first opportunity, divulged. When by way of response she screamed with shock, everybody in the café practically jumped out of their chairs and jostled and spilled their lattes. Philip assumed that to be a shriek of joy. Then she hauled off and took a roundhouse swing, barely missing his nose as he bent back and away. He knew how to avoid a punch. Then, immediately, she threw her arms around his neck and laughed and cried, pretty much at the same time. Those are all the facets of what they grew up labeling the Full Fitzgerald.

She sat back violently and let loose a torrent. "You kept this all under your hat? Since when? Never mind, I can do the math. Due date? You in love? You better be. Tell me about her. How long have you known her? Will I like her and of course I will. Though the woman's judgment is automatically suspect. Hooking up with the likes of you. And I've got just the book in mind for a prospective parent like you: *What to Expect When a Fucking Moron Dad is Expecting*."

"Sounds like I could use that."

There was so much ground to cover. Where to start? Philip issued the executive summary Ruth Report: all good with her and the baby kicking all night long to get out. Yes, and of course, he had deep feelings for her, of course he did. Yes, the two of them had history. Good history, mostly, he emphasized. One obvious, if secondary, subject loomed: Colleen asked if he were leaving the priesthood. Philip said he didn't want to act precipitously.

"Oh, sure, *precipitous* would be ill-advised," she said. "It's not like your life is going to change or anything, because nobody is going to notice diaper bags and think anything weird about a crib in the rectory."

"Wait a second, listen up, this gets interesting fast." In sum, while Catholics were not generally aware of this, and many would be scandalized to be so informed, the Church was nothing if not nuanced when it came to the subject of priests and the children they fathered. They had centuries of practice in this regard, though nobody could put a verifiable number on how many priests and their children there currently were. Philip read around in the dusty ecclesiastical tomes and consulted with an old, retired priest in the next diocese over who was a canon lawyer. "Hypothetically," he framed the issue for his friend, "what does canon law say about..." his situation?

"I'll presume you're asking for a scholarly friend, Philip."

To Philip's surprise, it turned out that canon law said...absolutely nothing. Though it did stipulate that priests' children neglected by their priest fathers were the moral obligation of the Church. Which was also quite curious, and subtle. As he researched, he discovered that over and beyond the edicts, it had been determined by long-established practice conducted in the shadows of Chanceries everywhere that, in circumstances such as these, a man could and should be a good priest *and* a good father to his child, even if he had to take leave of his clerical duties—temporarily or perhaps permanently. Every situation would be different, every thus-conceived family would pose unique challenges. The priest in question may have betrayed his promise of celibacy, which was grave on its own terms. But he could be forgiven if he were repentant, and at the same time he would be unequivocally bound by his sacred promise to love and care for his offspring. But *was* Father Philip repentant? It depended on the day, sometimes a qualified yes, sometimes an affirmative no. Behind the scenes, ecclesiastical processes evidently kicked in, and financial considerations, too, he would bet, but everything took place securely *sub rosa*. But maybe not indefinitely.

"Heaven forfend!" said Colleen. "You aren't implying Holy Mother Catholic Church is a racketeering operation, are you, Father?"

"You know who's been causing a stink, Colly? Right, the Irish, go figure. They want to protect the kids, to make sure they are taken care of, and to lift the shroud of secrecy and shame."

"Careful now, secrecy and shame are what totally make us Irish."

"There's gotta be a thousand kids with priests for dads in Ireland alone, they say, and who knows how many in America. Clearly, there's no one-size-fits-all when it comes to how the Church regards them."

"Now there's a bloody shocker, the Irish! Always ready to throw down for a reason, even a good one. I want to be there to help when she delivers."

"That's so great, so *Colleen* of you, to offer. But I think we'll do this on our own. We chose an OB/GYN out of town, and far from the diocese, and her hospital is where we're going to deliver. That way nobody recognizes me. I hope. But that's a chance we're willing to take."

To revisit her original question, no, Philip wouldn't automatically be drummed out of his pulpit and ceremonially stripped of his Roman collar at sunrise. Once they found out about the baby, however, he'd be relieved of his clerical duties, almost certainly at least temporarily, so he could attend to his child. But where exactly did he stand, ultimately, with his child and with his Church? Time would tell. He would work this out, because—because he had no choice.

—

PHILIP HAD APPRISED RUTH of what struck her as arcane Church subtleties that ultimately amounted to insignificance now. Here was the simple truth overriding doctrine and politics: the baby boy right now swaddled in Father Philip's ecstatic embrace. *Monsignor* Philip. She assumed Philip would do the obvious and right thing—the right thing by her and by their newborn child. In the moment, she was more concerned about something else: "I want to meet your sister. Have her come over, I can use the help. Can we count on Colly?"

"She's on our side, she'll hold her mud. She knows she has to keep this news inside the family tent, which is why I told her first. She'll make every Fitzgerald take a blood oath of secrecy, to swear on our mother's grave. And she'll figure out how and when to break it to my dad that he's finally getting the grandson he's been waiting on forever. Only he probably didn't imagine his dream would arrive courtesy of me." He stopped himself—he'd hit the unintendedly off-key note. "Courtesy of *us*," he clarified. "Because you know, never told you this other thing, Ruth, but when I held the baby the first time, I was seized by the strongest, strangest emotion, even as I was totally bowled over by the birth and being there with you. You know what else sneaked up on me, there in my green scrubs? It was about my dad. When the nurse handed me the child in the delivery room, that instant, I think I understood my father for the first time in my life."

"Look at that," she whispered, smiling in the direction of her little baby whose eyes were closed. "He's dead to the world, so peaceful. You have the magic touch, Daddy. I think he likes you singing to him. You should do that all the time." And she crashed down onto the couch, exhausted, as if she'd been shot. All she needed was a precious hour—if she were lucky, two. Please, she pleaded—to God and to Philip in case either was listening. And she fell into a deep, deep dream-drenched slumber.

Philip shuffled into the darkened hallway where it was cool and quiet, and he softly crooned while gently rocking his child: *"Baa baa black sheep, have you any wool? Yes, sir, yes, sir, three bags full. One for my master, one for the dame, one for Donovan Fitzgerald who lives down the lane."*

Chapter Thirty

Philip & Family
Two Years Later

E XCELLENCE, THANK YOU FOR seeing me." Philip didn't add what he was thinking: *And taking out time from marshalling your army of angels.*

"Certainly, Monsignor."

It was late morning when Philip met with Bishop Stanislaus Mackey, sitting across from each other in oversized armchairs in the dark red velvet parlor. This is where the bishop spent his private time for quiet reflection, and also where he took intimate, confidential meetings. Three incense-scented votive candles flickered on the credenza and dimly illuminated conversation and countenances. This is the special room where the bishop would sit with a family in mourning and commiserate, offering words of comfort and support, and more than words his silent presence, being with people in their abjection. Also a place where he would give personal counsel or express heartfelt gratitude. Sometimes a place to hear confession. Also where he would read, meditate, pray. And yes, of course, where the crowd of the bishop's angels regularly congregated. No phone, no computer, no booklets or breviaries on the table; heavy crimson curtains, a spray of freesias, whose syrupy bouquet threatened to overwhelm him.

—

For Philip, this time, no tequila fortification. A three-month sabbatical he took after the birth—a break granted by the bishop predicated on false claims (fatigue, a need for rejuvenation, in other words: lies)—created valuable time and space for him and the family, but left him longing for more. By the time he met with Mackey, he had been living, somewhat incredibly, his secret life, whose effort required constant vigilance, and that all-consuming effort had taken its toll.

"This has to stop, Philip," said Ruth more than once. "I can't do this, I don't want to be a single mom, I'm worn out waiting for you."

Of course, once the Fitzgeralds had heard the unbelievable news, and after they recovered from the shock, the happy shock, they banded together, tightening their circle, keeping sacrosanct the secret, and furiously pitching in: babysitting, shopping, doctor's visits, the entire gamut of baby world. Paddy couldn't snap enough pictures, though he could not show them to anybody who wasn't inside the family—for the time being, anyway. He was there every day. Along with Jonesy, he sat through the night with the infant boy when he fought off a series of withering ear infections, and no toy or pop-up book or cowboy sleepwear was left behind on the store shelf or the internet in his wake. Colleen and Caitlin were the unquestioned stars of the new Fitzgerald family show, and they stole as much time as they could away from Floozy's. Ruth had bonded with those two women and relied upon them for love, company, assistance, especially during all those times when Philip could not sneak away, drawn out of the home sometimes for days at a time to keep his clerical obligations. In general, the Fitzgeralds were united in their campaign to help the baby and his mother—and to shield Philip for as long as was necessary—and joined together in a common, furtive, confidential resolve, which, truth be told, was not new territory for them. Many an afternoon, Donovan would run up and down the rolling grounds of Haymarket, happy as can be, his grandfather in close pursuit. The boy had a family.

"I mean it, Philip," Ruth said with finality, "your family has been great, but this has to stop. When are you going to the bishop?"

Expert prevaricator Philip may have been, but he was now beyond exhausted living a lie that had become his truth, his doubled, his tripled, truth. That is, he was a father of a young boy and a mate to Ruth *and* he was a priest who had by sheer force of his will (or was it guilt?) maintained his duties nonetheless. Yet at the same time, he continually yearned for the relief of casting off this burden once and for all. It is well-known that there were more than a few rogue priests in Italy, South America, and elsewhere who maintained clandestine, thriving families while they served their parishioners faithfully. It was equally clear that Rome formally and unambiguously insisted upon priestly celibacy—and for the foreseeable future would continue to do so. The Church made room, however, for rare exceptions: such as Episcopalian priests who convert to Catholicism, who bring with them their families, not to mention Eastern Orthodox married priests. Whatever was going on elsewhere in the world, Philip couldn't imagine indefinitely doing what he had been doing, even if he was at heart simultaneously a priest and unquestionably familied.

—

"Something's on your mind, Monsignor?"

"I think the time has come, Excellence."

He proceeded to tell Mackey everything.

—

But everything? After speaking without cease for ten minutes, it wasn't quite everything. As far as Philip was concerned, nobody, not even this bishop, to whom he was answerable on multiple levels, needs or desires to know everything. And not everything is ever truly knowable. Yet it was enough, what Philip said, more than enough.

The bishop listened intently—he'd gotten progressively better at listening ever since the gala aftermath. He did not take notes, didn't fixate on details, didn't dwell on the historical sequencing of events and decisions and the systematic, sly abrogation of his priestly commitments, and didn't interrogate him. The monsignor's words seemed to settle heavily inside his chest. When Philip finished, Bishop Mackey sat back and closed his eyes. He looked as if he had been pelted by a hailstorm. He did have one important, to him, question, which he asked with his eyes reopened. "Why are you telling me this now, Monsignor?"

"You deserve the truth."

"You and I both always deserved the truth, Philip, so I'm asking you again, why now?"

Why *now*? It was simple and it was anything but. Because Philip wanted to play catch with his son at the park. Because someday he wanted to go to dinner at a restaurant with Ruth and the boy. Because he wanted to do the right thing by Ruth and by his Family Fitzgerald. Because he was tired of keeping secrets. Because he wanted to open up the windows and the doors of his life and stand in the light of day. Because he wanted to tell the truth to someone, to everyone. And finally because now was as good a time as any to begin his new life, now, as a dad. That is what he told the bishop.

They sat in shared silence until the cathedral bells tolled eleven. Philip counted, and he would remember the bells whenever he remembered this moment with the bishop.

—

DESPITE WHAT HE HAD been told, and despite his heartbreak, Bishop Mackey had an important request. He asked Philip to officiate at the grand new school dedication ceremony. Yet another surprise on the part of His Excellence.

"You would be perfect for the occasion. Truthfully, nobody else would do."

Philip was stunned. "Excellence, respectfully. Let's not be rash." He referenced his reasonable supposition that everyone could one day soon be catching on, if they hadn't already done so, as to his upended and notorious domestic circumstances, and also his worry he might sabotage if not sensationalize the proceedings, simply by virtue of being on the dais.

"I appreciate the element of risk, but we should take it, because it's like what your own father, Paddy, says all the time. No risk, no reward, right? This will be a great day for the diocese, and for your family, and let's not forget, there would be nothing to celebrate if it weren't for the Fitzgeralds—all of the Fitzgeralds, including you, Philip. So I would be personally gratified if you would consider. If the occasion goes sideways, and if anybody takes the public relations hit, it will be me, and you know how little I concern myself with PR. After everything else that's happened, that'll be like rolling off a log. If I've learned anything about public opinion, it's in the end not worth trying to engineer it. Time we do the right thing."

Philip marveled and he doubted. He himself now played an indispensable part in doing the right thing? That's what the bishop seemed to mean. Somebody as compromised as he? It was incredible, because the man's message distilled into an affirmation of the bishop's kindness toward his family and to him, personally. He pushed back half-heartedly:

"Do I have a choice?"

"God in His infinite wisdom and love bestowed upon us the gift of free will, so yes, each of us has a choice. You made your choice with your own life, and a rather major, consequential one at that. My choice consists of asking you to perform a task of some import. Yours, I hope, means accepting."

The gift that was free will was a gift except for when we don't have much of a choice, Philip considered. Some kind of infinite wisdom, the double-edged gift that whole free will thing was, something that had plagued the human race since the Garden of Eden, all the way up to now and especially for him. But as long as Mackey put it that way, he agreed to do what he was asked.

"And then, afterward?"

"Then," Mackey said, and paused, weighing his words, "then the time will have come. You should take a leave of absence, go on retreat to ponder what awaits you, and when you return you and I will determine where you and all of us go from there."

The bishop had no alternative to that course of action, and no reason to defer the inevitable any longer, and Philip understood Mackey all over again.

"You knew, didn't you, Excellence. You knew all along."

"To be clear, Monsignor, I gather this was no one-night stand. You have been keeping your fatherly obligations, caring for and loving your child, and looking to the child's mother, correct? Even as you betrayed your promise of celibacy."

Philip nodded, of course, yes.

"I'll be praying for you, Philip, and your child and your child's mother— for your whole family. A son needs a good father. Be a good father. You have sacred obligations to keep for your child and your child's mother and your vocation. Which is why you sought me out today, to confess as much. I will facilitate your laicization if that's the path to follow, and I will decide one way or the other upon my reflection. But whatever course we take, your primary obligation is to your child, priest or no. Because you are and will be, I don't need to remind you, a priest as long as you live, and forever after."

"I honestly don't know what I should do, Excellence. I will take my retreat, with your permission, and hope to discuss this with you upon my return—again, with your gracious permission, of course."

"Why don't we pray together, for your family."

Gravity pressed down upon him as never before and Monsignor Philip Fitzgerald dropped to his knees. He should have fallen already to his knees before Ruth. And a good father and a good priest? He wasn't so sure he qualified on either score. But Philip couldn't fault the bishop for praying for him and his family because, on the off chance it wasn't too late, somebody should.

—

IT WAS A GLORIOUS late-summer Saturday, and over a thousand had gathered on the stately, open quad of the gleaming new campus still very much in progress. Fitzgeralds were conspicuously present, guests of honor, along with other donors as well as the usual cast of local dignitaries, politicians, and clergy. Construction was not completed, but an astonishing amount of work had been accomplished, more than anybody might have hoped for, and there were more than adequate facilities for students and teachers when the school year began in a few weeks. The site planners and architects and construction crew had been fortunate. The weather had cooperated and as a result few work days had been squandered. There were still Bobcats and one crane grazing on the land, and the science building was not yet finished, and neither was the library—though it wouldn't be long before everything would be. The football field was freshly sodded, too, and between the goal posts and before the shiny grandstands it radiated a verdant glow. School would be opening its doors officially, and welcoming soon the entire school community. First day of school would take place a week later than they had initially planned, but in plenty of time for the academic year to begin before Labor Day.

Bishop Mackey approached the microphone at the podium on the makeshift stage before the new main school building and, after a few kindly words of welcome, he introduced Monsignor Philip Fitzgerald, who then stepped forward. He spoke slowly, self-confidently, without notes.

"Thank you all for being here on such a spectacular, gorgeous day. We all feel blessed to be in attendance. I'm myself honored to be here in a double, or triple capacity. First, as representative of the diocese and at the pleasure of Bishop Stanislaus Mackey, whose vision has inspired us every step of the way. Second, and very significant to me, as a representative of my father, Padraic Fitzgerald. His generosity has shown us all what it means to step up and fill the need. He has made possible, he along with a legion of fantastically generous donors, our beautiful new campus. Thank you, thank you, thank you, one and all. There will be many occasions in our future when we can celebrate you. I can also never forget that I'm also here as representative of my family, gathered here today, including those no longer with us in this world."

He stopped himself, a little catch in his throat. His chest expanded and his shoulders lifted, then he exhaled. He looked out across the assemblage, and he would make systematic eye contact with each and every one of the Fitzgeralds in the course of his little speech. His family didn't have the latest details, but they all knew Philip's days as a priest in the diocese would become more complicated still, as how could they not be? Ruth was there, too, with his and her young child, on the fringes, trying to keep up with him as he scuttled around, marching headlong into his terrible twos, indifferent to any ceremonies or remarks, including by his daddy looming in the distance. Ruth would make certain the boy would not run into his father's arms, and she would foreshorten their stay at the festivities, to take no chances.

Francesca herself was swept up in the moment, scanning the campus and trying to recall where it was on the twenty-five acres that she and Paddy drank the Brunello the day they laid the foundation of the deal that eventuated in today. If she had to guess, she would say they had conferred right over *there*, between the chapel and the cafeteria, where somebody planted a dozen mature, beautiful olive trees—something done, she would have surmised, at Paddy's behest. And that's where there was a small flat headstone to commemorate Dickens, who died in his sleep, forever a hero and her unforgettable, sweetest dog.

"We are all elated and humbled to witness what we, with God's blessing, have created: a new school, a school that has been remade. You know, a school is a remarkable place. Here's how remarkable. It's where the marvelous happens every day, and that is certainly true for our school. I suppose it's tempting to take for granted the goodness of a good school, but we know better. We know how far we have come to reach this point. A good school opens the heart and illuminates the mind, it reveals the workings of the fantastic creation that is our world, that is our earthly home for a while. There is nothing more sacred than the bond between a teacher and a student, a school and all the students. That's where the work of redemption and the love happen. His Excellence Bishop Mackey has caused a miracle to happen, and it's on par with the everyday miracle that takes place in a school."

He couldn't quite focus on the faces of Matty and Colleen, since they were far off in the distance, at the edge of the crowd, in the vicinity of the new gym. They were making their usual sort of statement, setting themselves apart from everybody else. They were Molleen and Catty, after all, the embodiment of the Afterthoughts, with no Claire in evidence. All he could glean this far away was that his brother, now that the loyalty oath was a dead-letter issue, was about to open his new classroom and continue teaching, only now as a department chair, and was staring down at the ground while his sister was peering up into the bluest of skies.

"The lessons learned at Holy Family High—well, our students carry them with themselves out into their lives, into their own families. They are all changed, and changed for the better. Same is true for our teachers, for our administrators, for our parents and families."

As for Philip's father, Paddy was flanked on one side by Caitlin, whose arm was locked around his jubilantly, assertively, and on the other side by Jonesy, whose range of emotional expression was ragged but unlimited and who had never signaled anything other than unease when it came to

Monsignor Philip, now holding forth up there and therefore vexing him. Jonesy had the idea, and not for the first time, that in another life he himself might have become a man of the cloth, and he would definitely be a better one than the priest at the podium polluting the air with his vainglorious words. And then, in quick succession, Jonesy laughed away that fantasy on the grounds it was ridiculous; if he had lived another life, he fully expected he would conduct himself in the same fashion all over again as before. As for Caitlin, her retrieved watch safe on her wrist, she was appropriately dressed for the occasion, chic and understated: a white linen pantsuit with blue silk scarf and a floppy blue hat shading her and shielding her fair complexion from the depredations of the merciless sun. Her physician had been stressing that she should take care, after calling her attention to some curious, early-stage dermatological changes that they would follow up on and vigilantly monitor.

Paddy looked over toward Ruth and smiled to see his grandson playing in the threaded shadows afforded by the shimmering, glimmering fifty-year-old olive trees he had imported and planted, trees that would stand there, like the school, for generations, for let's say forever as far as Paddy was concerned. And as Philip's boy scampered about, his own beautiful grandson, whom he had once lost hope ever to know, he recalled the wisdom of the Italians he lived by. Credit them for testifying that you plant grapevines for your children, olive trees for your grandchildren. Here at least Paddy got this one thing right. And in some awkward and strange and roundabout way, his son Philip had as well. Yes, it was a slight risk to have the child there, and the Fitzgeralds were unified and prepared to keep the boy distracted.

Paddy and Jonesy O'Dell exchanged a quick look and did not specify what they were both thinking, namely that near where Philip was standing and holding forth, under the earth beneath his feet, was the final resting place of somebody whose name nobody summoned to mind. "The meek shall inherit the earth," Jonesy often reminded anyone who would listen, a man who gave in to sentimentality when it came to poetry but nowhere else, "but not the weak, for they are toast."

"And finally, let me say, today my family also remembers my late beloved brother Anthony, alumnus of Holy Family, someone whose memory burns brightly every single day for the Family Fitzgerald, for me, and particularly for his cherished wife, Francesca. Anthony embodied all that is great about Holy Family High, and still does. So I am here as witness to the example of my brother's noble, virtuous life, whose impact we all feel and whose memory graces us forever. Ladies and gentlemen, all of us who love Holy Family High, it's now time to formally dedicate and bless this building." Then he cued Bishop Mackey. "Excellence?"

The bishop was brief, and to the point: "The new Holy Family High School is now open, and God bless the school and God bless all of us!" And out of the line of sight somebody—it was Baxter—pulled down the rectangular white tarp covering the bronze plaque mounted prominently above the entrance door, so large and imposing that everyone within a hundred yards could read it.

ANTHONY FITZGERALD HALL

Honor Faith Heart Service

Holy Family High School

Francesca gasped—she had had no inkling, which was Philip's and Paddy's intention. Her body shuddered with tearful, fierce joy and sadness mixed and brutally reconciled.

The school band struck up the alma mater, largely on key, as the red-and-white Holy Family High School banner unfurled from the building rooftop and fluttered on account of the cross breezes and the exuberant exhalations of the crowd.

—

"Thank you, Philip," said Francesca and clasped both his hands in hers. "What a beautiful occasion, Anthony would be so proud." She noticed the tears welling in his reddened eyes.

He didn't bother to articulate what he was thinking. All the buildings in the world, all the cathedrals, all the schools, all the museums, all the bridges, wouldn't make up for Anthony's not being there. He didn't need to say as much, it was obvious.

"Your dad looked emotional, you should check in with him."

In due time, he would. "I'm glad to see you here, Frankie."

"Tesoro, how could I not be?"

"My dad and Mackey agreed on the naming, but they vowed to keep it secret till today."

In response, her speechlessness was, as ever, eloquent.

Philip scanned faces nearby. She was unaccompanied. "Tommy?"

"Hard to explain. Maybe not. We were not meant to be. Story of my life. Ever since Anthony." In this way, she glancingly touched on her and Philip's history.

Funny how Francesca and Philip existed in a separate place exempt from the reach of the milling crowd, as, in truth, they always did.

"Miss you, Frankie."

"Me, too, but."

"I know, I know."

"We both know." She took a risk: "Are you going to get married?"

Philip half-expected the question, but he didn't have an answer for her today.

—

FRANCESCA WANDERED OFF AS an elderly gentleman in a motorized wheel-chair approached with zeal and determination, rakish green silk scarf boldly, and somewhat improbably, looped around his neck, as he came to a halt before Philip's feet.

"Your eloquence, Father, your pure Fitzgerald eloquence moved me. Because Anthony Fitzgerald, if you will permit me to say, Father, now there was a blood," he said, chest heaving, teeth clenched. "A savage lawyer, a mortal savage, an attorney who held his mud, smart and fair and honest and totally devoid of bullshit, excuse the expression, Father. And you are his brother."

"Honored to meet you, sir."

"Sorry to say, you and I met once, and I'm sad to note, at the cemetery, Father Philip, on that terrible day of interment."

"Remind me, you knew him how, sir?"

"From Limerick Jewelry & Loan, not that he was a client of my establishment. I was *his* client. Name's Slip McGrady, I'm the one honored to be here today, amongst the venerable Fitzgerald clan. Ask me, they should name the whole damn school after him, my alma mater, too, and then the town and after that the courthouse as well, because maybe justice would prevail at least somewhere in our godforsaken land. All babies born from now on should be named Anthony. I've been drinking today, but no matter. Best lawyer I ever knew, and trust me, I've had more than my fair share, so I should know, but you know what, he was even a better man. I miss him to this day. And he could talk, Mother Mary, I loved to hear the man talk. What I admire in a lawyer—what I admire in a *man*—is a man who finishes his damn sentences. Lots of men start sentences and don't know how to finish them. They trail off. The old dot, dot, dot. But start a sentence, finish a sentence! And see this scarf? I admired it on him one fine day, and he was a clothes horse in his bespoke super two-hundred-thread-count suits, and he said his loving wife gave the scarf to him, and I don't know why he did, but he took it off and gave it to me, just like that."

"That is a very fine scarf indeed, Mr. McGrady." He was thinking of getting one like it to give Caitlin, who fancied her scarves.

But Slip McGrady, inspired, took that as his prompt to remove Anthony's scarf from his own neck and, saying nothing further, hand it over to Philip. He accepted the garrulous man's gift—a gift that also importantly to him originated with Frankie—and solemnly draped his brother's scarf around his own neck. A reluctant tear rolled down his cheek.

"Oh, and Father Philip, if you're ever in the market for a fine timepiece for your wrist, it's Limerick Jewelry & Loan, you know where we are downtown, you could not have missed my billboards. Why, I'll personally never forget when your distinguished father, Mr. Fitzgerald, deigned to enter my store some years ago. He was looking for a special watch for a lady friend, he said. Man, he picked out a beauty, Piaget, practically new, sixty, seventy-grand retail, but with respect I gave him a deal. Much later on, circumstances afforded me the chance to assist him when this watch was briefly, dishonestly, out of his possession. In the spirit of today, Father, I invite you please to come take your pick of a timepiece, Cartier, Rolex, Omega, Panerai, whatever you fancy, be my guest, on me, if your vow of poverty permits, of course, but since it's on me, why should the Holy See in Rome find that a problem? Just ask for Slip, which is me."

"Rome, I'm sure, has more important business on its hands, and that's quite a temptation, sir."

"I'm practiced at temptation, Father, and a man my age who did a year in the clink wastes not a single minute of his time left on earth. Don't forget. Slip McGrady. Limerick Jewelry & Loan."

Slip McGrady was nodding and sadly smiling as he wheeled away, soon to be swallowed up by the throng that parted to grant him unimpeded passage.

—

Years before that commemoration, Francesca could not help herself. She had unsuccessfully struggled to make peace over where she left it with Ruth during that wrenching last session a few months earlier. So she reached out and pleaded to meet with her, and her former therapist agreed.

As they drank tea at a café on the campus of Saint Monica's College, Francesca acknowledged she had crossed the line with Ruth, as she had crossed so many lines with so many others in her life, but in that wretched moment this one mattered more. She had to admit that she regretted her behavior. She guessed Ruth was pregnant with Philip's child, and Ruth confirmed yes.

"If you were still my great therapist, we'd have many sessions on that subject," Francesca said.

"Oh, Frankie. If I were ever a *great* therapist, we wouldn't have any sessions. Sorry, that sounds wrong, but I am at a loss these days."

"Eight months now?"

"Of course, the baby, the boy means everything to me."

"A boy, marvelous. And he means everything to Philip, too, I'm sure."

"I am sure of that, usually I am sure of that, yes."

When two women like Francesca and Ruth share a history they cannot quite share, and feel a bond that disappointment cannot rend and truth cannot change, they might always have much, if not too much, to say to each other. There existed no perfect launch point or landing spot for the conversation they would have for the rest of their lives, and no prospect of ever returning to where they once had been. Such would be the case from now on for the two of them, and for all touched by the Fitzgeralds.

Francesca was curious if they had selected a name.

"Philip wants *Donovan*. Gaelic for 'dark chieftain.'"

"Name like that, the boy will fit right in."

PART THREE

Chapter Thirty-One

From the Donovan Fitzgerald Journals

The Family Fitzgerald house on Haymarket Hill had once been my home, forever teeming, forever driven, forever purposeful, equal parts laughter and tears; piano and whiskey and tenors and setters and bagpipes and soda bread, or so childhood recollections cinematically rolled by on the flapping family movie reel projector.

Fuck me, we are officially off to the races in a maudlin Irish start. What am I thinking, do movie reels exist anymore?

Sorry, that's the way it goes sometimes with us Fitzgeralds.

Let us have a minute to gather our thoughts, Donovan, and while we're at it, reclaim our self-respect.

Anything for you, boyo, anything. (Movie reel flapping, my God, embarrassing.)

⚴

Give it another go, shall we?

After I swooped off to college, I essentially never returned to Haymarket. I wasn't psychically wounded or disappointed or consumed by postadolescent rage, and I wasn't dismissing or repudiating anybody. I had no scores to settle, and no unpaid debts to collect. I was not confused.

I mean, I was confused, by which I mean I was fucked-up in, to me, a healthy way. Because, you see, the Fitzgeralds are my people and always will be, without whom I wouldn't begin to understand myself, assuming somebody like me ever had the capacity.

Was it as simple as that, someday we all have no choice but to move along? Nostalgia, that homecoming urge, does not seem to be in my genes, certainly not the way it seems for the rest of my relations, as you'll see. If this deficit constitutes a character flaw of mine, it is merely one of many, which you would discover should you foolishly survey my legion of exes.

Which reminds me, here's as good a place as any to make the first of what's bound to be a series of personal disclosures, or confessions, because what else is a journal for?

When I was much younger I suffered from Romantic Arrested Development Attention Span (RADAS), though not as much as my exes suffered from the syndrome—the term for which I invented—when I tormented them. Perhaps this boutique diagnosis signals a terminal condition, though it's premature to tell (this journal is still being written, after all, as you can see to your mortification). Nonetheless, back in college I richly earned my nickname: Donovan One Month, the significance of which must be self-explanatory. But one month is an eternity when you're nineteen or twenty or so, at least it was for me, when there continued to mystically appear one after another knee-knockingly gorgeous lassie in Irish Fiction Seminar or Honors Philosophy or Modern Poets or Byzantine Civ, and she offered up to me an enthralling new body of stories I desired to hear and probe and colonize. On second thought, please don't bother tracking down and afflicting my exes, I gave you all the sterilized instruments required to operate in this surgical theater, otherwise called my life, and besides, there's no need for you to reopen old wounds. That's my job.

╬

Now I'm not saying Haymarket Hill was an ordinary home, and maybe nobody's is, but neither am I implying that I ever endured a moment of emotional deprivation, much less abuse. Just the opposite. At some point early on, as early as five or six, I became conscious that I had, in a way, a multiplicity of moms: Aunt Frankie, Aunt Colleen, and Caitlin, all of whom lived on Haymarket alongside me and my mother, Ruth. I guess I could call her my birth mom, or my biological mother, but don't such terms sound awkward or downright antiquated these days? And I should toss into the mix the name Hilda, the kindly housekeeper and furnisher of secretive sweets, who was almost as closely involved with me till the day she left and returned to Chile blessed with, so I heard, a generous retirement package from my grandfather. I liked them all—no, I loved each of them, and almost as much as my own mom, and each of them I loved differently.

Let's indefinitely postpone consideration of my candidacy for beatification, however. Beginning when I turned ten or so and carrying into my protracted adolescence, I wouldn't say that I consciously played them off each other. But I will say this, that I knew if I strategically played my cards, I could arrange for whatever I wanted by appealing to the appropriate one for permission—the green light to go to the movies, for keys to the car, for spending money, for the answer to a tough test question, for some insight (invariably into a girl). But as Catholics say, you have a choice: you can ask for permission or you can ask for forgiveness. I know, wretched cliché. But guess which was my go-to. To be honest, I don't recall asking for much in the way of advice, and none of them were forthcoming in that department anyway. They were old school, like Paddy Fitzgerald, my ass-kicking grandpa who believed experience was the best if not the only teacher, particularly the experience of pain and failure and slip-ups. But I seemed to osmotically soak in what amounted to their counsel, all of it good and useful, though my childhood was not the typical one, or so I concluded when I observed how other kids lived. Aunt Colleen was the most permissive and free-spirited; Aunt Frankie, the most skeptical and analytic; and Caitlin, the one who might have had the biggest heart, the softest touch. My mother—that is, the one who gave birth to me—was a rock, a bulwark of unconditional love. She was also the most predictable. What I mean is, every subject for her seemed to require extensive conversation, deliberation, examination. So if I went to her, I knew it was going to take a while. That was OK, it was the price I paid for her once having been a psychotherapist—and I'm not complaining. If I may testify thus: I was remarkably sane and emotionally balanced, at least in the eyes of the girls I fell for who didn't fall for me, which explains why they didn't belly up to the bar and ultimately rehearse for the role of exes in the long-running hit Netflix series titled <u>Donovan Fitzgerald</u>. I count at least two lies in the previous sentence. Can you circle them?

I would be remiss if I didn't add in here that, for the most part, three of these four women were serially unattached to any romantic partner, at least as far as I was aware. I'm not implying I lived in a kind of convent, and I'm also not saying that I was an interloper in some Amazonian women's tribe. If they were embittered or despondent over this development, I must have missed it, as they never appeared to be lacking, emotionally, or thwarted or disenchanted. All I'm saying is that such relationships seemed to them by and large, well, irrelevant—or so it appeared. They had each other. They also had me, for what that was worth, and I guess there were moments when it couldn't have been worth much. (Consult the never-to-see-the-light-of-day self-help book <u>D. Fitzgerald's Adolescent Years: More Fun with Irish Reaction Formation</u>.) (The things you learn being the child of a psychotherapist!)

It might be inappropriate on my part to mention that Caitlin and my grandpa supposedly formed, according to Haymarket lore, at some point a tender, impassioned romantic partnership, something verging on coupledom or a type of unconventional marriage, loosely defined, but from my early days I never sensed anything but a profound friendship between her and him. Neither of them seemed dissatisfied, I have to say. And he slowly metamorphosed into what he is now: a very, very old man. He along with the women who lived alongside him seemed relieved, or resigned, to be done with the romantic phase of their lives. There are worse developments, I suppose, and not many better ones, if you ask me. ~~But given my current frame of mind, I wouldn't recommend you try.~~

I have no choice but to own up to this: I was to the manner and to the Fitzgerald manor born. There, that's my first and perhaps last Shakespeare allusion, as well as a lousy pun, but no promises. Being a Richie Rich manchild, the wealthiest kid in town—a factor that dawned slowly and then irremediably, like so many of my hardest lessons in life—I never lacked for company from the outside world. I was as curious about other kids' lives as they were about what they presumed mine to be. When my friends (I had a few of those) visited my house as I was growing up, real friends as well as the other kind, I would occasionally be asked, "Which one is your mom?" Sometimes I'd make clear it was Ruth, and sometimes, if I was in a mood, I'd say any or all of them. And any and all of those positions were true, as I said. None of my friends believed this made for an awful situation for me, and neither did I. I was lucky. You could speculate that a boy might resist, or at least tire of, so much female attention. Most boys would push back. I didn't. I was a pretty good son most of the time, and this was the family I was given. That was plenty for me. If I take a longer view, did my upbringing facilitate or complicate my adolescent or my later adult romantic relationships? How would I possibly know? And if I knew, I would not be in a position to say so. Not even in this journal of mine (which I cannot believe I am writing). The last name on my driver's license is Fitzgerald, after all. Which reminds me, I need to deal with my expired license—as soon as I figure out, what am I going to do with a car in Williamsburg?

Funny how coming back here now has brought back all these memories—and sent me to this journal to consider what they all mean.

There was more than enough room for everybody on Haymarket Hill. I forget if I ever counted, but there were something like thirty rooms and ten bedrooms spread out on three floors. You would think it would be uncomplicated to locate a zone of solitude inside the capacious environs, and you would be mostly correct. There were long stretches of my teenage years when I barely exited my own room, and when I spoke up, neither the Gettysburg Address nor the Sermon on the Mount ushered forth. Monosyllables became my default mode of discourse.

With so much space to roam the halls and the grounds outside, my grandpa began to do more and more often what he called "taking the sun." This was an image that I rolled around in my mind. If anybody could legitimately claim to take the sun, it would have been Paddy Fitzgerald, master of the universe. That is, he spent most of the nicer days outside, under the grand gazebo by the olive trees, blanket over his legs in his wicker chair, his head shaded by a nice straw fedora. This change occurred around the time of my graduation from Holy Family High School, at which point he seemed to lose interest in conversation, a big turn given how I remember him holding forth, center stage, at every opportunity when I was little. Only now he gave off the sense that he had already said whatever needed to be said. To be fair, it would have been tough for him to get a word in edgewise, I suppose, because all of the women—especially my mom—were big talkers. I have fond recollections of hanging around with him, letting the hours pass by, the silence being a relief. In his occasional voluble moods, he taught me how to play (and cheat at) cards and study the Racing Form. He wasn't the boastful type, but early on I picked up—from him or from all my moms—that he had been a very big player in his day, and later on I could confirm that was certainly true. The Fitzgerald name was plastered all over my high school buildings and fields, for one thing, and all over town, too. It wasn't much earlier before then when he and I would go have lunch at Noah's Boat House, where everybody seemed to regard him as a celebrity and I felt wildly lucky to be in his company, fantastically fortunate to be a Fitzgerald. That was the restaurant where when I was sixteen I had my first vodka martini at his earnest suggestion served up by his favorite waiter, an arthritic sprite by the name of Seany. And in due order my fourth martini, served up by the same now blurry white waiter's coat. And after that, my first sickness-unto-near-death hangover. Spoiler alert: it wasn't destined to be my last hangover. Since then, vodka has been my friend, the special sort of friend you're not so sure you ought to keep around, like the kind who always needs at-the-last-minute help moving and whose calls you let go to voicemail.

╬

About this journal of mine: a part of me feels self-conscious about the whole shaky memoir-ish enterprise. I have never kept one before, and who knows if I will continue to do so, or if this will be the last sentence I write.

╬

Consider yourself formally shit out of luck, my friend. I guess that wasn't going to be my final utterance.

I never understood the audience for such a thing as a journal, unless it was the writer himself. But you know what, Donovan? You overthink everything, including overthinking. A journal seems a fitting occupation all of a sudden. I'm not the first novelist who ever said that, fashioning my fiction, I can more confidently and candidly tell the truth. And I'll likely not be the last to claim that writing a journal, on the other hand, by virtue of revealing the so-called truth, is also a way to lie, if by lie I mean pretend I understand the supposed unvarnished reality that is my self-appointed task alone to illuminate myself. And I can prove that contention right here and now. The ultimate purpose of the no-holds-barred journal relies upon the illusion of somebody else reading the words composed solely for myself. And that makes you, not-so-gentle reader, a co-conspirator, if not my voyeur. I admire you,

~~or maybe it's that I'm fascinated by somebody who secretly peers from the shadows into other people's lives.~~

Shall we continue? Seems I have nothing better to do, and apparently neither do you, because here you are, going toe to toe with me. Be advised that I am heretofore operating under the impression nobody will read this, while in my mind I require you to be present and not quite accounted for, figuratively standing outside my bedroom window. It is a room bathed by the luminescence of my incandescent prose, and somebody please shoot me for invoking that ornamental image, and ham-handed enough in a plagiarized _A Room of One's Own_ sort of way.

I take that point, and I think I'll have to agree with myself.

Besides, what can possibly go wrong at this point? I guess we both shall see.

╫

The day I arrived the house was bustling as ever—Mom playing piano, Aunt Colleen working the garden, Caitlin and Aunt Frankie cooking up wonders in the kitchen with Hilda. I sought refuge from the buzz and the ravages of my jet lag and from not having slept for twenty-four hours or so. I went out to the olive grove and sat on the bench close to my grandfather.

"Grandpa, want to come back inside, watch a game?"

He shook his head no. I guessed he had watched enough games in his lifetime. Instead he preferred for me to keep him company. Not a lot to ask of his only grandson, and I was happy to comply. I never once considered asking him if he liked living with so many women, back when he and I were the only males, and he the uncontested alpha. I figured this arrangement wouldn't have happened in the first place if he hadn't given a thumbs-up. And now that he had come this far, I couldn't imagine his instituting any radical alterations to his domestic arrangements. Caitlin would always stand by him. And he seemed, in his own way, content enough, as content as a Fitzgerald permitted himself to be. Sometimes I felt remorseful that I had abandoned him to all these women when I went to college and afterward moved into my own apartment far, far away.

The birds were especially raucous that afternoon, signaling to each other, perhaps because the hawks were soaring overhead before dive-bombing and gliding too close to the ground, and the terrified squirrels were frantically darting here and there, seeking safe haven. Caitlin came out with a tray of Irish breakfast tea and scones, situating it between us. Growing up, I could hardly have failed to sense the tremendous age difference between her and my grandfather, even when she was a young woman and he already an old man. But in the instant it felt different, now that she herself was no longer young. She was always tender toward him, and he toward her, and I could grasp that the passing years had made her kinder and more considerate to him—but let's get this on the record right this instant: not in some caregiver-ish sort of way. It was much more intimate and knowing and loving than that. They may have never married, but that was nothing but a technicality; they were going to be together forevermore, and that forevermore was beckoning faster and closer on the horizon each day. I am sentimentalizing her or him or possibly myself, forgive me; long flight, no shut-eye, watching the Family Fitzgerald withering before my eyes.

Then Aunt Frankie and my mom ambled outside—they were distinguished amblers, as in stylish sashaying walkers, all swiveling hip and shoulder and fashion-forward footwear. We hadn't talked much since I got in late last night from JFK. Those two women always seemed to have a special sort of connection, which, though I never quite understood how deeply extraordinary that was, mesmerized me. They seemed closer to each other than to the rest of the family. I used to think they were conjoined on some primitive level by virtue of the fact that Fitzgerald blood was not coursing through either of them, but of course that was also true of Caitlin. I concluded the obvious, that Aunt Frankie and my mom may have felt a special kind of intimacy via the memory of my late Uncle Anthony, who was Aunt Frankie's husband and the older brother to my dad. In any case, those two seemed merged in some unspoken pact.

Yes, I made a point of telling everybody I flew from John Fitzgerald Kennedy Airport, which never failed to please my grandfather or any other Fitzgerald extant.

⚏

"Good flight?" Aunt Frankie asked.

"Give thanks to a Valium ten and two gin sodas, extra limes to battle the scurvy." I would regret the report. In my defense, they had irresponsibly run out of vodka, but of course that is no defense in this house.

"Gin, my God, don't upset your grandfather with your mongrel British concoction. Gin!"

In the moment, I realized all over again I had serious unfinished business with Aunt Frankie, and always would have. Shortly after I began college, her dad keeled over, dead, a man whom she loved, and I couldn't trouble my sorry ass to come home for the services. I wish I could explain the reasoning behind such a stupid, callow judgment, but that would be a flight into science fiction. Of course, nobody insisted I be there, but I should have put that together on my own, insofar as I owed Aunt Frankie that much—and more. Only now, it was too late to make things right. There's a terrible lesson contained therein, but that's the thing about some terrible lessons, that you never learn them in time in order to act upon them, which is the functional definition of a terrible lesson, I suppose. She was so important to me, throughout my life. I should have done the right thing then, but I didn't. All that's left is for me to be sorry, and to find a way someday to tell her so. You, yourself, dear imaginary reader and friend, have memories of mistakes you made during your younger years. Maybe you too are filled with regret, as I am, to this day, about one thing or another if not everything. But the older I get, I find the appeal of regretfulness diminishing. I intend that notion in both senses, according to the fancy-pants ambiguous syntax of that previous sentence: the appeal diminishes and/or the appeal diminishes me. Both are veracious propositions. And the older I get, I find it more appealing (and therefore less unappealing) to accept that I was indeed an asshole and that there's nothing I can do to rectify what I did wrong, except in one very limited way. That is, I can honestly report what I did if not why. That does sound self-serving, but it's also chastening to acknowledge the unpleasant truths about my own personal past. I can linger in the black-hole recollection of my rash, impulsive words and decisions, or I can do something about it. Not to go all like friggin' Montaigne on you, but it's not in my power to revise history, though it is absolutely in my power (and nobody else's) to give (quoting the French, sorry, genius) an "accurate accounting" of my life, which is shorthand for the uninterrupted series of fuck-ups I refer to as my once-upon-a-time so-called youth. Hey, did I, being the dumbass I obviously am, just stumble upon a sound rationale for writing these diary entries? One of us will have to get back to each other on that question. Fair warning: Don't even think about texting me.

But to return to the subject of Aunt Frankie, if I may: as a teenager I had the appreciation (not adequately enough expressed) that it was she who taught me how to operate a car, my dad being fairly totally out of the picture, but then again, the less said about my driver's education the better, because when I was in high school, it was I who totaled Caitlin's famous and beautiful Maz.

Long story, though not really anything but a predictable one: beer, babe, bong, the boring usual, and I was unbelievably fortunate to walk away alive. My mother cried for two days out of abject horror alternating with outbursts of fury, and I endured the baleful infinite anxious stares of Aunt Frankie and Caitlin and Aunt Colly and Hilda, all of whose painful attention left me no room for feeling anything but awful and not fearful for myself. Of course, my grandfather had a different take on the near catastrophe, not that he explained. He was most likely making a connection to my own father's/his own son's legendary car crash when he was roughly my age: like father, like son? God, I hoped not. My grandfather gave the assignment to his man, Jonesy O'Dell, who was always good to me.

"Oh, Donovan Boy, the pipes the pipes are calling." He took me out for a long walk.

"Mr. O'Dell, what can I do?"

"He that troubleth his own house shall inherit the wind, and the fool shall be servant to the wise in heart. Proverbs 11, Donovan, Proverbs 11, look to it."

"You must be talking to my dad."

"He was—and maybe he still is a Catholic priest, of the order of Melchizedek, true." Then Mr. O'Dell gave me a look that only in retrospect I understood was meant to convey incredulity as to the chances he would ever be freely consulting with the likes of my old man. "Please, for your own sake and your granddad," he said, "please do not troubleth his house." I didn't know what he was saying, yet I knew what he meant. "And you take better care of yourself from now on, your mother and your entire family love you too much to lose you."

The car—the beautiful car Caitlin and everybody loved—was junked, and not to be replaced, because, I guess, there was no point. The Maz was in every sense irreplaceable. Just like, from that day forward, illusions of my own immortality.

⚏

"Wish you could stay awhile, baby," my mother said the afternoon I arrived, but not in a critical way, because she wasn't like that to me. I had informed her when I booked my flight reservation that it would be only for a couple of days, that my book tour was taking me to Los Angeles, some readings and a few local cable television and public radio interviews, where I would ummm my way through one unanswerable question after another ventured by interviewers impressed by themselves and not me.

"How come no readings around here?" my other mom, Aunt Frankie, wanted to know. "We would all love to hear you."

"I listen to my agent and dutifully obey my publicist and my publisher's instructions. They tell me where to go, I have no clout." This was my first novel, and though apparently trade reviews were pretty good, so I was told, and some were starred and therefore deemed raves by my overjoyed publishing house, I had no juice. But the truth is, and I should be candid here, when we planned the tour I specifically requested not to do any readings around here. I didn't think I could, or should, read in front of my family. Writers are a strange breed, as everybody knows, and I am no exception. I didn't think that anybody would feel hurt by my story, or feel in any way assailed or criticized, it wasn't like that. My writing wasn't motivated by resentment, I had no axe to grind with my family, I had no hostile agenda, and I didn't feel sheepish about any racy, proprietary disclosures. I told the story I wanted to tell, and it was fiction. So no, the book was not exactly autobiographical, what they call autofiction these days, but if it were, it was only so to the extent that any first book is bound to be indirectly or allusively autobiographical. I was fairly confident I alone would be able to identify those subverted if not completely buried preoccupations. I rewrote the whole book, I don't know, twenty times over five years (I lost count to be honest and so did my computer), and if I ever reflected on the question, I was confident I had erased all traces of my personal past before it appeared in print. And if you are gullible enough to regard authors as trustworthy, then you should take that immediately to the bank. But me? I was not so sure.

Caitlin and Aunt Colly had sent me a photo of the book as it appeared featured in their Floozy's window. They had prominently arranged a looming stack. I had guessed that all of the family had read it, but I wasn't going to pursue the subject. As I said, writers are a strange breed. A peculiar tribe. Each of them a band of exactly one. We talked for a while, then the women headed back into the house.

My grandpa turned to me, lifted up his hand as if he were about to administer a sort of blessing, and then waved it through the air, encompassing the land and all the trees and flowers and all the memories and all the family history. He hadn't said more than two words since I had been back, and I sensed he had been awaiting his opportunity to be alone with me. If I knew anything about my family, I knew we were about to have a moment.

"I'm getting old, Donovan, my boy." His voice was strong and piercing, surprising as a nocturnal bird calling out, hidden by the night in the darkened trees. "Man my age, he takes stock. I think I must be how old, don't know, what?" He needed my help. Or more like he wanted me to think as much.

I knew how old he was and I told him.

"So it is. How did I manage to live so long?" It was less a rhetorical position than an actual query.

I told him I was glad he did manage, and I always would be.

"Well, I'm living proof only the good die young. But hear me out. Someday I'll be gone, fifty years give or take."

"At least."

"And this, this will all be yours. Yours and Caitlin's. I know you'll take care of your mother."

I wasn't ungrateful. If I am honest with myself, I might admit I was not shocked. My take on this development, which you likely won't believe: I didn't want this. Haymarket Hill rightfully belonged to the women, Caitlin especially, and my mom and Aunt Colly, not me. Aunt Frankie didn't have financial need, we all knew that. I would take up the subject with him later, because now didn't seem right. I wondered all over again if my wishes ever counted in this family. It wasn't always clear. That's maybe why I was a writer: my imaginary world was always mine and mine alone.

"Let's talk about it, Grandpa."

"Talk? You are your dear loving mother's only child, no doubt, with the glorious gift of the gab."

Now that the prospect of my inheritance was broached, funny how I connected it to that unforgettable conversation post-car-wreck debacle with Mr. O'Dell. I could not forget the phrase "inherit the wind," which I was still unsure I understood. Nonetheless I took the plain point: one cannot keep hold on the wind, and the troublemaker will end up with nothing.

"I was thinking about Mr. O'Dell, your old friend."

"Jonesy? Jonesy, man, haven't thought about him in ages. I guess we were, in a manner of speaking you might say, friends. Long ago Jonesy moved to Ireland, to the splendid rolling meadows of Dingle, God, cannot remember when. He wed a barmaid, a teenage mortal beauty to tell by the snapshots, had a slew of black Irish children and raised sheepdogs and lived in a hillside cottage he built himself. He wrote me a letter once to tell me how happy he was, that he remembered fondly the past, which makes one of us."

"Think he'll ever come back?"

"If he does, it'll be at the final trumpet. His wife sent me the announcement card for his funeral. Time moves on, like they say, Donovan."

"Never been to Ireland," I said, apropos of who knows what.

"I almost wish I had gone myself."

This revelation astonished me. "Wait. You've never been?" Wasn't such an excursion tantamount to sacred obligation for every proud Irish American?

"When I was your age, couldn't be bothered with the old country. It wasn't my country. Caitlin and I talked about making the grand tour someday, but we kept putting it off, what with this and that, the bookstore, my business, the school construction, everything, and now, now, doesn't look like it's going to be in the cards."

"Inherit the wind," I said, illogically enough, but then I feared, hurtfully.

"Funny. Jonesy used to say that all the time. But that won't apply in your case, I'll see to it. Your inheritance will be a little more substantial than that." But he had clearly entered into another zone. "I read something in the paper. Old people, or people who are heading toward the great divide, which is, guess you gotta say, the same thing. Anyway, these people choose to write their last letter. To sort of speak your piece while you're still kicking. Settle up, make amends, explain, forgive, get the record straight, solve any mystery, that sort of thing. Then you can set it aside for after you're gone or hand it over before. It doesn't have to be a letter, you can send it computer message-type thing."

"Nothing wrong with email."

"I don't know how, the computer message thing, but I was thinking. There's stuff I could say, so maybe I should write my last letter. I'm not too good a writer, not like you, Donovan, my boy. I was thinking, you could write it for me, or we can write it together, like one of those 'as told to' kind of books, like you see in supermarkets."

I told him of course, whatever he wanted.

"If there's anybody in the family who could, it's you who can help me say what I want to say about how I feel about the Family Fitzgerald."

And with any luck, I added to myself, about how he felt about his own life. At the same time, I caught myself wondering if I hadn't done something along those lines, in the story I told in my own book, which I didn't think he needed to read, because he had already lived it. We'd revisit the last letter at another time.

"Your father loves you, Donovan, my boy, only he doesn't know how to show it. Hell, he might not understand how much he loves you."

I almost wanted to argue with him, but decided no.

"My own father, he hated me, and I hated him. That's why I killed him."

My head seemed to combust, and it took me a minute to ask him to explain.

"I killed him. You heard me. Not hard to understand. I'd had enough of the belt, the teeth he knocked out, my mother and me, both of us had enough. And there he was that day, it was a Sunday, and my mother was in church, and he was hitting the bottle all morning, and then he stood up, stumbling, whirling and then he dropped, his head smashing against the potbelly stove, blood everywhere. And he lay there, unconscious. I could have run to get help, but you know what I did? I went outside and walked and walked, and hours later, when my mother came home, there he was dead on the floor. I was a fifteen-year-old boy that day. But that was the day I became a man. I never told anybody before. I suppose it doesn't matter much to anybody but me—and now you.".

I reached out to touch his hand, the paper-thin skin, because I didn't know what else to do after hearing his revelation. Did I think less of him, for his confession? I cannot say that I did. He didn't literally kill his father, but then again, he didn't really not kill him. Looking back, I ask myself why I didn't press for details, ask questions, probe into his motivation. I guess I didn't because I didn't want to be lied to by him.

"This memory of mine dies with me. It's time for telling truths. It has always been time to tell truths, I suppose."

I knew it would be a long while before I could find a place to keep his story. And now I see that I have found a place: inside the journal that is inside of me. At the same time, I didn't have adequate language to thank him for all he had done for, and all he meant to, me. He clutched my hand and held it tight for a long time, as if he were losing his balance and about to tip over. He had never been one for physical affection—at least for me, so this gesture carried strange, important weight. His grip loosened and he turned inward and silent, resuming the journey on his own private funicular train of thought. This didn't amount to his last letter, but he'd said his piece, for now, and for now is all we can ever do. Letter or no, he may have been communicating that Paddy Fitzgerald's lifetime work was almost finished.

"One other thing, Donovan, my boy." He pointed toward the olive grove he loved so much. "Day comes, plant me over there, under those pretty trees. And also, I'm warning you, no fucking bagpipes."

"Grandpa, what do you say we have lunch tomorrow at Noah's? Seany the waiter? You still like that place?"

"Ah, Donny, Donny, Seany and the old Boat House, they're both long gone."

I'm no hotshot baller of a publicity maven, all big black rectangulated glasses and suited up Chanel to my Fifth Avenue office. Yet I'd say that giving a reading on no notice is not the surefire method of guaranteeing turnout. I didn't see any way to avoid agreeing to Caitlin's ask. But the women in the family must have pinged everybody, because Floozy's Books was flash-mob packed. Are there still flash mobs?

Seems unlikely, but I am out of touch with all things contemporary. Yes, this is my subtle way of indicating to you that I truck exclusively with the immortals, and the immorals, the eternal verities. In any case, the Fitzgerald name, while it did not resonate in the hood as it once did, still tolled like a church bell beckoning the worshipful locals to services. Not that it mattered to me how many showed up. On the tour, I had given readings to a "crowd" of two, and once to a hundred. Felt pretty much same same to me. This is going to sound awful and entitled of me, and don't sell me out to my publisher, but I'm not sure I get why people flock to readings in the first place. It might be a function of their endeavoring to gain a glimpse of the flesh-and-blood author in their podcast- and NPR-loving hopes of understanding the story behind the book, as if there were such a thing, and if there were such a thing that it ultimately mattered. You know what's <u>behind</u> a book? No, really, tell me. What do you think is behind a book, and what does it mean, to be <u>behind</u> a book, because hell if I know. Confession: I myself hardly ever go to readings. Please keep that between us. I think books—and also please don't let on to my hardworking, kind, resourceful marketing, sales, and publicity people—I think books should, and can, stand on their own without my hawking them. That is an old-fashioned, ridiculous, and vain point of view, I realize, in this day and age, and an especially odd position to take for a novice novelist like me, a few years to go before turning thirty, a so-called emerging writer, and yeah, I know how lucky a submerging writer like me is. To help me and the book out, for instance, the publishing house staff constructed a supposedly super-duper website for me. I cannot tell you much about it, as I was too above-it-all to take a close look.

My grandpa was there at Floozy's, too, ensconced in his wheelchair. My mom said this was the first time he had come to one of these events, which made sense, insofar as a ninety-plus-year-old so-called supposed onetime loosely defined mobster wasn't their target demo (poor word choice, <u>target</u>). I heard he was the one responsible (well, it was his idea, but who knows who made it happen?) for setting out a table laden with Irish whiskey bottles and a rack of shiny clean shot glasses (<u>shot</u>, another problem). He and I ceremoniously clinked and wordlessly toasted each other before I headed toward the back of the store, where all the chairs were laid out, the warmth from my mouth oonching deep down into my belly. I knew I should have eaten something, but I can't when I cannot avoid reading in public. The Irish know a thing or thousand about their whiskey. If I was going to read, that wouldn't be the worst preparation. I swear I detected a droning hum in the room, which should reasonably be ascribed to the buzz of the Jameson-fueled audience.

Caitlin stood at the podium and instantaneously earned everybody's attention. She couldn't help it. As pretty as she is, she could stop traffic if she wanted to—something I would testify that I'd witnessed with my own startled eyes as an impressionable child—and I am confident she could accomplish this result, if not cause a minor car pileup of gawkers, even in her current condition. Her brilliant red hair existed exclusively in my memory and in vintage photographs, the chemo and radiation over the past few months having stolen hers away, and her head was proudly, defiantly wrapped in a sparkly, ruby-studded gold scarf. Treatment was going to give her, we all hoped, one or two more good years. But her voice was clarion and strong. She opened by saying that Floozy's was celebrating its anniversary, and she hoped to be here for years to come. She also said that opening the bookstore and keeping it going may have had its challenges, but it had been worth everything to her and Colleen in order to introduce tonight her favorite boy, now grown up and a writer, referencing, well, me. Then she delivered a touching introduction that you can imagine: local boy makes good in the big city, that kind of thing. Her testimonial amounted to an exaggeration, but well-intended and generous, as she never failed to be.

Caitlin was somebody you could not help but love, trust me.

Prior to my big homecoming, I had been living in an undoubtedly illegally sublet studio apartment in Brooklyn, and I was paying the rent on time though I was not on the A List of up-and-coming authors automatically invited to hipster parties. When I go out and see all those man-bun guys with Civil War beards streaming down to their sternum and the dazzling women rappelling alongside them while they're sipping on the IPA, I wonder where I went wrong, because that look must be the equivalent of Brooklyn babe catnip. Actually, I don't wonder where I went wrong, I <u>know</u>, and if you've been paying attention and if you read my book, so must you by now. Body ink would be advisable as well and ratchet up my desirability coefficient, though tattoos would raise all sorts of decision-making issues (like where and what and by whom and who cares?), but I'm not in the market for elective suffering or staph infection or extra-corporeal branding. Or it could be a lot simpler: that is, my body is a hallowed temple. You bet. Some kind of sacred site of worship. More like a <u>bare ruined choir</u>, which phrase everybody in the pub can now Google up on their phone, part of a line from a genius poet named Shakespeare (a second allusion to the Bard, and more proof not to trust me). But it always sounded to me like out of Keats, dead by the age of twenty-five, who didn't have a man-bun or a Civil War beard and passed over to the other side while pining fruitlessly for the love of his life. You know, there's an upside to everything. But enough with my whining. Those Brooklyn guys must have it all figured out, and I don't begrudge them, more power to them. Did I mention that one of them illegitimately sublet me his apartment? (Thanks and respect, Vinnie.)

In any case (pathetic transition, almost as horrible as "by the way," for which my brilliant editor would kick my lazy ass if she comes across this journal), my publisher expressed high hopes to sell the movie rights at a premium, and there is evidently a good deal of chatter in LA and New York. But as everybody knows, when it comes to the entertainment industry, it's all bullshit till it ain't—that is, till money changes hands. I do not enjoy what anybody would term a rabid following, but I did have a cross-eyed raccoon hiss at me outside a bar on Metropolitan Avenue, and I did have one energetic stalker slash troller on Facebook who may or may not actually have rabies. I did delete my account, which I never should have opened in the first place. Funny, I almost missed him or her or them or it.

‡

As Caitlin celebrated me, I was feeling—I don't want to say embarrassed, but ill at ease, like a kid at graduation with cameras clicking and flash bulbs popping. I was thinking something else: as it goes in the Bible, a prophet is without honor in his own country. And you know what, I was good with that, either way. And then she waxed very personal, and she spoke about how she and everybody in the family knew I would turn out much more than all right, and about how they were all proud. She didn't give up family secrets. If she ever decided to do that, her introduction might conceivably have concluded a week later in the grand jury. I'm not so sure how much Grandpa Paddy was taking in, but he would have put a stop right away to an excess of sentimentality or disclosure—unless he was the source. She did speak about how much she loved the book—the first direct indication she had read it. "I could tell stories," she said, "about how Donny as a little boy would read and write till he dropped to sleep at his desk in his room. We'd have to wake him up and put him to bed." But she didn't go on too long, thankfully. I would never fault Caitlin, who had a good heart and was always better to me than I and all the rest of us deserved. I didn't even mind the Donny. It had been a long time since anybody outside my family called me anything but Donovan—with one important, to me, exception, as you'll see.

Here's when the image of my Uncle Matty unexpectedly crossed my mind: like a slow armadillo on the Texas highways, splat, reek forever. So not in a pleasant way. I was glad he was not there in the bookshop. Nobody had seen this lost soul for many years, and he had attained a sort of legendary status since my youth. Last anybody heard he was in Santiago, Chile, making a living as an English language instructor. It could have been Buenos Aires, as with everything involving him, it was unclear. He and his wife (what was her name?) had long ago divorced, and there were rumors he had taken up with that crazy high school student of his who caused all that trouble. I didn't entirely credit the speculation. My vague memories of Uncle Matty indicate that he was beleaguered and damaged, but he wasn't insane, which is what it would require to have settled down with somebody like that girl—if the stories my mom told me were half true. Girl? She must be approaching fifty now. Besides, some people like him seem incapable of settling down anytime, anywhere—though I hear you: I should talk. I think her name might have been Tracey, something like that, but I cannot confirm, and nobody has mentioned her name in decades—identifying her as that nutjob runaway. I wish him well, but he and I have nothing to do with each other. Aunt Colly herself wrote off the poor guy. Thus it was that it occurred to me all over again that my grandfather had in some profound and final sense lost every single one of his sons: Anthony, Matty, and Philip, my father.

When the polite applause died down, I stood there. I don't know how to explain what happened, but I couldn't find my voice at first. I could see my mom proudly fighting off a tear, and Aunt Frankie staring at her fancy shoes so as to keep herself composed. Usually under these book-reading circumstances I can make a few lame jokes and, clearing my throat, just launch, trusting my book to do what it had done already, right there on the page, for better or worse, and so be it. If you're born a Fitzgerald, I guess, you are hard-wired to be self-assured or appear to be, or simply not give a flying fuck what anybody else thinks. Or at least to be adept at pretending not to give a flying fuck.

Only then, only then, only then it was not so simple. The problem was that I looked across the packed room of people in their folding chairs, and cast my eyes toward the people spilling out onto the street and standing near the store entrance. That's where he positioned himself, hands in pockets, wearing sunglasses to guard against the twilight's angling sun, my father.

╬

It had been a long time since I'd last seen him. Couple of times, true, he came to visit me in college. He didn't make my graduation, for reasons he never deemed essential to explain. That was fine. It wasn't like I was the valedictorian or anything. (OK, I was the valedictorian, which surprises me, too. I'm no JFK, no relation, so he didn't miss much of an oration. As I recall, I was ten cups of coffee into ironing out the creases of the hydrogen-powered hangover caused by excesses of the night before.) My mom was relieved not to see him at the commencement, but she never said as much, or if she did, I didn't register, having been shitface drunk or in bed with one girl after another all the conga-line weekend long. Fun times for the college boyo. If you may say so.

He and I had connected in the city a few times since the humid day of pomp and circumstance, spending a couple of hours together tops. Once over dinner, he did something pretty spectacular, I have to admit. He took this watch off his wrist and showboatingly handed it to me, a graduation gift, he said.

"Dad, get out of here, this is a goddamn fucking Rolex."

"Take it."

"Come on, this cost a fortune."

"Not really. This old parishioner friend of mine, named Slip McGrady, nice guy in the watch business, he gave me a deal. Put it on."

So I did. It was a beauty. At the time, I had no idea where, or if, I could wear such a flamboyant piece of jewelry. But you know, it was worth a try.

"You sure?"

He said he was. "You deserve it."

"Ever change your mind, you can have it back. This is a nice watch, Dad, and a fabulous gift, thanks."

For your information, it's on my wrist right now as I write. But after everything that would happen later, I would never again offer to give it back.

He was perennially on his way, elsewhere, somewhere, seemingly anywhere. Israel, Sicily, Ireland, Scandinavia, Malibu, Morocco, Bali, Tokyo, always tracking something I would not be made to understand. He had grown more and more restless, it seemed to me over the years, searching for who knows what or whom.

He had reminded me more than a couple of times he was still in his mind a priest, as if I could ever forget, and that he refused for a long time to accept being laicized despite being ostracized by the Catholic equivalent of the CIA. According to canon law, so he advised me, once a priest, always a priest. You might be shocked to learn how many priests have children, how many are married, have families on the side. They number in the thousands. Trust me. I didn't believe it, either, at first. He and my mom had lived together a while, partnered after their own fashion, till I was three or four or so, and one day he moved out, I guess—and as far as I knew, back into a parish, where he resumed his life as a priest for a while. Until, that is, one day he was no longer there in his rectory, putting on vestments for Mass, and was gone into the wind for a long time. Here's when I could show you my PowerPoint display of family photos, if I cared, or if I had them. That was when my mom and I moved to Haymarket Hill with my grandpa's urgent, sincere blessing, and there we joined Colleen and Caitlin and later on Frankie—our little tribe, the last living remnants of the Family Fitzgerald. Then later he took up residence nearby and we would intermittently see each other, throw the ball around, go to games, grab a pizza or burger, catch a movie, that sort of thing. My mother and he one day stopped battling, which was bad, and then stopped talking to each other, which was worse. My father was upset that she and I moved into his family home, but at the same time he was elated that I was there. The contradiction neatly summarizes my dad, and now that I think about it, every single Fitzgerald, living and dead.

Always a priest as he may have been, he was no longer permitted to dispense the sacraments, or wear the Roman collar, or to perform any priestly offices, of course, but they couldn't take away his priest identity. "A priest," he said, "is a priest for life." I have no reason to believe he considered himself a Catholic radical with a political agenda, pushing for reformation of the priesthood, making celibacy an option, urging for women to be welcomed into the ranks, that sort of liberationist agenda. At least he never talked along those lines to me. As a teenager I argued with him about Catholicism a few times, and it was unsatisfying. He vaguely defended the religion, to my irritated mystification. I railed against the hypocrisy and the hierarchy, with all the passion of the know-it-all I was, and doubtless am to this day. He listened, and wouldn't debate with me. As a result, I assumed he conceded I was ultimately right. I haven't been to Mass since high school, and I have no plans to start up again anytime soon. I was, and I am, done with the Church. And somehow he would never be anybody other than <u>Father</u> Philip. That he was also <u>my</u> father always made for complications, some obvious, some not so much.

Such as when we had an unexpected exchange about what amounted to what he characterized as his ultimate experiences as a priest.

I cannot reliably quote him wholesale and verbatim, but I vividly recall many of the details he narrated and certainly the gist. He explained that his most lasting lesson about faith and the religious life was taught him by his onetime bishop, a man by the name of Mackey. I cannot recall the man's first name. In any case, it was Bishop Mackey, you see, who was personally responsible for ushering my dad out of his clerical life. The word for that, and a funny word it is, is laicization—to depart the clerical life and become part of the laity, the people. Not that the bishop was a great spiritual leader or mentor, and not that he was a particularly effective diocesan leader, according to my father, who said he was actually a pretty flawed bishop—until, that is, the night something unfortunate, or maybe it was fortunate, happened.

Nobody knows, my dad said, what happened to the bishop after some big churchy shindig. Not me, he said, not even him, but he was never the same afterward.

Mackey's personal transformation took place that night, when he suffered a type of breakdown, when he was confronted in his limo in the middle of the night by someone he had supposedly betrayed. Details blurred in my dad's account and they blur to this day in my recollection of what I was told. I do have a vague recollection that my aunt, Uncle Matty's wife, whose name I have somehow misplaced, was somehow involved, and she played a crucial, mysterious part. According to my dad, Bishop Mackey came to Jesus. I knew what he meant, and who doesn't? He was never the same after. From that time forward, Mackey was both more and less himself. Before then he was ill-equipped to naturally inspire the faithful. But later, he could inspire the faithless, my father said, referring to himself. And I know I said a minute ago he might have been a poor excuse for a bishop, but he did guide the new high school, which became my sorry high school, into existence, when nobody had justification to believe it would ever happen. He got my grandfather to bend on his real estate deal, so legend has it, and if he hadn't done that—no new school.

Good or gutsy or imperfect man the bishop may have been, my dad considered him a worthy human being in the end, to him a kind of hero or saint. When he transcended his mantles of power and authority. When he went beyond his role and accepted his defects, affirmed his weaknesses—and my father's, too. In the end, Mackey was all about forgiveness. My father said that the bishop began to talk incessantly about, and with, the angels, which mystified my dad, but not Mackey.

When he pushed my father to face up to the consequences of his choices, which revolved ultimately around me, his son, and his being—and failing to be—a father to me and a husband to my mother. He couldn't keep living the lie of embracing the priesthood—his clerical life. But he made my dad understand he could start to live the truth of being a father—which he tried and often failed to do with me. The two of them grew close, years after my dad no longer maintained his formal priestly life.

So when the bishop lay on his hospital deathbed he sent word to my father, pleading with him to visit. And that's when he asked him to dispense last rites. This was what they used to call the sacrament of Extreme Unction. Strictly speaking, according to dogma and canon law, he always retained the ability to exercise such sacramental authority, dealing with one in extremis, Latin for dire straits.

"I granted him absolution, Donovan. I told him, 'Excellence, your sins are now forgiven.'"

"You absolved him," I said.

He got what I implied, and to his credit, he didn't defend himself, and he didn't explain, probably because where would he begin with me?

Then he performed the sacrament upon Bishop Mackey, praying and ritually administering the sacred balms. This occasion served as the opportunity for the bishop to underscore for my dad that he would always be a priest, for a priest is a disciple of Jesus, and therefore a man always in the desert following Jesus. Don't ask me to elucidate, because I cannot. The image of my dad walking in a desert feels all too right, however. And it seems it was then that the bishop thanked him again. And the man who used to be Father—I mean Monsignor—Philip Fitzgerald thanked the bishop for letting him be by his side at this hour, and they both gave thanks for the angels in their forever connected lives—whatever that could possibly mean.

My dad also reported that, as the sun was setting a few hours later, the bishop, palpably weakening by the minute, found the strength to utter one last thing, which was this: "Now what?" Then he crossed over to the other side, or at least that's how my dad characterized his parting.

Now what? As last utterances go, that strikes me as right on the damn money. It's a question and it's an assertion at the same time, a testament of disappointment and the declaration of wonderment, and an indictment, too, equal parts futility, anger, and expectation: all of which sums up many a man's existence. As my dad's favorite saint, Francis of Assisi, used to say, "Preach the gospel; if necessary, use words." To tell the truth, if I had a favorite saint, Francis would be mine, too. Then again, sometimes I feel like I have nothing but words.

"Why are you telling me all this, Dad?"

"So I will never forget and you will always remember."

There were many things my father told me over the years that I did not believe, and many more things he never said that I subscribed to more adamantly, but that last statement was a crucial one I did not contest. No hard feelings, I almost wanted to say to him and almost wanted to believe myself. But what he wanted me to understand was something he could not articulate, which was that he, with all his failures and despite every single one of his monumental fuck-ups, loved me, who was his son. You know, in the moment, I believe he believed that. But does he earn a pass? A participation trophy? Does anybody finally?

Talking with him that day, I couldn't shake the subject of the angels, thanks to the old bishop's tale told by my dad.

"You believe in angels, Dad?"

"I used to."

"I believe in them. I've seen them myself."

You know, when I opened my mouth there, part of me was messing with him. But then, once I said it out loud, I caught myself badly wanting to believe in them. And wanting to believe, I bet, is as close as we Fitzgeralds get to believing anything. That may be the working definition of belief. This goes along with that Now what? moment. More I think about it, nobody asks a question like that on the edge of the abyss, without half-knowing the unknowable and half-yearning for a confirming response. Now what? For the bishop, for my dad, for me, I don't think it's a rhetorical question. It's more like a dare. Go on, God, if you exist and especially if you do not, take your best fucking shot.

‡

There was the time I told my father I had begun to meditate and was growing more and more interested, after my own ignorant fashion, in Zen Buddhism. I'd read some books. Who knows, in the moment I might have meant it.

He laughed. No, really, he laughed at me, the suave condescending bastard. He went: "You know when a Fitzgerald will go Zen? When Jameson goes belly up, or in other words, never."

He moved again and again, taking up residence far-flung here and far-flung there, not that I had been to any home of his since before college. What did he do for a living? No idea. Not that I didn't occasionally inquire, and not that he ever directly answered me. He could have been an adjunct professor, he could have been an ad hoc preacher at some Protestant outpost—but I have no idea what I am talking about. One day it dawned on me, being slow on the draw, that undoubtedly his own father was financially sustaining him, which would have been no burden to my grandpa. If he had a romantic life, for a long time I was thankfully spared the details, until, you'll see, the day arrived when I wasn't—and my mom had no information she wanted to share, either. Prior to that moment, I never heard a name, and certainly never met anybody, but if I ever reflected on the issue, I had to assume he was never quite indefinitely, perfectly alone. Some men, seems to me, cannot manage that trick. Once I was enrolled in college, he remained in communication with me almost entirely via email, and every few months he'd shoot me a long involved message about what he was reading (philosophy, history, nonfiction, memoirs) and the exotic locales he had visited and the books and movies he recommended. I answered immediately. And he never followed up. I guess I easily exhausted the attention quota assigned me.

╫

Once we were having dinner at a cool bistro on the East Side, autumn in New York, let's all join in the old Frank Sinatra song, he and I and Darcy, to whom I was engaged. And with fanfare he announced he was working hard...writing a book (you guessed it). I didn't know how to take this news, or if it qualified as such, or if he was living, as I might have suspected, in yet another fantasy. No genuine writer would ask another writer to tell him about the book he is working on, certainly not before it's finished. One, it's bad luck. And two, talking about a book peels the magic away. And three, it's terrible luck. These are the views I held because I am a writer who happens to be a Fitzgerald—or that's the other way around. But if I didn't ask for details, that didn't stop him from telling me.

"It's a memoir. I am enjoying writing about what happened to me back then, those crazy times, the me I was, you know? I do worry about how your mother, and Frankie, and my dad, and my sister and brother will feel when the book hits the shelves. Everybody probably has a memoir bubbling up inside them. But if you cannot be brutally honest in a memoir, you shouldn't write it. You agree?"

First of all, he made the rash assumption anybody would rush out to buy and then by chance read such a book of his, much less my mother and the others he had identified. Second, and more to the point, I had no confidence he was writing that sort of book, or attempting to. Not that I thought he was lying, not really. He was trying to connect symbolically to my life, and in his fantasy life he was one of those people who think you can write a book in your mind before putting down a word on the page. Beyond all that, only a unicorn of a writer "enjoys" writing a book. Certainly there are good days, or I should say good minutes, sometimes stretching into an enchanted page or chapter, and that is something in the zip code of enjoyable, but it's not at the top of my list of descriptors of the writer's life. For another thing, delving into one's personal narrative is not for the faint of heart. Or to put that another way, the dickless. But I'm not disparaging women writers by summoning up crude boundary-riddled out-of-date psychosexual immature terminology, no way. Because that would be dumb. It would also lead to people attacking me for being insensitive and clueless, which is a waste of bandwidth, because there's a solid chance I am. Bandwidth: haven't heard that term for a while, either. There was one more thing about my dad's announcement. He didn't mention any anxiety about the book's reception relative to his son, me. How come he didn't care how I would take it? I'm reluctant to admit that my feelings were hurt. Then he surprised me all over again.

"Would you be willing to take a look, when I'm further along, close to finishing, before I send it to my agent? There's nobody's opinion I regard higher than yours."

I doubted his veracity (no way he had a literary agent) and said to myself <u>You have a funny way of showing how you regard my opinion</u>. I had published a few stories, won a little prize and then a fancy so-called "emerging writer" fellowship, and maybe he had by some accident actually read some of my work, though I didn't know for a fact.

"That's so exciting," said Darcy. "I would love to read the family story."

I wasn't so sure I shared that bright perspective, but I agreed to take a look. Did I have a choice?

"Wouldn't that be incredible," said Darcy, "if the handsome father-and-son team both published books? Isn't it fabulous, Philip, Donny signed his first book deal?"

First of all, <u>team</u>? Darcy never could hold her liquor, a problem I never had after college, where drinking had been practically my major. Second of all, he didn't know about the book deal because I hadn't told him, and I wasn't sure if, or how, I should break the news. Well, Darcy rendered moot an important decision on my part, and it wasn't the last time she would, as it would turn out.

My dad rocked back in his chair, as if he had taken a bullet, his mouth grimacing in a rictus-like smile. Something told me he was both pleased and downcast, and dinner proceeded to go on for what felt like a February in New York winter. He looked like a man who had been betrayed, and in a way I suppose he was. Betrayed by me, betrayed more by himself and his own illusions. I knew the feeling. If I were smarter I should have immediately carved out plenty of time in the future for paying a price.

To this day, you may or may not be surprised, he never did show a manuscript draft to me (whose opinion was regarded so highly) and to my knowledge, his book hasn't seen the light of day. It would be perplexing for me to read his memoir, if it were ever produced, so I didn't relish the prospect, even if I might learn more about him than I already knew, which would be easy to imagine, given that in many respects he remained opaque. I don't completely understand what I am saying, so you may be frustrated, probably not as much as I am, I'd lay odds. As I studied him across the table that night at dinner, Darcy—poor lovely Darcy who had had one too many—reached for my arm and squeezed gently, lovingly.

"When did you grow <u>that</u>?" I asked him because I had been waiting to pounce, so I pointed at his bearded face, and he preened by way of reply.

Darcy intervened and addressed him, because she never could resist any intervention: "I once tried to get Donny to grow a goatee. It's such a jaunty and sophisticated look." She'd had <u>two</u> too many. <u>Jaunty</u>. Still thinking about that sad defunct word.

My father looked like a lion, yes, though indeed more thick-waisted with each passing year, his face progressively more grizzled, yet the metrosexual, closely cropped salt-and-pepper beard was, to me, a recent, dashing, miserable touch. Facial hair, the stylized sort I guess, always strikes me as a cry for help. So yes, aging lion he may have been, but a lion is a lion nonetheless. For some reason this reminds me of when my mom and Aunt Frankie took me on a South African safari, a fantastic high school graduation, pre-college present. It was an amazing trip. The two of them were so close, it was very moving to observe their bond during our travels together. And South African wine is world-class, I hear, not that I'll ever approach connoisseur status, but I know what I like, and therefore endorse how beautifully that wine works its magic under the open starry night skies stretched out across the savannah. As for the safari, now that was quite an eye-opening experience. From the jungle-savvy guide, for instance, I learned that leopards are the reigning kings of the hunt. They go out looking for prey ten times—nine times they return with warm-blooded dinner in their jaws. Lions? No competition. Ten times out—nine times they slink back dejected to their den. This appalling batting average is likely no consolation to the single antelope or baby giraffe or hobbled zebra they drag down to the veldt for a feast. Please hold that thought.

╬

About six months after the bistro, as my book was fast heading into print, I got a call from Darcy. She and I had broken up. We pretended to be civil and to stay (cue the ominous background music) always friends. Nonetheless, her call registered as something of a shock. She was ten years older than I, and there might have been some generational tension between us—but I doubt that was the determining factor in the split. I can't say which of us had initiated termination of mission, but I do know I didn't fight hard to keep us together. She was, and is, a lovely human being, and even then I realized there was a very good chance I would always regret losing her and there was nothing I could do about it.

"Your father wrote me an email, Donny. You have an idea how he got my address?"

Her tone was both accusatory and quizzical—but I decoded her self-consciousness, and detected beneath it all her susceptibility to his all-star flattery. I could speculate there must have been some rogue cc'd email with both their addresses, and he had kept track—but I just work here so I don't know.

"He says he is heartbroken about us, guess he only recently heard, maybe you told him." I had done no such thing, so I had no idea as to his information source, unless he maintained provisional access to Family Fitzgerald news services. "And he wanted to get together to talk about putting us back together."

That sounded vaguely wishful on her part, as well as utterly strange to me as it pertained to his mission of mercy, a point which I made to her.

"But you know?" she said in a tone that indicated she was now about to reveal the true reason for calling. "Maybe I'm crazy, but I picked up a funny vibe, asking me out for a glass of wine when he was in town. Which maybe you knew about already."

I almost said, Jesus, be serious. With Fitzgeralds, everything is on a need-not-to-be-out-of-the-loop basis.

Instead I said: "Funny vibe how?"

"Do I have to spell it out? He's still a handsome man, a handsome man who knows he is handsome, and something tells me he didn't really want to talk about helping you and me get back together. Are you tracking what I'm saying, Donny?"

Let's assume she was being candid. Let's assume she was not trying to upset me. Let's assume good intentions for as long as we can—because we won't be able to do so forever.

My mom and Darcy had become close for a time after she visited us in Brooklyn, and my then fiancée was beginning her clinically supervised hours as a psychotherapist. Narcissist that I am, I wondered if the two of them could ultimately shed some diagnostic light on me, or compare their fascinating individual notes. Somebody should be able to do so someday. So Darcy's psychological training may have equipped her to suss out the undertones in my father's invitation. I would trust her when it came to her intuition.

But I wouldn't trust my father on anything in this realm. And by realm, I mean anything pertaining to a woman, or to his own son.

"Are you asking me what you should do? Or what you think I want you to do?"

"I don't want to be impolite. He is your father, and once upon a time you and I were planning to get married, if you recall."

I could have flipped a coin. I knew my opinion didn't matter to her or anybody, including my father, anymore. "I don't think you should go out with him."

"OK then. I won't. You miss me, Donny?"

"Like water." In the moment I meant that. There's no question in my mind I will always mean that.

"Same here. I guess we weren't meant to be."

I wish I knew why, but it was true.

She and my father did meet for that drink. At some point, I heard from a mutual acquaintance that she was dating again, and she was amazed to discover that Darcy had grown serious about a much older man.

Do I need to say who it was?

OK, if I must and if you insist, Donovan. It's obvious anyway.

I can fake being rational, if I have to. Their considerable age difference would have been hard to bridge, I suppose, and that bridge collapsed before long under the weight of—who knows what if not everything? Under the crushing weight of sleeping with the son's ex? That sounds pathetic, and I am punishing myself. I would bet anything that in the end he broke up with her, once his curiosity was satisfied, and after his desirability was confirmed by her in the usual way: in bed. Her friend told me she was devastated. Take a number, my dejected, tenderhearted Darcy. No one should be flabbergasted over this course of events. But now it was all over, they were done with each other, and by extension done with me, and part of me, I have to confess, was bitterly satisfied. Those two deserved each other. I am not being totally cynical, either. It never crossed my mind at the time to think about poor lions on the mostly futile hunt. One out of ten. Not bad odds, till they were yours.

Recently my mom mentioned that Aunt Frankie heard he had moved back to the town where we Fitzgeralds had resided forever, or somewhere nearby, on the outskirts, though she hadn't seen him. I wouldn't have been stunned to hear that he and Frankie were in conversation. They were once close friends, it seems, and she may well have been the only woman who loved him who, I had to presume, never slept with him. I guess even he had high enough standards not to sleep with his older brother Anthony's widow. He probably never called his own father or visited the house, even if he was still cashing my grandfather's checks. Some wreckages on the family shoals are unavoidable.

As I said, you can ask for permission or you can ask for forgiveness. But guess what? My father asked for neither.

~~My life can feel like a Russian novel. I detest Russian novels. All those unmanageable feelings and cummerbunds and revolutions and firing squads and snow. Steam trains chugging across the tundra. The gulags. Cameo appearances of the devil incarnate. The vodka. The duels in the meadow, the casualties bleeding out among the wildflowers. More vodka still. The box seats at the opera. The country homes, the dachas, going up in flames. The little boys in white sailor suits. The little ballerinas with gold ringletted hair. The French wines swirling in crystal goblets. Poached poisson and caviar and Dom Perignon. And squab, count on the squab. Black velvet drawing rooms. Roaring fire in the hearth and candles in the chandeliers and wolfhounds lounging on Persian carpets. The plunging knife. When nobody's looking, the gleam of the plunging knife.~~

At the Floozy podium, I gathered myself. It was a balmy spring night, and he was standing by the opened bookstore door to the street, half in, half out, a perfect metaphor for his relationship with me. Not sure he should stay, not sure he should leave. I met my father's gaze, simultaneously mirthless and inquisitive, defiant and vulnerable. Of course in the instant I helplessly imagined him with Darcy and her with him. I used to wonder what they said about me, because I doubted the subject of me was out-of-bounds. Some lesions can never be sutured. ~~I used to hate the two of them, in other words.~~

As for my book, in case you haven't bought it yet (and Jesus Mary and Joseph, what is holding you back? The hardback beauty costs less than two rounds of craft brews in Williamsburg, come on, big spender), I had dedicated it this way:

To the Good Family Fitzgerald

I wouldn't take that back, either. But in that moment, standing in front of my family and the people in my town, I realized, despite all my worst intentions, I had ultimately written the book for my father—or I could say against my father or on account of him, as if that amounted to a difference. It didn't feel like revenge, it didn't feel like justification, it didn't feel like victory. I didn't think: Dad, here's something you'll never produce in your miserable life, a fucking book. But it was your miserable son who produced it instead. And you know why I felt that way? Because I didn't have it in me to savage him. Because Darcy was the concluding episode of his inflicting himself upon me. When I had the chance, I had listened hard to him all my life, especially when he wasn't there, even when he wasn't talking to me. I've lived long enough to understand that fathers and sons—for all their familiarity and genetic similarity—remain mysteries to each other, which is both a blessing and a curse. But now he had reached that hazardous stage of life, when in spite everything that had happened between us I felt almost sorry for him. As everyone knows, nobody's more dangerous than a man who senses he is being pitied, and especially when he is pitied by his own son. There's no satisfaction to be gleaned by anybody here. But I wouldn't be me without him. Maybe that's his ultimate achievement, bringing into the world a son he does not know, all the while being a father who does not know himself.

I loved my mom, let's be clear, without qualification, and always will. In a moment of weakness or of indignation, I don't know which, I told her about him and Darcy. I shouldn't have; she was crushed for me, and for herself, too. That was when she said she regretted the day she first met him, because then our pain, hers and mine, wouldn't exist. But then I wouldn't exist and she and I wouldn't exist, either.

I couldn't tell if he and his father had made contact that night in the bookstore, because my grandfather was stock still, eyes closed, the Irish having taken its toll. I would never understand who Philip Fitzgerald is and what drove him to do the things he had done, but he was my father. Some wreckages keep replaying over and over again in our imagination. And we all know how it goes: that we cannot look away from them.

"I wrote this book, <u>A Love I Can Use</u>, and this is how my story begins," I said—and as near as I could tell, I said this out loud. I opened to the first chapter and, pretty much without prefatory remarks, I read. Some hotshot reviewer had lavished praise on the opening, but that was nothing other than a setup for skewering my ass: "The promising novel spiraled out of control by the end as the protagonist devolved into grievance and high literary, mannered incoherence." This was her phrasing, which imprinted itself in my brain. Too much anger, too much violence, she complained. If she only knew.

~~Hers was the first and last review I would ever read about my book, and you have no idea how much self-control that vow required. My streetwise editor explained it was no big deal, and if anything it would only increase sales, so don't take it to heart. More pointedly, she said, in general, authors who paid too close attention to reviews were doomed. "You don't write to please somebody else. That's a losing proposition. You wrote the book you needed to, so fuck anybody who can't take a joke." She added that the Hollywood A-lister they were negotiating with for film rights would not be discouraged by the gratuitous violence accusation if he ever learned of it; if anything, the opposite. And not that the violence was in fact gratuitous. I wished I could believe her. I also wished I could imagine an alternative. She and I have begun sleeping together, who knows where this will go, if anywhere. We should be careful, but we aren't. An acquisitions editor hooking up with a writer she had "acquired" would have her professional credibility called into question. My unprofessional incredibility is continually called into question, so I can relate. And questioned all over the place, by my dad, by Darcy, by that fucking reviewer, and especially by me here in this journal, which I should never have begun and which I should burn right now. No chance of this drama queen doing that.~~

I finished my fifteen minutes of reading at Floozy's that night, and I registered as if from far, far away the tender but sustained patter of applause, like raindrops on the roof. But I could not register approval, if that's what it was. Instead, I was feeling something else, something sadder: my family and I would never gather together ever again. My grandfather was losing hold on his life, his beloved Caitlin was facing down stalking demons, and I wouldn't presume either would survive the next twelve months. Aunt Frankie was seeking whatever it was she desired, and my hunch was she would find it. Uncle Matty was a continent away, but then again he always was, and now he would likely never return. Uncle Anthony was also here, ever present, if only as an inexorable, ethereal memory. Aunt Colly was nearby, too, situated behind the cash register, head down, pawing her eyes with the back of her hands. My mom was forlornly smiling, looking I suppose proud. I always loved her smile—I mean I always especially loved her when she smiled—even if I never once told her that. That's the moment I decided I would correct my oversight and tell her tonight when we all got home, as soon I found the opening to be honest with her for a change. After all, trite as it may be to say, it was true there was no time to waste.

I looked out across and over the gathering, and I could see my father, only now Aunt Frankie was by his side, and he bent his head down when she seemed to be speaking to him. I wondered what they were saying to each other, I wondered if I would ever inquire, I wondered why I should care as much as I did. In any case, that was my good Family Fitzgerald, the parts that never quite made a whole. And apparently I was there as well, the one Fitzgerald who told a story about a love I wished I could use, a story that it took my whole life to tell.

Don't get me wrong. I published a book, and that's not much to justify a life, assuming a life requires justification and who's to say it does not? More important than publishing a book, I think, is <u>writing</u> the book—well, important solely to someone like me. But I have no illusions. The world will not be better for what I wrote. But probably safe to say, it will also not be a whole lot worse, despite that reviewer's take. It will make no net difference, in other words, to anybody but me. Books die, writers die, readers die. Sell two copies, sell two million, makes no diff. But please go back, reread this paragraph from the top. You know what? I don't believe one single word of it. Spoiler alert, the last one in my journal: only an idiot believes a writer. So don't trust a thing I say, including this sentence.

That's all you got, boyo?

With respect, piss off.

About that last-letter concept my grandfather endorsed: We should jump on that right away. And now that I think about it, everyone—including you, whoever you are—should write their last letter immediately, while they are capable.

I'd agreed to take questions from the Floozy faithful as well as the Floozy faithless, and a few hands swayed shyly in the air, like tulips in the spring before retreating underground. Perhaps on this occasion I would have some answers for my audience, and maybe for myself.

Now what? I thought to myself, remembering those famous last words. <u>Now what?</u>

I looked for him on the threshold where he was lodged uncertainly before, my everlastingly liminal old man. I didn't see him, and I didn't see Aunt Frankie, either. He was once again gone. That is what he does. And I once again stayed. That is who I seem to be. There was nowhere else for me but right where I was. This was where, and maybe even why and maybe even how, I could look for love I someday could use.

Acknowledgments

For counsel, friendship, wisdom, and support of various kinds, the author is thankful to:

Regan McMahon, his editor

Ralph Long

Craig McGarvey

John A. Gray

Katharine Ogden Michaels

Monsignor Shane

Rare Bird Books: Tyson Cornell, Publisher; Guy Intoci, Editorial Director; Julia Callahan, Director of Sales and Marketing; Hailie Johnson, Editorial and Design Manager

Elizabeth Trupin-Pulli, JET Literary Associates

Keith Jarrett, *A Multitude of Angels: Four Nights in October 1996: Modena Ferrara Torino Genova*

"Who pushed me to complete this part of my fate? The angels. They include everyone around me; the audiences, the pianos, the sickness (angel of death?),....my manager and my wife (certainly not exactly in that order).

"I swear: the angels were there." (liner notes; May 9, 2016)

With appreciation to Dean Young for his music.

Ava & Raylan James

Patti James, great-granddaughter of Edith Maude Fitzgerald, as ever and always.